The Oriental Casebook of

SHERLOCK HOLMES

The Oriental Casebook of

SHERLOCK HOLMES

TED RICCARDI

RANDOM HOUSE / NEW YORK

Library of Congress Cataloging-in-Publication Data
Riccardi, Theodore.
The oriental casebook of Sherlock Holmes / Ted Riccardi.
p.   cm.
ISBN 1-4000-6065-6
1. Detective and mystery stories, American. 2. Holmes, Sherlock
(Fictitious character)—Fiction. 3. Private investigators—Asia—Fiction.
4. British—Asia—Fiction. 5. Asia—Fiction. I. Title.
PS3618.I27   O7   2003   813'.6—dc21   2002036947

Printed in the United States of America on acid-free paper
Random House website address: www.atrandom.com
24689753
First Edition

Book design by J. K. Lambert

FOR ELLEN

CONTENTS

The Oriental Casebook of

SHERLOCK HOLMES

PREFACE

FOR ALMOST TWO DECADES, I HAVE BEEN AWARE OF THE GREAT PUBLIC interest that surrounds the lost years of Sherlock Holmes. Indeed, those Wanderjahre between his disappearance at the Reichenbach Falls and his return in the case of Ronald Adair have occasioned much speculation in the press as well as in literary circles.

It is only now, however, that I am free, with Holmes's expressed permission, to bring before the public what I have termed here *The Oriental Casebook of Sherlock Holmes*. His further adventures in the Orient, in Italy, and elsewhere in Europe still await his final approval and will be published separately.

The cases here described took place or have their origins during those momentous years between 1891 and 1894, when Holmes, unbeknownst to the world at large, travelled the globe locked in mortal combat with some of his most implacable enemies. He began recounting these events to me shortly after his reappearance in London in the spring of 1894. Those first fall and winter months after his return were at times a period of deep melancholia for him, but the narration of his experiences often provided him with a measure of relief until new challenges from the world of crime made him active once again.

Many of the readers of the following tales will be already familiar with the dramatic circumstances of Holmes's disappearance in Switzerland and his return to London three years later. They were accurately if not fully reported in the press in Europe as well as in England. The reader unfamiliar with these events may wish to consult my more complete accounts in what I have entitled "The Final Problem" and

"The Empty House." These are still in print, and I have little to add to them.

At the risk of dwelling overly on the personal, however, it might be of some use if I add a word here of my own circumstances and actions after Holmes's disappearance. Those familiar with my previous writings will recall that Holmes and I had journeyed to the Reichenbach Falls with Moriarty fresh on our heels. Even now as I write, after several decades, the memory of those last few hours still haunts me. As Holmes and I walked toward the falls, a message from the proprietor of our hotel, delivered to us by a young Swiss servant, urged my immediate return. An Englishwoman in the last stages of consumption, it said, had just arrived and had requested the emergency services of an English doctor. With the greatest reluctance, I left Holmes in the company of the Swiss servant boy and hurried back. As I returned, I noticed a tall figure striding rapidly along the upper path of the falls, but I thought nothing of it, so intent was I to help a patient who might be on the verge of death. When I arrived at the hotel, Peter Steiler, the keeper of the inn, informed me that there was no sick person and that he had sent no message.

I realised immediately to my dismay that I had been duped and that the letter was a ruse. I fairly flew back to the falls, but I arrived too late. Holmes was gone; only his Alpine stock stood where I had left him. A note written by him and placed under his silver cigarette case explained that he surmised that the message from the hotel was a trick, but that he deemed it better if he confronted Moriarty alone in what he knew to be their inevitable and probably their last meeting. As I gazed over the falls thinking that Holmes had perished in that awful abyss, I was overcome by my own failure to realise that the tall figure who approached as I left was indeed Moriarty himself.

Grief stricken at the loss of the friend I valued most in the world, and filled with remorse at my own obtuseness, I returned to London, where my wife saw me through the first disconsolate days. The only ray of light in the darkness was a visit by Lestrade, who reported on the successful arrest of many of the Moriarty gang, all of whom had been already scheduled for trial. Unfortunately, several of the inner circle, including Moriarty, had avoided the net and were presumed to have fled England. One, Sebastian Moran, Moriarty's chief lieutenant, was also thought to have accompanied him to Switzerland. The others had scattered and were at large.

Despite my wife's ministrations and the distractions of my medical practice, both she and I realised as the days passed that something more was needed if I were to recover from my loss. Indeed, it was she who first proposed that I take a trip to the Continent and spend a few weeks exploring places that I had not visited hitherto. Placing my patients in the hands of a trusted associate at St. Bart's, I booked passage on a steamer bound for Naples and, shortly thereafter, found myself at sea on my way to the Mediterranean.

The stormy Atlantic did nothing to alleviate my sorrow, but after we passed through the Strait of Gibraltar, the clouds broke, and I began to recover a measure of that sense of well-being that the sun-starved Londoner experiences when he approaches the warmer climes of the south. The ship, the *Albrig,* was a Danish freighter bound for Alexandria and Constantinople, with a return in a few weeks to England. I disembarked at Naples and journeyed south along the coast, where I stopped for a time at Ravello. It was here that I first received word of James Moriarty's slanderous remarks concerning Holmes and his outlandish defence of his dead brother. Distracted from my sorrow by the gaiety of the Italians and my anger at Colonel Moriarty's absolute perversion of the facts, I here began to write in response my own description of those last few days in Switzerland.

Recovered somewhat, I returned to London, where I met with Mycroft, Holmes's older brother. I benefitted greatly by his many kindnesses, and on several occasions, he invited me to dine with him at the Diogenes Club. Although his corpulent appearance was so different from that of Holmes's spare and lithe figure, his mental acuity and habits of mind were so like those of his younger brother that they led me to feel that something of my friend still lived on in our world. During one of these meetings, Mycroft asked that I accompany him to the quarters I had once shared with Holmes on Baker Street. Before his disappearance, sensing that his meeting with Moriarty might not go entirely according to his desire, Holmes had left Mycroft instructions on how to dispose of his personal effects, including his papers. Among the most physically inactive of men, Mycroft had decided to leave things as they were for the present, paying Mrs. Hudson the modest rent until such time as his physical energy might rise to the point where he could begin the grim disposition of Holmes's effects. It was my first visit to Baker Street since Holmes's disappearance, and my eyes misted over as I entered, half-expecting to see my friend sitting in his accustomed place. But he was not there, and the ample tears of Mrs. Hudson on seeing me only confirmed what I then regarded as the greatest loss of my life.

In the spring of 1892, as well as the spring of the following year, I revisited the Reichenbach Falls. My grief and remorse had dissipated to a great degree, and it is still not entirely clear what inner compulsion led me back to that fearful spot. In part, I think, it was the indeterminate nature of Holmes's death. I harboured no doubts or suspicions that he was anything but dead. For me that was the bitterest of certainties. Beyond his Alpine stock, the silver cigarette case, and the note that he had left behind, there was nothing. He was simply gone. The glimmer of hope that I would uncover something more of him at the falls, that there would be still some unnoticed trace after the lapse of so much time, a further clue to exactly what had happened, lingered on. It was, of course, a failed hope. There was nothing but the menacing voice of the falls emanating from the abyss below. And, to speak with the utmost frankness, there was also the small but persistent illusion that I could relive my actions during those last minutes and change my decision to leave him, as I had, to confront his archenemy alone. This illusion too went in time.

During those visits, I stayed again at the hotel in Meiringen, and had long conversations with Peter Steiler, the innkeeper, especially about those last hours before Holmes disappeared. Without question, the figure I saw striding toward the falls was Moriarty, and the young Swiss servant who brought the note to me was obviously in his employ. The youth had appeared looking for work but the day before. Steiler, thinking that he looked honest enough, hired him on the spot. He did little to confirm the young man's story, however. He knew only what the boy told him, that he came from Bellinzona, the capital of Ticino canton, that his first name was Giacomo, and that he aspired to be a painter. He disappeared without a trace.

In the spring of '94, as the cruel days of April ended and the third anniversary of Holmes's apparent death approached, I determined to remain in England and not to visit the falls again. By now the passage of time coupled with the inevitable distractions of my practice had assuaged my grief. I began to allow the full and unguarded return of Holmes's memory without experiencing the searing pain that I had felt earlier. The interest that I had in crime while he was alive returned, for whatever else he had done, Holmes had conferred upon me such a passion for the criminal deed that I often felt compelled to follow in detail the more sensational cases reported in the London press. My constant companion in these cases was of course Holmes himself, with whom I now once again engaged in fruitful, if imaginary, dialogue. I heard his voice often as he repeated some of his most emphatic utterances, concerning his theories and his methods: "You see, Watson, but you do not observe"; "My method, Watson, is based on the detailed analysis of trivia"; "You know my methods, Watson, apply them." Although I had become sufficiently familiar with his methods during our time together, I remained slow in mastering their application. I solved no crime about which I read, nor could I voice convincing opinions about the solutions found by the detectives of Scotland Yard, whom Holmes had so often deprecated. Without him, the solutions of crime in London fell still to their hands. Lestrade, Tobias Gregson, and Athelney Jones were yet at work, the best of a bad lot, as Holmes had said so often, but necessary nonetheless.

And so, that spring, on a day at the end of April, my attention was directed toward the untimely death of Ronald Adair, the murder of whom had shocked much of London's fashionable society. So engrossed did I become in this awful crime and the details of its commission, that I ventured even to make a visit to Park Lane, the scene of the crime, compelled, I felt somehow, by Holmes's long influence upon me. I can still remember looking up toward the room where the victim had been found shot. As I gazed upward toward the unfortunate Adair's window, I must have moved backward slightly to balance myself, for I struck unintentionally into someone behind me. I turned to see an old wizened gentleman who had just bent over to gather up a number of books that he had dropped in our encounter. I leaned down to help him, but he was so unpleasant in his words and demeanour that I left him to fend for himself. I looked toward the house of Adair again and stayed on for a few minutes longer, listening to the idle gossip coming from the small crowd of curiosity seekers gathered below his house. I then turned and went home.

It was no more than a few minutes after I entered my quarters that there was a knock at the door. The maid opened, and I was surprised to find facing me the old man whom I had struck into, his arms still laden with books. He muttered an apology for his rude behaviour and said that he had recognised me too late as a neighbour, for his bookshop was nearby. He wondered if I might not like to purchase some of the volumes that had fallen from his arms. "These," he said, holding a few forward in the long fingers of one hand, "would fill nicely the space on the top shelf." As he spoke, I looked in the direction in which he was pointing. When I turned again to face him, he had disappeared, and Sherlock Holmes stood there instead, a broad smile on his face, the old man now a pile of rags and a wig resting on the floor between us.

I have never been able to say clearly what happened next. Holmes later told me that I went pale and fainted before his very eyes. I must have regained consciousness almost immediately, however, and once I had ascertained that Holmes was real and no illusion, I began the enquiries that in the end resulted in this volume. He told me how he had escaped Moriarty's hold on him at the falls, how the great criminal had fallen into the abyss, and that he had decided on the spot to let the world think that he had perished as well so that he could deal more effectively with his remaining enemies. He apologised for his long deception, but he felt that a sincerely grieving friend was necessary to his survival. He then spoke briefly of his travels, of his escape to Italy, his time in Tibet, and his visits to Persia, Mecca, and Khartoum. It was out of these very brief remarks that my enquiries grew, finally resulting in the present volume.

The world of crime is not a tidy one, and I would be remiss if I were to lead the reader to believe that these adventures were as neat in their solution as they sometimes appear to have been in print. Some of them took place over many years and appear here in perhaps what are far too tidy packages of condensation. I should note too that Holmes was often an unwilling partner in their narration, and it was with reluctance that he responded to my many promptings. Sometimes the relation of a single tale took many months.

Holmes has read through the entire manuscript. As in the past, he has chided me for what he considers to be my tendency toward romance. He would much prefer what he calls a "scientific approach," in which the detailed observation of fact and the principles of deduction are all that are given. Despite his misgivings, he has granted his approval, albeit reluctant, of these "fables," as he calls them. They appear here in the order in which he related them to me, not in the order in which they occurred. In recasting them for the reader, I have followed the principle of *ipsissima verba,* quoting Holmes's exact words wherever possible, using paraphrases only when necessary.

At Holmes's insistence, I have thrown some of the stories into later years, distorting somewhat the historical record. This has been done to protect those who survived some of the bizarre events narrated here. It has also been done to delude some of the criminals who still remain at large despite his best efforts. Since all the happenings recorded here took place or had their origins in the period between 1891 and 1894, the careful reader should be able to discern the pattern of true events. The reader who looks to these tales for historical consistency will be disappointed, however.

—JOHN H. WATSON, M.D.

THE CASE OF
THE VICEROY'S ASSISTANT

OR SEVERAL WEEKS AFTER HIS RETURN TO LONDON, MY FRIEND Mr. Sherlock Holmes had once again begun to evince those symptoms of melancholic lethargy which had led me on occasions past to increased apprehension about his mental health. He rarely ventured out from our quarters on Baker Street, consumed almost nothing despite Mrs. Hudson's stern admonitions, and spent most of the day staring idly into space. Occasionally, he would pick up his violin, tune it slowly, and attempt some mournful piece by Mendelssohn, but at the slightest rebellion from the instrument, he would fling it down and throw himself onto the couch, sometimes falling into a deep sleep. His only moments of enthusiasm came when the morning paper arrived. He scoured it quickly, his eyes hungrily searching for something that could satisfy his restless brain. Alas, however, most of the crime was of the most ordinary variety, and the absence of intelligent design behind any of it was apparent to him at once.

"I have destroyed my enemies, Watson," he said one morning over breakfast, "and in so doing I have perhaps destroyed myself. Look at this: a bank robbery in Charing Cross, a woman has murdered her adulterous husband in Oxford, and several drums of fertiliser have disappeared from a factory in Whitechapel. What is to be done?"

"Holmes," I said, "perhaps we should take an extended trip to the Continent. The grey weather in London is causing a melancholic state in you that—"

But he already seemed lost in his usual silence and vacant stare, and I knew by now not to irritate him when such a mood overtook him. I looked with dread also at his return to the use of cocaine, which as far as I was able to judge, he had avoided until then.

Unexpectedly, he said, "You are right, Watson. A change would be most welcome, but I haven't the energy for the Continent. Let us begin with a walk and then perhaps a concert. Sarasate is playing this afternoon, and if he is in form, it will be worth our while."

The stroll through St. James's seemed to do him some good, and after the concert we again walked, this time through Hyde Park. It was just before dinner when we returned. As we entered, I noticed that Holmes had inadvertently left a window open, and that a pile of papers had blown off his desk. I reached down to pick them up, and in so doing my eye was caught by a note written in a large and vigorous hand. It read:

My dear Holmes,

My gratitude for your help in the sad Maxwell affair. You have served your country well and have in no small way helped to preserve peace in the Empire. I wish you every success upon your return to England.

(signed) Curzon

The note filled me with the greatest surprise and interest. At dinner, I said: "My dear Holmes, you have never told me of your journey to India."

He looked up vaguely, but I could see a slight gleam appear in his eye.

"Ah, you saw the note from Lord Curzon."

I nodded. "Indeed, I did," said I with some annoyance, "and I must say that I am confounded. You have never given me even the slightest intimation of an adventure in which you helped to preserve the peace of the Empire."

"It was a most disturbing affair, Watson. Even now only Lord Curzon and I know the details, and if I may say so, in all probability I know more than he. If I tell you the story, Watson, you will be the third to know. I think it should be a long time before you bring it to public attention, however. The tensions between nations remain, and several parties still living bear the wounds of what was a most grisly affair."

He had begun to warm to his subject, and I could see that he was eager to relate to me what for him had been a most absorbing case. The vague faraway look in his eyes had vanished completely, and he appeared once again engaged with a worthy opponent, if only in memory.

"Of course," I said, "I shall bring nothing of this to public notice until you deem it appropriate."

"Very well, my dear Watson, listen then. It will probably do me some good as well, for lacking a new problem, I could do worse than retrace the steps of some of my most difficult cases of the past. In this way, I shall at least keep my brain alive until something worthy of interest appears here in London."

We moved from the table to our comfortable armchairs in the sitting room. Holmes lit his pipe after removing it from his slipper and began, his eyes bright now, his voice composed.

"I suppose, Watson, that I had better go back and review my travels after the death of Moriarty. You will recall that I mentioned on a previous occasion that I had journeyed to Tibet, where I spent two years with the head lama."

"Yes, indeed," said I. "You travelled as a Norwegian by the name of Sigerson. You then went on to Persia, visited Mecca, and then went to Khartoum, I believe."

"Precisely. You have a good memory, Watson. There was of course far more to my stay in that part of the world than I have related to you. That I visited Persia and Arabia is true, but I travelled by a most circuitous route. Upon leaving Lhasa, I gave up the disguise of Sigerson. As you know, Watson, I have a certain facility with languages. I had picked up a good deal of Tibetan in the monasteries and even studied the ancient Tibetan practice of concentrating bodily heat. It is a most useful and extraordinary technique, which I can still perform on occasion. Indeed, it saved me from two serious misadventures in the mountains from which I might have frozen to death. In any case, I donned a lama's robes and travelled with a merchant's caravan on the old trade route south, arriving after a few weeks in the valley of Nepal, where I rested in that most pleasant place at a Buddhist shrine atop a hill overlooking the city of Katmandu. Were it not for its xenophobic rulers,

Watson, I have often thought of retiring to that idyllic spot, for I know of no better place to spend one's declining years. To do so now of course one would have to remain forever as a lama or in some other appropriate disguise, for the present ruler, the Rana, does not tolerate easily the presence of Europeans.

"Although keeping a disguise at all times, I did identify myself at one point to the British Resident, Mr. Richardson, and was able to help him out of strange difficulties. That was the episode that might one day be entitled the case of Hodgson's ghost. Another case concerned the bizarre troubles of a French savant recently arrived from Paris to study ancient inscriptions in the Sanscrit tongue."

Holmes stopped to puff on his pipe. He eventually left Katmandu, he continued, and headed south toward India. Once across the border, he journeyed to Banaras, where he deepened his studies of Oriental body techniques.

"I found that after a few months of concentration I could control my breathing and heart rate to such an extent that even you, Watson, might declare me dead on your usual diagnosis."

"Extraordinary," I exclaimed.

"Yes, dear Doctor, extraordinary indeed. I have studied these and other techniques with great success, for in my line of endeavour, one can never foretell when such knowledge may be of use."

"And how did you acquire these techniques?" I asked.

"Diligence, of course, and a bit of luck in finding the right teacher. My interests are in the main practical, Watson, as you know. Whatever the metaphysical foundations of Indian science are, I am of course uninterested. Give me a technique, however, that will contribute to the success of my work, and I become a tireless pupil. Thus, yoga, Watson, the practical aspect of Indian science, became valuable to me: first, in the aforementioned power to feign death; second, in the ability to improve the science of disguise, to the point where the bodily illusions created could be assumed with little makeup or physical accoutrements of any kind. My purpose was of course a simple one: to keep alive in India, and in England once I returned, for unless I increased my arsenal of tricks, sooner or later one of my dedicated enemies would doubtless do me in."

Holmes's rather long introduction to the tale fascinated me, showing aspects of my friend's interests long hidden from me. After a few months of the most diligent concentration, he had acquired what he needed, and he felt he might be refreshed by social intercourse with some of his own countrymen. Knowing that he must still be on guard lest his enemies learn of his whereabouts, he determined to go to Calcutta, where he thought he would spend a few moments in the more gracious mansions of British India. And so, still in disguise, this time as a Hindu merchant, he took a rickshaw to Moghul Sarai, where he was to board the Tuphan Express, which would take him overnight to the capital of our Indian Empire.

"As my rickshaw pulled into the station, however, I felt the gaze of someone in the crowd staring at me. I soon saw that it emanated from the face of a fakir, someone unfamiliar at first, except for his eyes, which had a look of deep malevolence that I thought to have encountered somewhere before. Naked except for a loincloth, the holy man was powdered with white ash from head to toe. His hands and feet were bound with rope, and a chain from a neck collar attached his hands to his feet in a tight bunch. He appeared as if maimed and deformed, incapable therefore of motion of any kind except for the shuffling of his feet and the grasping movement of his fingers. Or so it seemed, Watson, for suddenly this repulsive creature, by sheer force of will, propelled himself high into the air, landing in front of me in the rickshaw. He stared at me hard for a moment, his contorted face almost touching mine, then jumped out with a resounding laugh and, with several incredible leaps, disappeared into the crowd. Most disagreeable it was, Watson, and even more so since I was certain that I had seen that face at the Ganges, and possibly before. As I boarded the train, I began the search in my memory for this man, for his look told me that I was no longer alone in India."

I was by now thoroughly engrossed in Holmes's adventure. I had myself served in our military forces in Afghanistan many years before and had always hoped to visit the eastern ramparts under our jurisdiction.

"I won't bore you with details of the city of Calcutta, Watson. Suffice it to say that, once one overcomes one's initial revulsion at the native squalor and becomes accustomed to the humid pungency of the Bengal climate, Calcutta appears a large, teeming metropolis, with most unusual possibilities for crime and evil."

Once arrived, Holmes threw off his disguise and became an Englishman for the first time in many months, creating for himself a new personality and occupation. He became Roger Lytton-Smith, recently arrived from London as a representative of a firm of chemists, Redfern and Russell, Kingsway, Finsbury, London. He took a room in one of the modest hotels off the Chowringee, and decided to enjoy the delights of this large city.

"I knew of no one there, save Reginald Maxwell—"

"*The* Reginald Maxwell?" I interrupted.

"I see," said Holmes, "that the case did have a certain notoriety even here in London."

"It is still a mystery to most of us. His death occurred so prematurely—"

"Yes, Watson, and I shall relate to you how and under what bizarre circumstances."

Sir Reginald and he, said Holmes, were schoolmates, and later attended the university together. After the university, they grew apart, but corresponded occasionally. Reginald wrote at one point that he had entered His Majesty's Foreign Office, that he had married, and that he probably would be serving for a number of years in distant parts of the Empire, most probably Africa and India. He was, if not one of our most intelligent diplomats, at least a man of charm and industry, and his qualities became rapidly known to Lord Curzon, who shortly after his appointment as Viceroy, requested that Maxwell serve as his personal assistant.

"You may well imagine, Watson, what a step forward this was in the man's career: to serve so closely to such a strong and important individual as Curzon, the representative of the King-Emperor in the Indian Subcontinent."

Holmes stopped for a moment to empty his pipe. The name he had chosen, Roger Lytton-Smith, was of course no accident, he said. It was the name of a third schoolmate with whom Maxwell and he had been fairly close. They had spent many hours together at snooker. It was under this name that he thought he would write a short note, knowing that Maxwell would be equally happy to see Roger, who if Holmes's information was still correct, was living happily outside London, working for Redfern and Russell, blissfully unaware that he was about to visit Lord Curzon's assistant.

"I therefore sent a note to Reginald, explaining to him that I was passing through Calcutta on my way to the Levant on business and that I hoped we might meet, if only briefly. He would of course recognise me instantly, but my true identity would be preserved until we were face-to-face. The following morning I received a reply to my note:

"Dear Roger,
  "So happy you are here. Come to my office at four tomorrow. I shall send a cab. It will be so good to see you.

"(signed) Reggie"

The ride was no more than a mile from Holmes's hotel. Maxwell's office was in a wing of Government headquarters, a little distant from the Viceroy's own offices. Holmes had only a moment's wait after his arrival before he was led to his old friend. The peon left, and as Holmes greeted him, Maxwell gasped and turned pale.

"Good lord! I don't believe it. Holmes! My dear chap, is it you? I thought you were dead!"

"A double surprise, eh?" said Holmes.

"Excuse me, my dear Sherlock, I am so taken aback by your presence that you will forgive me if I sit down. I was of course expecting Smith, a surprise in itself, but to see you, Holmes—and here, of all places."

Holmes explained to him in brief what had transpired since his disappearance and his reasons for wishing to preserve the impression that he was no longer alive. His desire to spend a few days among his countrymen after long isolation in Tibet, the Himalaya, and India itself had brought him to Calcutta and to his old friend Maxwell.

"Of course, I understand perfectly, Holmes. I shall open every facility here for you, including the Gymkhana. With your permission, I should like to advise the Viceroy himself of your presence and your true identity. I am sure that he would be most happy to meet with you and to learn your impressions of Central Asia. The Great Game, as they call it, is still afoot."

Holmes replied that he would consent to meet with the Viceroy if Maxwell so wished, and that he had no objection to revealing his identity in this instance, provided that he was referred to publicly at all times by the false name he had given. Maxwell agreed to use the utmost caution in this regard and would arrange for every social convenience for Roger Lytton-Smith during his stay in Calcutta.

The two old friends then reminisced about their university days. As they talked, Holmes observed Maxwell closely. He had changed somewhat from the "Reggie" that Holmes had known, as would be natural considering the number of years that had intervened. A bit stouter perhaps, and grey had begun to appear in his still full head of hair. During their conversation, however, Holmes became aware that his friend's grace and good humour disguised some inner turmoil. When he stopped talking, his smile dropped from his face like a mask, leaving in its place an expression of deepest conflict.

"I must meet with the Viceroy in a few minutes, my dear Holmes," he said. "As you may have heard, His Majesty King Edward will arrive in Calcutta shortly for an extended visit and darbar. His ship has been reported in the Bay of Bengal just north of Ceylon. He should arrive therefore in a few days. We have much to do in the meantime. However, would you dine with us tomorrow evening, about eight?"

He handed Holmes a card with an address in the Alipore district of the city.

"My wife," he said, "has heard much about Roger from me through the years and will want to meet him. She will be leaving the day after tomorrow for England."

"Indeed, I should like to meet her as well," said Holmes. "Will she be gone for long?"

It was at this point that the look of pain Holmes had glimpsed before covered Maxwell's face. His voice cracked as he said: "I am afraid that she will not be returning."

Holmes nodded but asked no more questions, for it was apparent to him that Sir Reginald's pain lay in his personal and domestic life rather than in his work, which had all the outward appearance of complete success. He took his leave, and was escorted out by the same peon who had led him in. He returned to the hotel, pleased at the prospect of being once again among his countrymen, but also uneasy about his friend's obvious discomfort.

"I should tell you, Watson, that this was the last time I was to see Sir Reginald alive."

By now Holmes had refilled his pipe, reached for the brandy, and poured us two full measures.

"Pray continue, Holmes. I gather that the case is about to take a most singular turn."

"Singular, Watson, yes," he said, "and most tragic. My first intimation that something unusual might happen came the following morning."

He had risen early, he said, and at breakfast was handed a note that read:

Dear Roger,

Something has transpired with regard to the important Visitor whom I mentioned to you, and so I must cancel, regretfully, our dinner together this evening. I hope you are not too greatly inconvenienced. I shall be in touch again shortly.

(signed) Reggie

The note was written in haste, and Holmes could see that the hand and mind that had composed it were intensely agitated. He could do nothing, however. He spent the day visiting the usual monuments, including the house of Job Charnock, the founder of Calcutta. He dined alone at the hotel, and then, rather than retire, took a long walk through small lanes and back alleys.

"It is a city that benefits greatly by darkness, Watson. As the black of night succeeds the dusk, it takes on an aura of magic and mystery that I have seen in few places. Women in silken saris, turbaned gentlemen, carried by the omnipresent rickshawallah, seem to float in the air. The smoke of the cooking fires is intense, the odours unusual with the spices of the East. As the evening moves on to night, a peaceful hush comes over the city, broken only by the occasional footfall of someone hurrying home."

In the intense darkness, he groped his way back to the hotel. It was about eleven when he entered his room. It was but a moment later that there was a knock. He had a visitor. He opened the door and saw there a woman dressed in black, her face veiled. She entered quickly, closing the door behind her. In the dim light, he could make out nothing except that she was tall and graceful.

"Please sit down, Lady Maxwell," he said.

The woman appeared startled by his addressing her by name. As she sat down, she lifted her veil and said, "You are indeed most clever, Mr. Holmes. How did you know who I am?"

"A mere surmise, dear lady, but obviously a good one. Only Sir Reginald and the Viceroy were to know of my presence. I doubt if an English businessman such as Roger Lytton-Smith would be receiving callers alone at night on his second day in the city, particularly a woman. It would be far more likely for such a visitor to come to Sherlock Holmes. Hence my well-founded surmise. That Sir Reginald also told you of my real identity is a small but unsurprising infringement of my request for secrecy."

Holmes confessed to me that not since the affair of Bohemia many years before had he met a member of the female sex of such beauty and attraction as Lady Maxwell. She had that rare quality found in some Englishwomen that joins the best features of our race with the grace of the highest breeding. As he observed her, he coldly lamented the early decision that had taken from him the possibility of a peaceful life of domesticity with a woman such as this, and led him to a lonely life fighting against the malignant evils of our times. He had little time to ponder such things, however, for the lady's state was one of great distress.

"What brings you here, my lady, in the dark night of Calcutta with all the attendant dangers and possibility of discovery?"

"Most assuredly, Mr. Holmes, I should not be here unless it were a matter of the greatest urgency. I am about to depart for England, but I am so unhappy about Reginald that I thought I might explain to you what has transpired in our lives that has forced me to leave. I am perhaps not without guilt in what I am about to tell you, but I hope that you will listen with sympathy and, I trust, with the thought of helping your old friend through what I believe will be a most difficult period."

"You may speak freely, madam, and I shall do what I can."

As she spoke, her dignity seemed to grow with her beauty, and Holmes could only be impressed with the honesty of the motives that had brought her on such a difficult errand.

"Let me start at the beginning, then. I was born in Yorkshire, in the small village of Wyck Rissington. My name before my marriage to Reginald was Jennifer Hume. My father, Jeremy Hume, had moved early in his life from Scotland to England, where he met and married my mother. He was a successful barrister, and I was raised with my younger sister in comfort and peace in the English countryside. Our life had all the outward trappings of familial happiness and was for the most part uneventful.

"My father loved us," she continued, "but was morose and rather strict at times, our mother understanding and patient. When I reached sixteen, my parents began to talk vaguely of my eventual marriage to the right person, but I made it clear to them that I would choose my husband myself, if I were to have one at all. My father, interested only in a good social arrangement that would be a match to his financial success, made it evident that he would certainly have the final word on who my husband was to be. There were a few scenes, as I am sure occur in many households, and there matters rested, for I was far too young for immediate concern."

A year later, however, she met a young man who took her heart. His name was James Hamilton. He lived with his mother in the next village. He had no known father, and his mother, once a person of some standing but now old and abandoned, was forced to take in laundry and to perform other menial tasks to support herself. There had been rude jokes also, passed back and forth in conversation, about old Rose Hamilton, but they were beyond Jennifer's comprehension. She had never met James, who was judged to be one of the handsomest lads in the region.

"One morning, I had gone to the fields not far from our house to pick wildflowers. I was standing near the road among the flowers when I became aware that someone was watching me. I turned and saw James for the first time and fell in love. He was tall, of slender build, with a beautiful open face, but what stole my heart, Mr. Holmes, was his smile and the clear earnest look in his eyes. We talked embarrassedly that day for a few minutes, as young people will do. He asked me if he could help me pick, and I nodded shyly in assent. He then accompanied me to the gate of our house and politely bade me good-bye. That evening I could not eat at supper, nor could I sleep for thinking of him and turning over in my mind everything that we had said to each other that day."

The next morning at precisely the same time she went out once again to pick the wildflowers. James Hamilton was there. It was apparent that he liked her company as well. Soon they were talking and laughing. Every day they met thus, sometimes a little farther off, without anyone the wiser.

"In a few weeks, even though I blush as I tell you, Mr. Holmes, our young love began to deepen into the inevitable passion to which we mortals are subject. I took my sister into my confidence, and she loyally protected us from intrusion during our trysts. For several months, I was happy in the sweetest love that any woman has ever known on the face of this earth. My darling James became to me my very life. Then one day my father discovered us. He made a terrible scene in which he heaped upon my beloved James every filthy insult with regard to blood and origin our English tongue provides. I tried to make him desist, scratching at him and giving him blows. My poor James stood by in stunned silence until my father's fury had run its course. Then he looked at me with the saddest face I have ever seen, turned, and walked proudly away. I tried to stop him, but he asked that I let him go, saying that he would write to me shortly. As he walked away, I felt my heart sink and I believe I fainted.

"I remembered nothing of how I arrived home. I awoke in bed, my mother sitting by my side anxiously. It was already the next morning. James had indeed sent me a note through my sister, who had given it to my mother for me so that my father might not see it. It read:

"My dearest love Jenny,

"Please know that I love you with all my heart and always will, but your father's insults have deeply wounded me, and I am determined to seek out my own father, whom I believe to be of gentle birth, and to earn a fortune so that someday we may live together in peace and happiness. Please wait for me, my darling, no matter how long it might take.

"Your loving,
"James

"The note produced in me a sense of panic despite its protestations of love. I leapt out of bed and ran all the way down the lonely path to James's house. He was already gone. The house contained only his mother, besotted after an all-night drinking bout. I tried to get her to talk, but it was hopeless. James, and all sign of him, were gone. I felt the despair and sense of sickening loss that only those who know the total destruction of their hopes can experience. I returned wearily to the house. That was thirteen years ago. I was not to see James Hamilton again until only a few months ago."

At this point, said Holmes, Lady Maxwell began to lose her composure. It was cold now, for even in Calcutta the temperature can go down in the dead of night in winter. Holmes had only some native arak, raksi as they call it, to offer her. She thanked him and took the merest sip, but the sting on her tongue apparently helped her to continue.

"I have told you of the frailty of a young woman, Mr. Holmes," she said wearily.

"I make no judgements on honest human weakness, madam. We are indeed all weak. But the actions caused by human weakness have inevitable consequences, often evil ones. And in these lie my peculiar interests."

"What has transpired heretofore," she said, "has had no irremediable consequences, but I am afraid of what may follow. It is to avoid any further harm that I have come to you."

As she continued, Holmes wondered what evil genius could have spun the web in which she had begun to find herself entangled.

After James left, she said, she had lived as if in a trance. She and her father hardly spoke to each other. Her mother and sister attempted to comfort her, in vain most of the time, and to their detriment very often, as she was subject to violent storms of tears and anger that left her exhausted. After about a year, she slowly began to mend. By now James's face had receded from before her to the extent that she could go out and lead an almost normal life. The days were bearable, but the nights still often unendurable in their pain and loneliness. She finished school and then was asked to take charge of the children of Mr. Edward Staunton, St. David's, Pembrokeshire, in Wales. She was glad to leave home and to have what became a most welcome change.

The Stauntons were a happy couple, she noted, with two delightful daughters, aged seven and nine. She and the Stauntons quickly grew to love and trust each other. Edward Staunton and his wife were the kindest of people, and their household was filled with light and good cheer.

"I had been with them for about three years when events again began to transpire which have brought me here tonight. It was Christmas, some nine years ago now, that Mr. Staunton invited a friend to stay for the season's festivities. He was an older man, a widower by the name of Humphrey Maxwell, a barrister at law, then living in London. He and his family had lived for a time not far from us in Yorkshire, and I of course knew his name, though we had never met. He was a tall, strongly built man in his sixties, but rather unpleasantly gruff in his manner. I remember not liking him at first, for there was something in his face that brought forth in me great anxiety, a look perhaps like someone I could no longer place. He was never anything but most respectful toward me, Mr. Holmes, and before he left he became attentive, even kind."

After the holidays, when he had gone, Mr. Staunton informed her that Mr. Maxwell had a handsome son, a recent graduate, who would be spending a week in the spring with the family. He said also that Mr. Maxwell had become quite taken with her and had remarked on how wonderful a daughter-in-law she might make. It did not take any great intelligence to understand what was afoot, she said. Mr. and Mrs. Staunton, with the very best of intentions, had decided that it was high time that she should marry and that they would take an active role in the search for a suitable husband.

"Naturally, Mr. Holmes, I had never divulged to them my love for James or the difficulties with my father. These were family secrets. For my part, I had decided to wait for James, or should he never appear, to spend my life in spinsterhood, for I could love no other man."

In the spring, she continued, Mr. Reginald Maxwell, son of Humphrey Maxwell, came to St. David's for a visit. He was a most attractive and intelligent young man, who, when she first saw him, made her heart race, for certain of his features so reminded her of James that she thought surely her mind was playing tricks. Reginald was only a few years older than she, in fact only a year older than James, and a young man of great prospects. He was a graduate of Oxford in law and had decided to pursue a career in government abroad. He was now in training in London and at the end of the year would leave for his first post, which was to be Nairobi. He was obviously searching for a suitable wife to accompany him.

"I turned out to be his choice. For whatever reasons, Mr. Holmes, Reginald soon fell in love with me and so filled that week's visit with his kind attention that I began to waver in my resolve. We took long walks along the Welsh coast, and we found each other good company. After he left, I began to doubt that James would ever reappear—all I had was the short note that he had sent me, a note so covered with tears and so pressed by my hand that it was nothing more than a crumpled wad of paper. Rather than spend a life living off some brief memories, perhaps indeed I should marry this man. Reginald returned for several visits, and despite his obvious love and attention, one thing was clear to me: I did not love him. I loved James, and I could not change that. Could I lead a life, married to a man whom I did not love, being at the same time secretly in love with another?"

By the late summer, she continued, it was apparent that Reginald would soon propose marriage. She had decided on a course of action in that eventuality. Should he do so, she would tell him that she had loved a man who left, that she thought that he would never return and was presumed to be dead. She would marry Reginald only if he understood that, and that she hoped someday to love him, but if they married he would have to be patient and give time for her love to grow and to overcome the past.

"On one of his summer visits, on a short walk from the house one evening, Reginald did indeed propose to me. I informed him of my conditions. He replied that he accepted them, enthusiastically even, for he loved me more than anything in the world and only being in my presence was enough to make him happy. I made the fateful decision then to marry Reginald Maxwell. I notified my mother and informed her that Reginald was to pay a visit to ask my father for my hand and that I had accepted his offer. Shortly thereafter, Reginald visited my father and received his immediate consent. My father appeared overjoyed at the prospect of the alliance, for Humphrey Maxwell had the required position and reputation in London society."

They were married, she said, in the early fall and took up residence in London. About a month after their wedding, Mr. Humphrey Maxwell fell ill. Reginald spent many hours with him and the doctors tried everything, but his heart finally gave out and he died within the week. Reginald was filled with sorrow at his father's passing, but soon thereafter the couple set sail from Southampton for Nairobi.

The trip was a long and beautiful one. Reginald, she said, seemed to recover from his father's death, but at times she became tormented, for she still felt deeply torn. He was very patient with her, for as long as she felt as she did she could not accept his conjugal advances. But as they talked, trust began to grow between them. He told her much about his family, for he realised then that she knew very little about him. They had been married so quickly. His mother had died shortly after his birth, he said, and he was raised by old family servants. His father, grieving profoundly for his dead wife, went on drinking bouts, had terrible brawls, and disappeared for weeks at a time. When he had spent his anger and grief, he returned to his infant son, on whom he lavished great attention and affection. Once, in one of his long descriptions, Reginald smiled and said for years he thought he might have a brother somewhere, for his father had often hinted, saying that someday he would tell him about his younger brother. It was finally on his deathbed he told Reginald that he indeed had a half brother, and that he should attempt to find him.

"Our life in Nairobi was pleasant, and I decided finally that my reticence and indecision were an unnecessary cruelty to Reginald, and we became truly married. I tried with all my strength to bury all thought of James. On the outside, we were happy and were considered to be a model couple. Reginald received several promotions for his service, and after four years, we were sent to Rangoon. We spent three years there. By now, Reginald was regarded by many as a future foreign secretary. It was at this point that he met the Earl of Kedleston, Lord Curzon, who upon his accession to the position of Viceroy, asked that Reginald be transferred to Calcutta to act as his personal deputy. Reginald and I were thrilled when we got the news, for it meant another major step upward in his career."

While they were in Burma, she said, and shortly before their departure for Calcutta, she received word of her own father's untimely demise. Her sister wrote that her mother was doing well under the circumstances, and that she should not try to return.

"My sister also enclosed a packet of letters for me. They were from James and had come to me regularly for several years. My father had intercepted all of them and had hidden them in his files. At his death, my sister found them and, with the most mixed emotions, sent them to me. You can imagine, Mr. Holmes, with what consternation I looked upon those letters. James had used various ruses, but my father had always succeeded in getting the letters before anyone else. There were fifteen in all. They came from all over the world, mostly America. The last was dated seven years before and was from San Francisco. It was the last because James had decided that I no longer loved him and that he would stop writing. Every idle moment I had I spent reading and rereading them for a clue as to his whereabouts, cursing all the time my father for what he had done to me and to James. Despite the deep despair that I felt, I managed to conceal my feelings from Reginald. We left shortly thereafter for Calcutta, arriving about a week later at the port at Hooghly. Quarters were already awaiting us, and the move was swift and easy."

At this point, said Holmes, Lady Maxwell paused for breath as if she were coming to the most difficult part of the story. He observed her closely as she fought to maintain her composure.

"Shortly after our arrival," she said, "we were invited to a large gathering at the home of a wealthy Indian trading family, the Shawsons, one of the leading families of Calcutta. There were many guests there, and the Viceroy and Lady Curzon paid a brief visit. As I stood on the verandah looking over the gardens, I felt a pair of eyes staring at me from behind. I turned. James Hamilton was standing there only a few feet away, the same look of love and disbelief in his eyes that he must have seen in mine. We could barely speak to each other, but we succeeded in arranging a secret meeting the following day. From that moment on, Mr. Holmes, I began a life of subterfuge and deceit here in Calcutta. James, with the same undying love that he has always felt for me, has pressed me to leave Reginald, and to return to England with him or, if that be impossible, to go with him to America, for he is now wealthy and we could live comfortably anywhere. I have decided on my own, Mr. Holmes, to leave Calcutta and to return to England. Only there, and alone, will I be able to decide what is right. I told Reginald that I thought it best for me to leave for a while, and that I would write to him as soon as I arrived in London. I of course did not tell him about James, but said that I had heard from my mother that certain problems had cropped up with the disposition of my father's estate and hence my presence was necessary. James has pressed me to tell Reginald all, but I have been unable to do so."

Then, she said, a few nights later, still unaware of her love for James, her husband informed her that he now had indisputable proof that he had found his long-lost brother: it was James Hamilton, the gentleman whom they had met at the Shawsons'. Despite her dismay, she managed to ask her husband if he were certain. He replied that his father had given him some strong clues and evidence which made it almost undeniable. It merely awaited some corroboratory sign from James, the nature of which he did not reveal to her.

"You may imagine my state of mind, Mr. Holmes, when I learned that the man with whom I was in love was the brother of the man to whom I was married. I have said nothing to James. I am more than ever determined to leave, for I cannot lead the duplicitous life of the last few months any longer, particularly under the latest revelations. In any case, Mr. Holmes, they will meet shortly, and I am afraid that James will not be able to contain himself and that the shock of hearing that he is Reginald's brother will lead him to reveal his relationship with me."

She was by now near the end of her story.

"Mr. Holmes," she said, "I am leaving Calcutta not out of cowardice, but because my respect for the man I married and my love for James have compelled me to go. I fear their meeting, and yet it is, I know, inevitable. I can only hope that your long friendship with my husband may be of some benefit to us all in this web of unsought relationships and that your wise counsel may be made available to all of us."

She stood up as if to depart. Holmes told her that he saw the clash that might occur and that he would speak to Sir Reginald as soon as he would see him. She bade him good-bye.

"I offered to see her to her residence, for by now it was quite late, but she declined, saying that she had learned to manage very well at night and that I should have no fear for her safety. I saw her to the door of the hotel. The staff was asleep on the floor, and we quietly tiptoed between them. I slowly unbolted the door, she turned to me, bade me again good-bye, put down her veil, and instantly vanished into the dreadful night. As I peered after her, the night air chilled, Watson, and though I am not a fanciful person, it was as if a forewarning of the tragic events that were to follow."

Holmes said that he then returned to his room. He had of course not told Lady Maxwell the details of his meeting with her husband, that he appeared beneath the surface to be extremely agitated, and what Holmes's worst fears now were: that Sir Reginald had learned not only that James Hamilton was his long-lost half brother but also that he was the lover of his most beloved wife. Only that knowledge could explain the look of despair Holmes had seen on his friend's unhappy face.

I watched Holmes as he stood up, placing his now spent pipe in its holder, and walked over to the fireplace. He stood there gazing into the dying embers and said: "It was a night of restless dreams, Watson, in which my brain wrestled unconsciously with the possible consequences of what I had heard that evening."

It was to be a short night, he said, for he awoke at one point in a start, his heart pounding at the end of the latest in a series of nightmares. It was about four in the morning. He could no longer sleep. He arose, washed, dressed, and was about to go out to watch the dawn when there was a strong knock at the door. He opened it to find a British soldier standing there.

"Mr. Lytton-Smith, Sergeant Laughton, sir," he said. "The Viceroy has asked me to accompany you to his office at once."

He handed Holmes a note. It read, with no salutation:

I request that you come immediately to me on a matter of the greatest concern.

Curzon

A cab was waiting, and they were taken directly to the Viceroy's private office. Holmes recognised where he was even in the morning darkness, for they were not far from where he had visited Sir Reginald. He was at once ushered into the presence of the Viceroy, who motioned all to leave. Rising from his desk, the Viceroy began to speak slowly and deliberately, in a tone filled with sorrow.

"Mr. Holmes, a tragedy of monumental proportions has occurred during the night, and I only hope that Providence has brought you here back from the dead in order to help us avoid any further evil."

"I am at your complete command, my lord," replied Holmes.

"In brief, then," he began, "Sir Reginald Maxwell, your friend and my trusted assistant, together with an English merchant, Mr. James Hamilton, were found dead in Maxwell's private office in the early morning hours. I have just come from the scene and, though I have seen my share of gore on the battlefield, Mr. Holmes, I have never seen anything quite like this. Both of them were shot and then beheaded. There are signs of a great struggle, for everything is in disarray. It appears to have been some kind of a cult murder, possibly a case of thuggee. There are imprecations on the wall in a local tongue, possibly Sanscrit, though no one can tell me definitely, that appear to indicate that the murders are also a direct attack on our rule. Some kind of obscene goddess holding a head in each of her hands is drawn in blood on the back wall behind Reginald's desk, with the words *Kali* and *rastra* written in the native script. Kali is the goddess of the criminal thugs, Mr. Holmes, and *rastra* the word for nation, or so I am told. We have no way of knowing at this point who perpetrated this dastardly act, but if it proves to be an act of terror by some of India's misguided political leaders rather than the wanton act of some insane intruders, the consequences for the relationship between us and the Indian people are grave. Whatever it is, I regard this as the most evil attack upon us since the Cawnpore massacre."

The Viceroy paused for a brief moment and then said in quiet anger, "I can only hope too that this was not meant as an act of welcome, so to speak, for His Highness Edward, the King-Emperor, who is scheduled to set foot on Indian soil in three days."

Pacing back and forth before Holmes, like an angry lion, he continued: "Mr. Holmes, it may also be that Reginald Maxwell and James Hamilton were killed by mistake, that I was the intended victim, and that it was the purest accident, the confusion of the mad beasts who entered the compound in the dark, that led to their slaying. In any case, I must act swiftly and ruthlessly in order to ensure that the perpetrators of this crime are brought to justice, that the King-Emperor is secure at all times during his sojourn to the Subcontinent, and that by extension British rule in India cannot be and is not questioned."

He stopped, and stood motionless before Holmes. "There are, however," he continued, "certain aspects of this crime that have made me hesitate before I act. One is that I am aware that Maxwell had recently discovered that Hamilton was his own brother or half brother. He at first seemed happy at learning this fact, but for the last few days, judging from his depressed mien, he seemed tormented, as if he had learned some awful secret as well. I do not know if the death of these men has anything to do with their relationship, and I ask you if you know anything that might shed light on the matter."

Holmes replied that he was aware of various possible relationships, but that he was not at liberty to divulge them at present, though he would do so if he thought they had any bearing on the case and such information would avoid further bloodshed.

The Viceroy replied that he appreciated such discretion and said: "There is, in the view of this office, Mr. Holmes, an aspect to this case that far outweighs any personal grief or loss that we may have to bear, for it involves a grave matter of state. One of the most secret files, containing animadversions pertaining to most secret matters of state now before His Majesty's Government, has disappeared. It is written almost entirely in my own hand. It was known only to Maxwell and to me. I gave it to him to return to its proper place yesterday afternoon. It is not there and, as far as could be determined, is not in his office."

"My lord," said Holmes, "you must tell me something of its contents, otherwise my investigation may be hampered."

The Viceroy looked at Holmes sternly, almost as if he had committed an impertinence, but then said quietly: "Mr. Holmes, I am bound by sacred oath to the King-Emperor not to reveal to anyone save my personal assistant the subject of such files. You should respect my desire to keep that oath. However, should you find during your investigation that you must know the contents for the larger good of the Empire, then I shall break my oath and divulge them, but only to you. Let it suffice for now to say that the documents concern the outbreak of war in Eurasia, a war which would have in my view the most tragic consequences for all mankind."

"What you have just told me may suffice, my lord. I think I should now have a look at the scene of the crime."

"There is one other bizarre aspect, Mr. Holmes," said the Viceroy, "that you ought to be aware of before you enter Maxwell's office. It may be an accident, but evidently the perpetrators of the crime confused the two men in the dark, placing Hamilton's head on Maxwell's body and Maxwell's on Hamilton's."

This latest revelation sent a shiver of revulsion up Holmes's spine, for he did not believe that this had occurred by chance.

"Who discovered the crime?" he asked.

"Lady Maxwell," replied the Viceroy quietly. "Poor woman. She apparently awoke in the middle of the night and, not finding Maxwell at home, rushed to the office, thereby walking into the scene of horror that I have described to you. She rushed out and collapsed into the arms of a guard, who immediately investigated and notified me. No one else has been in there except Laughton, my personal guard, the aide who brought you here. He has studied the local languages to some extent and was able to make a preliminary decipherment of the writing on the wall."

"Where is Lady Maxwell now?"

"At home under sedation and intense care. The doctors fear for her life and sanity."

Holmes's thought went to the moment just a few hours before when Lady Maxwell had disappeared into that dark night. Little did they know that the events that were transpiring as they talked would go far beyond any imaginable horror.

The Viceroy remained in his office, and Sergeant Laughton accompanied Holmes to Maxwell's private office, the same one he had visited only two days before. It was indeed a horrible scene. Blood was everywhere. The two dead men were lying on their backs, head to head. Their heads had, as reported, been transposed. Holmes could only think of Lady Maxwell at this moment and hoped that somehow her agony might someday come to a peaceful end.

"I shall not go over my investigation in detail, Watson. With my usual methods, I examined everything with the greatest care, taking copious notes on the positions of everything in the room. I paid the closest attention to the writing on the wall. It read काली., which, as Lord Curzon had indicated, spelled *Kali,* the word for the bloodthirsty goddess of the Bengalese, and राष्-, or *rastra,* the Indian word for nation, a reference presumably to the growing feeling for an independent nation run by Indians alone. There were a few details that intrigued me, however. Each syllable of the word *kali* had a dotlike mark after it, something unknown in the Indian scripts, and the word *rastra* was followed by a small dashlike sign, as if the word were incomplete. Perhaps the message would have been longer had the murderers not been interrupted during the writing. But as with the dots, unless I was mistaken, the dash did not appear to be part of another unfinished letter, nor was it part of the known conventions of the scripts with which I was familiar. The goddess drawing itself was an obscene stick figure, herself headless, blood surging up and out her gorge. In each hand she held a head. Crude figures, headless with blood surging forth from their necks, knelt in homage on either side of her. Another figure, apparently female from its dress, also knelt in worship to her. The hideousness of it all made me yearn for the crimes of London, which appeared staid by comparison."

Holmes left the scene and walked out on the verandah to ponder the evidence that he had assembled. There was already enough, he believed, for him to find the solution, if only he could piece it all together. Was it as the Viceroy suspected, a political act of terror, perpetrated by a vile cult of murderers hired by some misguided politicians desirous of frightening the British out of India? Or was it something else?

In an instant, as if his mind had anticipated it through the restless dreams of the night before, some of the puzzle began to fall into place. Holmes returned quickly to the Viceroy's office. Lord Curzon was with a secretary, but he sent him out as soon as Holmes appeared.

"I believe, Your Lordship," said Holmes, "that I understand much of what happened last night. I do not believe that it was an act of terror perpetrated by thugs or by thugs in the pay of politicians."

"Then what is it?"

"I shall be able to tell you all shortly. In the meantime, I want you to act as if this is, indeed, an act of terror, or a suspected one, and allow your investigation to proceed along those lines. Do as you would ordinarily under such circumstances: put troops on the alert and round up suspects. But on no account allow anyone to come to harm, for no one you will arrest will have had anything to do with the crime. Your men must be instructed to be firm but, particularly in cases of opposition and protest, extremely gentle. I ask you to do this so that the real culprit is put off and does not escape before we have a chance to catch him in his lair."

"How do you know he is not gone already?"

"He may indeed have already escaped and be beyond our reach. I have little doubt, however, that he has the secret file and probably knows of the presence of Sherlock Holmes in Calcutta. If I am correct he is waiting for me to bargain for the secret documents. He may want a large sum for their return."

"If we cannot apprehend him, we will pay, provided the contents have not been divulged. But where is he? Who is he? Or are there more than one of them?"

"There is at least one, the ringleader. He may or may not have accomplices, but they are not nearly as important, Your Lordship. I wish now to ask you to provide me with the best maps of Calcutta at your disposal. I shall need absolute quiet for a time as I work."

"You shall have it."

"While I am engaged, I shall need two other requests to be met. I should like an immediate investigation of Maxwell's staff to see if all are accounted for, including peons, sweepers, and other menial help. I am especially interested in knowing the whereabouts and identity of the peon who ushered me into Sir Reginald's office two days ago. This information may be brought to me while I am at work."

"What else?"

"I shall want three of your most trusted Gurkhas to accompany me to my destination, to my meeting with the culprit. They are to be dressed as peaceful pilgrims and to carry no weapons save their knives. I wish at all costs to apprehend this criminal alive. You can see from the deed that he is no ordinary malefactor but one of great cruelty and intelligence, with whom, if I am correct, I have grappled before. He is capable of the greatest violence, and there is no question in my mind that he would like to put an end to me."

"Holmes, simply give me the word and I can supply you with an entire regiment of Gurkhas."

"Your Excellency, I believe that three of your best men will be ample, even in these circumstances."

Holmes left the Viceroy and sat with the detailed maps of the city supplied to him. He pored over them until he found what he needed. It was as he had suspected. He surmised that the criminal awaited him at a temple to Kali, a temple to a particular form of this divinity, the one known as the goddess of the severed head. This was the message he had read in the drawings on the wall. Temples to this special form of Kali were very rare. Indeed, to this goddess, or Chinnamashtaka as she is known to her worshippers, there was only one possible temple, an old medieval shrine just on the northern outskirts of the city, isolated enough to provide safe refuge for the man Holmes wanted.

"As I finished my investigation," said Holmes, "Sergeant Laughton informed me that one of Maxwell's peons, Karim, a man described as a recently arrived Kashmiri emigrant, had not returned to work and apparently had disappeared. It was he who had ushered me in and out of Maxwell's office. That was all I needed: I now knew how the culprit had entered Maxwell's office and stolen the file. This Karim, said Laughton, had been hired because he came with excellent recommendations 'and seemed to be rather intelligent for a native.' It was difficult for me to control my urge to laugh."

It was about six in the evening when Holmes had finished his work. He went directly to Curzon's office. Three Gurkhas, now in the peaceful dress of Nepalese pilgrims, were sitting, awaiting his arrival. They rose as he entered. Curzon had personally supervised their selection.

"They are the bravest and the most skilled that I can give you, Holmes. They are a match for at least fifteen to twenty ordinary men, and I pity those who come in conflict with them."

Holmes looked at the men carefully. Curzon had indeed chosen well. Not only were they strong but they appeared calm. Holmes told them that they would be going to a temple, and that they were to worship in the ordinary way. He continued that he was trying to apprehend a dangerous murderer, that he wanted him taken alive if possible, and that they should be ready to come to his aid when he gave the signal: the lifting of his left hand to his ear. They appeared to understand. He described to them the man that he wanted. He was short, thin, fair skinned, and would be dressed as a yogi or fakir. He gave them minute directions to the temple, telling them that they should arrive separately. He would arrive shortly after them dressed as he then was. On no account were they to acknowledge his presence, but they were to keep their eyes on him at all times. At the signal, they were to seize the man to whom he was talking, if possible without injury to him.

"I took my leave of the Viceroy, and walking a safe distance from the palace, I took a rickshaw to the temple of the goddess of the severed head. It was a long ride, some five or six miles. I remember going through a Muslim quarter, with the attendant abattoir, filled with hundreds of vultures gorging on the remains of the day's kill. By the time I reached the temple precinct, it was dusk. Along the way, I had mentally reviewed the plan of the temple. It was a small shrine located in the middle of a rectangular courtyard. At one end was an ashram that housed the chief priest and some Hindu mendicants. I was sure that my quarry was living there in disguise."

As he spoke now, Holmes became greatly agitated, for he was reliving the final events of his long tale with an even greater vividness than before.

"I walked slowly up the few steps to the temple compound. It was almost dark. There was the usual evening religious activity—the ringing of bells, offerings, the wailing of infants. As I entered the courtyard, I tried to locate my Gurkha confederates but could not. I could only hope that they had arrived in time."

Holmes acted the part of the English tourist, curious, befuddled, without direction, for he assumed that his quarry would find him easily. As his eyes grew accustomed to the darkness, he could see the usual conglomeration of human derelicts that is so often present at places of this kind—the crippled, the limbless, the dumb, the starving. In the flashing of the oil lamps, he could also make out the temple, a gaudy and hideous affair, covered with skeletons, images of horrible spirits, and monsters of a repulsive variety. In the main sanctuary stood the headless goddess herself. Holmes stared at the image briefly, then became aware that a young girl, one of the many derelicts, this one dumb and dressed in filthy rags, had accosted him and had begun tugging at his coat, pulling him toward a large peepul tree that was situated at the back of the shrine. In the darkness he made out a figure seated in yogic posture under the tree, his face hidden by a shawl draped over the upper half of his body. The dumb child pulled Holmes in that direction, and the yogin motioned to him to sit down. The child brought two oil lamps, which provided the only light.

"Welcome, Mr. Sherlock Holmes." The voice had a pronounced foreign accent, and the speaker hissed the name through his teeth. "I was expecting you."

"So," said Holmes, "we meet again. If I am not mistaken, I sit before Karol Lissanevitch Rastrakoff, onetime member of the Oriental Institute at St. Petersburg, now secret agent for the Tsar in central Asia, an infamous figure throughout the murky underworld of Asia. We tangled in Tibet, Rastrakoff, and I would judge the contest a draw. Your message of blood was clear to me almost immediately, for your initials and part of your last name conveniently spelled *ka* and *li,* and *rastra,* the word for nation in the native tongue. I shall not waste time or mince words: I want the return of the file, for which I am willing to offer a reasonable sum and your safe passage out of India."

"Mr. Holmes, Mr. Holmes, please, dear sir, you move too quickly."

As he talked, he lowered the shawl from his face, and Holmes saw once again the cruel countenance that recorded so many evil deeds.

"A most impressive jump into my rickshaw, Rastrakoff. My compliments."

Rastrakoff smiled. "It was nothing," he said, "with our training. But we have more important matters before us. First, let me explain to you that I have no desire to bargain for the file. It is already on its way to its intended destination. It was of the utmost importance to my employers, and I stopped at nothing to obtain it. The deaths of Maxwell and Hamilton were unavoidable, for they entered the office unexpectedly after hours. They interrupted me in my search. I was able to hide when they entered, but then they began an interminable conversation, punctuated by Maxwell's loud accusations. I had little time to waste, and at the height of their argument I shot them both, intending at first to make the crime into one of murder and suicide. I then found the file. It was while I was seeking it that I thought of the grand opportunity that had been thrown my way. The file, once I had it, was my triumph. But if I could cause the Viceroy to think of this murder as an act of terror against Britain, then I would have caused even greater havoc among our enemies. I decided then to make the crime look like an act of thuggee."

"A foolish move," said Holmes, "for it did not look like such an act at all. Thuggee victims are strangled alive, Rastrakoff."

"Only one such as you would be aware of such niceties. Your countrymen are pitifully ignorant of the people they rule. It was only after I severed their heads that I decided the third part of my plan: to lead you here, for I had recognised you immediately upon your first visit to Maxwell. I reversed the heads, added the word *rastra* to my message, and arranged my initials so that they could be read in two different ways. I knew that you would read the message instantly. I gather now that I have been completely successful. The Viceroy has put all troops on the alert, arrested most of the political leaders of Bengal—and all on the eve of the visit of Edward VII, the so-called King-Emperor."

He stopped then and looked at Holmes, his eyes narrowing evilly. "And finally, I shall rid the world of Sherlock Holmes."

Rastrakoff squealed the last few words in a high falsetto, and the quick action that followed almost took Holmes by surprise.

"Rastrakoff lunged forward," said Holmes, "a dagger in hand. I fell back pinned to the ground, the point of the knife now grazing my chest. I was unable to free myself. Suddenly, I felt a shower of warm liquid that I at first took for my own blood. I looked up, however, to see Rastrakoff's severed head hurtling through the air, and I knew that the blood that covered me came from his open jugular. One of the Gurkhas, aware that I was pinned down, acting instinctively and with lightning speed, had rid the world of one of its archfiends."

Holmes's eyes were now ablaze as he recalled the perilous situation into which he had fallen. I listened in amazed silence and cold fear, for even though he was before me, he had related the last events with such intensity that I thought he might have been slain before me.

"The rest, unfortunately, is history. I reported immediately to the Viceroy that Rastrakoff was dead, and that he could call off the emergency. The file was already on its way to its destination and we had failed to recover it. When hostilities broke out between Russia and Japan thereafter, we knew that the documents had been used for their evil purposes."

Holmes had come to the end of his story. He smiled, and I could sense the irony that lay behind it. "That short war," he said with barely hidden sarcasm, "the first lost by a European power to an Asian one, will have untold repercussions for the white race as we move further into this century. Or so some historians will tell us."

"What an incredible story, Holmes. And to think that Maxwell and his brother were killed needlessly."

"Yes, my dear Doctor. Though there was more to that part of the story, a part which had to wait until my return to England. It was shortly before my meeting with you, Watson. You will recall that I was disguised as an old book dealer when we first met after my return?"

"Yes," said I.

"A few days before, I had journeyed to Yorkshire in the same guise, to find Rose Hamilton, the mother of James."

"Why on earth did you want to do that?" said I in great puzzlement.

"Because I had an idea, a mere suspicion, that Reginald and James were not brothers. I had examined them in death very carefully, and my knowledge of skeletal and craniological types had made me suspect that it was unlikely that they were related at all. And in fact there was something in Hamilton's face that struck me. There was a clear resemblance to someone, but it was not to Maxwell, though there was a surface simi-larity that had struck his wife early on. Upon my return to England, I went to Wyck Rissington in disguise, located the old Hume estate, the natal home of Lady Maxwell, and then found the house where James Hamilton had grown up. It was now an abandoned shack. His mother had died several years before in an alcoholic fever. Her place had been boarded up by a man in the village so that it would not be easily van-dalised. I entered the hut one night, prying off the boards nailed over a back window. I spent several hours looking through the woman's pos-sessions. There were many things there, among them hundreds of books, that indicated that Rose Hamilton had once been something other than what she finally became. There was also a small metal box in one of the drawers of an old cabinet that had been hidden amidst her clothes. Inside it was a small diary. It contained the information I had been hoping for. An entry, dated June 5, 1865, read: 'My little son, to whom I have given the name James, was born to me one week ago. His father is Jeremy Hume, who refuses to recognise him.' "

"Good lord," I cried. "Hamilton then was Lady Maxwell's half brother!"

"Precisely, my dear Watson. I had noticed the resemblance. Hence her father's violent reaction when he found that an amorous relation-ship had developed between them. It was during the telling of her story that I initially became suspicious. Hume, a man of position, could not admit either to his family or publicly that his liaison with the wench Rose Hamilton had produced unwanted progeny. Hence his violent outbursts and the actions that followed."

"And what of Maxwell's father, and the information conveyed to his son? Surely Maxwell believed that Hamilton was his half brother."

"I thought that this part of the case would be forever lost to us, since the last conversation between Maxwell and Hamilton was heard only by Rastrakoff. Its contents had died with all of them. Here again, however, my dear Watson, luck was with us, for another entry in Rose Hamilton's diary made it clear that, after the death of his wife, Humphrey Maxwell, Reginald's father, did begin to visit her as well and to take solace in her arms. When Hume failed to recognise his son, or to support her, Rose Hamilton turned to Maxwell, claiming he was the boy's father. Maxwell believed her, and secretly supported her and the child."

"Extraordinary," said I.

"Yes," said Holmes, "as I look back the story is perhaps unique in your annals. One day you might bring it to public attention."

"Indeed, I might. And what of Lady Maxwell?"

Holmes now looked out the window wistfully. He was silent for a moment. Then he said, "I wonder, Watson. I have often wondered."

THE CASE OF

HODGSON'S GHOST

I T WAS LATE IN MAY 1894 THAT THE DEATH OF BRIAN HOUGHTON Hodgson was announced in the London newspapers. One of the great Oriental scholars of the century, Hodgson passed away quietly in his sleep at his home in Aldersley at the age of ninety-four. His life had spanned, therefore, all but the last few years of the nineteenth century.

It was on seeing Hodgson's obituary that my friend Sherlock Holmes made the initial remarks that eventually resulted in this portion of the chronicle of his years in the Orient. In a most curious way, Hodgson played a large if indirect role in the singular events that I have set down here, but it was only after Holmes returned to England that he was to meet Hodgson in the flesh. In later years, my friend still referred to the great scholar of Buddhism and his lasting influence on the intellectual life of Europe.

Brian Hodgson was born in 1800 in Cheshire. When he was twenty-one, he joined the Indian Civil Service and was first sent to Calcutta, where he held a junior post. Shortly after his arrival, however, it became clear to his superiors that the climate and other discomforts of Bengal were serious impediments to his health. He had lost considerable weight, and there was talk of sending him home. He was posted instead to Almora in the Kumaon Himalaya, and when an opening appeared in Nepal, he was transferred with an appointment there as assistant to the British Resident, Edward Gardner.

It was in April 1823 that Hodgson left Almora for Katmandu. The journey was a difficult one. To reach the Nepalese capital, Hodgson had to brave the notorious jungles of the Tarai, where, in addition to the afflictions acquired in Bengal, he contracted one of the worst ailments of the globe, the aul, as it is known in those parts. He spent the first three weeks after his arrival ill with a high fever that kept him to his bed. Gradually, he began to mend, due largely to the ministrations of Mrs. Gardner and the salubrious climate of the mountains.

Upon his recovery, Hodgson rapidly became an energetic and trusted servant of the Company. So highly did his superiors regard him that Gardner, upon his retirement, recommended that he be appointed his successor. The recommendation was favourably received in Calcutta, and Hodgson, not yet thirty, attained the coveted position of British Resident to the Court of Nepal.

Hodgson was to remain twenty-one years in the post. During that time he pursued a double career. He was officially the Resident, representative of the East India Company to the Court of Nepal, and in this capacity, he became an intimate of the Nepalese rulers, in particular of General Bhimsen Thapa, with whom he wielded considerable influence. At the same time, he pursued a private career of science, immersing himself tirelessly in every aspect of the Himalaya, recording their history, languages, customs, and laws. His fame in Europe began with a series of papers on the religion of the Buddhists, then little known, which formed the basis of European research for many decades.

It was in 1843, however, that his policies and conduct came in direct conflict with those of Lord Ellenborough, then Governor-General of the Company. Hodgson was recalled, and rather than take the minor post that Ellenborough offered him in India, he resigned from the service and returned to England, where he devoted his time to scientific research on Asiatic subjects.

Some time after Hodgson's death, one night in the late summer of 1894, if memory serves, Holmes and I sat at home, quietly discussing his years of absence after the death of Moriarty. I remember the night vividly, for Holmes's latest bout with melancholia was unusually severe. In order to distract him, I prompted him with questions, hoping that they would result in a respite from the deep depression that had overwhelmed him.

"You have mentioned on several occasions, Holmes, that you journeyed at one point to Katmandu in the forbidden kingdom of Nepal, but it has never been clear to me what you did there or how indeed you managed to enter the country at all."

Holmes smiled for the first time in many days, and I saw that my prompting had the desired effect.

"There are few places, Watson, that touch one as deeply as Nepal. One of our countrymen has written that it would take the pen of a Ruskin or the brush of a Claude to do it justice, and in those judgements I must concur. The climate is salubrious, the natives friendly and as handsome as the landscape. They suffer, however, under the heel of a harsh and backward regime, and though it is in the interest of the Empire to support the present Maharajah, there is no question that the people would throw off his tyrannical yoke were it not for the support and friendliness that Government finds it necessary to display in order to preserve our interests."

As he spoke, Holmes became unusually expansive, and I realised only then the affection in which he held his mountain friends.

"As you may recall, Watson, I lived and travelled in Tibet in the guise of a Scandinavian explorer. Inevitably, however, my time in Lhasa was drawing to a close. The Regent, Gethong, who had been my friend and benefactor, had passed on, and although my enemies had largely scattered because of our combined efforts, they showed unmistakable signs of growing strength and order, and I knew that I should be an easy target should I choose to remain. I determined to leave, therefore, always aware of course that I was subject to deadly attack at any time. I changed my disguise and journeyed from Lhasa to Katmandu as a Tibetan lama. While resident in Tibet, I had acquired the Tibetan language and had studied the native Buddhist religion so that, should I choose to, I could be convincing in my expositions of doctrine to the lay folk of the country and to the lamas as well, some of whom I had bested in debate on a number of philosophical subjects. One day the Scandinavian explorer, Mr. Sigerson, bade good-bye to his friends and left. Coincident with his departure a lama from the north of Amdo arrived in Lhasa on his way south to Katmandu."

Holmes then recalled to me that he had been befriended by a

Nepalese trader long resident in Lhasa, and it was with his caravan that he made the difficult journey south. The trader, a Newar of the Tuladhar caste, had lived in Tibet for many years. His name was Gorashar, and he dealt in cloth and a variety of manufactured goods, including on occasion Russian weaponry. Holmes met him shortly after his arrival, and they soon became friends. Gorashar returned home to Nepal every four years, and it was fortunate that one of his trips coincided with the end of Holmes's Tibetan sojourn. Gorashar warned Holmes that he travelled at great risk and that discovery by the authorities in Katmandu would result in severe punishment. Holmes assured his friend that he was willing to bear the risk and that in any case his stay would be brief.

The journey was long and arduous, more difficult, said Holmes, than the one by which he had entered Tibet. From Lhasa they went to Shigatse, where they crossed the Tsangpo or Brahmaputra River, in one of those strange boats of yak skin that the Tibetans have manufactured from time immemorial. From this point they began the ascent to an altitude of nineteen thousand feet, a climb that strained the lungs of all.

"Many of the animals refused to go further," said Holmes, "and we had to search for fresh replacements. This caused endless delays. We finally crossed the pass above Nyalam, moving then to the village of Khasa, where we spent the night. On the following morning we crossed to Kodari, resting there for the evening. The following day we began our descent toward the kingdom of Dolakha, a few days' walk from Katmandu."

Holmes described the passing from Tibet into Nepal as a dramatic one. Though filled with astounding sights, Tibet, he said, is by and large a barren land of great immensity. Nothing there prepared him for the sight of the snowy heights of the Nepal Himalaya, the clear mountain streams and rivers that pass through them, or the lush vegetation that appears as soon as one begins the descent.

"To my knowledge, Watson, I was the first European to visit Dolakha, a forgotten kingdom of remarkable beauty, one even whose name is unknown to the civilised world. It was there that we began to recover from the rigours of our journey and I began to sense a well-being that I had not known for many years."

I smiled inwardly, for my friend rarely allowed himself to display his emotions, but in speaking of Nepal there was an exultant tone in his voice, one that I had not heard in a long time. He seemed to divine my thoughts, for he said, sternly and rather coolly: "Although I have often been amused by your portrayal of me as a cold calculating machine without emotion, I have chafed a bit at it as well, for it is of course untrue in one sense. I have emotions. In that I am like all other men. But they are completely in check and at the service of my brain. In that I am perhaps like no other."

I was amused by his attempt to attribute to my rather paltry literary efforts his own portrayal of himself as a thinking machine, but I did not join him in argument here, for I did not wish to interrupt him. Seeing that I had nothing to say, he grew pensive for a moment, then continued, as I had hoped he would.

"After our rest in Dolakha, we proceeded through Panch Kal to the old Newar town of Banepa, just east and south of the Nepal Valley. I remember clearly the morning there. We rose and bathed in one of the local dharas or fountains and then turned our direction along the road that leads toward Katmandu. The sun had begun to burn off the winter mist and it was still early when we began the final march. It was then that we saw the first signs of the beautiful villages that lie scattered across the landscape."

They climbed a small hill, passing a number of small brick temples. The fields were green, for there had been heavy winter rains. As they reached the top of a ridge, they turned and saw spread before them the valley of Katmandu.

"I must say, Watson, that I was a bit taken aback by its beauty, even more than by my first sight of Lhasa. There it lay, its golden pagodas, shining rivers, and verdant fields. I watched silently as our long party passed. Gorashar noticed my rapt attention. 'This is my home,' he said quietly, in his inimitable way."

For one of the few times in his life, said Holmes, his iron will relaxed and for a few moments he was at peace in a gentle world, one apparently without crime and its evils. He thought, for a brief instant, that he might remain in this place and devote himself to meditation and the contemplation of first principles, far from his enemies and unknown to them.

"For a few fleeting moments, these were tempting thoughts, but I quickly rejected them, knowing that once I had joined the struggle there was no turning back. I knew well that intelligent crime had begun to tire of London and the other metropolitan centres of Europe. Of course there is no end to the mayhem and the brutality of the London back alleys, but it is almost always the result of small frictions, with no overall pattern. If one wished to find the intelligent criminal, one would have to seek him out in the most unlikely of places. The more innocent the soil, the more likely it is to be sought by the criminal for his nefarious purposes. One had only to look at the innocent face of a Nepalese child, Watson, to understand what fertile ground the Himalaya might prove to be."

It was with these sobering thoughts that Holmes, not knowing what awaited him, walked the last few miles from the ridge near Banepa toward the city of Katmandu.

"I came out of my reverie sufficiently to notice that the caravan was well ahead of me. Gorashar himself had also tarried and was only a few yards ahead. He had been waiting for me. By the time I reached him I had sufficiently recovered, but not quickly enough to hide all my thoughts from his sensitive eyes. He said nothing, and I felt reassured by his presence."

They walked together behind the caravan, passing to the south of the ancient city of Bhaktapur and through the town of Thimi. It was late afternoon when they reached the outskirts of Katmandu.

"We were exhausted by our journey," said Holmes, "but exhilarated by our arrival. As our caravan passed through the city gates, we entered the main bazaar, and I caught my first glimpse of this new and vibrant place. Men and women bargaining, children at play, animals everywhere—there appeared at first to be no order to it all as each went about his task. I would have tarried here, but Gorashar was impatient to meet his wife and family, and so we continued through Indra Chowk to Khicha Pokhari, where his entire family had gathered in warm welcome. Gorashar and I were covered with garlands of flowers as we crossed the threshold to his residence."

Gorashar, Holmes explained, owned a small inn in the centre of town, where he also lived with his family. His lodgers were Indian merchants for the most part. He invited Holmes to stay, for in that way he could remain within the confines of the inn, venturing forth only when necessary.

"For the first few days, I limited my movement almost entirely to my room and the small but charming courtyard of the hotel, for I needed a more manageable disguise before I ventured forth. A Tibetan monk in this part of the city called for notice, and I felt that while the guise had been a convenient one for our journey, it was too difficult to maintain once one was in residence. In my few early forays outside the inn, I learned that Nepal was a land where the slightest change in the ordinary was noticed at once. The Tibetan monk had already attracted far too much attention. And so the need for a new and believable identity. You know well, Watson, my abilities with regard to disguises, and have remarked yourself more than once in your chronicles that the world had lost a great actor when I determined that I should devote my life to the study of crime. Yet, I must say, with regard to these abilities, that Nepal taxed my talents to the fullest. Although I am capable of shedding at least a foot from my height, I could never pass for a Gurkha. The build of these hillmen and their physiognomy are completely different from ours. Being a Tibetan monk or European trader was quite satisfactory for Lhasa and the subsequent journey, but far too confining for a stay in Katmandu. Sooner or later, I should be found out. The disguise of Sigerson, the Scandinavian scientist, which I had finally abandoned in Lhasa, I could not revive, for the Nepalese government does not allow Europeans into the country without elaborate justification or enormous bribes. I needed a new disguise, therefore, one that would at once arouse little attention and yet afford me the freedom that I needed to move about at will. I decided that I should have to become an Indian, for they cross the border in the Tarai freely, and that I would have to be one of high caste, for there would be no other that would secure my freedom of movement. The dark-skinned frail Bengali I immediately eliminated as well as the peoples of northern Bihar and Oudh. A Rajput prince? Perhaps, but I decided against it on the grounds that the Gorkhali rulers were said to be in constant touch with the Maharajahs of Rajputana and that I should be hard-pressed for elaborate fictions. South India I know nothing of, and besides, the Tamileans are darker complexioned than the people of the north.

"This reasoning left me with the Punjab and Kashmir from which to choose. Sikhs were too visible, and their small community would immediately find me out. This left Kashmir, and I decided the best disguise might be that of a Kashmiri merchant. The difficulty was, of course, that these merchants are nearly all Mahometans, and the activities of Mahometans are restricted by the Hindu orthodoxy of the Nepalese Maharajahs. In the end, I decided on the disguise of a Kashmir Brahman or pundit, one who had come to Nepal to study the languages and dialects of the Himalaya. I had met on my way to India a young Irishman from Belfast by the name of Grierson, who was conducting a linguistic survey. He had remarked to me that his assistants were mainly Kashmiri Brahmans, who were well educated, light complexioned, and well versed in English. I was also aware of the work done in Kashmir by the Hungarian scholar Aurel Stein, whose archaeological interest had led him into remote areas of the Hindu Kush.

"And so, my dear Doctor, I became, shortly after my arrival in Katmandu, Pundit Kaul, Assistant, Royal Linguistic Survey of India. I carried letters from both Grierson and Stein, forged of course, but convincing enough in their description of my character and assigned duties. So quick was my reasoning in all this that my decision took but a few seconds, the steps in my explanation to you being decided almost instantly by the mind."

Holmes recalled to me that he took the greatest care with the disguise, planning it to the most minute detail. One day, he said, the monk who had arrived from Lhasa bade good-bye to Gorashar's family and his few recent acquaintances and departed for India. Just after the police check post at Bhimphedi, however, he abandoned his robes, and clad in Kashmiri costume, he reentered the Katmandu Valley as Pundit Kaul of Srinagar.

"I shall not bore you with details, Watson, but I may say that it is remarkable what a beard, properly shaped by a local barber, Indian spectacles, and Kashmiri dress can do for one's appearance. I returned on foot to Gorashar's hotel, and though he knew of my plan, I was pleased that he did not recognise me when I entered. My disguise as an ageing Kashmiri pundit appeared to work very well."

Holmes now roamed the bazaar more freely, learning the maze of its narrow streets and alleys. In so doing, he concluded at once that the notion of a forbidden kingdom was the deliberate and well-calculated fabrication of a weak government which did not dispose of the means to defend itself from outside interference. There were many from abroad living in Katmandu, and it appeared that anyone who had the physical stamina and the will could enter Nepal. The length and success of his stay depended on the skill of his disguise, and the extent to which he was willing to profit by the corruption of local officials. Through the years, said Holmes, the Nepalese Government had kept an official record of foreigners afforded permission to enter the country. They numbered but a handful.

"So much for the humbug of governments, Watson. I can attest to the fact that the country was riddled with secret agents working both for and against our interests, and that I recognised several criminals of international repute living in the central bazaar, all rather recently arrived. In just two days, I had identified three Tsarist agents, among them the notorious anarchist and bomb thrower Kakovetsky, whose whereabouts had been unknown for many years. And there were others. There was Rizzetti, the poisoner of entire families, living as a shopkeeper; Thalmann, the inventor of the deadly Salzburg rifle, earning a meagre existence as an old map seller; Caspariste, a former groom in the stables of the German Kaiser suddenly gone mad, a trail of horrors from Riga to Messina the result, now running a spectacle repair shop; and the infamous Anna Miramar, the Spanish gypsy and murderer of Lord Harrow, now the rich owner of a brothel and the chief supplier of young Nepalese women to the bordellos of India. All of this, Watson, in an area smaller than the distance from Trafalgar Square to Piccadilly. Like a beautiful forbidden fruit, Nepal had begun to attract a large number of maggots, ready to feed on its soft sweet flesh.

"I shall not deny to you, Watson, the pleasure that I imagined in bringing these criminals to justice, but I realised the difficulty of doing so in a country where the criminal justice system was of a rather crude order. I sensed, also, rather surprisingly one might think considering my stated attitudes in the past, the absence of Scotland Yard, particularly of Gregson and Lestrade, for though I have been harsh at times in my judgement of their intellectual capabilities, their physical presence has enabled me to pull through many a narrow scrape. And, if I may say so, dear Watson, at times such as these, I missed your companionship and wished that you could share with me these strange moments abroad."

"How I wish," I said, "I had been there with you. But pray, continue."

"Once back in the solitude of my room," he said, "more trouble-some thoughts emerged in my brain. Why had these rogues gathered here? Was it merely the innocent soil? Was their presence here on the very edge of the civilised world due to accident, or was there some hith-erto unsuspected criminal intelligence lurking in the shadows, another prime mover of crime whose design was so subtle and so complex that perhaps even the major actors in his plans were unaware of his thoughts and actions, or perhaps even of his existence?"

So much did these and other like thoughts disturb him, Holmes re-called, that for several nights he slept only fitfully. One night, he awoke sometime after midnight. He dressed and read for a time by candle-light. He had borrowed from Gorashar an old tome, some essays of the British Resident Brian Hodgson, who had left Nepal many decades be-fore. He read several of these but quickly tired of them, and though his eyes ached, he could not sleep. He looked out his window. The city was quiet. The Clock Tower struck two. He peered into the pitch darkness and decided to walk into the bazaar.

"I descended the stairs, passed through the courtyard and into the front hall of the hotel, where I picked my way carefully, gingerly step-ping over the bodies of the servant boys asleep on the floor. I unbolted the door quietly and let myself out into the dark. You know my pen-chant for nocturnal wanderings, Watson. Each new city requires several prowls by night. It is the time when the scent of the criminal is at its strongest."

The night air was cold, damp with Himalayan mist. Holmes had wrapped himself tightly in a woollen shawl that left only his eyes un-covered. He wore a black cap, the Nepalese topi, so that he would not arouse suspicion in the event that he were seen. But he had little to fear, he said, for the night was moonless, the sky cloudy, and the dark night enveloped him immediately.

"The city was filled with stray and wild dogs who began their hor-rible yelping at dusk and continued until they fell asleep around mid-night. They were quiet now, but every so often one growled suddenly from the darkness. I moved on, tripping over the occasional person asleep on the ground. I made my way to the market square called Asan. There I perceived dimly a few people performing some nocturnal wor-ship, but except for the occasional tinkling of temple bells, the city had entered a silence as deep as the enveloping darkness. I walked slowly down a lane opposite the chief shrine, holding on to the buildings with my left hand as I tried not to stumble on the rough stones of the gully. The ancient bricks sometimes crumbled to dust at my touch, and invisible rodents scurried over my feet."

Holmes judged that he had wandered for almost an hour when the lane ended, and he found himself in the main square of the town near the old royal palace, the so-called Hanuman Dhoka, or Door of Hanuman, the Ape-God. The square itself presented an unearthly appearance in the night, its pagodas rigid and black in the enormous shadows, their idols barely visible. It was here, he recalled, that much of the bloody drama of Nepalese kings and princes had unfolded. In the centre of the square he saw the hideous image of the Black God. Even in the almost total obscurity of this night, the white of his eyes and fangs was visible.

It was only after he passed through this lugubrious scene that he noticed any further sign of human activity. Before him, just at the beginning of that portion of the bazaar known as Makhantol, he saw the flicker of a candle emanating from a partially open window. He heard voices, and speaking what he thought to be English. Curious, he went closer. An argument, quiet but deadly serious, was under way. Three men were seated round a small table, one facing outward in Holmes's direction. Holmes could barely make out his features, but in the intermittent flickering provided by the candle, Holmes knew he had seen him before. The others, their backs to the window, were wrapped in darkness.

The first man spoke in English but with a very heavy European accent: "No more, unnerstana? No more! I geef you no more—"

"These were his last words, Watson," said Holmes grimly, "for as he spoke, one of the men seated opposite him rose slowly. He was tall, far too tall for a Nepalese. I could see little of his face by the candlelight, but I saw his eyes. I am not a fanciful person, Watson, but they were enough for me to realise that I was in the presence of a formidable adversary. It took all of my self-control to prevent a gasp of surprise from issuing from my lips. The look of cruelty in his eyes was visible for but an instant, however, for in the same motion with which he had risen from his chair, he pulled a dagger from under his cloak and plunged it into the heart of the man in front of him. So quick was he and so surprised was his victim that the latter let out no sound, slumping in silence to the ground. The murderer withdrew his weapon from the dead man's chest, calmly wiping it on his victim's shawl, and disappeared with his accomplice into the night. As they withdrew, however, the candle flamed bright in the ensuing draught, and for an instant the faces of the murderer and his accomplice were partially revealed. They were both Englishmen without doubt."

Holmes was tempted to follow them, but they disappeared immediately into the dark labyrinth of the city. He found the door to the wretched victim's room and entered. The corpse lay in a pool of blood. The candle was still aflame, and by its light he recognised Rizzetti, the poisoner. The killer of many, he had come to a violent end, richly deserved no doubt, but one that was deeply troubling to Holmes for what it seemed to portend for his stay in Katmandu.

"I left Rizzetti to those who would eventually find him and walked back to my quarters. As I passed through the hotel courtyard, I noticed the slightest touch of light blue in the sky. I had been gone almost until dawn. No one, however, was aware of my nocturnal peregrination."

Holmes lay down on the bed, falling into a light sleep. He was soon startled awake by a strange clatter rattling outside his window. He looked down to see hundreds of pigeons gathered on the roof below, feeding on the grain that had just been thrown to them. It was a morning ritual, and he had not yet grown accustomed to the sound of large handfuls of maize, muckeye, as they called it, striking the tin roof. He peered out to see an old Newar woman above him, hurling grain from a verandah high above his room.

"The day had indeed begun," said Holmes, "too noisily perhaps for one who had been up the better part of the night. Morning worship had started all over the city accompanied by the ablutions of the Nepalese, including the vociferous removal of catarrh from the nose and throat. But so warmly human were these sounds and sights that they dispelled some of the apprehension engendered by the events of the previous night.

"There was a knock at my door, by now familiar. Lakshman, a small village boy who worked as a bearer in the hotel, was there with my morning tea. He was only eleven years of age, dirty, barefoot, but of great cheer and spirit. The Anglo-Indian breakfast of eggs and porridge was on the usual filthy tray, which he placed on a small table in front of my window. He smiled and left as quickly as he had come."

Holmes sipped his tea, ruminating on the events of the night before. His close scrutiny of the bazaar over many days had convinced him that he had identified all the European criminals in Katmandu. All were known to him, and not one of them matched the physical appearance of Rizzetti's murderer or his accomplice. No, these villains were not in the bazaar but had a refuge elsewhere. But where? Eliminating all impossibilities, Holmes arrived at a possible answer to his question: the British Residency itself, the only place where an Englishman could be lodged or could hide unobserved.

"As I sat there deep in thought, I noticed that the teacup and saucer had begun to jingle and the small table on which my breakfast was placed had begun to shake. The vibrations moved to my chair, and for a moment I thought that perhaps a cat or some other animal had been trapped under it. Suddenly, the entire room began to sway and the hotel itself seemed to move. The tray slid off the table, and I heard the crashing of objects outside my window and the voices of people shouting wildly. Then the shaking abated as suddenly as it had come. It took no time at all to realise that I had just lived through an earthquake. A strong tremor had passed through the city. I raced to the window. There appeared to have been no great damage, for everything I could see was intact. But people were shouting, and it was then that I heard something I shall not forget: the rhythmic, slow, mesmerising repetition of the syllables 'ah ah,' uttered over and over again in unison by what seemed to be the entire population of Katmandu. I learned later from Gorashar that this is the magic utterance of the people, spoken as they press their thumbs against the ground to stop the earth from moving under them any further."

It was not long before Holmes dressed and was on his way out. He could see that the bright Katmandu sun was already high in the sky as he walked through the courtyard. Gorashar stopped him and warned that he exercise all caution. The royal astrologers, he said, had seen a most inauspicious conjunction of stars and planets and foresaw the possibility of disastrous events. The morning's earth tremor was merely the beginning. Everyone in Nepal was now engaged in worshipping the gods in order to ward off further calamity. The entire population of the city was frightened, and in their fear could instantly blame any stranger. Holmes reassured Gorashar that he would be most prudent, and that he wished to pay his first call on the British Resident, Mr. Edward Richardson. Gorashar said that the city was filled with rumours concerning the Resident's health. According to these, he was very ill and would not receive anyone. Holmes insisted, however, and Gorashar said that he would accompany him as far as the outer wall of the city.

Just as they entered the place known as Bhotahity, a large procession stopped them.

"The Bodhisattvas have come to protect us," said Gorashar, with audible disbelief.

The procession was a compelling sight for Holmes nonetheless. Avalokiteshvara and the other chief deities of Buddhism walked slowly past, their robes barely concealing the more diminutive figures who walked within them, holding up the great weight of the statues.

Gorashar departed, leaving Holmes to watch the full procession. When it had passed, he walked through the old city gate and proceeded in a northerly direction toward the British Residency.

"The Residency," Holmes continued, "lies outside the old city walls, to the north, in a place that had once been infertile swampland and was considered by the Nepalese to be unlucky and inauspicious, haunted by demons. What events may have lain behind these quaint superstitions are well hidden in the recesses of Nepalese history, but even a casual observer could see that a succession of British Residents had turned the swamp into a small English paradise. The gardens were extraordinary and the Residency itself of the most pleasing dimensions. Much of this was the creation of Brian Hodgson, the second person to occupy the post of Resident, for he had spent more than twenty years in Katmandu. It was he who was first charged with turning the cursed spot given by the Nepalese into a place where our representatives could live in tranquillity.

"As I entered the Residency, I was greeted by one Shiv Shankar, the chief pundit, an Indian from Banaras. He accepted my letters of introduction without question and informed me that Mr. Richardson was still quite ill, but that he would see me, if only briefly. I saw a look of deep concern on the pundit's face as he accompanied me to the rear of the Residency."

Richardson was seated in the sun on the terrace. As Holmes came into view, Richardson turned stiffly and motioned him to a chair near him. He seemed to have been very ill, for he was emaciated, and of a deadly pallor. Probably a thin man to begin with, his recent illness had only made him appear even more gaunt and skeletal.

"Forgive me, Punditji, and welcome. I have not been well, and under the orders of the Resident Surgeon, Dr. Wright, I am not to exert myself at all, even to rise out of this chair for an honoured scholar such as yourself. I gather that you bring news of Mr. Grierson and Mr. Stein."

"I bring you warm greetings from both gentlemen," said Holmes.

"Ah," the Resident said, with a bit of effort, "Grierson! That ambitious young philologist, the one who is writing a book about all the languages of the Subcontinent! And Stein, whom I met in Kashmir. A funny little man, eh wot? With a funny little dog."

"But a man of intense energy and great intelligence," replied Holmes.

Holmes's mild contradiction seemed to disturb the Resident. It was as if the reference to Stein's energetic ways reminded him of his former self. He became silent, and stared into the far recesses of the garden. There was a further exchange of pleasantries, but it was clear that the Resident's energy had ebbed.

Rather than overstay his welcome, Holmes took his leave and expressed the hope that they would have occasion to meet again soon. So weak had Richardson suddenly become that he did not reply, and he bade Holmes good-bye with a feeble wave of his hand. In his eyes Holmes saw a look of despair, as if he were bidding farewell to any connections with the outside world that he once might have had.

"I returned to Pundit Shiv Shankar's study, where I spent the afternoon with him and a Nepalese scholar, one Gunanand, working on the philological tasks that Grierson had supposedly assigned to me. This work consisted of having the biblical text of the parable of the prodigal son translated into the various languages and dialects of the Himalaya. Simple but lengthy, this task gave me the pretext to pay repeated visits to the Residency. On that first visit, I also became acquainted with the work that the pundits were doing themselves. They were immersed in the innocent world of Oriental scholarship, preparing a translation into

English of a mythological history of Nepal written by Gunanand's grandfather, a translation which had been commissioned by the Resident Surgeon, Dr. Wright. But of my other concerns I learned nothing, at least not immediately."

Holmes now visited the Residency on a regular basis, and in the following days he became aware that the only other people living there, beyond the servants and the guards, were the aforementioned Dr. Wright and Richardson's daughter, Lucy, who had arrived only recently. She appeared to have had a very difficult journey, for since her arrival she had hardly ventured forth from her rooms except to spend brief periods with her father.

It was not long, however, before Holmes's initial surmise about who might be present in the Residency received some corroboration. One morning, after a brief discussion of philological matters with his pundit colleagues, he occupied himself with copying out in Roman transcription a Tibetan version of the parable of the prodigal son. As he sat there thus engaged, a tall, thin Englishman entered the room. Holmes recognised him immediately, his face one of the two that he had glimpsed ever so briefly by candlelight that night in Makhantol, the face of the accomplice in Rizzetti's murder.

The pundits rose as if on signal, and Holmes rose as well. He was then introduced to Daniel Wright, the Resident Surgeon. Holmes pressed his hands together in the usual Indian greeting.

"Welcome, Punditji," Wright replied. "I hear that you have become part of this learned circle."

"My knowledge is like a small drop in the sea of milk of their intelligence," said Holmes.

"Your modest response no doubt conceals its own sea of wisdom," Wright answered coolly.

For a moment, he scrutinised Holmes intently, but he seemed to find nothing unusual. Holmes returned to his scholarly tasks, and Wright began to engage the pundits with regard to their historical translations. Holmes observed all, his every word and intonation, every motion of his body.

"I was suddenly alive to presences so vicious, Watson, that instinct called forth the most acute reactions of the brain. Surely, now, the murderer of Rizzetti himself could not be far away, and I was already prepared for the inevitable encounter. I had passed muster for the time being, but I had no illusions that, with longer contact, something, some small slip, some unconscious movement, would give me away."

At this moment, Holmes looked at me and let forth a great sigh. His eyes then focussed beyond me into the distance as he recalled the events in that faraway land.

"Pray, continue, Holmes," I said, fearful that he would stop.

He rose from his seat and began pacing slowly back and forth in front of me as he spoke, his hands together behind his back. I watched him curiously as he relived this strange adventure. His lithe figure became catlike as he walked back and forth, the grace of his physical motions matching the spare logic of his narrative.

A young woman appeared at the door, he said. It was Lucy Richardson. She informed Wright that her father wished to see him. Wright turned and left at once.

"And who is this gentleman?" she asked, referring to Holmes but addressing her question to Shiv Shankar.

"This is a very learned gentleman who is spending some time with us. He is Pundit Kaul, of Kashmir."

Holmes bowed.

"Ah, yes," she said, "my father told me that he had met you some time ago. Welcome. I have just arrived and would benefit by your knowledge. Perhaps you might join us at tea today. I would so like to hear about your country, for I should like to visit there once my father's health improves. And perhaps I might learn about this country and its languages as well."

"I am at your service, Miss Richardson. I would be most happy to join you and provide whatever assistance you might desire."

"Please join us at four on the terrace," she said.

Holmes bowed again as she departed.

At tea that afternoon, said Holmes, were Lucy and the Resident, whose health seemed to have improved somewhat. Still unable to walk without some assistance, he appeared, however, stronger, and he spoke warmly about his daughter and how happy he was that she could visit him. Holmes talked of Kashmir, they about England, of which Holmes of course had to feign no firsthand knowledge. Wright appeared several times to examine Richardson. He seemed preoccupied and took little notice of Holmes's presence. Holmes continued to observe him closely, however, particularly his ministrations to Richardson, but he noticed nothing untoward.

Lucy Richardson remained close to her father, serving his every need. Holmes observed that she was very young, possibly not twenty, with dark chestnut hair and green eyes. But an anxious look occasionally appeared on her face which made her seem much older. She was obviously devoted to her father.

"Miss Richardson at one point asked me to accompany her to an adjoining garden," said Holmes. "We spoke for some time about my work, but several times she expressed great concern for her father's health. I professed to have a knowledge of indigenous plant remedies and the diseases to which they related. Katmandu was filled with rare plants, I told her, of both beneficent and deadly varieties."

As they returned to the verandah, the sun had set behind the mountains and it was already dusk, and night was about to fall. Miss Richardson went directly to where her father was seated. As she approached him, however, he sat up suddenly, a look of intense fear on his face visible in the twilight:

"He's there! He's there! He's come back!" He pointed toward the far end of the garden. Holmes looked but saw nothing.

Richardson had gone white. His breath came in fast gasps, and Holmes feared that he might expire on the spot. Dr. Wright appeared from the Residency and quickly administered a potion that seemed to calm him almost at once.

"We'll have no more of that," said Wright. "If there is any more excitement here, I shall be compelled to confine you to your room and to prohibit all visitors."

The Resident did not respond but seemed contrite. Several servants appeared and carried the sick man to his room.

Turning to Holmes, Dr. Wright said, "I am sorry for the incident. The Resident is very ill and on occasion suffers from hallucinations, but these are common to the severe fever that he has."

Holmes nodded in sympathy and said that it was time for him to depart. As he took his leave, Lucy Richardson turned and said: "Mr. Kaul, I have been invited by the Maharani to accompany her to Janakpur. In two days I shall be leaving Katmandu for the Tarai. I shall be gone for several weeks. I wonder if you would allow me to benefit from your knowledge of the religion of the Hindus. Tomorrow I plan a tour of the Shrine of the Sleeping Vishnu. Would it be presumptuous to ask if you might accompany me?"

"I would be most happy to do so," said Holmes.

He bowed to the Resident Surgeon and took his leave. A flicker of annoyance passed over the surgeon's face as Holmes accepted Miss Richardson's invitation, but the doctor hid his emotions instantly. Holmes returned to his quarters.

"The mystery had continued to deepen," he went on. "How had someone like Wright become a surgeon in the Residency? And where was the presumed mastermind of it all, the murderer of Rizzetti? And what was the nature of the Resident's illness? And what of his hallucinations? Or had he seen something real?

"I decided at that moment to ask my friend Gorashar to make some discreet enquiries in the bazaar. He was disturbed by my account and by the implications of my questions, but he agreed to find the answers I needed at once. He also told me that many Nepalese were very disturbed by the rumours that they had heard concerning the appearance of ghostly apparitions in the Residency, for they were considered to be further portents of impending disaster."

Holmes interrupted his narration and stopped his pacing. He sat down and fumbled in his slipper for his pipe and tobacco. He lit up, puffing slowly as the sweet aroma of his favourite mix began to fill the room. He sat lost in thought for a few moments.

"The following morning," he continued, "I met Miss Richardson at the gate to the Residency. She was accompanied by guards provided by the Nepalese Government, and a maidservant. We must have appeared a strange couple, thought I, this beautiful young woman with an ageing pundit, but I paid no attention to the curious looks we received along the way. It was a bright day in early February. The mist had burned off more quickly, and the sunshine was stronger, a definite prelude to the spring season that was to come."

The Sleeping Vishnu, said Holmes, lies at the very northern end of the Valley. The road is no more than a dirt path once one passes a half mile or so from the Residency. About halfway, their party rested in a bamboo grove known as the Bansbari. Lucy Richardson by now had asked much about Kashmir. Holmes spoke rather eloquently about that other Himalayan valley, and did reasonably well, he thought, for one who had never visited the place. He had prepared for far more tren- chant questioning on the subject than her simple demands afforded, however. When he finished, she became quite pensive.

"I suppose that you will be going back quite soon?" she asked finally.

Holmes replied that he had no plans beyond the completion of his assignment in Katmandu. He did not know when he would return home.

Miss Richardson spoke hesitantly. "I too am here for an indefinite stay. I fled England, Punditji, for I could no longer endure the situation that had come to pass in my mother's home." The young woman paused, her eyes searching Holmes's face. "Punditji, I feel that I must trust you. May I burden you with my troubles?"

A deep sadness had come over her, and Holmes saw that she had no one in whom she could confide. He was pleased that she had turned to him, for he suspected that part of the mystery might lie in her family's history, particularly in that of her father.

"It would in no way burden me. I am honoured to listen," he said.

Holmes sat quietly while Miss Richardson told her story. She said that her early years were spent in India, in Indore, where her father had his last post. When he was appointed Resident in Nepal, she was twelve years old. She was a happy child, but because there were no schools or tutors in Katmandu, it was decided that she should return to England for her education. Her mother had also decided to return, for though the subject was never discussed, she sensed a growing estrangement be- tween her mother and father. There was little talk between them, and though they never bickered in her presence, she often overheard heated exchanges from behind their bedroom doors. When the time came for her to leave, she found parting from her father particularly difficult, for it was not clear when he would be able to visit England, or indeed when she would be able to return to Nepal, if ever.

"My mother and I left Nepal a year after our arrival. The journey to England was a sad one for me, and England soon became a dreary bore. We settled in my mother's home near Oxford, and I attended the local schools until she decided that I should attend a boarding school near London. The school was a relief from my mother's constant overbearing presence, for it was very clear to both of us that we did not get along well. Holidays were more than enough time for us to spend together. As I grew older, I began to regard her with more sympathy than before, for I realised that she was a very lonely woman. Letters came regularly from my father directed to me instead of to her. All she received from him was a perfunctory note scrawled at the bottom, while the messages to me were filled with lively descriptions of Nepal and its people, and of the exciting life that he seemed to lead. I was particularly envious of his travels outside the Katmandu Valley, which the Rana now permitted more frequently."

It was well over a year before, she said, that she began to notice a change in her mother. She seemed brighter and happier than she had ever known her to be. And one night, Miss Richardson learned the reason. Her mother had taken a lover, a Mr. Morrison, a gentleman who had been introduced to her by one of her very old friends, Ellen van Maupertuis, a woman who had married a Dutch diplomat and was then living in Amsterdam. Her friend had met Morrison first on the island of Sumatra and had found him charming. He had travelled much and was said to run a business in Amsterdam which imported rare woods from the Dutch East Indies. Lucy's mother had invited him to dine with them on occasion, and at the beginning Lucy rather liked him, even though she made clear to her mother that she thought her conduct was reprehensible. He was tall and handsome and possessed what Lucy came to recognise as an incredible intellect. He seemed to be particularly strong in mathematics, but he could discuss almost any subject intelligently. Her mother was entranced. There was little that Lucy could do but accept the arrangement, and little that she could argue with when her mother told her that she had learned that her father had taken a Sherpa woman from the eastern mountains of Nepal as his mistress.

"Upon my return home after my last year of school," she continued, "I found that Mr. Morrison had moved into the house and was living with my mother. To the outside world, he was merely a boarder who lived in the guest cottage, a convenient pretence that satisfied local speculation and quieted much of the initial gossip. One day, however, he began to evince a great interest in Nepal and my father's work there. In explanation he pointed to a lifelong interest in the geography and the

Himalaya, which were still a terra incognita, as he called it, and specu-
lated that he might expand his business to include rare Himalayan
woods. Even though we had lived there many years before, he questioned us both incessantly, and seemed particularly interested in the
city of Katmandu and its overall plan. He began making drawings of the
streets and gullies of the city, which he showed to us for correction. His
questioning became almost brutal at times, and my initial feelings of
warmth toward him immediately turned to dislike when I learned quite
by accident that he had found Father's letters to me in my desk and had
read them through. I was horrified at the intrusion into my privacy.
When I confronted him with his disgusting conduct, he merely denied
it, saying that he had taken the letters because my mother had wanted
to reread for him one of the notes to her from my father. My mother
supported his explanation, which I knew in my heart to be untrue, and
I found myself unable now to talk to my mother except about trivial
matters."

One night, continued Miss Richardson, just before retiring, she
heard her mother and Morrison shouting at each other in the library.
He had been questioning her closely concerning the Residency itself,
its occupants, including the guards and the servants, the arrangement of
rooms, including the furniture. He also wanted to know exactly what
the gardens were like. She heard her mother plead with him, saying
that she could tell him no more, for she remembered nothing beyond
what she had already told him. At this he lost his temper and began
striking her. Lucy heard her pleas for mercy. She rushed to the door and
banged on it, shouting at him. There was only silence. Morrison
opened the door. Her mother was crying softly, her face bruised in several places. Morrison stood facing Miss Richardson, his face calm, his
cold grey eyes filled with an unholy satisfaction. She felt as though she
was in the presence of evil incarnate. She rushed to her mother's side,
and Morrison left without a word.

"My mother's bruises were shocking to see, but they proved not to
be serious. Had Morrison and she been alone, however, I had no doubt
that they would have been far worse. She said nothing to me until the
following morning, when she said sadly that she was unworthy of him
and that he had threatened to leave. I was overjoyed at his threat, but
my mother, totally under his sway, said that she would do anything to

please him and make him stay. That afternoon we learned that Morrison had indeed left the guest cottage with all his belongings, leaving no indication as to where he had gone. My mother was distraught, calling all known friends and acquaintances, but Morrison had disappeared, to where no one knew. As the days passed and he did not return, my mother became embittered, her anger being addressed mostly toward me. Months went by. No word came from Morrison, and my mother became disconsolate. We quarrelled constantly. It was apparent to me that the conflict between us would not resolve itself, and that I would have to leave. After a dreadful argument in which my mother accused me of turning Morrison's love away from her, I decided on my departure. I had nowhere to go except to return to my father. I wrote him saying that I was coming as fast as I could, and I took the first passage to Calcutta available, making the difficult land journey from there with an escort sent by the Maharajah."

When Miss Richardson had finished speaking, Holmes suggested that they continue on to the Shrine of the Sleeping Vishnu. A group of children had by now gathered about them. The children stared at them, laughing, and Miss Richardson smiled in return. Then a gong sounded, and the children motioned to them to follow. They climbed to the top of the shrine, where they looked down on a procession, one very like the one Holmes had seen at the city gate. Nine tall figures, with large brass faces, their bodies clothed in red robes, walked slowly to a small statue of the Buddha, where they bowed in silence. Holmes and Miss Richardson watched them until they disappeared in the distance. They then turned back, and by the time they reached the Residency, it was dusk, and the pundit took his leave. The next day, Miss Richardson left for Janakpur in the party of the Maharani.

"Lucy Richardson's disturbing story had served to confirm my worst fears," said Holmes. "Though I did not know it for certain, there was a growing suspicion in my mind that the mysterious and cruel Mr. Morrison might now be in Katmandu. Why else the great interest in things Nepalese? Perhaps he was the murderer of Rizzetti, and was directing Wright's actions within the Residency."

It was evident that Holmes needed to know more about Morrison and about the Residency, particularly its history. He recalled to me that he had confided his whereabouts to only one individual, his brother,

Mycroft. With the help of Gorashar he arranged for a message to be taken by a trusted runner to India, where it could be sent to London.

"I sent detailed enquiries to Mycroft using an old elaborate code that we had devised together. I took the added precaution of embedding the message in an obscure Himalayan dialect that I had found in a work of Hodgson's. Called Kusunda, it was known to almost no one. I signed the letter Hodgson, which would suffice for Mycroft to find the lexicon he had compiled."

"I then determined," Holmes continued, "that I must enter the Residency secretly at night and speak with Richardson himself, for his own version of events might be most illuminating."

Entering would not be a difficult business, said Holmes, for the Residency was not particularly well guarded. Two sepoys were at the gate during the day and three at night. He had noted on occasion that they sometimes patrolled along the walls but often neglected to do so. Scaling the high wall would be the main problem, but he had seen several places where this could be accomplished by climbing a nearby tree.

"It was well after midnight when I set out. The nocturnal scene of Katmandu by now had become well familiar to me. I walked swiftly through the city gate and continued on to the Residency. As I arrived I could see by the light of their lanterns that the three guards were fast asleep. Entering the compound would pose little problem. My only fear was unexpectedly running into Dr. Wright should he be with the Resident during the night. I decided, however, that it was well worth the risk. I scaled a tall tree, climbed out on a large limb, and jumped down to the wall. From it I could see the entire garden and the back of the Residency. There was a light coming from a window near the verandah, and as I drew closer I could see the Resident. He was alone and in his nightgown. I drew as close as I could. He appeared to be at work, writing by candlelight, engrossed possibly in the routine tasks that he had been forced to neglect during the days previous. Everything appeared calm and peaceful."

Holmes then heard a noise in the garden below. There, moving in the yard, was an immense human figure, well over six feet tall, dressed in black, inching slowly toward the Residency. He carried a lantern in his left hand and appeared to be searching the ground as he walked. His clothes were reminiscent of those of almost a century ago, and he had a long white beard. The figure interrupted its walk, stooped over, and began to moan. Then it stood erect and resumed its slow approach to the Residency.

It was at this point that Holmes saw the Resident move slowly, a pistol in his hand. As the figure drew nearer, Richardson rose, opened the door to the verandah, and walked out. He took slow, deliberate aim at the figure and fired. At such close range Holmes judged the shot to be a direct hit. The figure reeled slightly but did not fall. Again Richardson took careful aim at the head and chest, firing several shots. While their impact was visible, they did not stop or wound the apparition. There was only a strange, dry, cracking noise as the bullets hit.

Unable to halt the apparition, Richardson became terrified and rang for the servants, who came running. In the few seconds during which Holmes took his eyes away to watch the Resident, the figure in the garden had disappeared into the night. Holmes continued to lie flat on the wall to remain unseen. Richardson was helped back into his bedroom by two attendants. Dr. Wright came soon after. Holmes watched as he mixed a potion. He appeared calm and unconcerned as he ministered to the Resident. He removed the gun from the Resident's grip and left.

"I could not help but smile at this juncture," said Holmes, "for parts of this complex but elusive plot were becoming clearer now. Richardson was not having hallucinations. What he had seen was real and not the nocturnal imaginings of a feverish brain. As I looked through the window, I could see him lying in his bed, frightened, his only defence the pistol now gone. I now had to reach him. Fortunately, he was tiring and was beginning to doze off. Whatever Wright had fed him had begun to take effect."

When Holmes was sure that the Resident was asleep, he jumped gently down in the garden and made his way over to the verandah, from which he entered Richardson's room. He shook the Resident gently. Richardson was about to scream when Holmes put his hand over his mouth firmly and said: "Have no fear. I am a friend. You are not sick, nor are you having visions."

"Kaul!" he exclaimed. "How on earth did you enter?"

"All explanations at the proper time. Right now we haven't a moment to lose. Mr. Richardson, your life is in mortal danger. You must leave the Residency with me at once. Your absence will be for a short time, at the most two days, perhaps only a matter of hours."

"I cannot leave my post, nor can I leave my daughter."

"You have no choice. For the moment at least, your daughter is in no real danger, but you are. Trust me. Time is short."

These last words seemed to reassure. Holmes threw a coat over the Resident, who followed him out onto the verandah. Holmes insisted that they leave the way he had come. It was not easy for the Resident in his weakened condition, and several times Holmes thought that he might fall off the wall as they crawled to the tree that would lead them below. But the freedom that the Resident now felt had invigorated him, and once they lowered themselves to the ground, he walked briskly enough. There was no one out at this hour, and they entered the hotel and Holmes's room unseen by anyone.

"I decided at this point to identify myself to him, Watson, for I thought that the pretences I had set up were about to crumble under the force of events. He seemed highly sceptical at first, considering the news that had spread about my death, but a few details about the Reichenbach Falls and Professor Moriarty quickly assured him that it was indeed Sherlock Holmes standing before him."

"What is happening here in Nepal, Holmes?" asked the Resident. "Why on earth should someone want to injure me?"

"I have several theories, but I do not have sufficient information to decide between them. Let me hear your account of events."

The Resident began slowly, his words unclear at first, Holmes prodding him at times with questions.

"Despite your saying that you saw the apparition tonight yourself," Richardson said, "I still cannot remove it from my mind. I have been ill, very ill. At night I see these visions and cannot sleep. The hallucinations are spirits, according to those Nepalese who want us British out of their country, because our presence desecrates their soil. We must leave, otherwise we shall die here, they say. Dr. Wright says these visions are rather typical of Nepalese illnesses. Sometimes I feel better after his treatment, other times much worse."

"Are these visions all like the one tonight, or are there others as well?" asked Holmes.

"There is really only one," he said, "and you have seen it. It begins after I have fallen asleep. I am awakened by something, perhaps the strange creaking sound that the vision makes as it approaches. I see it vaguely at first through my window. Then there comes a dim light. It is a lantern carried by a tall, bearded figure dressed in black, wandering through the garden. Last night it came close. And I saw its face, the face of a withered old man. The servants say it is the ghost of one of the former residents, Hodgson, whose spirit has returned from England to search for his dead wife. They say that he will not leave until I leave or I am dead. At first I did not for a moment believe any of it, Mr. Holmes, but the visions continued and had a frightening reality to them, as you saw tonight. At times they have been so real, in fact, that I have been afraid of losing my mind. I am an excellent marksman, Mr. Holmes, and you saw yourself that bullets had no effect on the ghostly figure."

"I understand," said Holmes, "but pray continue, for the ghosts are indeed real and have a natural explanation."

"Whatever the nature of the phenomena, Mr. Holmes, I believe we are dealing with some evil presence that has come to Katmandu. I arrived in Nepal almost exactly eight years ago. Before that I had served in Rajasthan at our garrison in Kotah, then in Ajmer as an agent assigned to two princely courts, and finally in Indore. I was then offered this post and accepted with alacrity. My wife, however, was less sanguine, and it became clear that the narrow orthodoxy of the Hindu rulers, and the poverty of the bazaar and the countryside, led to a boredom that became intolerable to her. A marriage that had been more or less a social convenience fell apart under the strain, and after a year in Katmandu we parted, she returning to England, where our daughter was put in school.

"For the first time in many years, I felt free, and in a short time one of the servant girls here became my mistress. Her name was Maya, and she was as beautiful and kind as a gentle maid could be. Very soon, Maya became with child. This appalled me at first, but there was little I could do but what a Nepalese nobleman would do: let her have the child and support them both. Her family learned from her what had transpired and became furious. Their anger was subverted, however, by large dollops of cash which I contributed to their impecunious coffers, and they became not only reconciled but genuinely pleased at the result, for they are Sherpas, Buddhists by faith, freer in their social ties and far less under the sway of the Hindus than the other tribes of Nepal.

"The birth, however, proved to be extremely difficult. What had appeared to be normal in every way turned into a tragedy. The Resident Surgeon at that time, Mr. Oldfield, tried his best to work through the gaggle of superstitious women who attended, but despite the power of his medicine, Maya died in childbirth and the infant died with her. I was greatly grieved by her loss, for this gentle friend had filled my lonely hours with solace. Because she died in childbirth and because the child was that of a feringhi, she could not be put to rest according to the usual rites, so she and the child were buried in the Residency garden in the plot reserved for deaths here in the Residency. Except for Dr. Oldfield, who aided me in every way, I might have gone mad with grief. He nursed me through the worst and then unfortunately was reassigned to Calcutta. He was succeeded eventually by Dr. Wright, who has ministered to me through my present illness."

The visions, he continued, began not long after Dr. Oldfield departed for India. He was sitting alone in the garden one evening. The newly arrived Wright and he had supped together, and he had retired early. It grew dark, the wind began to blow rather hard, and the air filled with bats from the large jacaranda trees. Then he heard what sounded like the groans of a woman and an infant's wail. A figure, wearing English dress of a half century ago, appeared in the far corner of the yard, as if bewildered, looking, bending, searching. He carried a light.

"I stared in amazement, wondering how such a figure could have entered without my seeing him. I shouted first, but it paid no attention. I then rushed toward it, but by the time I got there, it had disappeared without a trace."

"Most interesting," said Holmes, "not unlike the disappearance that we witnessed tonight, though the bullets that passed through him may have made him travel a bit faster."

Richardson smiled for the first time and continued with his description.

"I first thought it was some sort of ruse and tried to put it out of my mind," he said. "But I was clearly frightened by something I remembered: it was an old wives' tale concerning Hodgson. It was said that Hodgson had a Nepalese wife who died in childbirth and who is buried in the garden. The burial of a second wife there, in the same ground, would cause an intolerable rivalry between their spirits and would cause his wife's spirit to summon him for protection. The tale must have had some subtle effect, for at the same time, I became racked with fever, horrible pain in every joint and muscle and pain in the very core of my stomach, as though I had been pierced by a flaming rod. And so there I sat, guilty of no crime, yet visited by an affliction that seemed to demand nothing less than my demise, at least until your arrival upon the scene."

Richardson finished speaking, and Holmes could see that by now he was exhausted. He summoned Gorashar, who after hearing of some of the events of the night, promised that he would have Richardson safely installed in his own chambers within the hotel, an area inaccessible to outsiders.

"Gorashar also had received answers to my enquiries," said Holmes, "and here, Watson, is illustrated one of those general truths concerning our relations with foreign nations that often go unnoticed: that what is common knowledge in the bazaar rarely reaches through to the isolated confines of our diplomatic enclaves. For what I learned was that the surgeon general Daniel Wright, appointed to join Richardson at the Residency, had been attacked and murdered shortly after he had crossed into Nepal not far from the Indian border. His place had been taken by an imposter, an Englishman whose identity was unknown. Yet another Englishman, also unidentified, had been observed at the scene of the crime, but his role was not clear. He was believed by some to be acting in concert with those in the palace who had decided to do away with the present Maharajah and replace him with one of their own family. Were the intrigue to prove successful, the new rulers would be far less friendly to British power in the Subcontinent. The appearance of spirits and ghosts within the Residency was widely believed by the population to signify some approaching calamity for them, whether political or natural they did not know.

"So much for the bazaar," said Holmes wryly. "The glance of evil intelligence that I had seen in the eyes of Rizzetti's murderer led me to believe, however, that he had his own selfish motives, and that even the Nepalese plotters were not safe from his designs."

By then it was early morning. Holmes left the inn and made his way to the Residency for his usual daily meetings with Shiv Shankar and Shri Gunanand. As he entered, it was apparent that something was amiss. Only Gunanand was there. He informed Holmes that the Resident had disappeared during the night and that his whereabouts were unknown. Dr. Wright was now in charge of the Residency and had gone to the Maharajah to notify the Nepalese Government of the Resident's disappearance.

Taking advantage of Wright's absence, Holmes went quickly to the garden, to the spot where the apparition had seemed to disappear. He found there an old dhara or watering place. Holmes climbed down the small set of steps that descended into the tank itself. Grass and other weeds had filled much of it, and it showed no signs of use. He looked closely at the old inscriptions first, then his eyes fell to the ground. Everywhere there were high weeds, the look of disrepair, of no movement or life for centuries. The gardeners had apparently avoided the spot. At one end there was the usual waterspout decorated with ancient gargoyles. Below it a stone bas-relief of the usual water sprite. The sculpture was quite beautiful, but what riveted his attention were two large stones beneath it that looked as though they had recently been moved. Fresh scrapes around their edges could have been made within the last twenty-four hours. Then he saw on the ground the most interesting thing of all: fragments of wood, or perhaps bamboo, that looked as though they had just been thrown there. He leaned down to pick up the larger pieces, carefully putting them in his pocket.

As he walked back through the bazaar, Holmes began to sift through what he knew. The so-called apparition had come and gone through the dhara, that was clear. The large stones were obvious. But from where to where, that was the question. How and where did this person enter the dhara from within?

When he returned to the hotel, Gorashar informed him that the Resident was resting peacefully, and that he was safe. Holmes then asked if he might avail himself of a small library of Asiatic researches that Gorashar kept in his private lodgings. Gorashar escorted him to the room, and Holmes began looking through the old tomes on Nepal.

"I began searching for clues to the ancient form of Katmandu. My eye was caught by a volume of essays, again by Hodgson. I grasped the volume and glanced over the table of contents. I read quickly through several articles, one on festivals and processions and another on the ancient agricultural implements of the Newars. I was soon caught by a title: 'On the Fountains and Possible Ancient Waterways of Katmandu.' It was a long, tedious essay, filled with detailed descriptions of the various fountains of the cities of the Valley, of which there are literally hundreds if not thousands that date from at least early Christian times. One paragraph, however, caught my attention:

"There is no doubt that a complex system of water supply linked the large public fountains both in ancient and in medieval times. The large terra-cotta water pipes were serviced by a series of tunnels. There is evidence that the system operated well into the eighteenth century. It was only with the total defeat of the Malla kings by the Gurkhas that this system fell into decay and disuse. Many of the old dharas, having lost their water supply, have turned into vessels of vile filth or have been abandoned to the growth of wild vegetation. If the present regime revives the system, it would be for its own purposes and designs, and it is eminently possible that these underground waterways and tunnels, still sturdy passageways, could be used for political intrigue and military surprise, techniques so successfully employed in the past by the Gurkhas. I am sure that, if one chose to, the Residency compound could be easily infiltrated in this way, but as yet I see no evidence or need for the present rulers to do so. Fortunately, the system appears to have been totally forgotten by the native population.

"I had found my clue, Watson. The Residency most assuredly contained one of the entrances to the old underground network. One could enter it with ease from the old dhara, either for invasion or to cause apparitions. If one knew the system, one could enter and leave from almost any point. This was the means by which Hodgson's so-called ghost had come and gone. The grounds of the Residency had indeed been haunted, from the very beginning perhaps, by a number of people working for their own ends. How Hodgson's ghost had come upon his discovery of this ancient network was not clear, but of his use of it I had no doubt. It enabled him to roam the city at will without fear of discovery. I now had to smoke him out or go in after him."

Holmes's eyes were now ablaze with excitement. He lapsed into silence for a few moments before he continued, reliving in memory those moments of turbulent emotion as he began to fit the pieces together. I said nothing this time, the look of anticipation on my face being sufficient to indicate that I wished him to continue. He suddenly became quite pensive and said: "I then began to wonder who indeed it might be. This was a master criminal. Was it this man Morrison, who had disappeared in England and had professed such interest in Katmandu? His name meant nothing to me, and the little that I knew so far—a businessman with dealings in Holland and the Dutch colonies—told me nothing. Yet, it is my calling to know what others do not. Could such a person be unknown to me?"

He grew silent again. I could see the intense struggle for comprehension that must have animated his face as he sat in that old lodge in Katmandu.

"I stared at Hodgson's words in that old tome, Watson, the smell of fifty years of Asiatic mould filling my nostrils. I sat foraging through my memory, checking every similarity, every detail that I knew or could infer as probable, against the activities of thousands of criminals. What I had experienced so far was uniquely singular. I then turned the question around, and asked it in a most general way: if I were to ascribe the aforementioned criminal activities to any one person, living or dead, who would it be? I could arrive at only one answer to that question, and it was most disturbing."

Holmes paused, waiting for me to give the inevitable answer: "Moriarty himself!" I ejaculated.

"Good, Watson, good, but not quite good enough. That Moriarty was capable of the grand intrigue I had uncovered in Nepal was indubitable. But it was also certain that he was dead. There was no possibility of his having returned from the Reichenbach Falls. No, Moriarty's bones were by now bare and chalk white at the bottom of that awful abyss."

"Who, then?" I asked anxiously. "Perhaps one of his lieutenants, some of whom approached him in ability? Colonel Moran, perhaps?"

"Someone who had the potential for just as great if not greater evil.

Not one of his close associates qualified, not even Moran. And, equally important, not one of them was present in Katmandu, as far as I knew. The criminals whom I knew to be there and recognised would be of the greatest use to a master criminal, but not one of them could have been described as such. No, Watson, I began to think of a very different person."

Here he paused for several moments. Then he began anew.

"I have often spoken to you of my brother, Mycroft, and how he shares, to an even greater degree than I, the abilities of observation and deduction that I have inherited. In the same way, Watson, there is, or was, one person, capable of more intelligent evil than Professor Moriarty: his brother, James. This conclusion came to me as I sat in Gorashar's study. You will recall, Watson, that James Moriarty wrote a defence of his brother in which he alleged that I had fabricated the whole case against him, that he was the innocent victim of the hallucinatory ravings of Sherlock Holmes?"

"Indeed, I do remember, and it was in your defence that I broke my silence and described the events as they were known to me until that time."

"Until this point, I only knew of James Moriarty's existence, for he had engaged in no criminal activities and had had little contact with his more academic brother. What had put him on his present path I did not know, but I was certain that he was my adversary. This belief was confirmed by the fortunate arrival of Mycroft's response to my message, which I deciphered at once. It read:

"My Dear Sherlock:

"My apologies. It took me a bit longer than I thought to locate a copy of Hodgson's lexicon of the language of the Kusunda, but once I did, decipherment was easy and your message quite clear. In answer to your question, Hodgson is still alive, though very old. He was too weak to converse at length, but he divulged the fact that he had taken a Nepalese mistress in Katmandu, and that she had died many years ago. This fact is known to several members of his family. There were two children from this liaison, whom he sent to his sister to raise and to school in Amsterdam. The children did not survive, for they were lost at sea off the coast of Ireland. Your other suspicions are quite correct. Richardson's wife is in the clutches of one James Morrison, who has become her lover. Of the greatest import to you is

the fact that in reality he is James Moriarty, the brother of your deceased nemesis. How he has recently been converted to criminal behaviour is most interesting, and I shall relate it to you when we meet. In the meantime, exercise extreme caution, for his whereabouts at present are unknown. I cannot trace him beyond a berth on the HMS Prince of Wales, *bound for Sydney, but stopping in Calcutta, which means of course that he may not be far away and indeed may be looking for you.*

"Mycroft

"I looked forward to meeting with Mycroft someday and hearing from him how he thought Morrison had become a criminal. But perhaps Mycroft's explanations were unnecessary.

"And here, my dear Doctor, permit me a brief digression, for what I say to you now occurred to me at that very moment as I put the match to Mycroft's message. Perhaps, Watson, good and evil are no more than natural properties, woven into our racial structure, indifferent in themselves, like the colour of one's eyes or the shape of one's nose. They may be indifferently combined with other traits. Some extraneous factor, perhaps a harsh experience, perhaps a chance meeting that enlivens one of these traits rather than the other, becomes the sufficient cause to determine a man's nature. Randomly created with a preponderance of good or evil, men become natural adversaries when these qualities are combined with intellect and will. It is then their intellect that identifies them to each other as mortal enemies, and the will that immediately opposes them. More than that is unclear to me, but my own experience supports what I have just said as a working hypothesis, one that I shall explore in retirement should that time ever come. In any case, I had now identified my implacable adversary, and had to assume that he might have somehow identified me. The final meeting was inevitable, the circumstances under which it would take place still unknown, and its outcome, whatever it might be, something that I faced by now with a certain equanimity."

I listened with rapt attention as my friend related to me these latest revelations. His theory of good and evil natures led me to pose a question: "Surely, Holmes, the inheritance of such traits as good and evil and the like means very little unless the sum of inherited traits is known. You have often remarked that Mycroft's abilities of observation and deduction surpass even yours, and yet, as you have also noted, Mycroft's lack of energy precluded him from any practical results in the field of crime detection. James Moriarty too must have differed in some way from his brother, the evil professor, that would have aided you in apprehending him."

Holmes smiled. "You are quite correct, Watson, and I thank you for your words of wisdom. Indeed, Moriarty frère had a severe fault. He possessed a violent and cruel temper that impelled him on to action that he would not have taken had his reason maintained control. The sudden and uncontrolled anger toward Rizzetti and the beating of Mrs. Richardson were two examples of this. I learned of a third that very day upon my return to the Residency. I had decided that, rather than let matters run their course, I would confront Daniel Wright and ask to be taken to Moriarty, alias Morrison. When I entered the Residency compound, I learned that Wright was in his study, having returned from his meeting with the Maharajah, and would see no one. After the guard left, I decided to enter his office unannounced.

"Wright was there, but he was dead. He had been stabbed in the same way that the foul Rizzetti had been. There were signs of a struggle everywhere. Uncontrollable anger at the Resident's escape had led Moriarty to kill his chief ally."

Holmes said that he examined the dead man and his clothing carefully. His private papers indicated that his real name was Saunders, that he had served in the Indian Army as a medical orderly, but that he had been discharged for violent acts against his men as well as financial improprieties. He evidently had been hired by Moriarty after his arrival in India, probably in Calcutta, where he had been living the life of a vagrant after his discharge.

Nothing among Saunders's effects revealed Moriarty's whereabouts. Holmes examined the contents of his medical bag closely. His search revealed a number of almost empty vials. They contained the minute remains of a number of poisons, some of which were locally prepared and of the greatest potency. Some of these Saunders had obviously fed to Richardson, in small doses, but sufficient to cause great pain, intense fever, and physical deterioration. Doubtless, they had been prepared by Rizzetti before his death.

"There was nothing else, except a rather odd passage written on a piece of paper on Saunders's desk. It appeared to be in Saunders's own hand. It resembled a passage from the chronicle that the pundits were translating. It read: 'And there shall be great bursts of thunder and light, vast explosions in the night, and a crazed Brahman shall kill an untouchable. And Kalanki shall ride into the city on a white horse. And the people shall rejoice in their new god, for he will reveal himself as the new Vishnu and their new king.' "

Holmes summoned the two pundits and asked them to take charge of Saunders's body. They were to notify the Nepalese Government of the recent events in the Residency. He asked them about the words on Saunders's desk, and they confirmed the fact that they were part of the prophetic passages from the ancient chronicle. Saunders, alias Wright, had been particularly interested in the prophetic passages in the book, but they did not know why. Holmes then took it upon himself to notify Lord Dufferin, the Viceroy, in Calcutta of the recent events. This he did in Richardson's name, using the wireless in the Residency.

"My hope of being taken to Moriarty had failed, and I now, alone and unaided, faced the monumental task of finding him, probably lurking in a subterranean lair somewhere beneath the streets and alleys of Katmandu. Saunders was the only one I knew who might have led me to him. I could not mount a search alone in such a labyrinth, for once I entered it I would in all likelihood never come out alive. No, I had to know beforehand where the minotaur had his lair and I had to lure him out."

Holmes's frustration turned to despair when he was informed by a sobbing attendant that Lucy Richardson had disappeared from the Maharani's party at the Chandragiri pass. He had to assume the worst, that she had fallen into Moriarty's clutches, and that he had been checkmated.

Holmes fell silent at this juncture, and I could see on his face the agony of despair that he had lived through at that dark moment. I had seen this only rarely in the past in England, for here he disposed of numerous resources that helped him in his battles, but in the alien world where he had found himself, he was thrown completely on his own. Unstated, too, was a paternal affection that had been awakened in him by Lucy Richardson, an affection which he did not mention but which played subtly on his face even now when he spoke her name.

"I questioned Miss Richardson's attendant closely," he said. "They had been walking in a temple area, she said, when they were unexpectedly parted by a crowd of people come to see a large procession of idols. The procession separated them, but she could still see Miss Richardson, who was talking to a Nepalese gentleman whom she followed through a small doorway. The procession of idols followed through the same entrance, which led into a monastery courtyard. Even though the attendant managed to reach the doorway, she was unable to find Miss Richardson or anyone who had seen in which direction she had gone. It was as if she had disappeared into thin air. The attendant then raced back to the Maharani to report on what had happened.

"I left the Residency and returned to the hotel. Gorashar led me to the inner room where Richardson had been hidden. When I saw him, I realised that his health had begun to recover, for his pain had eased considerably. I decided it best to tell him everything, including the possibility of Lucy's capture by Morrison. He was of course amazed at my long discourse and what it revealed to him about his wife's life in England and the sufferings of his daughter. He could shed no light on Moriarty's whereabouts, however, nor did he know anything of the underground system beneath the city of Katmandu."

Holmes returned to his room, still trying to find the clue that would reveal Moriarty's whereabouts and the grand design of his evil plans. He reviewed all in his mind: the murder of Rizzetti; the elaborate attempt to kill Richardson and to scare him with false apparitions; the murder of Wright before he arrived in Katmandu; the murder of Saunders, and the mysterious prophecies written on his desk in his own hand; and finally the disappearance of Lucy Richardson in a religious procession. As he turned these matters over in his mind, he scrutinised every detail that had been offered. It was then that he remembered the bamboo fragments that he had picked up in the old dhara in the Residency garden. Taking them out of his pocket, he placed them on the table. They had been smashed by Richardson's bullets, but the few pieces that fit together formed a curved piece about four inches long. Suddenly, as he stared at these innocuous fragments, they jogged something in his memory, something that he recalled reading in another one of Hodgson's old essays.

"Suddenly, Watson, I saw the pattern that had escaped me until then, and within a few seconds I saw the entire scheme, the whole ingenious mad plan. All was revealed to me. The only question now was whether I could act in time.

"There was a sudden knock at my door, and Lakshman appeared with a note. I opened it and read:

"My Dear Holmes:

"By the time you receive this, events will have moved far beyond anything that you can do to prevent them. I had suspected for a long time that you had escaped the Reichenbach Falls, but I finally became sure of your presence here through my interception of your message to your brother. You have done well in your disguises, but you have already caused me not inconsiderable inconvenience, and I shall be happy to settle with you in due course. In the meantime, I invite you to enjoy the drama that will ensue shortly. And, to allay any doubts that you may have had, Lucy is here beside me and sends her very best to you.

"James Moriarty"

As Holmes recited the contents of Moriarty's letter, he visibly turned pale, and I felt his overwhelming despair. So palpably did he re-live the events in his narrative that I found myself fearing the worst. It was only his presence before me that guaranteed the outcome. He had suffered a piece of very bad luck in Moriarty's interception of Mycroft's message, perhaps even a mortal one, but certainly an unforgivable one in his own eyes. His face and body sagged in front of me as he uttered the last words that Moriarty had written him. But as he approached the final events of his tale, he regained his confidence and continued his narrative.

"The last sentence, the reference to Lucy, made it imperative that I act with the greatest speed. I ran down the hotel steps, only to be accosted by Gorashar, who pleaded with me not to leave the hotel, for he said that a rumour had spread rapidly through the city that the Brahmanical predictions for calamity had fallen on this very night and that people were engaged in frantic worship to dispel the displeasure of the gods caused by the presence of the English, the feringhi mleccha, or barbarians, on their sacred soil. A Brahman, mad with fear, had just killed a kusle, an untouchable, in a rage over having been polluted by the untouchable's shadow. This incident had taken place not far from the hotel. This was taken by the people as the sign that Vishnu himself was to appear in his last avatar. After his appearance, the present era would come to an end, evildoers would be punished, and a new ruling dynasty would be installed. Gorashar himself believed none of this and considered it part of a plot to overthrow the present regime. He did not know who the actors were, nor where they were, but the most primitive emotions had now been unleashed and the people would listen to no one, neither the Rana nor the King himself, for their fate was also sealed in what was seen by a superstitious people as the end of the world. It was at times like this, said Gorashar, that he feared the violent emotions pent up for centuries in the hearts of a gentle but oppressed people. The priests had called for the entire population to assemble at nightfall in the Tundhikhel, the meeting ground that lies just outside the city, for a mahapuja, or great sacrifice, to pacify the god Vishnu."

It was already dusk, and Holmes could hear the footfalls of many people running to the great field or maidan. He had little time before it became dark. He pulled away from Gorashar's anxious grip and ran into the street. Everywhere people were walking toward the Tundhikhel. Each person carried a flaming torch of straw as he marched toward his destination. The city was as if in flames, as if every human being was drawn by the desire to void the priestly prophecy.

"I ran toward Asan," Holmes went on, "unnoticed by the crowd that hypnotically moved in the opposite direction, looking for the shop where I had once seen Thalmann, the Austrian gunsmith. The shop was closed, but I broke the lock to the entrance with no difficulty. No one was there—I was sure Thalmann was part of the evening's programme, as were the other criminals I had seen in the bazaar. I found what I had hoped to find, however. There, in a back room hidden from the street, Thalmann had kept several of the finest examples of his craft. I chose the best of the Salzburg rifles, itself the most accurate weapon then in existence. Thalmann had stored an endless supply of ammunition. I stuffed my pockets with bullets, wrapped the rifle in a woollen blanket, and made my way toward the Tundhikhel, now bright with tens of thousands of torches."

The heat was intense, said Holmes, and several people were already lying on the ground, overcome by the flames and smoke. Suddenly, as he reached the edge of Bhotahity, the first of several explosions rocked the city. The sky flashed bright with their light, and he was thrown to the ground by their force. People cried in fear but continued in blind flight toward the Tundhikhel. Holmes picked himself up and ran with them. When he reached the great maidan, he looked for a building from which he could see from above. He darted into a nearby house, vacant now, climbing the stairs as fast as he could. When he reached the verandah, he saw the crowds converging in the field, the priests exhorting them to hurry to perform the great offering. The entire maidan appeared to be in flames, as if lit by a thousand suns. The explosions he now saw were coming from the southwest, from the military cantonment, where large amounts of explosives were stored.

Suddenly, the explosions stopped. There was a dead silence, after which could be heard only the chanting of a priest and the crackling of the straw torches.

"Then came the sound of Vishnu," said Holmes, "the roar of a thousand conch shells. I looked toward the east. There riding slowly on a large white horse was a gigantic figure, four-armed, crowned with a golden helmet. He was accompanied by a large group of cavalry that rode behind him, dressed in ancient Hindu military regalia. The great white horse stopped before the crowd. The people bowed in awe. Great Vishnu had arrived. The crowd was as one as it waited for the divine message.

"I had but a moment now," said Holmes, his eyes ablaze. "I raised the rifle to my shoulder and took aim at the great figure, aiming directly at his head and chest. I fired and heard the impact of my bullet. I fired again as fast as I could. The figure reeled, trying to hold on to the reins, but the horse reared up, throwing the rider. My shots had blown away the top part of the rider's costume, revealing a common bamboo cage, resting on the shoulders of a tall Englishman, who now stood exposed to the enormous hostile crowd assembled in front of him."

The last avatar of Vishnu had been fatally exposed. His allies in the plot quickly abandoned him. His soldiers fled, and the crowd, seeing him and him alone as the perpetrator of this blasphemy, pulled him from his horse and, several drawing their khukris, swiftly despatched James Moriarty to his final destiny.

"I had still to find Lucy Richardson, however. I descended into the crowd and saw Caspariste trying to flee after having fallen from his horse. I grabbed him and, with a few threats, convinced him to take me to the dead Moriarty's lair. We entered the underground waterways through a dhara near the Mahakala temple, and walked by candlelight to a series of chambers that had been used by the ancient engineers of the city. There, still under guard, was a terrified Lucy Richardson. Once informed that the plot had failed, the guard fled, and Lucy accompanied me back to the hotel, where she rejoined her father. Caspariste I allowed to go free to seek his own fate."

The following morning, said Holmes, the Maharajah of Nepal, Bir Shumshere, announced the arrest of one of his younger brothers, for plotting revolutionary activities with an unknown mleccha, a heathen foreigner, who had performed a heinous deed by attempting to impersonate the great god Vishnu. They had wished not only to overthrow his government, he said, but also to create a state of tension between Nepal and the Government of India, and to destroy the trust between him and the Nepalese people. Henceforward, he said, even more severe restrictions would be imposed on the entrance of foreigners to the Kingdom, and those who had participated in the plot would be severely punished. He absolved the Resident, his family, and the staff of any complicity in the events of the last few weeks, and announced again his desire for the friendliest relations with the Government of India and the Queen-Empress, and that he had communicated directly with Lord Dufferin.

Holmes rose from where we had been seated. "There is more to the story, Watson, but it is late and perhaps you have heard enough."

Neither of us was ready to retire, and I suggested a stroll outside so that he could complete the tale. As we walked down Baker Street, I looked at my friend as he strode, tall and erect now, against the darkening trees and the star-filled sky. We walked for a time in silence, and he spoke only when we arrived at Trafalgar Square and then only in answer to my bewildered silence, for much remained that puzzled me.

"I assume, Watson, that you are sorting out your puzzlements. You have the narrative, and the clues, of course, but certain crucial deductions had to be made and, in fairness to you, could only be made on the spot."

"Tell me first," I said, "what you deduced from the bamboo fragments."

"Almost everything. You see, they connected three crucial elements of the mystery: the figure of Hodgson's ghost, Lucy's disappearance, and finally, Moriarty's appearance as Vishnu. This web of connections came to me as I stared at them. They were obviously the result of Richardson's bullet hitting the tall figure of Hodgson. Why had he not produced blood instead of bamboo with his bullets? It was only after staring at the fragments that I remembered the processions I had seen, and a note in passing in Hodgson's essays concerning religious processions among the Newars of Katmandu: the men dress as their gods by wearing bamboo cages on their upper bodies. These then bear the large head of the deity and the divine drapery. The effect is most dramatic: large, tall divine figures appear to walk down the paths of the old cities to the temples themselves. In the night they are quite striking. Fortunately, for the person underneath the head and clothes of Hodgson, Richardson did not aim any lower, for had he the result would have been quite different."

"And who was that person?"

"Caspariste, who admitted as much to me before I let him go. He is still at large, and was the only one of these rogues in whom Moriarty had confided. The same local custom was taken advantage of to capture Lucy Richardson, for as she was walking in the bazaar, a procession passed and she was whisked under an idol by one of Moriarty's henchmen, in this case a local soldier, who took her to Moriarty's hideaway. And, of course, I realised instantly that I could unseat Moriarty from his mount if I could but have the means. The Salzburg rifle, incidentally, my dear Watson, is a formidable weapon."

"I must say, Holmes, that I am still a bit puzzled by Moriarty's purpose. Why did he do what he did?"

Holmes laughed. "Ah, Watson, surely all of this had high stakes. As you know, we do not keep our Empire without a price, and we have many enemies within both the Subcontinent and Asia as a whole. We are the envy of mankind, but we must maintain constant vigilance. The plot in brief was to incapacitate the Resident and to keep him permanently ill and isolated, but not to kill him unless absolutely necessary. Then, during his incapacitation, to take over the Nepalese Government and to install a group friendly on the outside but inwardly inimical to British interests in the Subcontinent. From there, with the aid of unfriendly nations, to forge alliances with dissatisfied groups and princes elsewhere in India in order to drive us out. I can assure you that an alliance of Gurkhas, Sikhs, Mahrattas, and Afghans would surely give us a bit of a time. It almost happened a few decades ago. Your own experiences in Afghanistan should allow you to recall the price that we have often paid to keep our Empire at peace. The diabolical part of course was to prey upon the people, by using their superstitious fears, their own history and predictions in fact, to attempt to topple the present Government. Moriarty could not resist playing Vishnu himself, an incredible piece of theatre, I must say. In all likelihood, however, his worldly stakes were even higher than his divine aspirations: to become the leader of an independent India."

"Had you not been there, Holmes, I hesitate to think . . ."

"Curiously enough, Watson, had I not been there it probably would not have happened at all."

"Why do you say that?"

"Because Moriarty suspected that I was there, and even designed the whole plot in part as a confrontation between the two of us."

"Surely he knew that you were there after he intercepted your message to Mycroft. But how the deuce did he know that you were there before?"

"Only a surmise, of course, Watson, since we did not talk. But I confirmed it on my return to England. I knew that my disguise as a Scandinavian naturalist in Tibet had some bad moments. I had become famous in some quarters for my scientific work, and despite my best efforts to avoid being photographed, on several occasions this indeed had happened. I knew that at least one of these photographs had appeared in print in an obscure Himalayan botanical journal devoted to the work of Joseph Hooker, the great Himalayan botanist. Unfortunately, you may recall that Colonel Moran, Moriarty's chief henchman, still at large then, had specialised in the study of the fauna of the Himalaya. I had to assume that he kept au courant and that he might have seen this photograph, recognised me, and communicated his suspicions about my whereabouts. Moriarty's desire for revenge for his brother's death was very great."

"Intercepting your message was no accident, then."

"No, indeed it was not, but reading it and understanding it was another matter, Watson, and here I must say I did not understand this part of the puzzle until I returned to England. I first attributed Moriarty's success in deciphering the message to bad luck and his mathematical genius. That would have taken him to the point of revealing the text. But how could he have access to such a language as this one in order to read it? His success was at once complete and inexplicable. You will recall that I took peculiar pains to find a minor Himalayan dialect in which to write this language, to wit, the Kusunda."

"Yes, indeed. Surely, Moriarty could not have known that language beforehand."

Holmes smiled. "Here, Watson, under Lord Nelson's statue, I shall finish the tale for you."

We sat, watching the thinning crowd of late strollers. Holmes was far more calm now than he had been, but in the dark his eyes held their light, and I listened attentively.

"My first task upon my return to England was a visit to Brian Hodgson. Before I left Nepal, I knew that he was still alive, ninety-one years of age, still vigorous, but in declining health. I hoped that he would live until I returned so that I could clear up much of the mystery that related to the appearance of his 'ghost.' "

Holmes had no sooner disembarked at Dover than he made his way to the village of Aldersley, where Hodgson had lived since his return to England. He stayed the first night at the local inn, and in the morning made the necessary enquiries. Hodgson was indeed still alive, according to several villagers, and lived on a large estate about two miles from the centre of the village. Holmes sent word with a young village boy that he had just returned from Nepal and that he brought word of that country and greetings from some of Hodgson's surviving friends. He had an almost immediate and positive reply from the old man, who was most anxious to talk to anyone who came from that part of the world.

"That afternoon, I climbed into a cab and went to visit him. His estate began down a path that lay to the south of the village. The road to the main dwelling was lined with old oaks, and the house itself, when I saw it, was an imposing but unpleasant structure. Part of it may have dated back to Norman times, for it was made of stone, with small windows in turrets. I realised as we approached it, however, that it was vacant."

The cabby turned and informed Holmes that "the old gentleman" lived in a cottage farther down the road. Holmes could see the house, a simple English country cottage, surrounded by flower gardens. It was not unlike the Residency in Katmandu, and as he approached, the door opened and Hodgson himself came out to greet him. Holmes was taken aback at his appearance, for there before him again was the apparition that had appeared in the garden in Katmandu: a very tall, thin figure, slightly hunched, dressed in black with a long white beard. The hallucinatory Hodgson had been a deft and expert creation indeed. Holmes alighted from his cab and greeted him: "I bring you tidings from Nepal, from the Maharaja Bir Shumshere."

Hodgson smiled, grabbed Holmes's hand more vigorously than he would have imagined, and led him to his study. It was here that the great scholar Hodgson continued to work, still cataloguing the research that he had begun decades before. The two men talked for the rest of the afternoon.

"As we conversed, I became aware that he was the oldest human being I had ever known. He was wrinkled, arthritic, and obviously very frail. Yet, as soon as he began to speak, his years disappeared, and I was faced by a vigorous mind and a long interrogation. He was filled with questions about his beloved Nepal, and I tried insofar as I was able, to acquaint him with the latest political developments. But he had many detailed questions, about the Residency as well, about the bazaar, about the effects of the Mutiny, and the whereabouts of Nana Sahib and his retinue, about the Ranas and their rule. I described all that I knew to him, even down to changes in the Residency staff. He had not been there in fifty years, and yet his memory was wondrously detailed. He had forgotten nothing of that country, or of his years there."

It was toward the end of Hodgson's questions that Holmes felt confident enough to pose his own. Since they were of a personal nature, Holmes began by asking permission to probe into subjects about which Hodgson might wish to remain silent, adding that, if he chose not to speak, Holmes would understand.

"In order to clarify some of the events that transpired during my visit there, I should like to ask some questions that will enable me to bring to an end certain difficulties that have eluded solution until now. They concern your marriage to a native woman and your offspring from that relation."

Without indicating whether or not he was disturbed by the question, Hodgson rose from his chair and went over to the door, closing it shut.

"Unlike many of my countrymen abroad, I have made no secret of my early relationship. It is taken up, though not in detail, by my biographer, Mr. Hunter. It is, however, still a very painful subject for my present wife, and therefore, if we are to discuss it in detail, I should like to do so behind closed doors. And in confidence, of course."

Holmes explained to Hodgson that he had no desire to cause him or his wife pain, and that his interest had nothing to do with Hodgson's career or personal life but only with the light that his answers might shed on the mysterious events that still had not been resolved. Holmes added that, about the nature of those events, he preferred to remain silent, for disclosing them to Hodgson could serve no useful purpose and might add to the pain of his last years.

"As with so many things in life, Mr. Holmes," said Hodgson, "there is a great deal to tell and very little at the same time. You wish to know of my early involvement with a Mohammedan woman. I cannot imagine what significance to you such events of almost fifty years ago might have, but since I have nothing to fear and am not really curious about your reasons, I shall tell you all. Briefly, in my last years as Resident, I came to know a Mohammedan family that lived not far from the mosque that served the small community of Muslim merchants who lived in the city. The family was from Kashmir originally, a family which had gone first to Lhasa and then settled in Katmandu. So many generations back, however, was their Kashmiri origin that the family had little recollection of it, and considered themselves to be Nepalese in every way. The family was small, consisting of Salim, a merchant who dealt in saffron, his wife, and their daughter. I frequented their household, for I found relations with the Mohammedans far easier than with the Hindus, who often were subject to the severe restrictions of commensality and pollution where I was concerned. With my Mohammedan friend, I could be entirely natural and felt often far more at home in his humble dwelling than I did in the mansions of the rich.

"It was not long, however, before I became aware that my friend and his wife were victims of consumption, a respiratory affliction that is pervasive in Katmandu. My friend and his wife died after a few months, within days of each other, leaving their daughter an orphan. For reasons that were not clear to me, both her near relatives and friends within the Mohammedan community refused to support her. Unmarriageable without parents, she had no prospects, and I decided to have her live at the Residency. She was literate, trained by her father in Arabic and Persian, and I set her upon the study of some manuscripts that her father had shown me, in particular accounts of the Lhasa bazaar that her great-grandfather had written while living in Tibet. It was not long before our relationship began to change, however. From a rather distant one at the beginning, I found myself seeking her company, until I realised that I was becoming very attached to her. Our friendship and intimacy grew in the privacy of the Residency. She was very beautiful, and it was not long before I asked her to live with me as my wife. She was nineteen at the time, and I thirty-seven. We both knew that I could not marry her officially, since the rules of the Company as well as the Koran disallowed such relationships, but so happy was I that I vowed that, once I had completed my service, we would marry legally and would spend the rest of our lives together. That indeed was my intention, to which she acquiesced at once."

The old man paused for a moment. It was obvious to Holmes that he was approaching the painful part of his tale.

"The irregularity of such a relationship bothered few in Nepal," he continued. "They regarded it as an inevitable consequence of my presence, and found it appropriate that I had picked a Mohammedan woman. The choice muted any criticism that the choice of a woman of Hindu birth might have given rise to, where many who considered themselves part of Hindu orthodoxy regarded my presence as an affront to the sacred purity of the land."

They lived happily, he said, and in time she gave birth to two sons, two years apart, who were the joy of their years. Their time together, however, was cut short, for the disease that had taken her parents suddenly reappeared in Hodgson's wife, who, pregnant again, died in childbirth at the young age of twenty-five, exhausted by racking consumption. The infant, a girl, died with her. Hodgson buried them together in the small graveyard in the Residency compound. She left him brokenhearted, with two young boys, aged six and four.

"The boys were badly affected by their mother's sudden death," he went on. "I had been much absent because of my work, which took me often to Calcutta, and their dependence on her was almost total. Without her, what had been two joyful young children became silent and sullen. They barely recognised me and spent almost all their time with a family of servants, tribals from the Tarai, who lived in a small hut in the back of the Residency. There they played with the children in the family, learned their tongue, and almost began to forget English."

Holmes interrupted Hodgson's narration with a further question: "Might I ask what language the boys spoke with this family?"

Hodgson thought for a moment. Then he replied: "It is curious that you should ask the question. The family was from a remote area southwest of Katmandu. They came to me as beggars one day and because of their peculiar dress I asked them to stay so that I could investigate them. At first I thought they were of the tribe known as the Tharus, but it became clear to me that their language was very strange and seemed to be related to almost nothing else. Indeed, I later published the results of these efforts. They called themselves Kusunda, and their language the same. They were among the last of this tribe. My sons picked up their tongue rather quickly and spoke it well."

It was at this point, said the old man, that he determined his sons had best leave Nepal to be raised and educated in Europe, so that they could have the benefits of our civilisation. His sister, Ellen, who was married to a Dutchman and living in Amsterdam, agreed to raise them and arranged for their schooling there. Just short of a year after their mother's death, then, his sons and he travelled to Calcutta, where he placed them on a ship bound for Holland. They travelled in the company of an English trader, one Joseph Michaelson, who agreed to deliver them over to Hodgson's sister.

"That was the last time I saw them, for they never arrived. An enormous storm near the Scilly Islands at the entrance to the Channel forced the ship's captain to divert northward to St. George's Channel. In vain did the captain try to keep the ship in peaceful waters, however, for the storm's fury damaged it severely, washing many onboard into the sea. Mr. Michaelson, seeing that the ship was about to sink, climbed into a small boat with the boys and four other passengers. The boat made it safely to the Irish coast with three of its passengers, but

Michaelson and the boys were washed overboard with one other, lost, and never to be recovered. This news I obtained in Katmandu about six months after their departure in a letter from my sister, who had received word from one of the survivors by way of the ship's company. With my heart heavy, I went to my wife's grave and knelt there for a long time. It was many years before the grief was lifted from me."

Hodgson rose slowly from his chair and went over to a large almirah near his desk. He took from it a large album, which he handed to Holmes, saying: "You may wish to take a look at some of these drawings and photographs. There are herein the only pictures of my late wife and my two sons."

As Holmes looked through the album, the old man returned to his chair opposite, a look of great sadness on his face. Holmes became engrossed in the old volume, for these were perhaps the original photographs of the Residency, its staff, and other personages of Nepal, including a massive photograph of General Bhimsen Thapa, autographed for Hodgson.

"The history was of no interest to me, however," Holmes said. "I turned until I found what I had been looking for: photographs taken in Calcutta just before Hodgson put his sons on the ill-fated ship that carried them toward Europe. Among them were large portraits taken of the two boys, Joseph and James, separately, at the ages of seven and five. Despite their young age, there was no doubt as to who they were. The high foreheads, the piercing eyes, and the cruel mouths were unmistakably the same as those of my greatest enemies. The loss of a doting and loving mother, their abandonment to strangers by their father, and the deep scars left by the storm at sea, had so cruelly disturbed them that their intelligences became misdirected. They had survived somehow the great storm. Taken into some poor and miserable household on the Irish coast, they were raised in bleak and stony poverty. Reaching early manhood, they left the stern and cruel circumstances of their childhood that had all but made their future criminal careers a certainty, and entered the larger world of London and Amsterdam. Or so I surmised, for we shall never know this part of the story.

"I must have been engrossed in the photographs for a good long time, for when I looked up, the old man was sound asleep in his chair, his long white beard now touching his knees. I placed the album on a nearby table, and rather than trouble or embarrass him, I tiptoed out, closing the door behind me. That evening I returned to London."

With these words, Holmes brought to a close the long narrative of his sojourn in Katmandu. We sat for a moment, looking at the empty square before us, each absorbed in his own thoughts. Then we walked slowly home in the darkness.

THE CASE OF
THE FRENCH SAVANT

I HAVE WRITTEN, PARTICULARLY IN THE CASE CONCERNING THE Greek interpreter, of Sherlock Holmes's extreme reticence with regard to his early life and family. He rarely spoke of his relations, and it was only after I had known him for several years that I learned, quite incidentally after tea one summer evening, of the existence of Mycroft, a brother seven years his senior. On that very same occasion, he revealed to me that the majority of his ancestors were country squires who led lives appropriate to that station in life, but that his maternal grandmother was a sister of the celebrated French artist Vernet. In this way he descended from that well-known family of painters, and it was to this Gallic portion of his lineage that he attributed his analytic powers and his not inconsiderable musical talents.

I had no knowledge, however, until one afternoon in late April 1896, that Holmes shared to some degree in the painterly attainments of his French ancestors. A tiring day with several difficult patients had convinced me to leave my practice early, and I arrived at our quarters at around four o'clock. Holmes was not at home, and I found myself alone. A great weariness overcame me as soon as I entered, and I sank immediately into my easy chair. I was about to doze off when I noticed a large portfolio placed atop the papers on my desk. I slowly pulled myself back from the torpor that threatened to envelop me, and stretching over with the little energy I had left, I took the portfolio and placed it in my lap. A note was attached in Holmes's hand:

Dear Watson,

I thought I would allow you to peruse these sketches before I consign them to the fire. As honest reproductions of their subjects, they are not without merit, but they lack the necessary artistic inspiration. They were done while I was abroad and record a number of places in the Orient. For that reason they may be of interest to you.

I am nearing the end of a particularly tiring case, the denouement of which should occur around six this evening. It is a case that I predict you will one day entitle "The Case of the One-Armed Wife" should you choose to add it to your chronicles. Lestrade and the Baker Street Irregulars are on hand should I find myself in need of assistance. If all goes to plan, expect to see me by eight, when I hope we shall have supper together. I shall be famished and should like nothing better than to spend a quiet evening with you by the fire.

Holmes

I opened the portfolio thinking that I would concur readily in his judgement of the drawings. A quick look, however, revealed that he was no ordinary draughtsman, and that, as in so many things, he had a keen eye and a steady hand. All of the sketches were in pencil, most in black and white, some in colour, on what looked to be a kind of rice paper, thin and most delicate, of different sizes and quality. All bore short titles in Holmes's hand, with the date of execution and the initials S.H. in the lower right hand corner. I saw at once that they formed a visual record of his wanderings in Asia, an irreplaceable supplement to the accounts of his adventures with which he had reluctantly provided me from time to time after his return.

One of the drawings in particular caught my eye. It was one of the larger ones, done in subtle hues of rose, gold, soft blue, and green. I studied it for a few moments. The subject was the facade of a large pagoda temple with golden roofs, and built of what appeared to be rose-coloured brick. It was heavily adorned with sculpture that I judged to be in both metal and wood. At the entrance were a series of steps, at the top of which on either side sat a lion, presumably guardians to the entrance. Above the door was a tympanum filled with a profusion of mythological figures, all exquisitely rendered. To the left of the entrance stood what appeared to be a large pillar, presumably of stone, with an inscription carved on its surface. So delicately and precisely had Holmes drawn the ancient characters that anyone skilled in the script could have read it straight off the drawing. At the top of the pillar rested a golden disc. From its centre a beam of sunlight shone forth and appeared to be reflected to some unknown point to the right hidden from the observer. At the foot of the stairs a large kneeling figure with wings on its back, half man, half bird, could be seen. To its right at the bottom was Holmes's inscription: "Changu, S.H., 1893."

What transpired that evening with regard to the drawings is after so many years still rather painful to my memory, for Holmes was true to his word about consigning them to the fire. He returned as he had promised, promptly at eight, fatigued but obviously elated by his latest success.

"A cruel and evil wretch is now behind bars, Watson," he exclaimed, "and if justice is done in the courts, he will remain there, perhaps forever."

He washed quickly, and we sat down to the simple supper Mrs. Hudson had prepared. We then moved to our armchairs by the fire, where Holmes gave me a brief account of his activities of the day. Lighting his pipe, he then asked, "Where are the sketches?"

"Here," I answered, as I pulled them up from alongside my chair. "They are fine drawings, Holmes, unexpectedly good since I had no knowledge of your achievements in this regard. They show a remarkable—"

"My blushes, Watson," he said interrupting me. "Your judgement is no doubt sincere, but I do not share it. You may choose one, however, for your own to keep as part of your historical record."

I pleaded in vain with him to let me keep them all, but he insisted that they be destroyed save for the one that I would choose. I looked through them quickly again and chose the one marked "Changu."

"I shall keep this one," I said.

Holmes took the portfolio and, removing the sketches, threw them into the fireplace. I felt my eyes mist over as I watched the rice paper curl black, the flames quickly turning it to ash.

"At least tell me something about the remaining one," I said grimly, as I handed it over to him.

"You have chosen well, Watson, if I say so myself. It is indeed probably the best of the lot. Less stiff than the others, and the detail is quite clear," he remarked clinically.

"The temple is of course that which is known as Changu Narayan," he continued. "It lies a few miles north and east of Katmandu in Nepal, atop a hill. It has rarely been visited by Europeans. Your choice has historical significance as well, since the temple was damaged by an earthquake after I executed the drawing. This may be as accurate a portrait of it as we shall have. There is also a tale concerning it which you may want to add to your Oriental chronicles."

His pipe refused to light, and putting it down to rest, he smiled, knowing full well my interest in everything that he had done while abroad.

"You owe me at least that, Holmes, after destroying the sketches."

"My humble apologies, dear Watson. I had no intention of causing you undue pain. In any case, the incidents occurred shortly after the banishment of Hodgson's ghost from Katmandu."

I watched him closely and saw the by now familiar pattern as he readied himself for his narration, the gleam in his eyes, the hands brought together at the tips in front of his face, and the slight pause as he ordered the events through which he had lived.

"For a time, I continued to live in Nepal as Pundit Kaul of Kashmir. My disguise had begun to wear thin, however, after I aided the Maharajah, albeit indirectly, in rounding up and forcibly removing from Katmandu the remaining criminal elements that had been allowed to nest in his country over the previous decade. I took great satisfaction in this. Like stray wild dogs, these criminals were collected and brought in chains to the Indian border town of Raxaul, where they were released upon taking a solemn oath never to enter Nepal again on pain of death. A new edict was then promulgated by the Maharajah, under which the number of foreign visitors permitted to enter was further limited, and almost entirely to those who had official business with the Government."

"Shortly after this, our Government's Resident, Mr. Richardson, announced his departure with his daughter for England. Miss Richardson had prevailed upon him to leave in order to regain his health, and she also hoped for a reconciliation between her parents, despite the gravity of their past difficulties. Once the Viceroy authorised the Resident's leave, father and daughter left for Calcutta."

With no business pressing, said Holmes, he prepared his own departure. His next destination was to be Banaras, followed then perhaps by Calcutta. He was slow to leave the comfort of Gorashar's hotel and the beauty of the Katmandu Valley, however. It was already late April, and he had no great desire to experience the torrid heat of the Indian plains. Gorashar therefore easily prevailed upon him to stay a few weeks longer, at least until the advent of the cooling monsoon rains, for the old merchant wished to show him some of the artistic treasures of the Valley that he had not yet seen himself. Gorashar had lived some nineteen years in Tibet, so long away from his own country that he felt the pressing need to make an extended pilgrimage to its chief shrines.

Except for these visits to the countryside, Holmes's own days were idle. He had only his edition of Petrarch with him, and the few libraries in Katmandu contained little of interest. He had exhausted Gorashar's small shelf of books on Nepal. He continued to visit the pundits at the Residency, however, and it was they who suggested that on his tour with Gorashar he collect rubbings of the ancient Sanscrit inscriptions of the Valley. And so, Gorashar and Holmes, still as Pundit Kaul, added long walks through the valley to Balambu, Kisipidi, Dhapasi, and other ancient sites which had hitherto never come to historical notice.

"I had no idea that you have any knowledge of Sanscrit," I interrupted. "How truly foolish I feel now when I think of the remark in my earliest chronicle that your knowledge of languages was nil."

Holmes again took up his recalcitrant pipe and smiled as he placed it between his teeth. "You were quite right, Watson, when you made your assessment. At the time that we met, I did not know a word of Sanscrit, or any other foreign language for that matter. And as for Sanscrit, I no longer know it. Your use of the present tense, therefore, is inappropriate."

"But surely, Holmes, you cannot have forgotten it all," I retorted.

"It is hardly a matter of forgetting, Watson, for this implies a mental action uncontrolled by the will and reason. As you know I am a brain. The rest of me is a mere appendix, and it is the brain that I must serve.

And I must serve it well. It would be foolish, as I have often remarked in the past, to assume that the brain is a place of infinite space. A better image is of a small atelier, where the craftsman or artist keeps the tools necessary for the work at hand. The rest he must store in the recesses of the mind, ready for the instantaneous recall that necessity might demand. The dormant subjects thus are no longer known in the ordinary sense of the word but reappear only when use is imminent. Sanscrit will have little if any use in the solving of crime in metropolitan London, and so it is stored safely with other Asiatic subjects in the remote instance that it need be resurrected. In the Orient, however, one would be foolish to attempt success in my line of endeavour without the language fresh for use, and so I cultivated it, until my travels took me to parts of the globe where it was totally unknown and therefore quite useless."

I was about to comment, but Holmes rose to his feet and began pacing back and forth, his hands together behind his back, a slight smile on his lips as he recalled the tale that he continued to narrate to me.

One morning at dawn, he said, Gorashar and he left for Changu Narayan, stopping first at Bhaktapur, an ancient town some nine miles from Katmandu which he had not previously visited. He found its preservation, both in its architectural and its human aspects, most remarkable. It is a town, he observed, that preserves in precise detail a medieval way of life now lost in almost all parts of Europe. Gorashar arranged for them to spend the night there at the house of a close relative, a Tuladhar merchant. The following morning, again at dawn, they began the walk from Bhaktapur to Changu.

The temple lies at the end of a long ridge that begins north of Bhaktapur. Holmes found it a pleasant walk, and they reached the temple at around eight. Gorashar spoke almost constantly, telling Holmes in detail what he knew of its history.

"Here we shall see the oldest inscription in Nepal, one that has not been read fully as yet," he said. "It is perhaps fifteen hundred years old and records the mysterious death of one of our illustrious kings, a great and religious man by the name of Dharmadeva."

Dharmadeva died quite suddenly, according to Gorashar, and no one knows how or why, but it is still believed by some that he was killed by his wife and son, Manadeva, who immediately succeeded him to the throne. His wife was said to have arranged the murder with the aid of the king's brother. But the full truth was not known.

"As Gorashar spoke, Watson," said Holmes, "I of course became most interested, since I now had before me a possible murder, a royal one, that had not been resolved for fifteen hundred years. Perhaps, I thought, I should solve it."

"And add it to your sensational annals," I said laughing. "I never cease to be amazed at how these things fall your way. You no doubt thought immediately of parallel murders, in Riga, or St. Louis—"

Holmes grinned at my last remark, but then he said almost sombrely, "On the face of it, one can indeed feel a certain astonishment at how similar cases arise. But upon reflection, Watson, one sees that, whatever the time and the place, good and evil are linked in some inextricable way. They are perhaps drawn to each other by some third force, the nature of which is inevitable but barely discernible. One can only hope that in the battles that ensue, the forces of good are strong enough to prevail. Having chosen to do what I do, I have found it only natural that crime falls across my path, whether from antiquity or the present. All I must do is wait and the inevitable happens."

It was, in any event, with added enthusiasm, he continued, that he arrived with Gorashar at Changu Narayan. While his friend performed his religious rituals with the priests, Holmes attended to the business at hand, a minute examination of what he found before him: a magnificent edifice, adorned with metal and wood carvings, and a courtyard filled with some of the finest sculpture he had seen.

At first, said Holmes, the temple appeared as if filled with a jumble of deities thrown everywhere. Its surface had no unfilled space. All was covered in ornament and design. It was only after one observed it closely, therefore, that one realised that all was in order and that the shrine itself was an illustration in wood, brick, and metal of the Hindu's belief in the interconnectedness of all things, the harmony and illusion of the universe that he conceives and, to a large degree, shares with the Buddhist. The temple was, according to Holmes, one of the supreme achievements of Gorashar's people, the Newars.

"No other people on earth, Watson, has produced such intricate beauty in as small a space as the Valley of Katmandu. One trenchant observer has described it best as a kind of coral reef, built up laboriously over the centuries by unrecorded artisans. As a human achievement, it ranks with the creations of Persia and Italy."

"Good lord, Holmes, and no one even knows of its existence . . ."

"Let us not say 'no one.' A few, including myself, have been fortunate enough to see and to observe it. But permit me to continue, Watson. I returned to Katmandu with Gorashar that afternoon, but not without securing from the temple priests permission to return and read the pillar inscription. In this, Gorashar's help was invaluable, particularly his pledge to supply gold leaf for the roof of the temple. With this promise, the suspicious priests became my allies and promised every courtesy and help. It took me seven long trips to the temple to record what you have in front of you in that sketch."

The long inscription had drawn Holmes's immediate attention. The pillar itself was some twenty feet high, and the writing on it was in most places as clear as the day it was carved, a most singular case of preservation from the ancient world. At the top sat a metal crown, a large disc of burnished gold, about two feet in diameter. It had a penumbra of flames, and was no doubt a representation of the sun itself. At the bottom, Holmes noted, to his frustration, that the writing on the pillar extended below the ground in which it was placed. Unless it were dug up, that part of the inscription would remain unknown. Holmes spoke to the head priest about excavating the hidden portions. The priest became incensed, refused to discuss his request, and said that Holmes would be limited, as all observers, to what was aboveground. Holmes made no more of the matter.

The reading of the inscription fully occupied the next several weeks. So engrossed did Holmes become that he decided to stay for an extended time in a nearby village, in the mud and thatch hut of a Brahman who lived across the river to the west. The Brahman provided his meals and a clean bed. This saved the long daily trip to Katmandu and allowed him to view the temple and its pillar from morning to night. It was during this long stay that he finished the recording not only of the inscription but of the chief features of the temple and the artistic remains around it.

It was at this point that he began to take note of what until then had been entirely hidden from him: the relations between the temple and the natural world, relations that led him to renewed wonder at the achievement of the Newars. One day, as he sat copying the last few lines of the pillar inscription, he looked up and observed that the sun, now beginning its descent in the west, had been caught in reflection by the golden disc atop the pillar. The beam thus created was redirected into the temple courtyard. His eye followed it quickly to a large statue of Vishnu, where it came to rest brightly on a jewel placed in the god's forehead. From there the light moved once again, coming to rest this time on the right hand of a small statue of Ganesh, the Elephant God. The light rested in this way for only a few seconds and then disappeared. As soon as it faded, a young boy, half naked and clothed only in rags, appeared and effortlessly scaled the pillar. Upon reaching the top, he gave the disc a slight push, slid down, and disappeared silently.

"This must be the beam," I said, pointing to Holmes's rendition of it in his drawing.

"Yes, you may imagine it hitting the third eye of Vishnu and the hand of the Elephant God just outside the drawing. But, as in many instances, Watson, here again you have seen but not observed."

Holmes took the drawing from my hand and said, "Look again, my good Doctor."

I took the drawing back and stared at it. This time I noticed that a portion of it had been folded over and secured to its back. So carefully had this been done that one hardly saw that the picture could be extended from behind.

"Let me undo it, Watson. The hidden portion is secured in a particular Nepalese way, and your tugging at it may harm it."

Holmes held the entire picture up to me, and it was now even more wondrous than I had thought previously. The light from the sun, visible only as a brightness in the sky, flowed in reflection directly from the golden disc to its two recipients, Vishnu and Ganesh, all rendered with the greatest beauty in the extended picture.

"Extraordinary, Holmes. What is the meaning of this? And what of the boy?"

"More of him later, Watson. Suffice it to say that he appeared periodically during my remaining visits, scaled the pillar, touched the disc, and slid down and left."

Holmes said that he studied the beam of sunlight very closely, noticing how it struck the same places on the statues and then faded away almost immediately. In this, there was obviously some as yet hidden significance. He gave it little thought at the moment, for he was preoccupied with recording the inscription itself.

On completing his record, he found that Gorashar's account of the death of King Dharmadeva was substantially correct, if incomplete. The inscription stated that the unfortunate king had gone to his pleasure garden, where he was found dead by his wife, Rajyavati. She sent news to her son, Manadeva, who was at once declared king. She herself planned to die in the funeral pyre of her husband, but her son, pleading with her, prevailed upon her to retire into widowhood. And so, like the celebrated Arundhati of Indian legend, she remained alive but in the seclusion of chastity.

Written much after the events and at the order of Manadeva himself, however, the inscription recorded none of the persistent doubts about the mysterious way in which his father had died. The rest of the inscription merely recorded King Manadeva's own exploits and said nothing more about his father, Dharmadeva.

"An odd business, Holmes," said I, "rather at odds with Hindu custom, I should think. A king who dies suddenly and unexpectedly, a wife who does not follow the usual rites of suttee, and a son who suddenly becomes king and explains nothing."

"Yes, Watson, a story so lacking in detail that any interpretation could be given to it. But I must confess that I had begun to tire of the work. I suddenly felt the need to leave Nepal and to move on. Gorashar had completed his pilgrimages, and I had seen more than enough of temples and sculpture. The monsoon had begun, and the rains were unusually heavy so that the most recent trips to Changu had become very difficult. And with the sun blocked by the clouds, I could not further my investigations into the mysterious reflections of its rays."

Without prolonged study of the temple, he continued, he did not think that he could solve the mystery of the death of good King Dharmadeva. And so he put his things in order to be ready for the first break in the rains, bade good-bye to the pundits in the Residency, and spent his last days in seclusion in Gorashar's establishment.

In a short time, the sun came out from behind the clouds and the sky cleared. He decided to leave still in the guise of the pundit through whose identity he had become known, and to change only when he had crossed the border into India.

On the evening before he was to leave, however, he found a note addressed to him from a scholar visiting from Paris. It read:

My dear Pundit Kaul,

I have learned through the offices of the Maharajah Deb Shumshere and the Rajguru of Nepal of your presence here in the Valley. I understand that you are performing some philological tasks for Grierson. I would like very much to meet you and to share your knowledge of the country and its history. I myself am investigating the ancient inscriptions of the Valley, and if you have come across any in your wanderings, I would be most grateful for your information and advice. At present, I am the guest of the Maharajah and am staying in the guesthouse at Thapathali. If I do not hear otherwise, I shall call on you tomorrow morning at seven. With my most distinguished sentiments,

(Prof.) Sylvain Lévi

Holmes received the note too late to inform Lévi of his imminent departure, and so the following morning at seven he found himself unavoidably at tea with the learned French savant. Lévi was, according to Holmes, a most entertaining fellow, very much aware of his intellectual gifts. In his late thirties only, he had already published learned articles on Indian history and religion. He proudly presented Holmes with copies of two of his works, *La Doctrine du Sacrifice dans les Brahmanas* and *Le Théâtre Indien,* neither of which particularly took Holmes's fancy, but for which he thanked the good professor. In turn, Holmes handed him his rough readings and translations of the Sanscrit inscriptions that he had found in the Valley, including the one at Changu. He no longer had any use for them. Lévi thanked him profusely for them, but noticing the latter, he remarked, "I have no need of this one. I already have it—and more."

Holmes continued pacing back and forth, his hands together behind his back, a slight smile on his lips as he recalled the tale that he continued to narrate to me. Lévi was an intelligent man, he said, but he showed a strong disdain for the local population that made his presence at that moment unpleasant. He criticised the government and its officials, and the priests of the country, especially those at the temple at which he was pursuing his scholarly investigations.

"These ignorant priests have tried to thwart me at every turn," he said. "My greatest desire has been to read the pillar inscription of King

Manadeva that stands in front of the temple of the god Changu Narayan. Manadeva was one of the great kings of antiquity, but little is known of him. As you may know, there is a portion of the inscription that lies below the surface, buried and unread for centuries. I tried in a friendly way to convince the priests that I should be able to excavate and read the inscription in its entirety. They refused. They would not even allow me into the temple area, saying that as a foreign barbarian I would desecrate and pollute it. Sacrebleu! Can you believe such ignorant superstition? I finally convinced the Maharajah of the importance of my work, and he sent several soldiers into the temple to dig it up. The priests were furious, but there was nothing they could do. In a few hours, I had a complete rubbing of the inscription, including the buried portion. It is mon triomphe!"

Lévi's eyes glowed with a sense of victory, and Holmes remarked that he was very fortunate to have arrived at the time that there was such a Maharajah as this one. But Lévi scoffed and said that anyone would have helped him, knowing that he was the best of European Sanscritists.

"And I have still not been allowed into the temple compound to study its treasures. The family jewels of Manadeva are reportedly there, hidden somewhere. But I shall find a way. Ah, ces prêtres—"

Holmes had tired of this gentleman. He stood up, extended his hand, and bade him adieu. Lévi took his leave, and Holmes went about his affairs, his departure now delayed by a day. He spent the rest of the afternoon with his friend Gorashar, who had promised that he would accompany him to Bhimphedi, the last post in the hills before one descends to the Tarai and the plains of India.

"It was early the following morning, as I prepared to depart, that I received an unexpected visitor. Lakshman, my servant, scrambled up the five flights of stairs to my room and announced breathlessly that there was a messenger from the Maharajah, who insisted on delivering a note himself. I told Lakshman to accompany the messenger to my room. Soon I was face-to-face with a member in full regalia of His Majesty's Royal Guard."

The soldier handed Holmes an envelope that bore the official seal of the Maharajah, Deb Shumshere Jang Bahadur Rana. The note was short and was written in what he took to be the Maharajah's own hand:

M. Sylvain Lévi, the French scholar, has disappeared without a trace. He left his quarters late yesterday afternoon and has not been seen since. Please come at once since I believe that you may be of assistance in locating him.

Deb Shumshere J.B.R.

The messenger told Holmes that he was ordered to accompany him without delay. And so, his departure thwarted once again, Holmes found himself on another, most unexpected, adventure.

The trip from the hotel by carriage to Thapathali, the Maharajah's residence, was normally of very short duration, but this time it took almost a full hour. The monsoon had struck again that morning, and the roads of Katmandu were flooded and thick with swirling mud. They passed through the imposing gates of the palace and rode through the front gardens to the verandah.

The Maharajah Deb Shumshere stood there waiting, surrounded by servants and umbrellas to protect him from the rain, but as soon as the carriage stopped he jumped forth and pulled the door open himself, escorting Holmes inside.

It was Holmes's first taste of this kind of Oriental splendour, and he found it most impressive. They walked through a large receiving hall filled with the luxuries of every country of Europe, then through a room that marked the love of the hunt, the shikar of the Ranas. The remains of tigers, leopards, and antelope, the great beasts of the southern jungles, were everywhere. They passed from there into a small room, which Holmes assumed to be the Maharajah's own study.

"I know who you are, Mr. Holmes, and that is why I summoned you. Your secret is safe with us, however."

Holmes was not surprised by his words, for he knew that it would have been foolish to think that he could maintain his secret indefinitely. An indiscreet word at the Residency would have sufficed.

"I believe that it is indeed time for me to leave Nepal," he said.

Holmes watched him closely to see the effect of his answer. The Maharajah was a small, dark man, but with an enormous head, upon which played a roundish face that had more of intelligence in it than the cruelty usually associated with his kinsmen. His eyes narrowed as he spoke.

"You are, as usual, correct. It is time for your departure," said he, "and I will see that you are aided on your journey. It is probable by now that more of your worst enemies know of your survival, and so I deem it best that you leave. But you will always be welcome here. We are indebted to you for your service to us in the recent matter at the Residency, and in the assistance which you gave to us in ridding our country of a number of unwanted pests. There is, now, however, the rather delicate problem of the missing Frenchman. I am distressed to tell you that my agents have failed to locate him, and therefore I must enlist your aid, even if it means postponing your departure once again. His disappearance is an embarrassment in itself, but even more so because the French Ambassador to India, M. Bertrand, is due to arrive in Katmandu tomorrow with Prince Henri of Orléans, on an important diplomatic visit. The recognition of our independence by France is one of my chief goals, Mr. Holmes, and I can hardly tell the Prince and his ambassador on their arrival that the greatest Sanscrit scholar of France is unaccounted for."

Holmes asked him what information his agents had been able to unearth.

"What my agents have uncovered, Mr. Holmes," replied the Maharajah, "is that after his return from his visit to you yesterday, M. Lévi lunched with his wife here at my guesthouse. Madame Lévi then retired for an afternoon rest. When she awoke, she found that her husband was not there. She questioned the servants, who said that he had left alone at about three. This was in no way unusual, for she was used to his habits of work, which left her to her own devices for the better part of the day. 'Mon pauvre mari travaille toujours,' she had said to me on their arrival. She only became alarmed at nightfall, when he had not returned. That is when she notified me of his absence. My agents learned that he travelled by rickshaw to the great Buddhist shrine at Bodhnath, where he was observed transcribing Tibetan inscriptions. He wore, as he has regularly since his arrival, local attire, including the Nepalese black cap, or topi. He was last seen before dusk leaving Bodhnath on foot through the great southern gate."

"What chances are there that he was abducted to embarrass His Majesty's Government?" asked Holmes.

"This is always possible, of course, but we should have been made aware of this by now by his abductors. I doubt this, therefore. My men have entered every house at Bodhnath. As you know, the inhabitants there are almost all poor peaceful Tibetans and would have little reason to harm him. No, something unexpected has happened that has put him beyond my spies. Mr. Holmes, we must find him. I can assure you that in this you will have my every assistance. You may have as many of my men as you need."

"I shall do my best," Holmes said, "but I shall work alone. I should like, however, to visit Madame Lévi, before I depart."

Holmes was led directly to the guesthouse, where he found Lévi's wife staring mournfully out the window. As he entered with the Maharajah, she began to weep. She was not a pretty woman but one of rather coarse features and of a kind of stoutness that one associates with French peasant stock. It was clear as soon as one saw her eyes, red and swollen from her fits of grief, that she had nothing to do with her husband's disappearance. Because her English was poor, they spoke in French. She said that she knew no more than what she had told the Maharajah, that her husband had returned from his visit with Pundit Kaul, mentioned to her that he had much work left before their departure, and after lunch retired to his desk, where he was when she retired for the afternoon.

Holmes then asked her permission to examine Lévi's desk and the work that he was doing before he left. There were no notes to his wife of any kind, no messages, nothing to indicate where he had gone. But as he had indicated to Holmes in their conversation, he was still preoccupied with Changu, its treasury, and its pillar inscription.

As Holmes examined Lévi's work, however, he noticed that Lévi had placed a large exclamation point next to a line in the inscription, a line that Holmes remembered, and a question mark next to one that he had not seen before, one which must have been found on the excavated portion of the pillar. It seemed that he had most emphatically understood the first but not the second.

Here Holmes paused for a moment. "Here, I must risk boring you, Watson, for the words are important to the solution. The line with Lévi's exclamatory mark read in Sanscrit in part:

> . . . raja udyanam iva tridivam gatah.

"These words mean literally, 'the king went to the other world as if he had gone to the pleasure garden.' "

"How odd," I said, not a little confused but amused as well as the strange words rippled off his tongue mellifluously.

"But the line questioned by Lévi," he continued, "read:

"sah sevina senagartibhis ahsevarpun hsivrihab.

"Its meaning? Well, my dear Watson, I was for the moment baffled. It made no sense, and appeared almost as a meaningless series of syllables no matter where it was broken into words. So supple and flexible is Sanscrit, however, that, with enough time, a variety of translations might be possible. In any case, I surmised that Lévi had seen a connection between the two lines and that he had gone to Changu to investigate. I also reminded myself of a general truth that had become apparent to me during my stay in Nepal: that nothing there was simple."

By this time my mind was reeling from the complexity as well as the speed of Holmes's account. That part of it was in Sanscrit did not reassure me in my attempt to understand what was happening.

"I am more than a bit confused, my dear Holmes. A king was apparently murdered fifteen hundred years ago, and a French scholar has disappeared before your eyes. Yet somehow their fates are intertwined. And somehow the fate of both men is buried in some difficult lines of an inscription in Sanscrit."

"Excellent, Watson, excellent. You have seen through to the crux. In the first line, Lévi had seen something that no previous commentator had seen."

"And what was that? Perhaps the king merely died of natural causes, and it means only that he died as if he had been at play, at perhaps some wanton sport," I ventured.

"And that is the way it was often construed in Nepal. But Dharmadeva was, by tradition at least, a paragon of virtue, probably incapable of the kind of vice that would do him in. Still there was something strange about the words, I thought, as if through their very strangeness the poet were pointing to something unusual. Perhaps there was a clue to his death in this phrase, perhaps a pun, a dual meaning. All of this, however, I retraced in my mind when I saw the words marked in Lévi's manuscript. Had he realised something that I had not? As to the other line, he had not deciphered it, nor could I!"

And yet, the inscription and Lévi's notes to it were the only clues Holmes had. He took the paper with his notes from the desk, folded it, and put it in his pocket for further study.

"I should say here, Watson, that I had in that piece of paper all that I needed to locate Lévi, but I had not seen through to the end. Without knowing where it would lead, I decided to go to Changu, following what in my best judgement might have been Lévi's footsteps. Reassuring the frightened Madame Lévi, I left the guesthouse and walked directly north, taking a path that led me through the ancient communities of Hadigaon and Vishalnagar."

By now the heavy rains had subsided, and the sky began to clear. As he walked, Holmes reviewed his conversation with Lévi, recalling in detail the scholar's words concerning the jewels of the ancient Nepalese kings. Perhaps greed, coupled with his outspoken contempt for the temple priests, had placed him in an awkward, even dangerous, position. Had he found the great treasure-house that he had mentioned? Had he entered it?

Crossing several streams, Holmes arrived at the Buddhist site of Bodhnath, his first place of enquiry. Here he questioned some beggars as to whether or not they had seen a foreigner. They said that indeed they had, that he was dressed in Nepalese clothes and that he was walking east along the main road when they last saw him. This corroborated the Maharajah's information and extended it a bit. Holmes was pleased, for he knew that his decision to proceed to Changu was the correct one.

By now, it was close to sunset, and he quickened his pace. The road entered the Gokarna Forest and was strangely empty, silent except for the sounds of monkeys and birds. Light flickered dimly in only one small house, and he knew that the road itself would be plunged into darkness before he reached his destination. He pushed on, confident now that if he was to find Lévi, he would find him, dead or alive, at Changu.

Just after a sharp turn in the main road, where it continues north to the small town of Sankhu, he took a fork to the right. This path, if memory served, led directly to the Manohara River and eventually to the Changu temple. He climbed a steep hill, then descended past a small village. All was dark, and the village appeared as if suddenly deserted.

When he reached the river, Holmes could see across it to the hill atop which the temple sits. The river was swollen by the rains, and it was only with a great deal of effort that he managed to cross it. The water was warm, but thoroughly unpleasant, for it was filled with debris brought down from the mountains by the rains. Things of all sizes and shapes, of all consistencies, touched and flowed against him. Soaked to the skin, he staggered across and, without stopping even for a breath, began the steep ascent to the temple.

It was almost dark, but even in the ensuing twilight, Holmes was aware that a large number of people were ahead of him on the path, and that pilgrims were streaming into the temple. The villages he had passed through were dark and deserted for a reason: their inhabitants were on their way to Changu with everyone who lived nearby. Something of importance was about to transpire.

In the darkness, Holmes fortunately passed unnoticed. Once at the top of the hill, he worked himself slowly into the crowd that now sat tightly arranged around the temple. The priests, their heads newly shaven, and in white robes, were leading a chant that he recognised at once as an ancient funeral hymn. Indeed, a cremation pyre had been prepared in front of the temple. The priests, three in number, had opened the inner sanctum of the temple, exposing to view the golden image of the god of Changu Narayan himself. As they chanted, several men carried in an effigy of a man, dressed in Nepalese attire, amazing at first look in its likeness to a human figure, but one that was clearly a mannequin made of straw. The figure was brought to the priests, who chanted over it in Sanscrit. Then it was placed in a supine position on the pyre, its hands crossed as if in prayer. It was only when the figure was lying down that Holmes noticed it wore on its face a pair of European spectacles, very much like those the French savant had worn to their meeting. It was the first clue he had upon his arrival, one which made him fear that he had arrived too late.

The crowd grew silent at this moment and stretched forward, not wishing to miss even the smallest detail of what was to take place next. Large drums began a low, steady rhythm, and the priests continued their chant. Then, one of the men who had carried the figure to the pyre stepped forward and, walking over to the head, smashed its face, including the spectacles, with a rock. Taking a torch from a member of the crowd, he lit the pyre. The straw figure went up in flames. In an instant nothing at all was left.

Having watched the fire devour its victim, the crowd vanished silently into the night. Holmes remained behind, crouched in the dark behind a wooden door from which he could watch the priests. These three, placing the idol of Changu back in its sacred location, closed the inner sanctum. Then passing a few rupees to the men who had carried the straw effigy, they departed, each by a different gate. The men, counting their wages, also quickly dispersed, and Holmes was left alone in the temple grounds.

Holmes feared that he might now have lost the trail to Lévi. The ritual he had just watched was disquieting, for it was an unusual one, obviously marking a death, and if his suspicions were correct, the death so marked was that of Sylvain Lévi.

The moon was bright, almost overhead now, and he could see clearly. There was almost no sound, except for the bats that flew everywhere, hovering constantly near his head.

As he debated his next move, he suddenly heard soft footsteps and the sound of voices from behind the temple. Taking care to remain hidden in the darkness, he moved slowly to where he could see to the other side. There, in the dark, he made out an old man and woman in Nepalese dress walking toward the pyre. The woman carried something in her arms, possibly an infant. The man, lame in his right leg, staggered slowly forward. He was assisted by a half-naked boy, the one whom Holmes had seen scaling the pillar. He could see from a distance that there was something wrong with the man's left arm as well, for it hung from his shoulder loosely. Having come to the front of the temple, the man sat on one of the temple steps. Holmes could see now that the woman was carrying a child. Handing it to her companion, she began poking and sifting through the still burning embers left by the cremation. Few words were exchanged between them, and occasionally a soft cry came from the infant.

"I recognised them all now," said Holmes. "These were, I had come to know from my previous visits, a family of untouchables, persons who must scavenge to live. Forced to subsist at the margins of Hindu civilisation, they were also known by the Sanscrit term *sandhyaloka,* 'people of the twilight,' those who appeared in the evening and disappeared at dawn, performing their assigned tasks all but unseen and unheard in the half-light of morning and the half-dark of evening."

A piece of good fortune, he thought, for these people well might be his last hope of discovering what had happened to Lévi. If his calculations were correct, Lévi had arrived in the vicinity of the temple just at sunset the day before. A bit of luck and they would have seen him.

When she had finished her task, the woman took the few coins that she had found amidst the ashes and turned them over to her companion. Taking the child once again, she and the old man began to retrace their steps, leaving the temple by its eastern gate.

"I followed them quietly. When they had proceeded about fifty yards down the slope, I overtook them and, seizing them both from behind, firmly but not so roughly as to harm them or the babe, forced them to the ground. So surprised were they that they both let out a cry, which I was able to cut short by a quick reassurance that I meant them no harm. The boy tried to run off, but I grabbed him by the arm, and he stopped."

They spoke in an archaic form of the Nepalese tongue, said Holmes, filled with those pathetic forms of respect that mark the great fear the illiterate outcasts have for their literate superiors. In a short time, however, they were sufficiently reassured by his repeated words that he meant them no harm that they were able to devote some of their attention to his enquiries. He also had placed several silver coins in their hands, more than they had seen in a lifetime of scavenging, and this too had the needed calming effect.

"I explained to them my search, and at first I met with resistance. They had seen no one. After a moment, however, the woman told me how sick and hungry the infant was, and that it was their grandchild, whose mother had died the previous day when the child was but a month old. I told them that I would give them sufficient assistance for the child, but that they must help me as quickly as possible. I placed several more coins in their hands, and the old man, rising to his feet, told the old woman to stay where she was. He motioned to me to follow."

Despite his age and infirmities, the old man walked down the hill quickly, speaking in a low voice as he and Holmes descended. The boy followed him close by. In a short time, they came to a clearing, filled with large wildflowers that glistened in the moonlight. In the centre was an ancient banyan tree. From it were hanging a variety of votive objects—statues and pictures, even ordinary pots and pans—all brought there in honour of the dead. Suddenly, the boy left the old man's side and climbed the tree. There, halfway up on a central limb, hung a silver disc. The boy turned it slightly, then jumped down and returned to the old man.

"Your friend is not far away, but by now it is too late. This is the udyana, the pleasure garden of our ancient kings. Your friend has gone to the Tridivam, the treasure-house of death, from which he cannot exit. He is dead by now and will not return."

The words he used chilled Holmes's blood, for in the archaic form in which they issued from his mouth, they were very close to the ancient words in the inscription of King Manadeva. It was apparent that Lévi, unable to contain his desire to know, had waited until dark and set out on his fateful path alone. He had followed the path of the ancient king Dharmadeva.

Seeing the look of despair on Holmes's face, the old man drew him closer to the tree. There, in the dark, he could see that there was a shrine built into its trunk. A stone image of the god Vishnu, in the form of one of his avatars, the Wild Boar, stood astride the universe, a figure of the goddess Earth sitting in comfort on his shoulder.

"This is the pleasure garden, the udyana of the ancient kings," the old man intoned again. "Below it is the Tridivam, the otherworld or heaven where their treasures are stored. At the beginning of this yuga, only the kings knew how to enter and how to leave, for as soon as one person enters, the entrance closes, and one can only exit through another place. The secret was passed from father to son in the royal line and later among us, the twilight people, from father to son. King Dharmadeva entered often, but for reasons we do not know, one day he did not return. And so the secret among kings died with him. Since that time a few, greedy for the treasure that lies inside, have come to understand how to enter, but none has ever returned. They have all died within. Your friend entered. He too has not returned. I know, for we showed him how."

"Then show me how he entered, for there is no time to waste," Holmes admonished.

The old man obeyed.

"Lift the Earth from her place," he said, pointing to the figure sitting on Vishnu's shoulder.

Holmes did as the old man said, raising the figure with his hand. It moved upward at his touch, then of itself fell back in place. There was suddenly a sharp noise, as if a giant spring had been released by the movement of the image. Then the great statue of Vishnu moved ever so slowly, as if of its own accord, then swinging rapidly inward to the left, leaving a small opening in front of it, large enough for one man to crawl down into.

The old man pointed to the black hole.

"That is the path to the Tridivam, to the treasure-house and to death, the path of your friend," he said. "If you follow, the opening will close as soon as you pass within. Even if I open it again, you will not be able to return by this path. The return is by another way. I entered once, but out of fear I climbed out before my head was covered. I escaped, but Vishnu bit me and took all the strength from my arm, and I no longer remembered how to return."

"My dilemma was immediately apparent, Watson," said Holmes calmly. "I was sure that given enough time I would be able to extricate myself from this so-called treasure-house, but I had no way to judge what lay below, nor how much time I would have before I succumbed either to lack of air or water or to some preordained scheme of death arranged by the bloodthirsty and greedy despots of the past. No sound emanated from the dark space below, and I presumed that Lévi was either dead, too weak, or too far away to be heard. Should I enter, or should I report back what I then knew to the Maharajah?"

As he stood there in thought, Holmes noticed that the moon had risen to the point where its rays were beginning to hit the temple. A moment later the moonlight, filtering through the leaves of the tree, struck the disc. As if by magic, it fell reflected onto the third eye of the statue of Vishnu and then the figure of Ganesh, striking his right hand. The astronomy of the temple, its relation to sun and moon, to night and day, to a whole series of opposites, struck Holmes, and he understood what he had to do in order to grasp the meaning of the second line of the inscription. He took out Lévi's notes and read the cryptic line backward, from right to left. It read in perfect clarity:

Bahir vishnupravesha / bhitra ganesha nivesha

which means simply: "Enter by the Vishnu outside; Leave by the Ganesh inside."

Holmes looked around. He was alone. The old man and his family had quietly slipped away. The opening was still there.

"At that moment, I chose to enter, knowing full well that I might be wrong, that I did not know with any certainty how I would escape if the opening closed above me, but knowing also that I had been through narrow escapes before, and that my brain had at the last moment saved me."

He peered into the abyss, then lowered his feet into it and slowly let go. He fell only a short distance onto a dirt floor. He could still see the moon in the sky through the opening above. He was now in some sort of pit. A large statue of the god Ganesh stood inside where he had entered. Holmes smiled at him. Then the sky above him disappeared. The opening had closed, and he heard the god Vishnu moving back to his earlier location.

Holmes gazed into the darkness. There was a corridor in front of him, at the end of which he could see a small light flickering. All else was darkness. He walked slowly toward the light. The corridor was narrow, but the ceiling high enough for him to walk without bending over. The air was damp and stale.

As he approached, he could see that the light emanated from a small tuki, or oil lamp placed on the floor well ahead of him. Beside it, as if asleep, was the figure of a man. As he neared, he saw that it was Lévi, alive or dead he did not know. He lay there amidst untold treasures— gold, jewels, precious stones, sculptures and images of every sort— strewn everywhere, all sparkling in the flickering flame of the lamp. There was no one else.

As he approached him, Holmes realised that the French scholar was in a deep sleep, breathing slowly and comfortably. In front of him was a large sheaf of paper. Holmes was amused by his scholarly dedication, for rather than find his exit, he had begun to record what he found. He had fallen asleep with exhaustion, his pen still in hand.

Holmes took a moment to observe what he saw. There were treasures, to be sure, everywhere, jewellery, coins, images, manuscripts in abundance. But his eye was drawn by a skeleton seated on a throne, covered in now crumbling attire, a gold tiara on its skull. This was presumably the ancient king Dharmadeva, who had entered never to return, eloquent testimony to the difficulty of exiting alive. Taking the lamp, Holmes examined the walls and floor of the room for any indication of a hidden opening. He found nothing, save the bones of others who had wandered in but had not been able to exit.

As he finished his preliminary examination, Lévi stirred and awoke. Holmes went over to him.

"Ah, my dear Kaul! How good to see you! I must have fallen asleep. How clever of you! When did you arrive?"

"Only a few moments ago," said Holmes, "but I must tell you frankly that I am most anxious to test my idea of how to exit."

Holmes explained to him that the Maharajah had summoned him and by what reasoning he had been able to follow him, taking the inscription on his desk as his chief clue. Holmes's tone of voice was one of irritation, for he made it clear that his quest had inconvenienced them all, even possibly costing them their lives.

Lévi smiled and stood up. "You need not worry, M. Kaul. I am not nearly as brave as you. I am but a simple scholar, and I never take large risks. You see, I was almost sure how to leave before I entered. Granted, I took some chance, but I was very certain. I have already been out twice this very night. The air in this small space is limited, and I would have been asphyxiated by now. But look, I have completed a preliminary inventory of what is here—there are over one hundred ancient sculptures alone, and the manuscripts number in the hundreds. Just a few more notes and we shall leave—in time for me to greet Henri, the Prince of Orléans."

Lévi spoke the last few words with a grin, and Holmes had no recourse but to wait until he had finished his tasks. As he wrote, Lévi continued to speak: "There is a third person of importance here with us, M. Kaul, the illustrious King Dharmadeva, who sits there, dead for almost fifteen hundred years. I examined his remains very carefully. He was murdered, M. Kaul, but before he died he wrote out his own account of what had transpired. It is a long tale of intrigue, but more of that on our way back."

Lévi pointed to a manuscript of birch bark that lay near his papers. He then carefully packed his notes and the manuscript, and, taking the lamp, he motioned to Holmes to follow down the corridor whence they had come. As they approached the end, Levi took from his pocket a large metal key and placed it firmly in the right hand of the large statue of Ganesh that Holmes had seen when he entered.

"The key!" exclaimed Lévi, "another lucky find. But of course, any long object would work."

Loud reverberations were heard, and the sky appeared in an opening above their heads. Lévi motioned Holmes forward and, standing on the shoulders of Ganesh, Holmes pulled himself up through the hole. Lévi followed quickly. Within seconds, they stood breathing the fresh early morning air, and the opening from which they had exited had disappeared without a trace into the temple wall.

It was just dawn, and the sun was about to rise. Nepal was covered by a thick silver mist. Unnoticed in it, they made their way back to the Prime Minister's palace, which they reached just as the mist burned off in the sun. On the way, Lévi explained his discoveries.

"You see, M. Kaul, I had available to me the entire text of the inscription now, due to the excavations that had been performed. I was now able to read anew. King Dharmadeva's own writing also cleared up many difficulties. It enabled me to translate to the end."

In his last few words, peculiar in their intent, Holmes realised how Lévi had learned what he knew, and how he had known the way to escape from the abyss beneath the temple, for he had guessed the same just before entering the treasure-house.

"You mean that the entire inscription is also a composition that can be read in two directions, one that, therefore, can also be read from right to left. I surmised this, just as I entered," said Holmes.

"Indeed, Monsieur, that is precisely what I mean. It came to me as I worked at my desk. So excited did I become that I left without saying anything to my poor wife. Nor did I register it in my notes. This inscription is a brilliant work, written by a poet who had complete knowledge of the Sanscrit poetic system. Reading in the ordinary way, beginning at the left and reading to the right, one has one reading. Reading it in reverse gives you a totally different, but completely coherent, if not always grammatical, composition. Almost no one knows this, of course, since the beginning of the inscription had been buried for centuries. Reading in the usual way, from left to right, one had the public account of events. Reading from right to left, from the end forward, one had the private account of what had happened . . . and the secret of how to leave the treasury. The first line excavated was the clue."

"And who was the poet who composed this and how did he come to know what he knew?"

"We do not know his name, and so he remains unknown. In answer to your second question, he was obviously someone well placed at the court, someone who knew the royal family intimately and could observe them closely without rousing their suspicion. Obviously of the Brahmanic caste, he may have been a teacher in the royal palace. The first line of his work read backward immediately struck me: Enter by the Vishnu outside; leave by the Ganesh inside. It was a clue to the meaning of the whole and was all I needed to have the courage to enter. Once there, I saw lying in the dust at the feet of Ganesh a great key. I placed it in the space in his hand made for it, and suddenly the way out appeared. I had tested the meaning of the line, and seeing that it worked, I began the examination of this secret treasury. It was almost immediately that I noticed the dead figure of Dharmadeva seated on the small throne to one side. He had in his hands a birch bark manuscript, which I took at once and read. It gives in detail his own account of what happened at the court, and how he found himself trapped in the treasury."

Holmes listened as Lévi continued his account.

"Dharmadeva was a king whose sole interest was in justice and in noninjury to living things. As he grew older, he became in his thought closer and closer to Buddhism. He refused to send his army on missions of conquest and started the building of temples and monasteries. His interest in the gods began to waver, and he grew estranged from his wife, Rajyavati, whom he had once loved but now treated with respectful distance. Rajyavati, of a character different from that of her husband, had a love of royal power that he did not share. One day, Dharmadeva summoned her and told her that he had decided to give up the throne and announce his abdication. He had decided to become a monk and to enter a monastery. He expected her and their son, Manadeva, to follow him in this. Controlling her anger at his words, Rajyavati gave her consent, but decided secretly that Dharmadeva must be removed. With Dharmadeva dead, Manadeva would become king, and she would rule through her son, who followed her every whim. She took as her chance the day when the king walked in the royal temple garden and visited the treasury to bring the annual gift of gold to the god Vishnu. She requested that she and their son be allowed to enter the treasury since this would be the last visit before they entered the monastery. Once inside the treasury, the unsuspecting king revealed to them the secret of how to leave. He showed them the key. Manadeva then hit his unsuspecting father from behind on the head, rendering him unconscious. They left him for dead and returned to the palace. Dharmadeva awoke to find himself alone and without the key. Realising that his fate was sealed, he wrote as fast as he could an account of what had happened, an account that was unknown and unread until now."

Lévi stopped for a moment as if in deep thought. "And, as luck would have it," he said, "Manadeva had dropped the key on his way out. Had he known that it was there, Dharmadeva could have escaped his fate. Too fearful to return to the scene of patricide without the key, Manadeva issued a royal edict forbidding entrance to the treasure-house during his lifetime."

"An incredible tale," Holmes remarked.

"Yes. I shall write it up in the *Journal Asiatique* and send you a copy."

"I shall enjoy it immensely," said Holmes.

By then they had reached the palace. Holmes bade good-bye to M. Lévi and returned to his hotel.

The next morning a group of soldiers arrived from the Maharajah's palace deputed by him to accompany Holmes to the Indian border. As he had promised, Gorashar accompanied him to the rim of the Valley. By midday, they reached the top of the Chandragiri pass. Holmes looked down and said good-bye to the valley of Katmandu and to the dear friend who had brought him there. He then turned his gaze southward, toward the plains of India.

I found myself at this moment gazing at Holmes's drawing.

"Who would have thought, Holmes, that so much meaning could be contained in this temple, and so easily hidden from us?"

"Light and word had come together in this temple, Watson. The words of the inscription were registered in its astronomy, if you will, in its relation to the sun and moon and other stars. The people of the twilight were the guardians of the relation, there to make sure through the millennia that the minute adjustments necessary to the preservation of its meaning were made. Indeed, these people, the lowliest of outcasts, made the system work and kept well its secrets. Lévi and I saw what is only a small fragment of a vast machine. But enough, Watson. It is late, the tale is told, such as it is."

Holmes suggested a walk before bed, and we went out into the early spring night. He said no more concerning the French savant, but instead spoke rapidly about his latest enthusiasm, the polyphony of Orlandus Lassus. Then we talked of many other things, none of which merit recounting here. It was almost light when we returned, and as we mounted the steps to our quarters, Holmes quoted two lines of the greatest of Italian poets:

> Così andammo infino alla lumera
> Parlando cose ch' il tacere è bello.

AN ENVOY TO LHASA

N THE PAGES WHICH I HAVE DEVOTED TO THE ADVENTURES OF Sherlock Holmes, I have often alluded to the contradiction between the impeccable order of his logical faculties and the extraordinary disorder that he allowed to reign in the world of physical objects immediately about him. Such thoughts again crossed my mind one morning as I looked up from my book and watched my friend slouched low in his favourite armchair, his eyes half closed, his mind apparently far distant. A year had passed since his return to London, and he was in the grip of another of the long melancholic fits that still seized him from time to time.

It was now the spring of 1895, a day in late March to be exact, and as the rare London sun began to pour through our sitting room window, I again looked up and cast a glance around our quarters. As my eyes moved over them, I was struck this time not only by Holmes's continued untidiness but by his ability to maintain such familiar disarray almost unchanged over many years. It was as if in the depths of his boredom he had somehow managed to cultivate a hidden order within the clutter.

As usual, his papers, chemicals, and test tubes were scattered everywhere. His cigars were still in the coal scuttle, and his tobacco was tucked into the toe of one of his Persian slippers. There were some new elements in the overall design, however, added in my absence no doubt during his more disconsolate moments. One of his recently acquired criminal relics, what appeared to be a large, sharp tooth, had now invaded the butter dish. A few bullet holes in the form of a *P* and an *M* had been added to the wooden mantel, this time presumably in honour of the present prime minister, and his unanswered correspondence was still pinned to the wall by a knife. It was only when I looked at this last object more closely, however, that I noticed another alteration, seemingly slight at first but important enough in the entire picture. The knife on the wall, originally an old jackknife, had been replaced by a different instrument, what appeared to be, from where I was seated, a knife of an entirely novel character, one with a golden handle. A quick glance about the room informed me that the jackknife had been transferred to the breakfast table, where it had been thrust to the hilt into an open jar of marmalade.

Curious about the provenance of the new knife, I walked over and pulled it from the wall, inadvertently letting the correspondence flutter audibly to the floor. I heard Holmes suddenly pull himself up in his chair.

"Boredom"—he sniffed—"is the only true gift of the gods, Watson. And the gold knife is from Tibet, should you be at all interested. It is a most unusual weapon. Note the distinctive fullering of the double-edged blade and the initial letter *S* that appears on the quillon. These details tell us immediately that the blade is of recent English manufacture and, judging from its slight curvature, a modified version of one of Major Henry Shakespear's deadly creations. The gold handle was of course cast in Tibet, possibly hundreds of years ago."

I made no immediate response to my friend's remarks but returned to my chair to examine the knife. It had a blade about seven inches in length of fine steel that was embedded in a slightly shorter handle that appeared to be of solid gold. The handle showed almost no signs of wear but bore decorations and an inscription. I noted what appeared to be the sun and moon, and the fylfot as it is known in British heraldry, or Buddhist swastika, here presumably a religious symbol, and an inscription in beautiful, elegant characters that I could not read. The language I assumed to be the Tibetan.

"Indeed, I am most interested, particularly if there is a tale associated with it," I answered belatedly, with feigned indifference.

"Then even though your never-ending curiosity in my exploits threatens my beloved Demoiselle Ennui," he said, "I shall tell you the tale of the gold knife and my trip to Lhasa."

He tossed the morning papers that had lain across his chest onto the floor. The boredom suddenly left his eyes, and I could almost see his brain running through the sequence of events that had transpired several years before as it reached his lips. I was inwardly overjoyed at his sudden decision to reveal his life in Tibet, but I did not press him, lest he draw back as he had done several times in the past. He had mentioned his life in Lhasa only in passing, the first time in his brief account of his escape from the Reichenbach Falls. But until now, he had resisted all attempts on my part to wrest from him even the smallest portion of his Tibetan adventures. I knew only what I had previously reported to the public: that he had lived there under the name of Sigerson, a Norwegian explorer and naturalist.

"You see, Watson," he began, "my trip to Lhasa was due not to any whim of mine, but to a secret mission which I undertook under the highest authority of Government. If I have shown a certain reluctance to divulge the details until now, it is because several principals in the matter would have been injured by their disclosure. This morning's paper announced the death of the last of these, and so I am now free to add these exploits to your chronicles."

He took the knife from my hand, moving his long, thin fingers slowly along the blade.

"As I have related to you before, except for the late, unlamented Colonel Sebastian Moran, Moriarty's chief henchman, only one other person was sure that I had survived the fateful encounter at the Reichenbach Falls, and that was my brother, Mycroft, to whom alone I communicated the fact of my fortunate but unexpected survival. It was shortly after my arrival in Florence a week later that I informed him that I was alive. A few days later, I received a message from him in the secret code that we shared, saying that special emissaries of Government were on their way to see me:

"My dear Sherlock,

"It was good of you to inform me of your final victory and survival in the battle with your great adversary, but in truth I expected no less of you. My compliments. The world is surely a better place now that Moriarty is no more.

"This is perhaps not the best moment to intrude upon your privacy or to add to your woes, considering your recent escapades, but a matter that will be before you shortly is of the greatest urgency. It involves a mission of extreme importance and great danger. I shall understand if you decline, but I believe that you are the only individual I know capable of bringing it off. You must forgive me, therefore, for having suggested to the authorities that you would be the ideal person to execute it. Representatives of the highest authority are on their way to you to discuss the matter. Please consider it carefully, Sherlock, for in addition to taking you far from your known enemies for a time, it will enable you to serve the most pressing needs of the Empire. It involves a long trip to one of the remotest corners of the civilised world. Expect to hear shortly, therefore, from a certain Florentine gentleman, one Signor Berolini.

"As your executor, I have taken charge of your personal affairs, which I trust will be in good order when you eventually return. A distraught Watson has just placed your obituary in the papers and is now writing up what he believes to be your 'final problem.' Although my sympathies go out to him, I agree with you that the deception of a sincerely grieving friend is necessary to your long-term survival.

"Mycroft

"I was immediately gratified by my brother's expression of trust in me," Holmes continued, "but I confess that I felt no immediate enthusiasm for the mission he mentioned. Mycroft, as you know, is the most brilliant mind available to our government. Indeed, as I have remarked on previous occasions, in some important ways he *is* the British Government. His message to me held important clues: the remotest corner of the civilised world could only mean somewhere in Asia, and in Asia most probably Tibet, that perennial goal of the romantic Englishman. But I assure you that what transpired in Tibet, or in any other remote corner of the world for that matter, was then farthest from my mind. After Moriarty's death, having dodged the rocks thrown down on me by Colonel Moran, I had taken to my heels, torn and bleeding, and had done ten miles in the darkness over the mountains before I boarded a train to Italy. The reaction of a terrible weariness was upon me, and I knew that I should be limp as a rag for many days to come."

Holmes suddenly rose and began pacing back and forth in front of me. He did not have to wait long, he said, to find out more about the proposed mission. It was toward evening a day later that the portiere in the pensione where he had taken a room handed him a note:

Please meet me at seven this evening at the Piazza della Signoria about the urgent matter of which you have already been informed. Under the Medusa head.

Suo dev. mo

Sg. Berolini

The last reference was of course to the famous statue of Perseus by Cellini that still graces the central piazza of Florence. And it was to that place that Holmes walked slowly from his pensione, arriving at exactly seven o'clock. He placed himself near the statue and looked around. It was the hour of what is known in Italy as the passeggiata, and the square was filled with strollers walking arm in arm. Among them he saw a single figure striding rapidly toward him, a short, rather stout man, wearing a black overcoat and a fedora.

"I am Signor Berolini." He bowed, addressing Holmes in measured but almost flawless Italian. "Please follow me," he said. They walked over to a nearby bench not far from the piazza, where they sat and conversed.

"But you are an Englishman nonetheless," Holmes replied, a bit sardonically perhaps. The man was a bit taken aback by his remark.

"How on earth did you know?" he cried out, breaking suddenly into English. "I have gone to great pains to create an Italian identity."

"Then begin by taking the added trouble of employing an Italian barber to shape your moustache instead of trimming it yourself."

Seeing that the man was crestfallen, Holmes did not continue in this vein, for he saw no reason to destroy his already injured confidence.

"My name is really James Munro," he said with a tight, embarrassed smile.

He handed Holmes a card that identified him as an agent of our foreign ministry, permanently assigned to the Italian peninsula. Holmes did not remark audibly on this part of his disguise, nor that he easily deduced that Munro had worked in Scotland Yard for a number of years.

"We shall leave here separately," said Munro, having recovered his composure, "and meet again in one hour at the address on the back of that card. Please memorise it. Any cab will take you there."

He removed the card from Holmes's hand and replaced it in his pocket. Rising quickly, he tipped his hat with a cheerful "Auguri" and disappeared into the crowd. Thoroughly amused, Holmes sat there for a few moments alone, contemplating the piazza. Then he hopped into a cab, asking the driver to take him to the assigned address.

It took Holmes almost an hour to reach his destination, a large villa beyond the old city limits on the southern route toward Rome, not far from Montepulciano. It was already dusk, and the shadows of the Italian pines were thrown softly everywhere by the golden setting sun.

Holmes alighted from the cab and was again met by Berolini, who stood at the gate, opening it as he approached. Holmes followed him down the main path to a large villa that sat a few hundred yards back from the road behind a large garden. They entered and proceeded to the library, in which two gentlemen, highly placed at the time in the British Cabinet, were already seated. Holmes recognised both of them instantly, and has asked that I not reveal their identities. One of them, a ranking member of our Foreign Office who still carries great weight in the upper circles of Government though he has since resigned, began the discussion.

"Mr. Holmes, I am here to explain to you in detail the mission to which your brother has alluded in his message to you. I sincerely hope that you will agree to take on the tasks that I am about to describe. Should you decline, however, I trust that all that transpires between us will be irrevocably forgotten and dismissed from your mind."

Holmes nodded in assent. "You may speak frankly, Your Lordship, and I shall consider most seriously whatever you propose. I can assure you that should your mission not suit me, I shall immediately dismiss it as well as any recollection of our meeting here this evening."

"Then listen most carefully, Mr. Holmes. As you may be aware, the threat to our Indian Empire from the designs of other Oriental powers continues to grow and perturb those of us who have the grave responsibility of maintaining our vast Empire in safety and order. Although the entire Subcontinent has been pacified internally for some time, the threat continues to grow from outside. The Russians, the Japanese, and at times those who manage the flickering energies of the Chinese Empire stand ever ready to take from us what is by now rightfully deemed ours. They see our Indian possessions as the likely sources of their own eventual enrichment, knowing little of the costly civilising burden that we carry there. Although the defences of the Empire in India are strong, the threat grows in Central Asia, an area that, as you know, is almost totally closed to us and still little known at best. The Tsars have continued to conquer and plunder the region, moving their borders eastward to the confines of Tibet, where they already have their resident agents. The Japanese, their eyes constantly on a weakening and starving China, have already shown signs of increasing interest. You have no doubt heard of the notorious Dorjiloff."

"He has a well-known criminal record, achieved long before he disappeared into the wilds of Tibet," said Holmes coolly. "Dorjiloff is a man of the greatest intelligence and is extremely dangerous. He is wanted for a particularly brutal murder in Riga. I have grappled with him in London, albeit at a distance and unfortunately without lasting success. His reincarnation as a government agent has amused me for some time."

"He has been in and out of Lhasa for several years," continued the minister, "during which period our relations with the Tibetan Government have come under serious strain. The Viceroy is already of the strong opinion that this agent and his gang, pursuing aggressive Tsarist policies of expansion in the Orient, have moved the Tibetan Government away from its traditionally neutral stance to one that could foreseeably cause us great trouble along our Himalayan border, thereby sowing the seeds of dissatisfaction in the plains of Hindusthan as well. The ultimate objective is of course obvious: the removal of Britain as a power from the continent of Asia and the unlimited expansion of the Tsarist dominions. I myself regard the latter as almost unthinkable considering our present strength. But I am also a person of prudence, one whose task it is in government to make sure that not even the slightest step along this path is taken."

"I understand your concerns," said Holmes. "What, then, are the immediate circumstances that have brought you here?"

"Recent events led us at first to believe that matters were about to improve. This past year, the Chinese Government agreed to a treaty that would begin the regularisation of our relations with Tibet. In order to stabilise these relations, we asked that the treaty be signed as soon as possible. The Chinese agreed, but they have only nominal control over the Tibetans and could only meekly request Tibetan compliance. Indeed, the ever-weakening Chinese Government proved too feeble to obtain Tibetan consent. As soon as certain elements within the Tibetan Government unfriendly to us became aware of the provisions of the treaty, they began, deliberately and presumably with the aid of agents such as Dorjiloff, to undermine it. Boundary markers were uprooted and destroyed, border patrols were attacked, and most impudently, English merchants were prevented from plying their trade. The most egregious example of this dastardly conduct occurred when the only road from Tibet to the market of Yatung, which had been thrown open to trade with India by the stipulations of the convention of 1810, was permanently blocked by the building of a wall. Letters from the Viceroy protesting this action to the Grand Lama in Lhasa were returned unopened.

"In order to convince the Tibetans that deeds such as these could only prove harmful in the long run and that it was in Tibet's interest to sign the treaty at once, a treaty that in my judgement is most generous to Tibet, a special envoy was sent to the Grand Lama with the specific purpose of explaining our present position directly and without ambiguity. The emissary was Sir William Manning, one of the most sober of our diplomats, whose experience began in the Central Provinces and included a distinguished period of service in Kashmir. We had every hope for his success, but except for a brief note sent by Manning himself to the Viceroy announcing his safe arrival in Lhasa, nothing has been heard of him. A year has now gone by since his arrival, all requests from us have gone unheeded, and the Tibetan Government professes no knowledge of him or his mission. Furious with what he considers to be Tibetan duplicity, the Viceroy has now requested permission to send an armed force to take the Tibetan capital and put an end once and for all to Tibetan machinations. Her Majesty's Government, however, is reluctant to do this without one last approach to the Tibetan Government. It is the general opinion in London that a war in Tibet is to be avoided at this juncture, if at all possible. Despite our military supremacy in the region, it would be a costly affair, causing severe repercussions among the warring tribesmen in Central Asia, all of which we would regard as undesirable. We are well aware of our losses in Afghanistan and do not wish to repeat such unfortunate episodes. An invasion would come only as a last resort.

"The mission which we propose to you, therefore, Mr. Holmes, would have several goals: to find Manning or learn what has happened to him; to have the treaty signed or, barring that, to recommend to us a course of action, including, if you deem it necessary, an invasion of Tibet, for which undesirable eventuality we are prepared. And, finally, of course, to do whatever might be done to neutralise the effects of Dorjiloff and his allies. Until now, there has been no one whom we could oppose to the dexterity of this Buriat lama, no one who might bring some sense to the turbulent children of Tibet. We believe that you are among the very few who might accomplish these things.

"Mr. Holmes, should you agree to the mission, you will have the full force of Government and their resources behind you. I should advise that in all dealings with the Tibetan Government you keep to the specific identity that we have chosen for you and confirmed in the documents: if you accept the mission, you will be known as Hallvard Sigerson, Scandinavian explorer and naturalist, and incidentally secret envoy in the employ of the British Government. Your true identity as Sherlock Holmes is to be kept secret and revealed only if necessary to the success of the mission. This I would presume would be your wish as well, judging from what little Mycroft Holmes has let us know of your immediate desires."

Holmes listened intently to the minister's every word. Despite his fatigue and reluctance to undertake any arduous assignments, he was most intrigued. He had thought of a long trip to a quiet corner of the world where he could recover and plan the demise of his remaining enemies in the Moriarty gang. Why not Tibet? The suggested journey not only fit his plan to avoid his enemies for a time but promised to be a mission of the greatest interest. It also gave him an official disguise, invaluable to him at this dangerous juncture in his life. He therefore did not hesitate.

"I agree to the mission, Your Lordship, but I shall need immediate assistance. I should say, immodestly perhaps, that for a variety of reasons my knowledge of some aspects of Tibet is already considerable, and I shall not bore you with the many reasons why that is so. I would attempt nothing of this kind, however, without the most painstaking preparation, preparation which, under circumstances such as those that may befall me during the mission—conceivably those of life and death—must reach to the most minute detail."

The minister smiled when he heard Holmes's acceptance and, in answer to his last words, replied: "Easily done, my dear Holmes, far more easily done than you would have thought. First, accept this portfolio. It contains official copies of the treaty to be signed, copies of the charge to Manning as well as the details of his mission and itinerary, and secret exchanges concerning Tibet between ourselves and the Chinese."

As he spoke, he handed Holmes a large folder containing the official papers.

"Enclosed also is what I trust you will find to be more than adequate compensation for your efforts and for your expenses to Lhasa and return. There are also your personal documents identifying you as the Norwegian naturalist Hallvard Sigerson. And now, let us proceed to the adjoining chamber."

They moved to the next room, one smaller than the library, but one also lined with books. It was the second minister who spoke at this time.

"Thanks again to your brother, Mycroft, Mr. Holmes, we were able to locate our meeting in this villa, the home of Count Giancarlo Possenza d'Este, one of Italy's greatest explorers and scholars of the Orient, and a good friend, I might add, of Mycroft's and mine from the Diogenes Club in London. It was in anticipation of your assent to the mission that his estate was chosen for our meeting. He himself is absent from Italy, but he has consented to full use of his collections. This room contains substantial collections in several languages on the history and peoples of Tibet and adjacent regions. There is, in my judgement, no better library anywhere. In your stay, an active brain such as yours should be able to absorb and retain as much as it needs. Notice, too, that these drawers contain detailed maps, the best now available, on Tibet and on Lhasa itself.

"We have made arrangements for you to live here until your departure from Italy," the minister continued. "Berolini is already seeing to the removal of your bags from your pensione so you needn't return there at all. You will have in all six weeks here. You will travel then to Naples, and thence to Brindisi, where you will board ship for Bombay. Once there, you must seek advice from the Indian Government—the Viceroy himself will be in charge of your mission—as to how to proceed and what the best route to Lhasa will be at the time of your arrival.

Best of luck to you, my dear fellow, and I earnestly hope for your safety and success."

They shook Holmes's hand vigorously as they departed.

"I was left alone, Watson, elated at the prospects of my new adventure, but still feeling the exhaustion of the previous days. By this time it was almost eleven, and fatigued by events, I decided to retire. A knock at the door came just as this thought occurred to me, and one of the servants appeared and showed me to my quarters. A heavy languor enveloped me, and I went smoothly into the first real sleep since the death of Moriarty."

The following days were for Holmes, as he recalled them for me, a vigorous assay into the Oriental literature on Tibet and its neighbours. Each day he spent long hours poring over old histories and maps, taking notes, memorising routes, passes, and altitudes. Since he was to travel in the guise of a Scandinavian explorer and naturalist, he made certain of his familiarity with what was known of Himalayan geography and its flora and fauna. He read not only Hooker but also, and not without a certain irony, the works of his remaining chief enemy, Colonel Moran, who had spent long years in the Himalaya. He studied the language and its peculiar script and read the classic accounts of the missionaries Orazio della Penna and Le Père Huc. By all these accounts, the journey to Tibet was a most dangerous one. Indeed, it was in the text of Huc that he read of the curious misadventures of the first Englishman to visit Tibet, a certain Clement Moorcroft, who was, according to the good friar's account, killed by bandits as he attempted his return from Lhasa. Not an appealing precedent, Holmes thought.

It was the more recent accounts, however, that provided much of what he needed to understand the present situation in the country. They described a most complicated political arrangement. The Grand Lama, the titular ruler of the country, was still a young boy, and the power of his office was wielded by a regent, one Gethong Tsarong. Little was known of the latter except that he was the most feared individual in Tibet, known for his ruthless methods and great cruelties. His power seemed to be diminishing, however, for in addition there now lived in the Potala itself, the residence of the Grand Lama, this strange presence who bore the name of Dorjieff or Dorjiloff, the deadly agent alluded to by the ministers from London. In strategic but temporary collusion with the Tsarists was the Imperial Government of Japan, the latter pressing its influence through a weakening China. The two governments, Russian and Japanese, appeared bent on wresting control of Tibet from the Tibetans themselves and dividing it between themselves. How long it would be before the interests of these two powers diverged into open conflict rather than remain in the uneasy cooperation that they now professed depended largely on the cleverness of our own policy. Holmes was indeed walking right into the Great Game in Central Asia.

"I had tangled with Dorjiloff earlier, though we never met face-to-face," said Holmes, relating to me what he knew of his adversary from earlier episodes. "Dorjiloff was a man well into his fifties by now, but his origins were mysterious. He himself claimed to be of Mongolian Buriat origin, born in Siberia east of Lake Baikal. His youth was misspent, and he soon ran afoul of the Tsarist police. He was arrested for murder and petty larceny and sent to a labour camp in the Urals. From there he escaped and came to London, where I first became aware of him. You may recall the unresolved murder of Sir Samuel Soames, Watson."

"Indeed, I do. Soames was a wealthy merchant of Liverpool, who was stabbed to death by a street thief—in Russell Square, if I remember correctly."

"Excellent, Watson. It was no street thief who perpetrated the crime, of course, and I traced the murder to a secret society of Russian agents operating in London, of which Dorjiloff was a prominent member. Unfortunately, he avoided my net and escaped to New York, where he engaged in forgery. He eventually made his way to San Francisco, then Shanghai. From there he returned to Russia and hid in a Buddhist monastery at Urga. There he convinced the ignorant monks of his religious propensities and began his study in earnest of the Buddhist religion. Following his ordination, he left Russia and travelled in Mongolia, taking the Tibetan name of Ghomang Lopzang. Arriving at last in Tibet itself, he entered the monastery at Drepung as an authority on metaphysics and philosophy. During his stay he went often to Lhasa, where he began to exercise great influence over the Regent and thereby upon the child who was the Grand Lama. Undetected by the Russian authorities, he returned to Moscow, where he became famous as a religious teacher under an assumed name, that of Dorjiloff, or Dorjieff, a Russified Tibetan name that means 'Man of the Thunder Bolt.' In this guise, he came to the attention of the superstitious Tsar himself, who brought him to the Russian palace, where he exerted a strong influence. In both Russia and Tibet, he soon achieved renown, and now works actively for Tsarist interests."

I marvelled at Holmes's account and the wealth of detail that he commanded about his enemies even after so many years.

"So much for my chief adversary, Watson. I won't bore you further. Let it suffice to say that by now Lhasa had begun to present sufficient criminal interest for me to wish to go even without my official task. I hoped to find Manning still alive, for I doubted that the Tibetans would have risked the killing of a British envoy, unless, that is, someone such as Dorjiloff had him killed or killed him himself. Such an act would bring direct intervention of the Viceroy, and whatever Dorjiloff's desires in this respect, my study indicated that the Tibetan Government itself was one whose character was if anything restrained. The old Regent still wielded the chief power and influence, and it was with him I wished to deal, if I could get near him. He apparently received almost no one and remained in the Potala, where he dictated the life of Tibet."

Holmes ended the account of his researches there. He added only that he emerged from the long days of study fully confident in his ability to accomplish his task. True to the minister's promise, Holmes was taken from Count d'Este's villa to the central station in Florence, where he boarded a train for Naples. There he switched to another that took him overnight to Brindisi. A small American freighter, the SS *Downes-Porter,* awaited him there, and he boarded in the early morning. That evening he was bound for Alexandria and then Bombay.

The trip was uneventful, and Holmes spent the long idle hours imposed upon him in further study of the notes and documents he had with him. Among them were several photographs of Manning and Dorjiloff. He also had photographs of the Grand Lama and his family. The Regent, however, as far as Holmes could ascertain, had circumvented all known attempts to photograph him, and Count d'Este had registered none in his collections. One of the family photographs, however, contained a figure who, Holmes was fairly certain, was the Regent Gethong Tsarong. The photograph showed a tall, rather gaunt man standing next to the child chosen to become the Grand Lama. He wore thick glasses, and his hair in a braid tied round his head. The picture was faded and improperly focussed, and Holmes found the man's features there displayed most curious. He also had made detailed diagrams of the Potala, the residence of the Grand Lama, both its outer ramparts and its inner corridors and rooms, which he committed to memory. It was this kind of knowledge, become almost instinctive so well had he drilled himself, that would give him the ability to move quickly in dangerous circumstances.

"We docked in Bombay just over three weeks after our departure from Italy," he continued. "By this time, I was in despair over the ship's food, the enforced rest, and the small talk of the few uninteresting passengers. I was delighted therefore when we first glimpsed the Bombay harbour in the early morning mists. It was my first taste of the Orient, Watson, but I must say that initial delight soon passed into disappointment. Architecturally, in its grandiose public monuments, Bombay attempted to be another London, but succeeded only in being one drab and run-down, a metropolis totally misplaced in the tropical climate of western India, filled with teeming millions living in the streets trying to survive the vicissitudes of an indifferent fate. The rains had been heavy, and the city was soaked through. The air was wet and reeked of humankind and its myriad activities, and I found myself eager to leave on my mission."

Holmes's first task was to meet with officials of Government, but they were at once unhelpful and unconcerned. What appeared as a grave problem in London impressed no one in Bombay as urgent. Indeed, Lhasa seemed farther from Bombay than it was from London. In addition, the Viceroy himself had been called out of India unexpectedly; he was on his way to Burma to tend to a crisis in Rangoon and was therefore unreachable. If Holmes was to keep to his schedule, therefore, he would have to pick his own route and travel to Lhasa on his own. Out of several routes, he chose one of the shorter ones, and the very one taken by Manning. This passed through the eastern Himalaya and led directly to the Tibetan plateau. From there, he would travel in an easterly direction to the sacred city of Lhasa.

With this route in mind, Holmes boarded a train to Darjeeling, and from there, with a guide and a group of porters, he began the ascent, sometimes on foot, sometimes on horseback, through Sikkim and the Chumbi Valley, thence to Shigatse and Gyantse. It was in Shigatse that he met a group of Kashmiri traders on their way to the holy city, and they kindly invited him to join their caravan.

"It has been said, Watson, that no stranger can enter Tibet without the knowledge of the Tibetan Government. And yet, in travelling with this large caravan, I entered unobserved. I was not questioned at the various check posts, and at almost every point I was allowed to proceed without difficulty. Only on one occasion was I noticed, and that was just outside Shigatse, the last post before Lhasa. I produced the documents of the Scandinavian naturalist Hallvard Sigerson, and stated that I was on a scientific mission to collect botanical and zoological specimens from the Tibetan plateau. I passed through without delay and continued on with my Kashmiri friends. The Tibetans appeared to have a high regard for Scandinavians, and looked upon them without the suspicion that they reserved for British citizens and those of the major powers. My special status as an emissary of the British Government I was to reveal only to the authorities in the Potala, and I kept it hidden from the police at the border. Having passed through this last post, I was finally in Tibet, and as I gazed around me, I felt a singular elation, no doubt intensified by the great heat of the sun and the high altitude."

The Tibetan plateau appeared to Holmes as it has appeared to so many travellers: a vast expanse of empty land, beautiful and severe, at times forbidding. Fierce winds blew, and the sun scorched him and his companions, blistering the skin, almost blinding them as it shone from the high vault of cloudless sky that seemed unending. The air was thin and deficient at the higher altitudes, and the way therefore exhausting. Holmes survived, miraculously he thought at times.

When they reached the valley of the Brahmaputra, Holmes had seen the worst of the trip. Though it is situated at almost twelve thousand feet, this valley, in which lies the capital city of Tibet, was filled with vegetation, and the caravan travelled with far greater ease than before. One morning, shortly after they had resumed their journey north beyond Gyantse, the city of Lhasa appeared, or rather, the Potala—that immense edifice that houses the Grand Lama—first became visible in the morning sun atop the hill on which it sits north of the city. It was in stark contrast to Lhasa itself, which soon appeared at the end of a broad avenue lined with large trees, and it was not long before the caravan entered the central portion of the city.

"Lhasa, my dear Watson, is no more than a small town, housing only a few thousand inhabitants in its stone houses and narrow lanes. Its appearance is better from afar, for closer inspection reveals a city covered with soot and dirt, with no orderly plan. The streets are full of dogs, some growling and gnawing bits of hide which lie about in profusion, emitting a strong charnel house odour. Despite this rather gloomy appearance, my first impression was overall a good one, for the poverty and primitive way of life notwithstanding, the people were friendly and courteous, varied and colourful, and the city was filled with the activity of an amiable, even innocent, humanity."

Holmes was taken first to a small lodge where foreign guests were housed before they met their official hosts. It was from here that he made his initial attempts to make contact with the Tibetan Government. His papers were politely accepted by an official of the Potala, but he was informed that he would have to wait until the Regent himself reviewed his documents before his work could begin. It was apparent that Tibetan officialdom, although now aware of his mission, had not yet agreed to receive him. When he asked to meet with Mr. Manning, the official checked a list of foreign visitors and duly informed him that no one by that name had ever visited Lhasa. He was most cordial but firm, and Holmes knew then that his work would take extraordinary patience.

In the delay, he was afforded the time to explore the city and to begin private enquiries about Manning, who now, it seemed, would be difficult to trace. In trying to locate him, Holmes spent the early days of his stay learning every inch of old Lhasa. At its centre lies the most sacred of Tibetan temples, the so-called Jor-khang, a most ornate edifice, heavy with incense and filled with monks, pilgrims, and the sacred idols of a superstitious people. Around it and in the adjacent alleys are the shops, residences, and offices of much of the Tibetan Government. These are all housed in grey stone buildings, with which Holmes soon became thoroughly familiar. No one here knew anything of Manning.

"Those first days in Tibet," he continued, "also taught me of things that I had not met in the countless books perused in Italy. Like all things human, the Tibetan character is complex, with much that is good in it, perhaps more than there is in ours. But there is a dark side as well, of which they are very much aware—of anger, greed, cruelty, lust, and mental as well as physical disease. The religious system is a highly developed one, with spiritual attainments that far surpass our meagre efforts. But the Tibetan life, despite these accomplishments, is, for the majority, of extreme difficulty and poverty. Tibetans are farmers and herders ruled by clergy and aristocracy, who together set the rules by which the majority lives. In some cases, these rules are extremely harsh, resembling the criminal law of our own medieval epoch. The rack, the ordeal, various ancient tortures such as disembowelling, dismemberment, and public executions, are all practiced for the most heinous of crimes. The harshness of these rules appears to have little effect on the criminal classes, for crime is widespread and gangs of thieves and murderers roam the countryside, giving grief to villagers, merchants, and priests alike. No trade route is truly safe, and the large caravans that travel between the Tibetan plateau and the Indian plains are usually well armed.

"Despite its isolation and reputation for impenetrability," said Holmes, "I soon became aware that Lhasa housed a number of people from other parts of the world. There were a variety of merchants, mainly Kashmiri, Nepalese, and Chinese, for the Tibetans in Lhasa are loath to engage in business on their own. There were also a number of Europeans. Some of these were engaged in honest activity and researches concerning Tibetan belief and practice. Among them were Sandor Halévy, the great student of Tibetan literature, and Marie le Carré, an exuberant and eccentric disciple of Buddhism from Provence. But others had bribed their way in with the collusion of corrupt officials. I quickly spotted Sackville-Grimes, the most dangerous of arsonists; Platon Gilbert, one of the cruellest murderers of modern France; the infamous German counterfeiter Wilamowitz-Moellendorf, and finally, Sviadek, notorious as the Gallician cannibal. These and others were there as long as either money was to be made or they were protected by the Tibetan Government, petty criminals and quacks most of them, who lacked the means or the energy to leave and so found themselves to be longtime residents of the so-called Forbidden City. None of these either, when interrogated, professed any knowledge of William Manning."

It was well within his first fortnight that Holmes met Gorashar, the most successful merchant of Lhasa and someone who was to be of invaluable aid to him. Holmes was taken to his house by one of the Kashmiri merchants with whom he had travelled. Gorashar was a Newar from Katmandu, a short, dapper man whose intelligent and impish eyes said at once that he believed in nothing and trusted no one. He welcomed Holmes warmly, offering him a rare Russian cigarette, and Holmes felt at once comfortable in his presence.

In the evening, Holmes soon learned, Gorashar's lavish home near the Jor-khang became the site of an elaborate salon, which almost all of the peculiar denizens of the city attended. Evenings there included banquets and games of mahjong and gambling in almost all its varieties, all of which were accompanied by the constant consumption of intoxicants, either in their local manifestations or in the more exotic varieties that Gorashar imported through his agents in St. Petersburg. The air was always thick with the smoke of tobacco and Indian gunja, and the ears were often assaulted by a band of Indian musicians from Calcutta who attempted peculiar Oriental renditions of the seductive ditties that one associates with the demimonde establishments of London and Paris.

"As you might well imagine, Watson, this other Lhasa did not possess an atmosphere that I found in the least congenial, and were it not for my mission, I would have removed myself at once. It was clear to me, however, that Gorashar's establishment was more than just a place for an evening's entertainment. It was, among other things, a feast for the eye of the detective. I found myself constantly drawn to it during my stay. The room was filled with the riffraff of four continents. What a delight, dear Watson. Here, in this large and crowded room in one of the most isolated corners of the globe, there mixed together the most dangerous criminals with the worst mountebanks and pious bewilderers known to the civilised world. Some of them taxed even my powers of observation. Imagine a host of criminals and quacks who had taken on exotic disguises—shaven heads and eyebrows, glass eyes, wigs, long beards, scars and tattoos, fake limbs causing the oddest limps, canes and crutches of exotic manufacture. On several occasions, I sat contemplating the scene before me, wishing that I could have uninterrupted observance. Remote Lhasa, the romantic destination of every middle-class heart in England, had become a cesspool not unlike London, far smaller perhaps, but one with its own poisonous aspects, one in which the profound religious life of the Tibetan people served as the scenic landscape for the nefarious activities of international roguery. So many who had apparently disappeared from the face of the earth were here, perfecting their disguises in this exotic land before they returned, transformed, they hoped, beyond recognition. And to my delight, neither Scotland Yard, the French Sûreté, nor the New York Department of Criminal Investigation had any inkling of their whereabouts."

I could not help but interrupt Holmes at this point in his story.

"Extraordinary luck, Holmes," I said, laughing, "considering your interest in disguise and charlatanry."

"It was a room of Cagliostros, Watson, and I add the curious but interesting morsel that, according to some philologians, *charlatan* is the only word that comes into English from the Mongolian."

We both laughed heartily, and he continued.

"But of even more importance, Watson, was the fact that Gorashar's salon was also one of the places where the most important matters of state were transacted. Monk, merchant, secret agent, Tibetan as well as other officials, mixed and made the arrangements that influenced the lives of the Tibetan people, almost all of whom were ignorant of what transpired late into the night in the confines of this one house. No contrast was greater than that of the daily life of the ordinary Tibetan, with its hardships and religious piety, but with its mirthful laughter as well, and the evenings at Gorashar's, where the piety of the monk, the mysticism of the saint, the integrity of the ruler, and the honesty of the peasant were often transformed into their dark opposites. One would have thought that in this atmosphere I would have come upon a clue, a trace, a word slipped into a conversation even incidentally, about Manning, but there was nothing. This absolute silence paradoxically became itself the only clue: it was as if a command had been issued on high that even the name Manning was not to be uttered. If the silence was absolute, then so must have been the fear."

The first weeks passed, and Holmes's frustration grew. Yet he knew through his long experience of crime that if he persevered, his very presence in Lhasa would eventually force something to the surface. One day, there was a sudden and abrupt change, he said. Events began to move rapidly, so rapidly that within two days he saw the first dim outline of what had transpired before his arrival and what was about to unfold before him.

The first of these events was most extraordinary. One morning a curious scene, seemingly unrelated to his mission, led him to the first clue. It was near noon, and he had walked already for almost two hours through the crowded bazaar to the outskirts of the city. A sentry, stationed near the city wall, prevented him from venturing any further, and he turned back. The sun was already almost too bright to endure, and he sat under one of the few nearby trees. As he enjoyed the cool shade, he pondered the sentry's refusal to allow him to go any further.

At that moment, a large man appeared in front of him dragging the remains of a dead yak, leaving it to rot only a few yards away. A group of wild street dogs that had followed, ravenously hungry, began greedily gnawing at the abandoned carcase. Suddenly, a group of vultures gathered in the sky above and descended, their large wings flapping furiously. These obscene creatures, abhorrent in their habits and appearance, began to fight for their rights to the carrion. A battle of loathsome proportions ensued, said Holmes, a battle in which the dogs, smaller in number but no less ferocious, were forced to retreat from the scene by the talons of these demons from the sky.

In defeat, however, the wild dogs took their toll: one of the vultures lay mortally wounded, blood flowing from its neck, a strange unearthly noise emanating from its beak. As soon as they had finished with the yak, the other great birds descended on their moribund companion, and in a few minutes had reduced the unfortunate creature to a second pile of bones gleaming in the noonday sun.

"It was only then," said Holmes, "after the vultures had flown away, that I noticed something stuck to one of the dead vulture's talons. It had glinted in the sun. I walked over and saw that it was a piece of metal. I tugged it free. It was a brass button, obviously of English manufacture. There were several black threads still attached to it. It bore the letters *WM,* the initials of William Manning. I placed it in my pocket for later scrutiny. As I turned back toward the city, I found myself staring straight at the Potala. Only then did I sense how that immense edifice dominated not only the city of Lhasa but my mission as well. The secret of Manning's disappearance may very well lie within its walls, I thought. Eventually, if all else failed, I would have to gain entrance to it and pursue my search within its vast chambers."

Holmes returned to his lodging, pondering the strange mono-grammed button and struggling with the implacable silence that Lhasa presented. How did the button find its way to its gruesome location? For the first time since his arrival, he feared for Manning's life.

Toward nightfall, having made little progress, Holmes decided to attend Gorashar's soiree once again. As he walked into the great central room, he saw Dorjiloff for the first time. With him stood a short, sallow man whom Holmes recognised as his chief accomplice, Rastrakoff.

Dorjiloff had been in Drepung and had just returned to Lhasa. Behind him in the dimly lit room, Holmes could see through the thick smoke a ring of dark shapes formed by the criminals and cranks whom he had come to observe in the holy city.

As Gorashar introduced him to the Russian agent, Holmes noted that Dorjiloff was shorter than he remembered but still resembled closely his old photographs. He was dressed in robes of Chinese red and gold brocade, and his bald head, dark pointed beard, and dark eyes gave him such a strong satanic appearance that Holmes almost laughed outright. This Tartar Mephistopheles still moved with singular grace, however, thought Holmes, and his robes did not hide his lithe and muscular build. Dorjiloff nodded pleasantly enough at Gorashar's words of introduction and looked directly into Holmes's eyes.

"Let us speak later, Mr. Sigerson," said he. "Our common interests give us much to talk about."

"I am at your disposal," said Holmes.

"Later, then, when the crowd has thinned," replied Dorjiloff.

Holmes nodded in assent, and Dorjiloff was suddenly embraced by Mirbeau, a French doctor recently arrived to treat the Grand Lama for an undisclosed ailment.

Holmes retired to a dimly lit corner of the room, his eyes never turned for very long from the figure of Dorjiloff. Around Holmes now was the constant chatter of thieves and mountebanks, and for a moment he listened with amusement to their words, chuckling quietly at the imbecilities of the criminal world. It was at that moment that Gorashar found him in the smoke-filled darkness. He had with him a young Tibetan woman, whom Gorashar introduced as Pema, a princess of Amdo, a northern province of Tibet, and wife of Pasang, a princely official in the Tibetan Government who had been recently reported killed in a battle in Kham. She stood silently, clutching at Gorashar's arm. Nervously glancing around her, she said in a whisper to Holmes, "He is still alive."

Holmes was about to speak when Rastrakoff suddenly appeared at Gorashar's side. The princess became at once visibly uncomfortable. She seemed anxious to communicate something further, but after her quick whisper, Rastrakoff took her firmly by the arm, bade good-bye to their host, and led her away.

Several other guests left shortly thereafter, and as the crowd thinned, Holmes noticed Dorjiloff staring at him from across the room. He motioned to Holmes, who joined him.

"So, Dr. Sigerson, you are a naturalist and explorer, I understand."

"Yes," Holmes replied. "There is much to study here in Tibet."

"I study only Buddhism," said Dorjiloff with a laugh. "But I pay great attention to all visitors. Tell me about yourself, Mr. Sigerson."

As he spoke, Holmes was aware that Dorjiloff examined and weighed every word he uttered, for he was there to make sure that no one entered Tibet with interests inimical to those of Russia.

"Wherein lies your main field of enquiry, Dr. Sigerson, in plants or animals?"

"In both," Holmes replied.

"How so?"

"Because I am interested in poisons . . . and their antidotes."

"How interesting, Dr. Sigerson. And which poisons in particular?"

"There are many here in Tibet. Belladonna I see grows everywhere, and certain arachnidae seem to have proliferated."

"You know of the wolf-man?"

"Yes, of course, a deadly species, but imported from outside . . . like certain snakes."

"Ah, then, you must be familiar with Kruger's work."

"Yes, *Giftschlange und Schlangengift* is one of the few volumes I have brought with me."

"And you know Gunther's work, of course."

"I worked with him in London."

"He is the first to report on—"

"*Agkistrodon himalayanus,* the Himalayan viper. According to Mellins, the great herpetologist of China, a recent import . . . from Mongolia."

"You know the story—"

"Yes," Holmes said, smiling, "the king cobra hidden in the golden funerary urn. A distinct surprise."

"Still there are few snakes in Tibet."

"The examination of that assertion is at the core of my research. I shall present you a copy of my monograph when it is complete."

"I shall be most honoured, Dr. Sigerson. As to your explorations, have you visited the Garden of Punishment here in Lhasa?"

"Not as yet," replied Holmes.

"You may find it of great interest. Special permission is required to enter. I go regularly. It is most instructive, for it is where Tibetan justice is dispensed. Behind high stone walls, the criminals of Tibet and other transgressors are punished. Today some wandered with cages set about their heads, their hands unable to reach their mouths, so that they must rely on the charity of people to survive. One of them was near death. In Tibetan eyes, his crime was particularly grave: he used a gold alloy in his paintings of the Buddha rather than the pure metal. The buzzards sit and wait for him to expire."

"Most interesting. I should like to visit indeed. No doubt there are some whose crimes are particularly grave in your eyes as well."

A look of anger passed over the Buriat lama's face.

"Perhaps," he said. "One further question. You are familiar with the work of Sebastian Moran?"

"In all its aspects," said Holmes.

"So am I," said Dorjiloff.

"By the bye," said Holmes with a smile, "I bring you greetings from the family of the late Sir Samuel Soames of Liverpool . . ."

Dorjiloff's face darkened, but he did not reply, for at that moment Gorashar announced to those who remained that the Regent Tsarong had arrived. Everyone rose at once. Two guards with drawn swords entered, followed by the Regent himself. Those who remained in the room bowed as he passed.

The most powerful man in Tibet walked slowly and deliberately, nodding only once so that the remaining guests would take their seats. Except for the red of his robes, there was no colour beyond silver and white. He was as tall and straight as anyone Holmes had seen in Tibet, thin to the point of emaciation, so that the lines of his skull stood out boldly on his shaven head, from the back of which hung a long silver braid. His face was indeed that of the old battered photograph, far older but the same imponderable one. His eyes were grey behind his spectacles, bright with a silver light, what the Tibetans refer to as the light of asceticism. His skin was exceedingly pale, almost translucent, and he had a full white beard of the greatest fineness that partially hid his mouth. He wore the simple robes of the monk. Though he walked with long, firm strides, Holmes judged him to be well into his eighties. He took his place with the Grand Lama's brother and sister and began to play the Chinese game of mahjong.

In a few minutes, Tsarong beckoned to Dorjiloff. He in turn summoned Holmes, and they sat in Tsarong's small circle. Gorashar acted as interpreter.

"Mr. Sigerson, I welcome you to Lhasa," said the Regent softly in Tibetan. "Your stay will be a fruitful one. And a long one, if you choose."

"I thank you for your kind words," Holmes replied. "May I know when I may pay an official visit to the Potala?"

"We are aware that certain tasks may have been assigned to you. The Tibetan Government has decided, however, that it will receive no official guests until further notice. In your case, you are welcome to pursue your researches. As long as your purpose remains a scientific one, you will be welcome. Any change in your activities, however, will result in immediate deportation outside the confines of Tibet."

Dorjiloff smiled. The Regent's face remained expressionless. To Holmes, they appeared to be at one, for what he had communicated to the Tibetan authorities in secret was known to Dorjiloff as well. Apparently bonded in the mysteries of Tibetan mysticism, the Regent and the Russian monk were acting in concert, their aim to bring Tibet under the protection of the Tsar, and to block British entrance into Central Asia. Sobering, too, was the thought that the Tibetan Government had now refused to deal officially with a British emissary, though a secret one, recognising only the disguise of the scientist, not the identity of the agent.

The Regent nodded, ending the interview, and Holmes rose and left the circle. The Regent left shortly thereafter, with Dorjiloff in his company. Holmes stayed on, and it was well past midnight when he said good night to his host. Gorashar smiled and said, "You have enjoyed the evening."

"I have indeed. And I hope that I may continue to come."

"My home is open to you. And so that you reach safely to your lodging, I will send my servant with you."

"That will not be necessary," said Holmes.

Gorashar smiled again. "I fear that it is," he said as he let forth a puff of smoke from his cigarette.

A sturdy young Nepalese boy appeared from the shadows, and Gorashar instructed him to accompany Holmes to his quarters. The boy was from the hills of central Nepal and belonged to a tribe called Gurung. His name was Purna Lal, and he was later to become indispensable to Holmes.

As they left, Holmes saw that the darkness was pitch-black in the narrow lane ahead of them. Purna Lal walked in front, silently checking the path as he went. Holmes found his way even in the dark, however, having trained himself to do this over a number of years. Still, he was grateful to have someone to accompany him. They had just reached the end of the lane when, in the moonlight that now flooded their path, Holmes saw a dark figure grab Purna Lal from behind. Holmes rushed forward instinctively, but the Gurkha needed no aid. In a swift movement, he disabled his assailant and was about to despatch him when Holmes caught his arm, holding a khukuri at the ready, in midair. The large knife fell to the ground harmlessly, and Holmes found himself gazing at a prostrate Rastrakoff, his face filled with terror at his close brush with death. Holmes held him as he tried to rise. He ordered Purna Lal to bind his hands with his scarf.

"This way," whispered a voice in the darkness.

Holmes turned and saw the princess Pema standing behind him. Dragging the unwilling Rastrakoff with them, they followed her to the end of the lane, where they entered a narrow courtyard and then passed into the hall of a large and regal house. The princess directed them to a small antechamber.

"Do not release him," she said, glowering at Rastrakoff. "He is a murderer who should be destroyed!"

"Fear not, madam, he will not trouble us further," answered Holmes.

"He is one of those responsible for the cruel plight of Manning," she said.

"How so?" asked Holmes quickly, for her remark was the first direct reference to the British agent that he had heard.

"From the day of his arrival," she said, "Manning lived nearby, in a house owned by my husband. We were introduced to him by the merchant Gorashar. We found him to be a most congenial guest. We had no idea at first that he was an agent of the British Government. Gradually, he became a close family friend. When my husband was killed in Kham, he was a great solace to me and my family. It was not many days before your arrival here, however, that at the instigation of this man, he was arrested and taken, finally, to the Garden of Punishment, where he now lies close to death. An order was issued by the Regent that the presence of Manning in Lhasa was not to be acknowledged by anyone. Even his name could not be uttered on pain of death. I have tried to keep him alive by paying the guards to feed him, but I have been prevented from seeing him myself more than once."

"Why was he arrested?"

At this point, the woman hesitated and appeared to have difficulty in continuing her story. "Manning had become enamoured of me," she said with difficulty, "but kept his affection to himself. When the news of my husband's death arrived, he showed the greatest kindness to me. Then, after some time had gone by, he revealed his affection and asked me to marry him and to leave Tibet. Since no Tibetan woman of the nobility may marry a foreigner, I refused. Rastrakoff learned of Manning's offer to me through a treacherous servant, who overheard our conversation. The matter became public, and not even the Regent could intervene on his behalf. There was an outcry. I was protected by my family's position, but Manning was placed first in a prison cell in the Potala, then in the Garden of Punishment in an iron cage in which his arms were pinned. He is there still. He cannot eat or drink unless he is fed. He is helpless. My servants say he is now near death. He has been taunted, tortured, beaten, and is no longer himself. They say his mind is almost gone."

At these words, Rastrakoff became agitated. "Manning is a British spy," he hissed, "and deserves his fate. And you also are a British spy," he said to Holmes as he vainly tried to free himself from Purna Lal's grip.

"You are in no position to engage in idle accusations, my dear Rastrakoff," Holmes responded, "for in addition to doing the dirty work of the Tsar, you have a previous history that unfortunately for you is even more sordid than your present occupation. Must I remind you of the murder of General Richter in Ulan Bator, in which you played a major role? Or, more recently, of the assassination of Prezhevalsky the younger in Canton?"

"How did you know? Who are you? You are not a naturalist nor are you a Scandinavian—"

"Who I am is of no immediate relevance to you—except that I intend to turn you over to the Chinese authorities in Lhasa once the Manning affair has come to a close. Purna Lal, keep close watch on him. I must leave now, and I do not know when I shall return. Should I not return by the morning, I wish you to take this man to the office of the Chinese Amban with this note."

Holmes hastily scribbled a message describing Rastrakoff's crimes in China. Turning to the princess Pema, he said: "We have no time to lose. Take me to Manning."

"Follow me," she said. "I shall take you to him, but we shall have to bribe the guards. Let us hope that he still lives."

They went out again into the cold air of the night, making their way down the dark lane whence they had come, past the Jor-khang, and into a wider street that led to the outskirts of the city. They soon reached the place where Holmes had been stopped by the sentry, the great stone walls in front of which he had witnessed the vicious battle between dog and vulture. Just beyond was the so-called Garden of Punishment. The princess handed the chief guard a few Indian rupees, and they passed through the gate.

"I must say, Watson, that even though I have experienced a number of horrors in my time, I found this place singularly abhorrent. The punishments were of the most brutal and primitive kind, as bad as Dorjiloff had described, and reminiscent of the worst of medieval Europe. Most of the prisoners had been maimed in one way or another and were either in chains or on racks with cages encasing their upper bodies. Each was kept there by the crippling visited upon him and the promise of a few morsels of food fed once a day."

They walked past several men who were in various stages of near death, groaning in what might have been sleep had their circumstances been different. The princess Pema led him to a dark figure lying under a large tree. His upper body, including his head, was encased in a cage of iron, his head covered with a black hood. Pema sobbed, and Holmes asked her to remain at a short distance. Holmes removed the hood. The man was dead. He was emaciated to the limits of mortal desiccation, and his eyes bulged from his skull. He had been badly beaten, and clawed by vultures in anticipation of his death. It took little to release him from the cage, for it was easily lifted over his head. As Holmes did so, the man slumped to the ground.

Holmes proceeded to examine the man thoroughly. He had been dead for only a short time, for the body was still warm. He was undoubtedly European, but he was so thin and bruised that he was almost unrecognisable. He was dressed in Tibetan clothes, but underneath was an English coat: one of the buttons was gone, and Holmes noticed that those that remained were identical to the one he had pulled from the vulture's talon. Indeed, he heard the fluttering of wings in the tree above and, looking up, saw the companions of that dead vulture, ready to pounce on the hapless corpse in front of him.

"At that moment, I was sure of only two things, Watson. The man was dead—and he was not Manning."

Holmes said he then moved quickly and led the princess Pema, now sobbing bitterly, gently away. Before it was fully light, they returned to her house. Rastrakoff had fallen asleep, Purna Lal's eyes glued upon him.

Holmes leaned back in his chair, and I took the moment to interrupt him with my own thoughts.

"Extraordinary, my dear Holmes. But the mystery has only deepened and become even more confusing. You have at this juncture one of the chief criminals in your hands, but a commonplace rogue, nothing compared to Dorjiloff. And the mystery of Sir William Manning is murkier than ever. You have been led to a dead man by the Tibetan woman, but he is not Manning. Obviously she thought he was Manning. And if she thought he was Manning, then surely others would have thought so as well, even Dorjiloff himself. You saw this immediately and without ever having laid eyes on Manning. How on earth did you deduce that the dead man was *not* Manning?"

"Simple, my dear Watson. I am perforce a student of the human face and skull. It is one of the less pleasant aspects of my work that I often have to identify someone after severe mutilation has occurred. You may recall that I had begun the study of photographs of all the principals while still in Italy. Despite the emaciated appearance of the dead man, I could still make out the basic physiognomy. There was only the most superficial resemblance, the kind of resemblance that might fool a layman but not a trained observer, particularly one who had made a special study. The dead man was put there at some point to deceive. But by whom? And again, where was Manning? At this point I did not know. But I was now almost certain of two things: one, that Manning was still alive and two, that Pema, who loved him, did not know this and thought sincerely that Manning was the dead man. She had taken me there fully convinced that we would find him. But he had been removed from the cage before his death and a second man put in his place. The deception was meant to fool even the woman Manning loved."

"Who then was the dead man?"

"That was the easiest part of the mystery, Watson. It was Sackville-Grimes, the criminal arsonist, who had come to an unfortunate but hardly undeserved fate. He had been brought into the imbroglio merely because he was an Englishman and a suitable substitute for Manning. He resembled Manning in a rather crude way, and I recognised him with difficulty but emphatically. I must say that, knowing what I did of his evil career, I did not mourn his fate."

"I must say, Holmes, that the whole affair is bizarre. I sense a sure and powerful hand in all this, perhaps Manning himself and his as yet unknown allies."

"Not bad, Watson. Your conjectures are well founded, and I regretted greatly then, as I do now, your absence. In a place like Lhasa one needs all the help one can get, and your assistance would have been greatly appreciated."

"I would have been of little help, my dear Holmes, I am afraid, beyond giving you a bit of morale and some physical support now and then," said I.

"It is no small thing, Watson, to employ my methods in a place as different from London as Lhasa."

"I should think that the transition would have been very difficult," said I.

"True enough," he replied, "but the question is why. Clearly, the laws of deduction and observation hold, for they are of universal application. But I had to be alert to the particulars of Tibetan existence to understand where to apply them. In addition, I realised that, despite my penchant for working alone, I had often used Scotland Yard, particularly its two most able detectives, Gregson and Lestrade, as foils against the false solutions that often present themselves to the investigator. In Lhasa I had no interlocutors at all. My methods, therefore, faced their greatest test. It was my brain and my brain alone that had to find solutions in an increasingly hostile milieu. Finding Manning or learning what had happened to him proved to be my greatest problem. From what evidence could I begin to deduce his fate?"

"A most difficult problem, if I do say so, my dear Holmes," said I.

"Yet, Watson, no sooner had I asked myself these questions than I realised that Manning could only have escaped a cruel fate with the aid of others. In no other place in the world, perhaps, Watson, does one so immediately feel oneself to be an intruder. Yet, I thought, surely British interests must be supported by some in Tibet. I had followed in Manning's footsteps, I had essentially the same mission. I knew the same principals in the drama that Manning knew. Among those common to us surely there were those who might be friendly."

It was precisely at that point that it occurred to Holmes that the short little man from Katmandu, the merchant Gorashar, might provide him with some needed information. It was now almost dawn. The princess Pema had retired. Directing Purna Lal to take Rastrakoff to the residence of the Chinese Amban, Holmes returned to the home of Gorashar. He found the merchant seated in a small room, going over the previous day's accounts with Pushkar, one of his assistants. Gorashar looked up and said, "Let us have tea."

"I need your help," said Holmes. "I must find Manning."

"Ten minutes for tea," said Gorashar, avoiding Holmes's plea by blowing a puff of smoke from his cigarette.

They sipped their tea, not the Tibetan salt tea but the *garam chai* of India, at what was for Holmes an entirely too leisurely pace. Then Gorashar stood up and said, "You come."

Holmes followed him down a long corridor that led out to a small courtyard. On one side was a large stone sculpture of the Buddha. Gorashar led him to the wall behind it. There, unconcealed but also not particularly noticeable, was a small door. Gorashar opened it. Bending as low as he could, Holmes followed him through, straightening up into what was a small but pleasant room. Seated at the far end, looking haggard and thin, was a gentleman that Holmes immediately recognised as Sir William Manning. Holmes looked at Gorashar with a mixture of surprise and gratitude. Gorashar smiled and left them.

"Sir William," said Holmes, "finding you has not been easy. Indeed, I had begun to think that you might be dead by now. I have here a letter from London which will explain to you who I am and the circumstances that have brought me here."

Manning took the letter, opened it, and read it anxiously. As he read, Holmes noticed that his face relaxed somewhat and he became more at ease.

"So, Mr. Holmes," he said, "you follow in my footsteps. I must tell you that my own mission has been an utter failure. I am fortunate to be alive, and thank God, I am about to depart. The Regent, whom I have never met, has agreed to allow me to leave secretly with the proviso that I divulge nothing of my stay here to the outside world and that I never return to Tibet."

"That means that you may still talk to me."

"I have little to tell, strangely enough. So deeply disturbing has been my stay here that my mind already appears to have erased of itself the details and even some of the major events of my sojourn. One year ago, I arrived, as you may well know from your own voyage, sick, tired to the point of exhaustion, but with a sense of exhilaration at having finally reached the forbidden city of Lhasa. I was met by an official of the Potala, who took me to my lodging, and I turned over to him the letters concerning my mission. I sent a message to the Viceroy informing him of my arrival, but I was allowed no further communication with the outside world."

Days passed, he said, and no call came. He was well cared for and carefully watched since a guard was posted in front of the house where he lived. One day, after several protests, he was told that the Regent would see him at last. But the meeting never came. After four months, he became somewhat restless, even belligerent. On one occasion, he walked unannounced into the office of a high-ranking monk, demanding his help in getting the meeting to come to pass. He pounded the table and shouted, but his anger only produced uneasy laughter and deep embarrassment on the monk's face. He went home, empty-handed and humiliated. He had become a boisterous annoyance for the Tibetans instead of a silent one.

"Shortly after my arrival here," he continued, "I met the princess Pema, and became totally enamoured. She was married, however, and I kept my affection for her to myself. I respected her husband deeply. He was a brave man who was charged with protecting the eastern borders of Tibet against rebel incursions, incursions that were never announced but occurred with increasing frequency. Unfortunately, he was killed during an ugly battle in Kham. Pema came to rely on me in those early days of her grief, and I did all that I could to help her. Eventually, a relationship of intimacy developed between us. Rastrakoff, who unbeknownst to either of us, had had me watched from the moment of my arrival, learned of our growing relationship and informed Dorjiloff, who used it as a pretext to have me arrested. For two months I was a prisoner in the dungeons of the Potala and then in the Garden of Punishment, where I fully expected to die. My arms were stretched forward in a rack, and an iron cage was put over my head. Feeding myself was impossible. I was given nothing to eat or drink except when some kind soul took pity upon me. Pema tried to get me freed, but in vain. Knowing the purpose of my mission, Dorjiloff fully intended to have me dead so that he could precipitate a crisis with our Government. Despite the prohibition on her entering the Garden of Punishment, Pema came one night to me. I was by this time almost delirious with pain and hunger, and I only recall bidding her good-bye. I must have lost consciousness, for I remember nothing until I awoke here in this room. I know that I was probably near death when someone must have taken me from that terrible prison and brought me here. Thanks to the ministrations of Gorashar, I have recovered much of my strength. I have now received written orders to leave the country as soon as possible. This is the only official acknowledgement of my visit here. My mission has been a total failure."

Holmes listened with the greatest interest as Manning spoke, for his story showed that the original decision to kill him, made probably by Dorjiloff himself, had been rescinded.

Holmes paused for a moment and then pulled the brass button taken from the vulture's talon from his pocket. "This must be yours," he said.

Manning looked at it curiously for a moment, and then said, "No, it is not mine, despite the initials. I have never seen anything like it before."

Holmes smiled, for it was then that the idea he had when he first saw the button came to final fruition. Manning was not the centre of this Tibetan drama. He was, if anything, a victim, as so many had been in the past, of events that were controlled by others. As Holmes realised what had happened in Tibet, a whole series of ironies revealed themselves, and he knew that he had but one course of action.

He took leave of Manning, who he believed was now as safe as he could be in the city of Lhasa, and returned to Gorashar's own quarters. There he told the merchant that he needed his help once again. Holmes looked directly into Gorashar's eyes: he was determined to enter the Potala that very night and to meet the Regent face-to-face. Gorashar looked at him quizzically; then he smiled and said, "You very intelligent man. Many things knowing you are."

A rather devilish grin broke out on Gorashar's face. He revealed to Holmes the easiest way to enter undetected. After midnight, the guards were generally asleep, those at the north entrance being the laziest. Dressed as a monk, Holmes should have no difficulty entering and then moving about, for there were few guards inside, and the patrols passed only once every two hours. Gorashar reviewed with Holmes the general plan of the palace and the location of the quarters of the Grand Lama and the Regent. Then, he provided him with all he would need in the way of disguise, including a monk's robe that would suit his frame. It was at that moment that he took from a drawer in his desk the gold knife that served as the occasion for this story.

"Please take this and keep it with you. You may need it . . ."

Holmes took it with gratitude, for he had no weapon of any kind, and the knife provided him with at least a fighting chance should he be attacked.

"Show it to the Regent as soon as you enter," he said.

The rest of the day passed quickly for Holmes. Then, in the dead of night, dressed in the robes of a monk, he left Gorashar's residence and walked quickly through the dark streets of Lhasa to the foot of the Potala. He felt his way around the west wall to the north side. There he saw a narrow stone staircase that led halfway up the massive building to what appeared to be an entranceway. There was no one in sight, and the night was completely still. He climbed the stairs as quickly and quietly as he could. To his delight, he found the door unlocked. It led directly to a dark corridor, dimly lit by a series of oil lamps placed at long intervals along the wall. A monk passed in prayer but was so engrossed that he noticed nothing.

From some distance ahead Holmes then heard the drone of the monkish chant of Tibet. He judged that he was close to the Grand Lama's quarters. So far Gorashar's directions were exact. He had instructed Holmes very carefully with regard to the Regent's quarters: the second door after the chanting room. The Regent slept there alone, with no guard.

Holmes passed the monks in their chant and arrived at the Regent's door. He opened the door. There, seated at his writing table in the flickering light of an oil lamp, observing him impassively in no great surprise, sat the Regent of Tibet, the great Tsarong.

For a moment that seemed an eternity, they stared at each other, neither speaking. Holmes entered the room. Sitting opposite the Regent, he took the knife from his pocket and placed it on the floor between them.

"Well done, Moorcroft," said Holmes in English, deliberately and slowly, "your impersonation has been perfect. Little did we suspect that Britain has had a friend in high places in Tibet these many years."

There was no immediate reaction. So complete was the Regent's composure that for a moment Holmes thought his surmise to be incorrect. Slowly, however, a slight smile crossed the old man's face, and Holmes could see his lips begin to form hesitantly the syllables that reached them, as if the language he was about to speak had not been used for decades.

"Who are you?" he asked slowly. The words were perfectly formed, but Holmes heard the accent of the distant past in them, and a voice that had not used English for over half a century.

"Who I am is of little importance. If you must know, my name is Sherlock Holmes. My mission is that of which you have been informed."

"Sherlock Holmes is dead," said the Regent emphatically.

"One should not believe all that one hears. I am amused that the report of my death has reached as far as Lhasa, and doubly amused that someone such as you, who was reported dead many years ago, believed it. How odd that we should be seated here together in the Potala, two Englishmen who have so successfully manufactured our own deaths that we are believed by all the world to exist no longer."

"An odd coincidence, indeed," said the Regent bemusedly, "although I have been dead for almost fifty years longer than you. And how long do you propose to prolong your own death?"

"Provided that you and I come to an understanding not to reveal each other's circumstances, I shall remain in my present state indefinitely, or at least until I have rid the world of several archcriminals, some of whom are my personal enemies, dedicated to my demise. A few of them have taken refuge here, as you probably know."

"I am aware of the presence of these Western criminals, and have found it most annoying. As to you, I shall be completely silent. You may continue as Mr. Sigerson, and as such you may stay in Tibet as long as you please. I shall help you in every way. I have not been pleased about the influx of riffraff from America and Europe into Tibet, and I have done everything to prevent their entry. In some cases, however, I have found their presence useful."

He smiled as he uttered the last few words.

"Like Sackville-Grimes," said Holmes.

"Like Sackville-Grimes, of course. But I would include Dorjiloff and Rastrakoff. These are the mercenaries, pretending to be other than they are. But Tibet in many ways has become a land of pretence, a land in which nothing is quite as it seems. To Lhasa in disguise: is that not the cry? . . . Everyone is in disguise," he said.

He paused for a moment, then continued: "I of course came in disguise myself but stayed so long that the disguise became reality. At a certain point in my stay, I found myself suddenly thrust by events into the middle of Tibetan politics. I did not shirk the responsibility that fell on my shoulders. When the present Grand Lama comes of age, that responsibility will end. Through these many years, I have worked to keep Tibet out of the clutches of its neighbours, and I have instructed the young lama in the politics of independence. But I do not know whether or not the Tibetan theocracy is ready to assert itself sufficiently to guarantee its independence in the future. This is why I have relied heavily on a friendly neutrality to the British through the years. My years of effort may in the long run prove to be in vain. The Russians, the Japanese, the Chinese, are all ready to pounce . . . but more of that later. How did you come to know my identity? Almost no one else knows, so you must have reasoned it out yourself."

"In my profession, it is the smallest things that often make the difference," said Holmes. He reached into his pocket and produced the button that he had found in the vulture's talon. He handed it to the Regent.

"Ha!" the old man exclaimed. "A mistake on my part, but something that I thought necessary at the time. But still, I want to hear your reasoning."

"It is clarity itself," Holmes said to the Regent. "My methods are based on the minute observation of trivia, in this case a button, innocuous in itself. The button bears the initials *WM,* obviously coincident with the initials of William Manning. But close examination of the small threads left in it, together with its somewhat antique appearance, led me to hypothesise that the button as well as the coat to which it had been sewn was made in the early part of the century. You will notice that the button also bears inside the inscription of the maker, Rollins and Company, a company that disappeared several decades ago. If this came from Manning's jacket, he would of necessity have been wearing an antique piece of costumery, highly unlikely judging from what I had heard of his sober ways. When I found the coat itself on the dying form of Sackville-Grimes, I knew that something was amiss: it was meant to identify Manning to those who wished to believe that Sackville-Grimes was Manning. But who could manipulate things in such ways? Who had such power? And who might have such a coat? Here one had to look at recent Tibetan history as well, the broad picture if you will, as it coincided with these minute bits of evidence, for despite the wishes of Dorjiloff to the contrary, Tibetan policy had more or less followed British desires over the last few decades. What if this was not accidental but was due to the firm intentions of someone high in the Tibetan Government? Suppose that person was the Regent himself? Suppose the Regent did not wish to see Manning die but wished him only to leave? Suppose the Regent himself had arranged to have Manning removed before death and the coat put on the body of the moribund Sackville-Grimes as an added indication of his identity?"

And here Holmes paused and said slowly, "And suppose that the Regent himself were an Englishman? An absurd thought? Yes, absurd, but were it true, who might that Englishman be? Who might fit the historical record as well as the initials on the button? The name of the early adventurer Moorcroft immediately comes to mind, but his first name is Clement, and so there is a difficulty. But Moorcroft sticks in one's mind because his death is unexplained and uncertain, a casual mention in the diary of Le Père Huc, the well-known French monk and traveller. 'He died while leaving Tibet . . . that is all we know. . . .' All of this came to me in a flash, far faster than the time it takes to relate my reasoning."

"Enough!" the Regent interrupted. "Well done, Holmes. I see why your reputation grew so quickly. If you must know, the coat with the buttons belonged not to me but to my father, William Moorcroft, and of course I did not die while leaving Tibet. I left the papers of Clement Moorcroft on the body of a dead friend and reentered Tibet in disguise with a group of Newar merchants led by Dharma Ratna, the father of Gorashar. It was Dharma Ratna who retrieved the knife that you have placed before us from the dead body of Farouk, the assassin of my own father. On learning my story, he kept my secret, and returned the knife to me. Later, I gave it in friendship to his son, Gorashar, a man who has remained my confidant. I have been in Tibet ever since, and I became through the years a Tibetan. The story of my life here is of course unique, and I may divulge it to you someday."

The Regent then rang a bell, and two guards carried in a figure, bound and gagged, whom Holmes recognised immediately in the dim light as Dorjiloff. The Regent walked up to him, removed his gag, and slapped him across the face with all his still considerable strength.

"You have tried my patience these many years, Dorjiloff," he said in Tibetan, "and I have suffered your cruelties and stupidities in my country as long as they served my broad purpose. They no longer do. You are to leave Tibet now and forever. I have arranged an escort that will take you to the Russian border. Do not return upon pain of death."

Dorjiloff tried to free himself, but to no avail. He said nothing coherent, for the insult of a slap across the face had angered him beyond words. He cast a malevolent look in Holmes's direction before he was carried out. Holmes never encountered him again but later learned that in attempting to reenter Tibet he was killed on the spot by border guards, thus bringing to a futile end a career dedicated to the cause of evil.

"I think, Mr. Holmes," said the Regent, "that it would be best for us to limit our direct contacts in the future, considering the complexity of the political situation here. You may stay as long as you like, and I will provide you with every facility to continue your botanical and zoological studies, and incidentally to rid us of some of our more nefarious visitors."

"I agree to that. We can continue to communicate through the one person that both of us trust in Lhasa."

"Gorashar," he said.

"Yes," said Holmes, "Gorashar."

Holmes stopped for a moment to light his pipe.

"A most engrossing tale, Holmes."

"Indeed, Watson, and there is little more that need be told. Sir William Manning and the Tibetan princess Pema left Tibet and are now living here in London. I see them on occasion. Unfortunately, Dorjiloff's accomplice, Rastrakoff, escaped, to my chagrin, and I was to deal with him later. I myself remained in Lhasa for almost two years and was able not only to bring several other criminals to justice but also to assist in preserving the delicate relations between Tibet and our Government. I then left on my long journey in the Orient, which eventually brought me homeward. It was on the final leg of my journey that I learned, to my great sadness, that the Regent had died just after the new Grand Lama came to office."

"And what did you learn of Moorcroft's own life, Holmes? How on earth did it happen that an Englishman became the Regent of Tibet?"

Holmes walked to his desk and pulled from a drawer what appeared to be an old manuscript.

"Here, dear Watson, is Moorcroft's own statement of his life in Tibet up to my departure. Perhaps you will find it of interest. You will see that he was a most improbable Englishman. He gave me his account just before I left Lhasa. As an explanatory postscript you will find it most valuable. You will notice some differences in our recollection. Do not try to reconcile them, for each of us is entitled to a good story told for his own purpose."

He smiled as he uttered the last few words, for I knew that he often thought I should limit my accounts to the barest essentials necessary to the introduction of the principles of observation and deduction. I smiled back, but said nothing, and began to study the thin volume that had been placed in my hands.

The manuscript was an old Indian notebook, of the kind that I later learned is manufactured in Indore in the Central Provinces of India and readily available in Bombay. The leaves were smooth and of a bright yellow paper, the cover of a bright crimson cloth. Around the whole was tied a piece of white string. I untied it, opened the cover, and began to read, written in a beautiful, archaic, though shaky hand, the long entry that follows.

II

THE DIARY OF GETHONG TSARONG

In this my eighty-fifth year, I, Gethong Tsarong, Regent of Tibet, set down here, for those who may be interested, a short account of my life. I entrust this document to one person, my friend Hallvard Sigerson, whose property it thus becomes and who will be free to publish it after my death in any form he chooses, provided that through its publication he deems no harm will come to Tibet or its people.

My life has been a long one, and though it did not begin in this ancient land, I have spent most of it here. I find it difficult to write in English after so many years, during which I have not spoken or heard my own tongue but for a few moments, and so my hand shakes as I write, not only because I am old physically, but because my mind works slowly, trying as best it can to wrest words from the dim storehouse of a wandering remembrance.

I was born in 1810, the only child of William Moorcroft, a seaman of Cornwall, and Jane, his wife. My father and mother were first cousins, but did not resemble each other. I never knew my mother, for she died shortly after my birth. My father, who was only twenty-one years of age at the time of my birth and had no other children, placed me with his cousin, my mother's older sister, who lived with her husband and family in a modest house in London. I was well cared for and came to love my aunt and uncle as my parents.

It was through my aunt that I learned the little I know of my mother. She was said to be a tall, dark English beauty, with olive skin and long black hair, which she often wore in a braid down her back, other times looped tightly around her head. I was said to resemble her in many ways. My aunt remembered that I was born with a full head of black hair, like my mother's. In explanation of our appearance, my aunt told me that my great-grandfather was a man by the name of Ogachgook Bradford, an American Indian of mixed origin, who had come to England with William Bradford, one of the governors of the Plymouth Colony of the Massachusetts Bay Company. Ogachgook had taken Bradford's name and remained in England. It was from Ogachgook that my mother's and my dark appearance was said to derive. I know little else of Ogachgook except that he was the son of an Indian chief called King Philip by the colonists, but known among his own people as Metacomet, son of Massasoit. There was some family speculation that the name Moorcroft is derived in some way from Metacomet.

I saw little of my father for the first five years of my life, for he was almost always at sea. His grief at my mother's death seemed never to subside, and he later confided in me that it caused in him an almost constant wandering. He came to see me as often as his travels allowed him, and I looked forward to his visits with great joy, for we prowled the city together for long hours, and when I tired he would pick me up and carry me for long distances.

One day, sometime in my eighth year, my father announced that he would like me to accompany him on his next voyage. Assuring my aunt that I would be well cared for, he took me with him to his next ship, a large frigate bound for the Americas. And so, as a very young boy, I began my travels with a voyage to the New World. I remember little of this trip, except that I took ill shortly after we left port. My sickness did not abate for several days, for the sea was rough and we had to pass through a great storm.

As we approached the continent of North America, the scent of pines filled the air, and the sun broke out from behind the clouds that had covered it for so long. We docked in Boston, and went ashore the following day. We were there for three weeks before we set sail again. We travelled south to New York, and it was here that my father decided to stay in America rather than return to England. After a few months of city life, however, his restlessness set in again, and he decided to seek his fortune elsewhere in America. We started west, journeying through Pennsylvania, Ohio, and Illinois, then through the Mexican territories, finally reaching the coast of California. Here my father tried to become a rancher, and for a year he tended the cattle of a prosperous gentleman. But my father's desire for the sea could be postponed only so long, and after almost four years in America, exhausted by the toil necessary to keep us alive, he once again took us to sea, this time across the Pacific, where we sojourned in the Sandwich Islands, Deshima, and then the coast of North China. Eventually we wandered from Hong Kong to Macao and to Singapore, where he took employment on a ship bound for England.

By this time I was twelve years of age, and my father thirty-three. We were as close as two brothers and had become inseparable. My father decided, however, that I needed schooling, so he tried to leave me with my aunt again so that I could be placed with a tutor, but I refused to stay without him. And so for one year he remained with me while I improved my knowledge of English, Greek, Latin, and mathematics.

It was during this period that my father met a Persian gentleman engaged in commerce and trade in the Caspian Sea. His name was Mr. Barzami. Impressed with my father's experience and energy, he offered him a lucrative position as his permanent representative in London. The position necessitated first, however, an extended stay in Persia at the company's offices in Tabriz. Because of the dangers of travel, my father was reluctant to take me with him, but I refused to stay behind and would have none of it. After a week of argument, he, I think rather happily in the end, agreed that we would continue our adventures together. In a few days, Mr. Barzami arranged our travel to Tabriz. We landed in Constantinople, and from there we journeyed through the Ottoman territories of Anatolia and Armenia, finally arriving at our destination. Mr. Barzami had arranged much for us. We were given a large bungalow with sunny, comfortable rooms. Outside was a most beautiful garden, and so for the first time in our lives we lacked for nothing. I was placed with a local tutor, and in time I came to speak the Persian language with great fluency.

Almost one year after our arrival, Mr. Barzami, instead of posting my father to England, asked if he would accept a position in Bombay. My father reluctantly agreed, considering the many kindnesses and opportunities that Mr. Barzami had visited upon us, and in a few weeks we left our idyllic existence in Persia and headed for India, where we arrived some three weeks later. Here we were again well treated, for Mr. Barzami had his agents meet us and provide for us.

It was here in India, not long after our arrival, that my life was changed forever and embarked upon the strange course that it has now almost completed. One of my father's first duties was to establish contact with merchants to the north, particularly in Kashmir. And so one day we boarded a crowded train to Pathankot in the Punjab and then began our long trek to Srinagar, the capital city of Kashmir. It was along this route that we were set upon by a gang of thieves. My father was killed and I, badly wounded, was left for dead. I remember nothing except a blow to the back of the head and then darkness. We were found by a group of Kashmiri merchants returning home. My life was saved by them, and they transported my father's body to Srinagar, where he was buried in the English cemetery. Through the ministrations of the family of one of the merchants, I eventually recovered, but I suffered a severe amnesia for at least a month. When I had recovered sufficiently, the merchants told me what had happened. I was filled with grief for my father's death. The merchants said they knew that we had been attacked by the gang of Farouk, the cruellest of the robbers of Kashmir and the one they feared the most.

I vowed revenge. I knew that I should not be able to rest until I had brought my father's killers to justice. And so, in the hope of finding the murderous brigands, I stayed in Kashmir. I was fourteen years old, strong and growing stronger. I informed Mr. Barzami of what had transpired. He tried to convince me to return to Persia, but in the face of my steadfast refusal, he relented and arranged for my father's funds as well as a generous gift to be transferred to a bank in India so that I could draw on them to help me trace the bandits.

The Farouk gang soon abandoned Kashmir, for so horrible had their depredations become that the Company deputed a military detachment to Kashmir to apprehend them. Farouk and his men fled into the mountains, and nothing was heard of them. I waited in Kashmir for news of them, but they seemed to have disappeared into thin air. The military detachment remained and seemed to have so frightened the gang that their activities ceased almost entirely.

After almost a year of waiting, I decided to accompany my Kashmiri friends on a trip to Lhasa. By now I spoke some Kashmiri in addition to Persian and could travel unobtrusively. The route was the usual one from Srinagar, and we reached Lhasa without difficulty. I became immediately at home with the Tibetans and their country. I left Lhasa often to travel in the distant corners of the country, spending weeks with yak and sheep herders in Amdo and Kham. When it came time for our caravan to return, I decided to remain. Bidding good-bye to my Kashmiri friends, I stayed behind and continued my solitary travels. Eventually, I made my resting place in Amdo, in a small village where I was welcomed most warmly. I lived with a certain Gyerong and his family. Gyerong was only two years older than I, but he had a wife and three small children. Through the years that passed, Gyerong and I became almost inseparable.

It was after five years of living in this way among the Tibetans that I decided to return to India. By now, my life had become so thoroughly Tibetan that I felt little connection with my past life, but the revenge I had promised myself for my *father's* death still haunted me. One day, I told Gyerong of my obsession, and he became the only one who knew my dark desire. He cautioned me and urged me to give up the idea, for it was an unworthy goal. To kill, he said, was against Buddhist doctrine. I tried to remove the desire from my heart, but my obsession would not leave me. I decided to return to Lhasa and there to decide my next move. Before I left, Gyerong gave me a knife with a golden handle as a token of our friendship. He said that the knife had been handed down for many years from friend to friend. The knife, as far as he knew, had never been used in anger or violence, and despite its fierce nature as a weapon, it had often had the effect of calming the anger of its possessor. I took it and thanked him profusely, but I felt no calming effect from its presence.

When I reached Lhasa, I learned that the Farouk gang had reappeared. A caravan of merchants on its way to the city had been attacked. The gang had fled Indian territory with a British detachment in hot pursuit, but they had outpaced the soldiers and made it to safety in Tibetan territory. It was reported that they had made their camp near the ancient city of Guge.

I decided to leave Lhasa at once for Guge, for I felt that fate was leading me to my goal. I joined a caravan going west. The leader of this group was a wealthy Ladakhi merchant, who unwilling to take any risks, had hired a heavily armed escort for the journey, consisting mainly of retired soldiers from eastern Tibet. We encountered no difficulty at the outset, and five days into our trip we camped near Guge, to the south of the town. The attack came swiftly. Thinking us to be another barely armed caravan, the thieves fired a volley of warning shots and did little to hide their positions. They appeared together in front of our group, demanding that we surrender to them. Farouk himself sat proudly on horseback. Our riflemen, ready for any such contingency, wasted no time in opening fire, and the first shots took their toll. The thieves were completely taken by surprise and tried to flee, but most of them were gunned down. Farouk himself fell from his horse during the first few minutes of the battle. He staggered about, trying to rally his men, but to no avail. I raced toward him, my only weapon the gold knife. I grabbed him, and there ensued a fierce struggle between us. Despite his wounds, Farouk was still extremely powerful, and it was only the strength of my obsession that enabled me to overwhelm him. I plunged the knife into his heart, and with a terrible groan, he fell and passed from this existence.

I myself must have blacked out after the struggle, for when I became conscious I found that I lay amid the dead, the only person alive. The caravan had scattered, and I was alone. Farouk's body was next to me, and his eyes stared at me in the evening darkness, his face a mixture of mockery and pain. What had I done? I had killed a man in revenge, but he still looked at me defiantly. At the time of his death he had no idea who I was, and would have laughed had he known. I tried to console myself with the notion that I had rid the world of a great fiend. But as the night fell, I became filled with strange feelings of emptiness and the utter futility of the obsession that had led to the pointless hatred which had drained me for so many of the years of my youth.

I fell into a deep sleep, and when I awoke in the morning, my mind was clearer than it had been since my father had died. Farouk was now only a decaying corpse. I left the knife in his chest for someone else to remove. I decided not to return to the world of my youth ever again, not to India, or Persia, or Europe. I would remain in Tibet for the rest of my life. Clement Moorcroft, whose existence had faded so much during the last ten years, was now no more. I placed my official papers inside the coat of a badly disfigured thief who was about my height, and turning east, I walked toward Lhasa, to begin anew my Tibetan existence.

It was a long and lonely walk. Upon my arrival there, I learned casually in the marketplace of the reported death of a young Englishman named Clement Moorcroft. His body and papers had been found by a group of Lhasa traders led by a merchant named Dharma Ratna, who came from Katmandu. Except for the gold knife, which eventually was returned to me, he turned everything over to Colonel Gillespie, the leader of the British military detachment that had chased the Farouk gang into Tibet. Gillespie had all of the dead buried there at the site of the tragedy. I returned to Amdo, and the few people who knew of my former existence.

I had been gone only a month, but terrible changes had taken place. An epidemic of cholera had wiped out most of the village. Gyerong, my friend, was dead. Only his wife and one of his children, the boy Pasang, survived. They were weak and close to starvation. It took me several days to bring them back from the brink, but within a week of my careful ministrations they had gained much of their strength, and were out of danger.

Because of my success with Pasang and his mother, I soon found myself treating others who had survived the epidemic. I told the headman of the district of my intention to stay indefinitely, and he welcomed me, saying that I should become the husband of Pasang's mother. Pasang's mother and I readily assented to this since a great affection had developed between us, and I settled down as a family man and sheep herder in Amdo.

For over thirty years I led this life. Pasang grew up into a strong, handsome young man who became a soldier in the Tibetan army. His mother and I had several children together, but late in our lives she gave birth to a child who reminded us so much of Gyerong that we named him after my dead friend. We called him Tenzing Gyerong. Tenzing was a special child from the first, remarkable in his intelligence and physical precociousness. He was a great gift as I began to near old age.

During the same year as Tenzing's birth, we learned that the Grand Lama, the so-called Dalai Lama, had died, and the search for his successor had begun. As the reader may know already, it is the belief of all Tibetans that the soul of the departed lama reappears in the body of another, usually a young child, who must be found and identified. This child then is designated the new Grand Lama. In this case, the search was an extensive one, but discouragingly difficult for the monks assigned to the task. Time and time again the monks thought that they had found the Grand Lama's successor, only to be disappointed in the last stages of their search. And so several years passed and the Grand Lama's successor had yet to be found.

One day, three years after the search had begun, the committee of monks appeared in our village. There were three of them, old and senior monks of the Gelugpa sect. They came because they had heard rumours of the very bright child Tenzing who lived somewhere in Amdo. They came to our house and told us immediately of their mission. Tenzing saw them as he was playing with his friends and ran toward them, smiling as if in recognition. He suddenly seemed to all of us older than his four years. We went inside together and the interview began. The monks had come with some of the personal possessions of the previous Grand Lama—his quill pen, a small silver bell, a manuscript of the Mangalasutra, and a small silver statue of the Tathagata. Tenzing, as if recognising them, said that they were his. Increasingly encouraged by the results of the interview, the monks continued to ply our little son with all manner of questions. He appeared to give adequate answers to all of them. Finally, they asked to see his feet, to see if the infant shoes of the previous lama would fit. The monks looked at us as they took out the velvet slippers and told us that the previous lama had very narrow feet, unlike a Tibetan's. The senior monk looked at me and said with a smile, "The Tibetan foot is flat on the ground from end to end, and has three equally projecting toes. It is as square as a brick, but look at these shoes. They would never fit such a foot. The previous Grand Lama had what we call ar-ya pu-ta, or the foot of the Aryan, like the Buddha. Let us see if these slippers fit your son." Tenzing showed his feet, and the monk slipped the shoes on them. They fit perfectly, and at this moment the monks rose as one and bowed to Tenzing, who had passed all tests. The boy was asked to leave the room, and there ensued a long conversation with his mother and me over the time and circumstances of the child's birth. The monks then went outside to talk to other villagers and to survey the landscape to see if it fit with what the last Grand Lama had said would be the place of his rebirth. They returned in an hour to tell us that they believed that Tenzing was the next Grand Lama. So sure were they that they would dispense with the usual formalities and ask us to return to Lhasa with them. The ritual and legal authentification of Tenzing as the new Grand Lama in Lhasa took but a short time so strong was the evidence, and the installation ceremonies were held shortly thereafter.

And so from a small village in Amdo, where I had lived so much of my life, I was transported to the Potala, and to a powerful position within the Tibetan hierarchy as the Grand Lama's father. The Regent appointed to serve during the child's minority, an old man named Rinchung, died within two years, and I was chosen to succeed him.

By then I was thoroughly familiar with the inner workings of the Tibetan Government, and the conflicting desires of monk and layman, of aristocrat, peasant, and nomad. And it was then, too, that the first threats of foreign penetration began to affect the well-being of my adopted country. The British to the south insisted that their merchants be allowed to import the most abhorrent of foreign goods—liquor, opium, and firearms. I was able to block much of this, but the British became increasingly threatening. I began to see in the new overtures from the Russian and Japanese governments the only effective counterweight to British power. I soon realised, however, that the goals of these governments were equally if not far more dangerous to Tibetan interests and to Tibetan independence, for they were anxious to remove British power from Asia and to divide the spoils, including Tibet, between themselves. Only the Chinese were no longer of concern, for despite the presence of the Amban in Lhasa, their own growing internal weakness led me to disregard them, except when I found them useful.

I thus found myself in the difficult position of preserving Tibetan independence by avoiding embroilment in the rivalries of the Great Powers. I made a decision early on to educate my son in such a way that he would be aware of these problems when he came of age. In this way, I would leave Tibet with a leader who could act wisely during the great storms of the next century, storms that would sooner or later engulf even Tibet.

The first great crisis of my regency came in 1891. The Grand Lama was still young, and I was already eighty-one. The Russian agent Dorjiloff, whom I had mistakenly allowed to enter Tibet, had ingratiated himself with a large number of monks and agents of Imperial Japan, and had emerged as a powerful influence among an ambitious group of aristocratic Tibetans. They wished to form an alliance with the Japanese to remove China as a political power and to restore Tibetan hegemony over large areas that had been incorporated into western China. Considering the political and military power of Tibet at that time, the latter was a silly fantasy, but it so entranced the ruling nobles in Lhasa that I had difficulty at times in reining them in. I had placed trusted associates into positions of authority within the army, including my adopted son Pasang, whom I had sent to Kham to pacify and regularise the border with the Chinese. But rude, pompous, and unaware of the consequences of their actions, some of the leaders of the Tibetan army on their own attacked a group of British merchants who had crossed the border. They had been encouraged in this I later learned by Dorjiloff. The army's action violated the treaty of Yarlung, and it not only raised a British protest but brought about a crisis of authority within the Tibetan Government. The army officers had acted without my knowledge or permission. I had them immediately arrested and executed for insubordination. To counter the influence of the Japanese agents, I had Dorjiloff brought in honour to the Potala, where he was installed as a supreme teacher of philosophy. I did this at great risk, for it meant inordinate Russian influence, but it also meant that my agents could watch him more closely. I decided to ignore the British protest until I had successfully dealt with the agents. I surmised that, despite the seriousness with which the raid on its merchants would be viewed in the English Parliament, the British Government would not invade or attack us until the situation had reached a much more serious stage.

In this my supposition proved to be correct. The British were angry, but they temporised and decided to send a mission in the person of William Manning. With his arrival, the situation became very dangerous. When Dorjiloff learned that the British had sent a diplomatic mission to Lhasa, he was greatly disappointed, for he had hoped for a military attack. He decided to kill Manning, disfigure his body, and announce that Tibet was now in open defiance of the British Government. This would result almost certainly in a British attack on Tibet. Learning of their plot, I had Manning brought to a secret location, where he was put under heavy guard. The house that he was placed in was owned by Pasang, my foster son, and his wife, the princess Pema. Except for these two, no one knew Manning's whereabouts.

Dorjiloff was foiled for a time, but soon his agents learned where Manning was. Still his guard was so strong that he was in little danger until events took a disastrous turn. Not long after the news that Pasang, the husband of Princess

Pema, had been killed in battle in Kham, Manning confessed to the princess his love for her and proposed marriage. Somehow this avowal became known publicly, and there was a general outcry. Dorjiloff came to me to denounce the presence of a British agent in Lhasa and to make sure I knew that large crowds had gathered around the Jor-khang to protest the union of a Tibetan woman with an Englishman. I issued a decree of silence, ordering that neither Manning's name nor anything concerning him could be uttered. I had no choice but to put Manning in a cell in the Potala, where I made sure that he was well cared for. He was kept there for several months, and the memory of his presence began to fade. In the meantime several letters came from the British Government enquiring about him. I ordered that no reply be made to any British demands. Suddenly, however, there appeared in Lhasa another diplomat, this time a Norwegian explorer and naturalist by the name of Hallvard Sigerson, another with a secret mission. I refused to see him formally but learned that he had come with the specific purpose of finding Manning. It was also clear that this mission would be the last before the British sent a military expedition. I now had two British diplomats to protect from Dorjiloff and his associates.

I decided to act in a way which was filled with risk but one which if successful could protect Tibet and my own authority as Regent. Under no circumstances would I permit the death of William Manning. Indeed, I realised that he must leave Tibet at the earliest opportunity. To get him out of Tibet alive, however, I had to convince Dorjiloff that he was dead. I issued a secret communiqué, but one that purposely reached their ears the moment it was issued, that Manning had been tried and sentenced to die by a Tibetan tribunal and that, in accordance with Tibetan law, he had been sent to the Garden of Punishment. There he would remain until dead. They were informed that they would be allowed to identify his body if they so chose.

I had Manning immediately transported to the Garden and put in the torturous bamboo cage, one of the great horrors of the Tibetan imagination. I had no intention of having him die, however, and after several days, when I was told by my agents that he was beginning to suffer unbearably, I had him removed in the night, and Sackville-Grimes, a notorious criminal of London who had found his way to Lhasa, was put in his place. Grimes had been mortally wounded in a fight, was near death, and bore an uncanny resemblance to Manning. In my desire to make sure that Dorjiloff and the other agents were convinced of the identity of the dead man, I remembered an old piece of clothing belonging to my father, William Moorcroft, that bore the initials WM on its buttons. I had Sackville-Grimes clothed in this coat. Manning was spirited away to a secret location kept by my good friend the Newar merchant Gorashar.

But my plans went awry. I was notified during the night that Sackville-Grimes had died. Rastrakoff, the agent of Dorjiloff, had been sent to verify Manning's death, but had been overpowered and taken prisoner by Sigerson. Although I had good hope of deceiving Dorjiloff with the dead Sackville-Grimes, I doubted if Sigerson had been fooled, and I had no idea if he would make his discovery public. I decided to act quickly. Dorjiloff, Rastrakoff, and their associates, as well as Sigerson, must leave Tibet at once. I issued orders for their immediate arrest. Dorjiloff was found in his cell in the Potala and was subdued only with a great struggle. Sigerson had disappeared from his quarters.

I ordered a search of the city for Sigerson, but he was nowhere to be found. I decided to direct the search myself, even if it took all night. This Scandinavian emissary had acted with remarkable resourcefulness, and I realised then that this was no ordinary agent, and no ordinary naturalist as he claimed to be.

It was just before nightfall that I received a message from Gorashar, the Newar merchant who had been a friend for many years: "Sigerson will come to you. I have given him the gold knife." I was astounded at the note, for it meant that Gorashar had found Sigerson to be worthy of the greatest trust.

I then ordered the search to be abandoned, the guard to the Potala to be relaxed, and that a tall stranger should be allowed to pass. I sat on the floor at my writing table, waiting for our meeting. I dozed, and it must have been almost the middle of the night when he walked in. We stared at each other for what seemed to be an interminable period. I studied Sigerson's face, his gaunt figure, his aquiline nose, and his penetrating eyes. He looked almost familiar to me, as if I had seen his photograph or read a description of him somewhere. His eyes stared into me, and I shall never forget the words that he uttered to me: "Well, Moorcroft . . ." It was the first time that I had heard my English name uttered in over sixty years. Sigerson then identified himself as the English detective Sherlock Holmes, and I remember little of the conversation that ensued, except that out of it came a lasting friendship and a useful alliance.

The conversation was violently interrupted, however. Dorjiloff had escaped his guard and burst into my room, pointing a gun at us.

"Neither of you move," he hissed. "I heard your little conversation before I entered. What a great piece of fortune! To remove from this life not only the fake Regent Moorcroft but also the counterfeit diplomat Holmes!"

He took aim and was about to fire when Holmes, moving with the speed and grace of a great cat, fairly flew through the air, knocking Dorjiloff to the ground, the pistol flying across the room toward me. Holmes had the gold knife at Dorjiloff's throat, but Dorjiloff's formidable strength was too great, and Holmes found himself overpowered. Dorjiloff seized the knife and was about to plunge it into Holmes's heart. I fired directly into Dorjiloff's chest, killing him instantly. He slumped to the floor, Holmes grabbing the knife from his hand.

"A very close call, my dear Moorcroft, and one not so very long after the struggle at the Reichenbach Falls. It is enough to make one think of changing one's profession," he said, catching his breath, "except that by persevering one has the opportunity to rid the world of a few of its devils."

"He is the second man I have killed in my life, and I am not pleased at my action," I said. "But such is my fate."

I summoned the guard. Dorjiloff's body was removed. Later that day, Dorjiloff's remains were prepared according to Tibetan custom for offering to the vultures at the Place of Silence, and the Russian Government was notified of his death and funeral. That very day, William Manning, the envoy to Lhasa, was escorted to the Indian border, where he continued his journey to Delhi and then to England. He carried with him secret documents signed by me outlining in detail the events of the last several years and a declaration of hope for a period of tranquil relations with the British Empire. He was followed shortly thereafter by the princess Pema, who joined him in Bombay, from where they departed together for England.

Sherlock Holmes remained in Tibet for almost another two years, during which time he, under the guise of the Scandinavian naturalist that he had assumed at the outset, carried out a variety of studies. He and I met often but secretly, and we became close friends. At the end of this period, he left with Gorashar for Katmandu, the first stop on his long voyage back to England. He carries with him this note on my life, which, depending upon his wish, may see the light of day in some distant moment in the indeterminate future.

Holmes had sat at his desk immersed in work while I read the account contained in the Moorcroft document. He sensed my having finished the reading, and turning said, with an affectionate smile, "Oh, by the way, Watson, the knife is now yours."

THE CASE OF
ANTON FURER

I T WAS IN THE SPRING OF 1884 THAT SHERLOCK HOLMES FIRST mentioned the name of Anton Furer.

"Remember it well, Watson," he said grimly, "this man has a brilliant future in crime unless he is apprehended soon. I myself have been on his trail several times in the last few years, but he has always eluded my grasp. Someday, however, I shall rein him in."

I felt the same iron determination in his words that I noted only when he was after an opponent he deemed worthy. It was well over a decade later, however, that the matter was finally resolved. In going over my notes for this episode, I found that Holmes had given me early on a short sketch of the beginnings of Furer's career.

Furer, as his name would indicate, was of German extraction. His father had been born near Hamburg, where he had been a petty dealer in antiquities. The family immigrated to England some years after the failed revolution of 1848, and settled in London. Anton was born soon after their arrival. The father, Julius, opened a shop in Finsbury, but it was a failure. Unskilled in English and impatient with his life, the elder Furer borrowed heavily and rapidly found himself in debt. Unable to discharge his obligations through honest means, he embarked upon a career of burglary and theft. Here his luck was better than it had been in honest business. He began by pilfering antiquities from other shops, then moved on to housebreaking, stealing from large mansions in the city as well as in the countryside. He formed a small gang who continued the dirty work of thievery for him while he himself became the chief purveyor of these stolen goods to collectors in America.

From an early age, Anton helped his father. Beginning as an apprentice to one of the gang members, he rapidly learned the skills of burglary and the quick disposal of stolen treasure. So skilled did the gang become that very often there was no trace of their illegal entry, only a blank spot where a painting was missing from a wall, or an empty space on a bedroom table where a jewel box had once stood.

Julius Furer, now at the height of his career, invested his ill-gotten gains in legitimate business and purchased a large house in London, where he rapidly became one of the city's most celebrated hosts. By this time his depredations had become truly international. Several thefts from the Louvre, including the removal of Massigny's *Adonis* and Vernet's *St. Sebastien,* were later found to be the work of the Furer gang.

After several years of uninterrupted success, father and son finally overstepped themselves when they tried to intercept a large shipment of Egyptian antiquities destined for the British Museum. One of the gang was seized and confessed. Julius Furer was arrested, convicted, and jailed. He eventually died in prison. Anton, however, being in Alexandria at the time of the discovery, escaped into Upper Egypt and disappeared entirely. He was presumed to be dead, supposedly having been killed by one of the gang who had escaped with him and was later apprehended in Addis Ababa. Holmes alone believed that he was still alive, for he sensed his presence through the bald reports in the newspapers of art disappearances and archaeological depredations throughout the world.

"But are you sure, Holmes?" I asked him one day. "How do you know that it is indeed Furer who is behind these crimes?"

The latest report was before us, one that spoke of the disappearance of several pieces of sculpture from a museum in Constantinople.

"Mere child's play, my dear Watson. If one follows a particular criminal for a time and carefully studies his methods, it is easy to recognise his hand at work, just as if one had a photograph of the scene at the time of the crime. In this way, one easily distinguishes between criminals. Thus, I know for instance that Furer is involved in the murder of Roger Dannett, but not in the recent attempt to steal several antiquities from the Victoria and Albert."

"For the life of me, I do not see his connection with Dannett," I said.

"You know my methods, Watson, apply them," he said impatiently.

I was about to object that knowing his methods was useless without his genius and encyclopedic knowledge, but even as he spoke, the far-away look that I had seen so often on previous occasions had already passed into his eyes, and I knew that I would hear nothing more from his lips that day. His great brain was already absorbed in the solution of some other crime, and it would remain so until he had solved it or had gone as far as he could without moving from his favourite armchair.

Holmes never mentioned Anton Furer again, and it was only a decade or so later, after Holmes had returned from the Orient, that I learned of Furer's subsequent career. It was late in the afternoon one day in June 1895. It had been a particularly warm day. Holmes had been excessively moody and complained about the lengthening days and his inability to sleep. He had once again taken to cocaine. As I was expostulating on its bad effects, Mrs. Hudson knocked and announced that a gentleman was here to see him.

"Halloo, Watson, perhaps I shall not need the drug after all. You may save your remonstrances for another occasion." He passed to me the card which Mrs. Hudson had just given him: Col. C. H. Ridlington, O.B.E., Ret., 5th Royal Gurkha Rifles, Old House, Bourton, Gloucestershire.

"Do show the gentleman in, Mrs. Hudson."

Colonel Ridlington was a tall, florid man of once muscular build attested to by his military carriage, but he had grown an enormous paunch, which bore witness to a very sedentary life in recent years.

"Please sit down, Colonel Ridlington, and allow me to introduce my trusted friend, Dr. Watson. You may speak before him with the same confidence that you do before me."

"Thank you, Mr. Holmes. I should like to say at the outset that what I am about to tell you is rather trivial on the surface, and I hope that I shall not be wasting your time by relating the matter."

"I shall be most happy to give you my opinion as to whether the case is trivial or whether it has a deeper aspect to it," said Holmes. "What appears to be unimportant to the layman is often of vital interest to me."

"Very well, then. Let me explain why I have come to you. I served in our Indian army for thirty years before I retired at the beginning of this year. I was stationed throughout the East, but the last five years were spent in Nepal, where I was put in charge of Gurkha recruitment. I lived in Katmandu but often visited other parts of the country, including the Tarai. It was a rather easy existence, if I say so myself, for I saw no combat and did not fire a shot except on shikar in the jungle. My acquaintances in Nepal were many, but they were confined almost entirely to the military class and the rulers.

"It was with a certain surprise, therefore, that, a few days before my departure, I found seated across from me a Buddhist monk who spoke excellent English. He told me that he was a native of the Katmandu Valley, a Newar, and that he had studied in Ceylon and had travelled as far as England, where he had met with many interested in the Buddhist religion. He had just returned to Nepal, and having visited the Buddha's birthplace at Lumbini, had taken up residence in a small monastery on the Svayambhu hill. It was while circumambulating that great shrine he said that he had been presented with a stone sculpture of the Buddha. The donor was a rich Burmese pilgrim who through piety wished that the statue would someday be revered in the West. Having learned from one of the guards at the Residency of my imminent departure, he asked if I might take the sculpture with me to England, where it would be claimed by a monk now living in London and leading a small group of English Buddhists in the study of the Doctrine. The name of the group was the Oriental Society of London, with their shrine near Russell Square on Bedford Street. He assured me that the statue was of no consequence from an artistic point of view but that its safe arrival would do much to increase the compassion of the small band of followers of the Buddha now studying in England.

"So earnest and sincere did the monk appear that I informed him that I would be willing to take it as part of my personal belongings, but that I should like to see it for myself before I gave my final consent. The monk appeared the next day, and it was as he had said: a modern reproduction in stone, done by a mediocre craftsman in the ancient city of Patan, and standing about thirty inches high. I accepted it and arranged that it be packaged along with my possessions. I gave it no further thought."

"A most interesting beginning. Pray continue, my dear Colonel," said Holmes.

"I arrived in England just two weeks ago and settled in the small village of Bourton in Gloucestershire. My family had kept a house there for many generations. Being the sole survivor and unmarried as well, I had inherited the entire estate directly upon my father's demise five years before. I had kept an old housekeeper to look after things while I was abroad. It was unsettling to learn, therefore, when I arrived, that the housekeeper had died the year before and the house had been unattended for many months. It is a rather large mansion, Mr. Holmes, built by Sir Roger Ridlington, my ancestor, in 1779, and it showed the neglect that a recently impoverished family had been forced to ignore. I spent the first day clearing a living space for myself amidst the dusty clutter. On the following day, as I had been informed, my personal cargo promptly arrived, and I set about sorting through the souvenirs and possessions accumulated in my thirty years in the Orient.

"I am not a collector, Mr. Holmes, and so I was somewhat startled when I saw the number of objects that I had managed to accumulate through the years, thoughtlessly I might say. I promised myself that I would dispose of much of what now struck me as quite useless. I sorted rather quickly, and by evening I had managed to open everything and find at least a temporary dwelling for most articles of importance. It was at this moment that I remembered the Buddhist monk and his request. I searched through the remaining crates, unpacked the Buddha, and placed him gently upon a table in the drawing room. I then wrote a short note to the monk resident in London to whom it was to be delivered, informing him of the arrival of his charge and asking him to retrieve it at his earliest convenience.

"After a late supper, I continued my work. To my surprise, in one of the last remaining crates there was another figure of the Buddha, identical to the first in every way, at least to my unpracticed eye. I was a bit annoyed at having another piece of stone to store in what was already becoming a sea of odd objects. One Buddha on display was enough, I thought. Where to put the second one? I was rapidly running out of space to put things. It was then that I remembered that one of the mantels in the great hall had a secret compartment behind it. Removing the second Buddha from its crate, I placed it in the secret place away from sight, and put the empty crate in a storage closet."

As I listened to the Colonel's account, I threw an occasional glance at Holmes. At our visitor's last revelation, the look of disinterested amusement that had played across his face had been replaced by the deepest concentration.

"By this time it was very late, and I had had enough," said the Colonel.

"It was about midnight when I retired, and I slept quite soundly. I rose at about eight the following morning and went into the kitchen to prepare some tea, when I noticed that the back door was ajar. I remembered distinctly having locked it before I retired. Someone must have entered during the night, I thought. I hurried quickly to the drawing room to see if I had been vandalised. Everything, however, appeared to be in good order until I noticed, to my chagrin, that the stone Buddha was missing from the table where I had placed it. Someone had indeed entered, but I had been fortunate, for whoever it was had mistaken a rather shoddy modern copy for a work of art. Nothing else appeared to be missing."

"Most extraordinary, Colonel Ridlington," said Holmes. "I am afraid that your account thus far leads me to believe that there is some danger to you. May I suggest that you employ a guard immediately to watch your house?"

"I have taken some precautions, Mr. Holmes, at least for the time of my visit here. Had matters ended there I would not be with you today. I spent the following day in routine business in the village. I was gone for about four or five hours. When I entered the house, I saw that the Buddha had been returned to its spot on the table in the drawing room. Nothing else appeared to have been disturbed until I observed that someone had entered the storage area where I had placed the empty crate that contained the second Buddha. Whoever had entered had hoped that the break-in would not be immediately noticed. The lock had been broken but closed to avoid detection, and the door had been shut tight. When I pulled it open, however, I found that what I had carefully stored had been thrown about as if someone had searched in a great hurry. It was then that I saw that the crate had been smashed and broken into. The burglar had failed, however, to find the second Buddha. It was at this point that I decided to present the matter to you for your judgement."

As he came to the end of his story, Colonel Ridlington leaned over and opened his briefcase. He took from it a red cloth.

"I have neglected to inform you of one curious matter," he said, handing the cloth to Holmes. "When I examined the first Buddha after it had been returned, I noticed that its bottom surface had been shattered and that this cloth had been stuffed into it. Whether it was there before the statue was removed from my house or placed there afterwards, I cannot say."

From where I was seated I could see that the cloth was quite large, possibly a blanket.

"Odd," said Holmes, as he felt the cloth between his fingers, "among the finest weaves I have ever seen, absolutely tight, Watson. Note the two gold cords that extend from the centre."

"It appears to be something between a blanket and a robe," said I, "but what?"

Holmes pondered the cloth for an instant longer. Then I saw a look of recognition arise on his face. He smiled and said, "Most interesting, my dear Colonel. I would like you to leave it here with me for the time being, for it may prove to be of some use."

"Please keep it as long as necessary," replied the Colonel.

Holmes folded the cloth neatly and placed it next to him on his armchair.

"And what do you think of my little problem, Mr. Holmes?"

"I can assure you, Colonel Ridlington, that what you have presented to us is hardly a trivial matter," said Holmes, "but that, with a bit of luck, we may be able to resolve it quickly. I should like to accompany you to your home in Gloucestershire so that I may have a firsthand look at the premises. And the two Buddhas, of course."

Holmes turned to me and said, "Watson, this is a case in which I must ask you to remain here and not accompany me. I request only that you leave with us now and return at once through the back entrance, making sure that no one sees you reenter. Remain inside until I reappear. And, Watson, once you have returned, I must ask that you remain in the bedroom with the curtains drawn till dawn, when you may move about freely in the front rooms as well."

I was at once mystified and disappointed at Holmes's request, for I had hoped to accompany him in what appeared to be a case more interesting than I had originally thought, but I did as he wished. I knew also that it would be hopeless to ask for an explanation.

The two of us left together with Colonel Ridlington. As we approached the crowd on Oxford Street we parted, and I reentered our quarters from the back. By this time it was evening, and I was almost certain that I had entered unseen.

I passed a difficult night, for the summer heat did not abate in the darkness. I finally sat on the floor below the window with a candle, trying to read my medical journals. I must have fallen asleep at last, for when I awoke it was early morning. The candle had burned down to nothing, and I was stiff from having lain on the floor the better part of the night. I arose and went into the drawing room, my mind filled with Ridlington's odd story of the previous afternoon. Holmes had not returned, and I presumed that he was still in Gloucestershire.

It was about eleven in the morning when Mrs. Hudson appeared and said that two deliverymen were downstairs with a large parcel for Mr. Holmes. I directed that they be shown up. As they entered I paid little attention, for an article on tropical diseases of the kidney had caught my eye.

"Where to, guv'na?" said one of them, a rather old man dressed in tattered clothes. I motioned to the centre of the room and kept on reading. The old man handed me a pen and a delivery slip to sign.

"Sign here, quickly, Watson," said a familiar voice, "for we haven't a moment to lose."

I looked up in disbelief. As the old man straightened up, he seemed to shed years, and I knew that I was looking at my friend.

"Holmes!" I cried.

"Correct, Watson, correct! And my colleague in the transport business, Mr. Tobias Gregson of Scotland Yard."

Gregson removed his deliveryman's cap and bowed. "My pleasure, guv'na," he said.

"Holmes, for the love of God, you owe me a bit of an explanation. Why such a trick?"

I was annoyed, not so much because I had failed to recognise him but because I had been doubly fooled and had to suffer through Holmes's obvious sarcasm and Gregson's deep satisfaction.

"Please accept my apologies, Watson," said Holmes with a broad grin. "You have played a vital role so far in this affair and will continue to do so. Please accompany Mr. Gregson into the other room and exchange clothes with him. And pack a further change of clothes, your own, into this sack and bring it along. I shall explain all in due course."

As he spoke, Holmes went over to the settee, moved it, and then lifted the floorboards. It was an old hiding place that he had used on many occasions in the past. He placed the package in the large space below, replacing the floor and the settee in quick, deliberate motions. He then peered through the curtains at the street below and smiled thoughtfully.

I did as he requested, and with his help looked as much the deliveryman as Gregson, who remained behind, hidden in my bedroom.

Holmes's conduct so far I found bewildering, and as usual in his haste he chose not to offer any information. We crossed Baker Street, then proceeded through a back alley to an abandoned building, where Holmes picked the lock and we entered easily. Here we changed into our street clothes, leaving the deliverymen's uniforms in a heap on the floor.

"There is little time to talk, Watson. We are close to a final meeting with an archcriminal. It will be dangerous, but I believe we have every chance of success."

Now in our usual dress, Holmes and I went out on the street and walked home. Holmes's eyes scoured every passerby, but we did not stop until we had reached our quarters.

"And now, Watson," said he as we entered, "unless I have misjudged, the bell will ring in a few minutes, and Mrs. Hudson will usher in our next guest."

Holmes sat down in his armchair, placing the red cloth that Colonel Ridlington had left behind in his lap. He fingered it gently and wrapped one of the golden cords around his wrist.

In less than five minutes the bell sounded, and Mrs. Hudson, a perplexed look on her face, said that there was a gentleman to see us. She ushered in a Buddhist monk in saffron robes. His face had a definite

European cast to it, despite his shaven head and the other accoutrements of his religion.

Holmes's eyes flashed with the delight of a fisherman who has just felt a great tug on his line.

"Watson," he said almost gleefully, "I would like to present to you Mr. Jack Evans, who if I am not mistaken, hails from Salt Lake City. He is wanted in America in seven different states for burglary and illegal entry. He has been one of the mainstays of the Anton Furer gang."

The monk's demeanour changed as soon as Holmes had identified him.

"I'm not here to argue with ya, Holmes. Where's the stuff? Furer sent me, and this time he ain't kiddin'."

The absurd contradiction between the monk's costume and his rough American speech brought a smile to my lips. But it was short-lived. The door to the flat was suddenly thrown open, and another monk stood before us.

"And this," said Holmes, without turning around to look at the intruder, "is the infamous Anton Furer, the chief art thief of our time. My compliments, Anton, on your having evaded arrest for so long. I am delighted that your love of art irresistibly brought you here. Please be seated."

"I have no time to waste, Holmes. This is the last time that you will have interfered with my plans. Please, we are both armed, and neither of us is prepared to leave without the object for which we came."

Furer was taller than I expected, thinner, more desperate looking than I had imagined, with eyes that darted quickly through the room, examining everything in sight as he spoke. As he searched, he found nothing, and an oath passed through his lips.

"Where is it, Holmes?" he asked.

"I am afraid that it is not available for inspection," said Holmes, lighting his pipe. "Evans, dear fellow," he continued, "be so good as to look out the window onto the street. If you do, you will notice that this building is surrounded by police."

"He's bluffing," said Furer.

"No, he's not. Raise your hands, please."

The words came from Gregson, who had suddenly opened the door as if by signal from Holmes. The bewildered Evans dropped his gun. In an instant, moving on him like a great cat, Holmes knocked the gun from Furer's hand and threw the red cloth over his head, pulling tight the gold cord that he had wrapped around his wrist. Suddenly choking for air, the hapless Furer fell to the ground, gasping, desperately scratching at the cloth to remove it, but in vain. Holmes watched in triumph the figure writhing at his feet, and after a few seconds more, he pulled the other golden cord, releasing the cloth from Furer's head. Unable to breathe at first, Furer panted on the floor, groaning and choking alternately. It was several minutes before he recovered.

"A royal experience for you, dear Anton, though an unpleasant one, I am afraid. You were just introduced to the infamous blanket of Kanishka, the one with which the ancient emperor was smothered to death. One of the more dangerous of Oriental antiquities, I should say."

Holmes stared down at his old quarry, then helped him to his feet.

"I invite you, Anton, to look below if you wish. I assure you that even had you been able to murder us your arrest was inevitable. I should tell you also that those colleagues of yours who had infiltrated the Oriental Society of London have been apprehended as well. You know, you really should have learned by now."

An evil scowl covered Furer's face, for Holmes had entrapped him easily, and so great was the anger that shone through his eyes that I imagined he would have torn Holmes and the rest of us limb from limb had he been able to free himself. Gregson handcuffed him and Evans, and led them into the street, where they were immediately taken to Scotland Yard.

"Well, Holmes, you must be pleased with yourself. A very easy end to a long career of criminal activity. My congratulations and, if I may add, my mystifications. Somehow I feel as though I have missed most of what this is about."

"You have, Watson, and through no fault of your own. Most of what transpired over the last two days is simply the end of a very long sequence of events, the larger part of which took place in India some time ago, a part with which you could not be familiar. Perhaps it would be of interest if I related to you those portions of the story that remain hidden from view."

"Indeed," said I. "It would be most helpful."

"But first, a look at the treasure that eluded Furer's grasp and eventually led to his downfall."

Holmes removed the settee from its place and quickly lifted the floorboards. He removed the package that he had stored below and un-wrapped it, revealing an image of the Buddha. Holmes turned it on its side and tapped the bottom with his fingers.

"It too is hollow, as I thought," he said. "Watson, quickly, let me have the large shears from your bag."

I tossed them over. Holmes took them and broke a hole through the rather thin plaster that covered the bottom. In a few minutes he had carved a larger hole, revealing a space inside the statue in which we now could see a rectangular object, a box of some sort. As soon as the hole was large enough for it to pass, Holmes inserted his hand and pulled it forth. His eyes were bright with excitement.

"Now," he said, "Watson, if I am not mistaken, we have here one of the great treasures of the ancient world."

He laid the object on the table, and proceeded to unwrap it. A golden object, a small chest, appeared, covered with magnificent designs. There was some ancient form of writing on it as well.

Holmes smiled. "I had this almost in my hands several years ago, and thought that it might be forever lost. Do you know what it is?"

"I must say it is impressive. Is it perhaps a reliquary?"

"It contains a number of the royal jewels of Kanishka, king of the Kushans, a warlike race who controlled a vast empire that stretched from northern India well into central Asia almost two thousand years ago. There is an inscription on the cover in their script, the Kharosthi, if memory serves, which bears testimony to this. Let us remove the cover and see what it contains."

It was indeed as Holmes had claimed. The box was filled with the most beautiful gold jewellery, studded with rubies, sapphires, and emeralds.

"Look at this, Watson," he cried. He was holding a large ring of gold. It had two beautifully intertwined serpents carved on its sides and at its top the swastika, the ancient symbol of good luck. It glistened in the late afternoon sun that was now streaming through the window.

"Try it on, Watson," he said, dropping it into my left hand. "It is a rare opportunity to share the experience of a king of antiquity. Yours will be far more pleasant than that of Furer."

I tried the ring on, and scrutinised it closely for a moment. It was beautiful to behold, but I remained untouched. Holmes continued to

examine the box. He had removed the jewellery and now stood holding it to the light, then to his ear. I saw him press with great force on its
left side. There was a sudden noise, and I heard him utter a short cry of
delight.

"Aha! Watson, there is more. Look, a false bottom. Let us see what
else there is."

Holmes took the false bottom from the box and placed it with the
jewellery on the side table. There was revealed a small cloth bag, made
of brocade, and what appeared to be a small scroll fashioned out of a
material that I could not immediately identify. Holmes unfurled the
scroll, upon which there were some ancient characters.

"Birch bark," he said, "one of the most ancient writing materials.
And a short inscription in the ancient Prakrit. Let us attempt a reading
before we consult the experts at the museum." Holmes held his glass to
the scroll, concentrated deeply for a few moments, and then said:

"Write this down, Watson, for I can read almost all of it: 'The jewels
of Kanishka are nothing compared to this, this lock of hair of the Buddha Shakyamuni, the Enlightened One.' So, we now know what the
bag contains, a true relic of the Buddha himself, perhaps taken at the
time of his enlightenment, or perhaps at his death. It is not for us to
know, Watson. I suggest that unbelieving infidels such as we not open
the bag, that that be done by others closer to the ancient forms of belief
than we are."

He placed the bag and the scroll back in the reliquary and restored
the false bottom to its original place. "It is growing late," he said. "Perhaps we should dine, and over a good cigar and a brandy I shall tell you
how all of this came about."

II

"AND SO, WATSON, FURER IS NOW WHERE HE BELONGS—IN THE HANDS OF THE
authorities, his long criminal career finally at an end."

I watched him as he lit his cigar, relaxing in his favourite chair. His
eyes were bright, and he could scarcely contain his pleasure.

"I appreciate your elation at the outcome, my dear Holmes, but certain parts of the affair continue to elude me. How did you know that

Furer would fall so easily into your hands? And how did you know what was hidden in the second statue? How, indeed, did you know that anything at all was contained in it?"

Holmes heard the slight irritation in my voice, which I had taken pains to conceal, but unsuccessfully, for I was still smarting from my failure to see through his disguise and that of Gregson. His tone of voice became even more self-satisfied, and I felt as if salt was being poured on my wounds.

"As to your first question, Watson, it is simplicity itself. One must know one's criminals. That is all. Furer was a thief, to be sure, but he had a well-developed aesthetic sense, a sense of symmetry, shall we say, that in the end was his undoing. He walked into our quarters as I walked into his camp in the Tarai several years ago. He also possessed throughout his career a deep sense of invincibility that on occasions past had led him to risk his life foolishly. I knew therefore that he would want to close the circle with me, so to speak. And he did, to his final defeat, I'm afraid. As to the other questions, well, my dear friend, knowing my powers of deduction, I venture to say that I would have quickly deduced the fact that one of the statues contained something unusual from the circumstances of the case alone. In this instance, however, I actually knew it. Indeed, I had been expecting its arrival, though the exact time and place were unknown to me. As Ridlington spoke, I assumed that the first statue was a decoy in which unknowingly the unique red cloth had been placed. Once the good Colonel had told his story, I saw how the matter would end. The visit to Gloucestershire merely corroborated my hypothesis and permitted me to take possession of the second statue, the one that Furer was so determined to get his hands on. Still, you find the entire case puzzling, Watson, simply because you lack the beginning."

Drawing in his breath, Holmes suddenly stood up and said: "Watson, it is a beautiful June evening. It will be light for several more hours. Let us stroll toward Green Park, and I shall relate to you the earlier portion of the Furer case."

The evening was as beautiful as London provides. The streets were filled with men and women strolling happily, some arm in arm, some walking with their dogs, with children playing summer games, and the other happy sounds of a people at peace. It was only when we drew near the park that the crowds abated, and Holmes continued.

"The story begins at a most unusual point. It commences just after the affair concerning Reginald Maxwell."

"You mean that this story begins when you were in India?" I asked.

"Indeed, it does, Watson. You will recall that while I travelled in India, I had assumed the name of Roger Lytton-Smith?"

"Certainly I do," I replied.

"After the Maxwell affair, I continued to use that name and identity. It was convenient and, above all, believable. I bade good-bye to the Viceroy and continued my journey. I travelled west by train. My intention was to spend some months in India before I entered the mountains of Afghanistan.

"My first stop after Calcutta was the obvious one: Banaras once again, the holiest city of the Hindus. The ride on the Tuphan Express from Calcutta was uneventful, and as I recall, I lodged at the Clark's Hotel, one of the more comfortable establishments in our Indian possessions.

"I had determined that what I needed was a moment of tranquillity after the episode in Bengal, and so I stayed close to my quarters, venturing forth only in the evening. I spent much time recording the events that had befallen me during the last several months. I spoke to no one except those serving me at the hotel, who were efficient and unobtrusive. The air was cool enough in the evening, and I sat in peace on the wide verandah until dark, when the mosquitoes finally became unbearable.

"On the third night, I wandered on foot into the city. Like all cities of India, it has those nocturnal characteristics that give it a sense of mystery: darkness, the human voice disembodied, the shuffling of countless naked feet, the barking of dogs, the shrieks of jackals and hyenas. But it is still in essence a village, lacking in the metropolitan aspect. It is after all a religious centre, one of the most revered sites of the Hindus and one of the most ancient cities of the world.

"I wandered through Godowlia, the town centre. From there I went to the Ganges, to the Dasashvamedha Ghat, one of the great bathing places. It is here, Watson, that the pious Hindu plans to arrive at his last moment, knowing that to leave this mortal coil here is to guarantee his eternal salvation and liberation from this vale of tears, or samsara, as they call it in the Sanscrit tongue.

"As you are well aware, Watson, I am not a religious person, and after a few days my interest in the bizarre religiosity of Banaras began to wane. When I returned to the hotel after my third night of exploration, I decided to move on. My departure was suddenly postponed, however, by events that began to transpire the following morning.

"I arose early and breakfasted not at Clark's but at the Hôtel de Paris, an establishment peculiarly named considering its location just across the main cantonment road. It was a most pleasant building, however, and its front gardens were filled with bougainvillaea and jacaranda flowers, bathed in the soft morning sunlight.

"As I entered, I noticed a man and a woman, the woman English, the man Indian, seated in a corner of the verandah, engaged in what appeared to be a deep and most serious conversation. The man I judged to be about forty years of age. He was well dressed and, judging from his carriage, of high caste Hindu background. By his build and accent I deemed him to be Bengalese. The woman was somewhat younger and rather frail. She was pale, and her eyes, red and tearful, indicated that she had been crying."

As Holmes observed them, the woman suddenly arose, as if in anger, and strode into the hotel. The man appeared surprised at her action, but did not attempt to follow. He rose slowly from his chair, his surprise having retreated into sadness, and left.

"I then went directly to the breakfast room. It was shortly after the bearer had brought my tea that the same woman entered and took her seat at a table near mine. I could thus observe her closely without seeming rude or intrusive. I deduced much from her appearance. She was a youngish woman, in her early thirties perhaps, aristocratic in her bearing, married, most probably to one of our government officers, and was someone who was experienced in India, since she spoke Hindustanee to the bearer, and it was decent enough. The deference and familiarity with which she was treated indicated that she was a person of some importance and that she had been in the hotel for several days. That she was under some great strain showed from her face, which contained an expression of great sadness and fear. She occasionally wiped a tear from her eyes, and I noticed that she ate none of the food that was placed before her. She fingered her wedding ring constantly, and looked repeatedly out the window toward the entrance to the garden, as if she hoped to see someone appear."

The breakfast hour was now drawing to a close, said Holmes, and there was no one in the dining room save the turbaned bearers who stood guard, ready to satisfy their smallest want. He decided then to approach this woman and learn the cause of her grief. He quickly penned a note to her on one of his calling cards, and handed it to one of the bearers for delivery:

Please forgive my intrusion into your private thoughts, but I could not help notice that you are under a great strain concerning the whereabouts of your husband. Perhaps we might talk on the verandah over another cup of tea before the sun gets any higher. I may be of some help to you in finding him.

The woman was at first startled by his note, almost angered by it, and Holmes could see in her eyes the suspicion that this stranger had something to do with her husband's disappearance. For how else could he know what her worry was? Suddenly her face became impassive, almost grim. She looked up and nodded to him. Holmes asked the bearer to bring tea to them on the verandah.

"You appear to be a complete stranger to me," she said. "And yet you know something about my husband's disappearance. You therefore must be part of the plot against him. Tell me where he is. I implore you."

There was a desperate look in her eyes as she spoke. Holmes had reasoned correctly.

"You are correct, madam. We have never laid eyes on each other, but I can assure you that I do not know where your husband is. I do not even know his name. What I know was merely based on what I observed."

"Observed?" she asked sardonically.

"Surely it takes no great talent to observe a woman fingering her wedding ring in great agitation and looking toward the entrance to the hotel for someone to appear to deduce that that someone might be her husband, that he has not come, and that his failure to arrive has caused great consternation in his wife. The staff appears to know you well, and so I reason that you have been waiting for many days. Your fear is now that something dreadful has happened to him."

"You are very clever for a chemist," she said.

"I have had other occupations in the past. Perhaps, madam, I may gain your confidence by showing you this."

It was a note of thanks and warm praise from the Viceroy for help in a minor affair in Patna, addressed to Roger Lytton-Smith. When she had read it, Holmes said, "I can assure you, madam, that you may speak to me in all confidence and that I have no interest other than seeing your husband restored to you."

She smiled wanly. "For the first time in many days, I feel as though there is some hope that I may find my beloved Vincent."

"Please tell me everything from the very beginning," said Holmes.

"I have been in India with my husband for six years," she said. "We have lived in Calcutta and most recently in Delhi. My husband is Vincent Smith, director general of the Archaeological Survey of India. Our years here, until recently, have been very peaceful and filled with satisfaction, for I share my husband's interests in historical matters. Unlike many of our countrymen who come here, we have not been separated by my husband's work. He has shared his enthusiasms and discoveries fully with me, and I have tried in my small way to aid him to the limits of my abilities."

"Your husband's writings are well known to me," said Holmes. "Pray continue."

"As you may know, my husband has dedicated his life to the reconstruction of Indian history and to the preservation of India's monuments. He is now writing a volume on the early history of the Subcontinent that I venture to say will become the standard work on the subject for many years to come. In composing his account, Vincent was satisfied with much of the earliest history, but felt that there were very real gaps in his knowledge of early Buddhism. He became intent therefore in expanding the investigations of the survey into the Nepalese Tarai, where hidden in its jungle confines, he believed, lie the archaeological ruins that would provide the answers to many historical problems. More than with any other subject in his career, I found him to be almost obsessed with these questions. He thought about, and talked about, nothing else."

It was when her husband was in this rather delicate state of mind, she said, that there appeared one day at the survey an Englishman, recently arrived in India, who claimed to be a trained archaeologist looking for work as a field investigator. He displayed excellent credentials, and even though he was not previously known to anyone at the survey, he was immediately hired. He said that he had recently worked in Hanoi with the French, and after a stay in Hong Kong he had decided to ply his trade in India. He had excellent references, for the French scholars appeared to have written for him most favourably. He had an encyclopaedic knowledge of antiquities. He claimed a great deal of knowledge concerning the geography of northern Bihar and the Nepalese Tarai, of which he said he had made special studies. This latter fact brought him immediately to the attention of her husband, who after a brief interview employed him on the spot.

"His name was Anthony Fordham," she continued. "To me from the beginning this man was a disturbing presence, a handsome, smooth, rather oily gentleman, who I felt in my bones could not be trusted. But he immediately gained my husband's confidence, and the two became almost inseparable. Their talk was constant, and Vincent took to inviting him to our home on a regular basis. I was most uncomfortable with this new friendship, for on the few short occasions on which I was left alone with him, Fordham looked at me so voraciously that I felt compelled to leave the room."

Her husband refused to hear her doubts, berated her for her fears of Fordham, saying that he thought her suspicions and worries unfounded. For the first time, she became distanced from her husband and replaced somewhat in his attention. The more she saw of Fordham, however, the more she felt that he could not be trusted.

"It was with a sense of relief, therefore, that I learned that Vincent had decided to send Fordham to the Tarai for a preliminary survey of Buddhist monuments. Permission for the expedition had come from the Nepalese rulers after a long interval, and Fordham left with a single assistant, this now about three months ago. He refused a large party of workers from the survey, saying that he would be best served by workers hired and trained on the spot."

A month later, her husband reported elatedly to her that Fordham had made great discoveries, including ruins that predated the historical Buddha, a rather sensational discovery in itself. Fordham's drawings and diagrams were quite detailed. Considering the report a major addition to the world's knowledge of Indian antiquity, her husband scheduled it for immediate publication without review.

"Six weeks ago," she continued, "Vincent returned home in a state of utter dejection. He said that Fordham's report had just arrived from the printer's and was about to be distributed when he suddenly noted some troubling discrepancies in its presentation. In consultation with his chief assistant, Mukherjee, it was decided that Fordham either had made some major errors or had perpetrated a colossal hoax. Although the report had been printed, Vincent determined to delay its publication until an *in situ* investigation could be made. Fordham had recently failed to respond to any of his messages and could not be reached. Only Mukherjee was now aware of the possible hoax, and in order to avoid his own embarrassment as well as embarrassment for the Government as a whole, Vincent decided that he had best make a field investigation himself.

"Mukherjee went ahead. He wired a few days later from Patna that the sites visited by Fordham had been systematically looted by him and a gang of henchmen, that the sites had been all but destroyed for archaeological purposes, and that Fordham had disappeared and probably left India with whatever booty he was able to remove from the ruins. This confirmed my husband's worst fears. He still felt compelled to go to the site himself, for his sense of betrayal was acute.

"Two weeks ago, he departed, leaving Mukherjee in charge of the survey, and, on the pretext that he wanted a few weeks to write up his own archaeological notes, left for the Nepalese Tarai. He promised to wire me as soon as he arrived. But after his departure, I received no word. After ten days of silence, I decided to follow him. Mukherjee accompanied me this far, and has implored me to go no further, for he deemed the natural dangers of the Tarai alone sufficient to deter me. He said that he would notify the Government of what had happened and would send a party of police and sepoys after my husband, but I have steadfastly refused to allow this. My husband wanted to avoid the Fordham affair becoming public knowledge at all costs. And so I find myself in the unenviable position of going to the Tarai jungles alone in search of my husband. It was Mukherjee whom you may have seen earlier with me in the garden. He is still trying to stop me, but I wish to leave for Patna today. From there I shall go to the Tarai."

Toward the end of her description, Holmes could see the fear that gripped her soul emerge on her face.

"I do not think that a venture into the Tarai is a wise one, madam.

The natural dangers of the Himalayan marsh alone should indeed give you pause. And I should be derelict if I were to allow you to continue to believe that your husband may be in the hands of a mere archaeological charlatan. He is, possibly, in the hands of an archcriminal who is most dangerous. The man who calls himself Anthony Fordham is in reality Anton Furer, a thief and plunderer who continues to devastate the archaeological and museum worlds for his own purposes. The false name Fordham is one that he has used on several occasions in the past. I am fully aware of his activities in Hanoi and Hong Kong. The letters from French scholars are forgeries, of course. The French Sûreté has put out a worldwide alert for his capture. It is unfortunate that word appears not to have arrived in India."

She appeared even more frightened than before. "Will he harm my husband?"

"Not until he finds what he is after. We can only hope that he is not already far away in another country plotting other misdeeds and that he has yet to find his prize. Perhaps he needs your husband to find it, perhaps to identify it. In any case, it is imperative that I talk to Mukherjee, and that I go to find your husband."

"Only if I go with you." She uttered the last few words with such firmness that Holmes knew better than to try to dissuade her.

"I do not think it wise for you to come, but I shall not try to stop you if you insist. In any case, I should like to meet with Mukherjee as soon as possible."

Mukherjee had not yet left Banaras, and he appeared at Holmes's hotel within the hour. Mukherjee knew intimately the areas of the Tarai which were of concern and mentioned specific places where Smith might be. He brought with him detailed maps.

"As you know," said Mukherjee, "the area of the Tarai with which we are concerned is very difficult, and we have only begun our archaeological explorations there. The Nepalese Ranas for many years were quite rigid on this point: no entry under any circumstances. For some reason, however, they relented recently, and allowed this expedition."

Holmes smiled at his last words, for it was obvious that some minor figure in the Rana palace had been enticed by Furer with promises of great rewards and had wheedled what he wanted out of the Maharajah.

"A system of rewards is at work here, Mr. Mukherjee, and I don't doubt that Furer will have promised to share his booty with various individuals. Who is the Rana in charge?"

"The area is under the jurisdiction of General Khadga Shamshere, who has absented himself most of the time on shikar. He was present when the first discovery was made: that of the Ashokan pillar at Rummindei. That discovery, as you know, identified that small village as the birthplace of the Buddha. But the General quickly lost interest and allowed Fordham to continue without supervision."

Mukherjee pointed to the map. "The area of exploration is this, circled in red. It is the area between the village of Rummindei, the birthplace of Siddhartha Gautama, the Buddha, and Tilaurakot, the village that probably contains the remains of his father's city. It is between these two sites that the initial investigations were to be made. Once he had made a preliminary survey in this area, Fordham made brief forays in every direction. In several places, he found substantial ruins, which unfortunately for the future of archaeological exploration, he destroyed in what appears to have been a greedy hunt for unknown treasures. All the sites have been disturbed in whole or in part. Knowing the nature of Buddhist ruins, however, I may say that he has misjudged, for it is rare that anything of worth is contained in them."

"And yet," said Holmes, "he continues to look for something, something perhaps of enormous value which would compel him to stay despite the dangerous circumstances. Something keeps him there, this rogue orientalist."

"I have an idea, but it is only a suggestion."

"And what is that?"

"The Piprahwa casket."

"And what is that, pray tell?"

"There is an ancient tradition, still current among Buddhists, that after the Council of Kashmir sometime in the first century B.C., the Emperor Kanishka journeyed to the birthplace of the Buddha and left a gift in memory of his visit, a casket in which jewels of the greatest value were placed, jewels which formed part of the royal Kushan collection. At the same time, relics of the Buddha himself were placed with them in a small cloth sack. The casket was first held in veneration at a stupa near Rummindei, but later it was moved to the city of Kapilavastu, which is where the Buddha grew into manhood and journeyed forth in search of enlightenment."

jew
reli
Fur
dhis
finds
form
Kapi

"N
Tilau

"W

"W
Vincer
to our
knowl
ing Vir
Fordha
herjee.

"It is
hands,

three days. Holmes would travel separately, hoping
tance they so sorely needed-from a friend whom
influence in the Tarai.

"It was by now late in the day," said H
Smith left at once, in time to board the
them to take the last boat across th
doing, they could easily reach
Rummindei on the follow
the hotel."

Holmes waited
loose shirt and tr
that time of
grew dark
where
Ind

...pilavastu, or better Tilau-rakot, since I am sure that it exists by its ancient name on no map and is known to no one save the antiquarians. It is there and perhaps only there that we shall confront Furer."

"I will not stay behind, Mr. Holmes. My duty is to Mr. Smith."

"I was about to say that you could be of inestimable help in our adventure, Mr. Mukherjee, as you have been so far. Yes, indeed, you must come; you must accompany Mrs. Smith and keep her away from danger. And I shall travel by a different route."

Mrs. Smith seemed overjoyed at the thought of leaving Banaras and at the prospect of helping to locate her husband. Holmes was less sanguine, however, knowing that Furer was a hardened criminal, capable of any treachery and cruelty. Indeed, there was always the grim possibility that Furer would find whatever he was searching for before they arrived. In that case, Holmes was sure that Furer would not hesitate to kill Smith and leave his corpse to feed the jackals of the Tarai. But there was no better plan at this point. He instructed Mukherjee to travel with Mrs. Smith by the most direct route to Rummindei, the village where the Buddha had been born, and that they would rendezvous there in

to obtain the assis-
he knew to be of great

olmes. "Mukherjee and Mrs.
next train to Patna, thus enabling
e northern rivers that evening. In so
ne village of Besarh by the next day, and
ng. I bade them good-bye in the garden of

ntil dusk, then slipped into the night wearing the
ousers worn by Indian men. It was disguise enough at
ay, and it would at least facilitate his movements when it
. He hailed a rickshaw that took him to the railway station,
he boarded the train to Motihari, a small town not far from the
ian border with Nepal.

"The car was crowded, and I sat with an Indian family that kindly shared their food with me. When they left the train, I was alone. You may wonder at the perils of the venture I had undertaken, Watson—"

"Indeed," said I, "it is beyond my comprehension. How did you expect even to find Smith, let alone deal with Furer?"

"As you know, Watson, I am adventurous but not foolhardy, and I rarely enter into a matter unless I am reasonably sure of the outcome. In this case, the odds against success were immense, and in all candour, I would not have undertaken the matter save for one thing: I had an ally in the Tarai upon whom I could rely for assistance. If I could find him, he would be of immense aid. His name was Balaram, and he lived in a village called Hariyarpur, not far from Motihari, the main rail stop in the region."

Holmes had met Balaram on his trek south from Katmandu, he said, and Balaram had invited him to break his journey and rest at his home. During his stay, Holmes learned that Balaram commanded the wide respect of the local people, who considered him a rajah of sorts. He came from an ancient family of mountain kings, but his father had been exiled from the hills by his enemies and sent to the jungles of the Tarai in the hope that he and his family would die of the terrible diseases and climate. They survived and prospered instead. Balaram succeeded his father as zamindar and travelled often to visit his various holdings, journeying always as a common man to learn what transpired in the region. In this way he had obtained the affection and loyalty of all who lived under his protection.

"It was night when the train pulled into Motihari," said Holmes. "Luck was with me, for I found at that late hour a tongawallah who knew the road to Hariyarpur and was willing to take me there. I climbed into his ancient vehicle, and we set out at a good speed in a westerly direction."

The road at first was smooth enough, for it was the main route through the region, but soon they turned north toward the Nepalese border. They entered a thick forest, and the path became rough and badly rutted, so that the horses were forced to no more than a walk. As they crossed into the Tarai, Holmes noticed the large white stones that marked the Indian border, and he knew that he was not far from his friend's house. In another hour, he found himself walking through Balaram's rose garden toward his large mansion. The house was dark as Holmes mounted the steps, but in short order, a servant appeared and assured him that his master was there. Holmes was ushered into the drawing room, and in a few minutes a sleepy Balaram greeted him with a warm embrace.

He was a large-boned man, said Holmes, with a large head covered with thick black hair, greying at the temples. He had a round, protruding stomach and spindly legs, on which he moved surprisingly quickly and with grace. His eyes gleamed in the darkness of the room, and Holmes could see his white teeth as he smiled in greeting.

"I am here on a matter of the greatest urgency," said Holmes, "and I need your immediate help."

"Tell me," said Balaram.

As Holmes spoke, the expression on Balaram's face became grim.

"You have a difficult mission," he said. "I have seen this man, this Anthony Fordham, as you call him. 'Mardan,' he is called by the people, or 'gift of death.' He has pillaged everywhere, destroyed temples, reduced villages to ashes, taken the people's gods and sent them away. He has at his disposal several gangs of dacoits who do his every bi' ding, and he rewards them handsomely for their plunder."

"His crimes are everywhere the same," said Holmes, "for perpetrated his evil deeds wherever he has gone. He has cᵣ swath, and in doing so has killed many."

Balaram listened intently as Holmes described some of I

horrible acts. When Holmes had finished, he said nothing for a moment, and his expression grew grave.

"You cannot succeed alone. You must have help," he said. "Come, we must go at once."

Holmes followed his host through the rose garden to the stables. There Balaram kept his elephants, from which he chose the largest for their jungle voyage.

"He will take us anywhere," said Balaram with a smile. He mounted easily, extending a hand to Holmes. As the elephant clambered back to its feet, a servant handed rifles up to each of them.

"Let us see," said Balaram gleefully, his mouth filled with pan, "what trouble we can make for this feringhi."

The moon now was a thin white crescent, brilliant in the almost cloudless sky. Holmes listened intently to the forest, the rustle of the wind, the owls and other night birds, the scurrying of small creatures, and watched with a certain amount of attention the occasional pair of yellow eyes that stared intently after them and then moved on.

The elephant followed closely every signal of Balaram, and Holmes soon became used to its movements. An hour into their trip, Balaram slowed the massive beast and changed direction, moving now to the west. Soon they reached a village. Balaram signalled the elephant to stop. They dismounted and were instantly greeted by three men, naked except for loincloths. They moved noiselessly, and Holmes judged them immediately by their features and dark colour to be of the Tharu tribe, an ancient race of the Tarai.

Balaram questioned them for several minutes before he turned to Holmes and said: "These men had originally been part of Furer's archaeological team, but they left when they realised that he was pillaging everything he found, including their own shrines. They have complained to the local police, but to no avail. The police are afraid, for Furer now has as his chief ally Gagan Singh, the leading dacoit of this area. His gang of twenty-five are now with Furer in Tilaurakot, five miles from here. With him is Smith, who has been badly treated, and since last night, Mukherjee and Mrs. Smith, who were captured just after they alighted from the train in Gorakhpur."

As Balaram spoke, Holmes realised that the situation had worsened considerably. "All is not lost, however," said Balaram. "There is indeed someone who can help, and that is a young officer here, a member of the Ahir tribe by the name of Jang Bahadur. He is incorruptible, one of the few who has refused the blandishments offered him by thief and government official alike. They have sent word to him, and he should arrive shortly."

In but a few moments a young man strode up, a rather burly fellow with an almost miraculous black moustache. He wore the uniform of the police. He smiled as he entered, flashing a large set of white teeth. Jang Bahadur bowed and then spoke quickly to Balaram, who then addressed Holmes.

"Aware of Fordham's depredations over the last month, Jang Bahadur has raised a group of some sixty armed men, who are ready to accompany us to Kapilavastu. We shall surround Fordham and his gang, since they can have little inkling of our presence as yet."

Balaram quickly described the route and their plan of attack. Holmes expressed his keen desire to enter Furer's camp and deal directly with him. He was an old enemy, he added. Holmes also explained that there should be no shooting unless absolutely necessary and that more important than the capture of Fordham was the safety of Mr. and Mrs. Smith and Mr. Mukherjee. Balaram assured Holmes that once the men were in place, the plan would go according to his wishes.

"Jang Bahadur agreed to meet us near the Furer camp with his men just before dawn," said Holmes. "Balaram and I and the Tharus who had joined us walked out of the hut into the cool night. The elephant was left behind in the village.

"Despite his age, Balaram travelled in the jungle at great speed. He knew the area well, for he had grown up in a village not distant from his present home. I could do nothing but follow. The jungle was dark, and the only things visible were the dirt path and the white turbans of the men before us.

"Three hours of this and we were close to our quarry. We came to a clearing near the outskirts of Tilaurakot. Balaram entered a small hut and motioned me to follow. In a few minutes, Jang Bahadur entered. He announced that the Furer camp was now completely surrounded by his men, who were fully armed. Neither Furer nor Gagan Singh and his dacoits could escape. The rest, he said, was now up to us."

Holmes and Balaram proceeded to enter the camp, moving as close as they could to the central fire. Except for a guard, the entire group appeared to be asleep. Smith, his wife, and Mukherjee were huddled together on the ground, not far from the fire, their hands and feet tied. The dacoits lay asleep everywhere. There were several tents, in one of which Furer presumably slept, and in another Gagan Singh, the head of the dacoits, also unaware of what was taking place.

"I decided then on a dramatic but rather reckless move. I walked directly over to the guard and told him in Hindustanee to take me to Furer. So startled was he by the sudden appearance of a tall Englishman in the middle of the jungle that, rather than give the alarm, he simply led me over to Furer's tent. Furer was asleep, a rifle beside him. I pulled it away, and he was instantly awake. It was too late. I held the gun to his head.

" 'Move ever so slowly, Furer. Quietly, not a word.' He did as he was told. I must say, Watson, that rarely in my career has anyone's face shown the disbelief and fear that Furer's displayed when he recognised me as I held the rifle to his left temple. He shivered with fear but watched carefully for the slightest hesitation on my part. I motioned him to untie his prisoners, which he did with great despatch. I motioned the frightened Smiths and Mukherjee to follow Balaram. We walked past our men into safety. By now, Furer had turned white, as if he had seen a ghost."

It was at this point that things took an unexpected turn, said Holmes. Furer, overcome with fear and knowing that he had been outwitted, turned and bolted back into the camp, screaming to his men that they should wake up and fight. But the warning came too late. Unwilling to allow their escape, Jang Bahadur and his men took full advantage of their position. What followed was an inevitable massacre. The entire gang of thieves and murderers was wiped out as they rose from their beds.

"Leaving the Smiths and Mukherjee with one of the Tharus as guard, I rushed back into the chaotic scene. By the time I arrived, it was all over. No one had escaped. In the early morning light, the grisly picture was clear. Twenty-four dacoits, including Gagan Singh and Furer's three European henchmen, lay dead. A fourth, severely wounded but alive, was the only survivor and was taken for questioning. To my great consternation, however, Furer had escaped. He was nowhere to be found. He had taken advantage of the brief moment given him before the firing began to plunge alone into the jungle. Whether he crouched nearby or was still running aimlessly in the wild, I had no idea.

"I decided to let fate take its course. Should Furer survive, I knew he would cross my path again. We made no attempt to locate him. A message was sent to both the Indian and the Nepalese authorities to be on the lookout for him, but he had made good his escape."

They camped that night in the safety of their escort near Simraongarh, and the following day arrived at the Indian border, where Holmes bade good-bye to Balaram and Jang Bahadur, and left with the Smiths and Mukherjee for Delhi. It was during this train ride that Holmes learned from Vincent Smith the details of his ordeal. Threatened with torture constantly, he had however managed to lead Furer astray until by accident they stumbled upon the stupa that housed what Furer had been looking for: the casket of Kanishka.

"You may imagine my consternation, Mr. Holmes, when I saw this most valuable treasure of ancient India fall into his hands. He gloated over it constantly until the uncomfortable moment came when he realised that he no longer needed my presence. He cruelly discussed a variety of ways of despatching me, including leaving me in a wounded condition for the wild animals to devour. Only the capture of my wife and Mukherjee distracted him long enough to avoid my execution. He then sent one of his henchmen, Aubert, off with the casket. It is lost to us now, but someday I hope that we may recover it."

"Of this, I have little doubt, though it may take time," Holmes replied. "You may be sure that Balaram and Jang Bahadur will do all they can to trace it and to return it, perhaps for safekeeping in London."

Holmes's sojourn in Delhi was short, and it was only just before he was to leave that Smith informed him of the latest concerning Furer. He had been seen moving toward Katmandu but had disappeared once again. The Nepalese authorities had been notified, but no reply had been received from them. Furer had again outwitted all who had tried to apprehend him.

"And so, Watson, we come to the end of my account of the events in India that led to the apprehension of Furer here in London many years later."

"A most incredible tale, Holmes. And how did you know that the Buddha contained the casket? And why were there two Buddhas?"

Holmes laughed. "There may be more than two. But I leave the answers to these questions to you, my dear Watson. It was all a very simple matter of deduction. Come, it is late, and I have talked enough. If we hurry, we can still enjoy an ale before we return home."

And so we walked quickly to Holmes's favourite pub near the British Museum and forgot about Anton Furer.

THE GIANT RAT

OF SUMATRA

I N READING OVER THE MANY ACCOUNTS THAT I HAVE PLACED before the public concerning the exploits of my friend Sherlock Holmes, I have noted that their pages contain many references to cases as yet unpublished. For reasons of discretion, almost all of these tales will forever remain untold. Only one of them, "The Adventure of the Second Stain," did I decide long ago, with Holmes's expressed permission, to publish at the appropriate moment.

Another of these cases, I now find, fits the present annals so very well that its publication in them is quite necessary if Holmes's experiences in the Orient are ever to appear in their entirety. The episode took place during Holmes's lengthy voyages in the Dutch Indies. The reader may remember that I have alluded to it once before, in the introductory words to the strange case of the Sussex Vampire. The story concerns the ship *Matilda Briggs* and the giant rat of Sumatra, a tale for which Holmes then believed that the world was not yet prepared. Indeed, no other case undertaken by him before or since shows so clearly the dreadful effects of the contact of primitive peoples with European civilisation.

In presenting this adventure, I have chosen to let Holmes speak for himself. The original is written in his own words, the manuscript of which he gave me after his return to England. Addressed to me, it was set down in his careful hand during some moments of calm in Singapore before he boarded a ship destined for the Levant. The prose is in Holmes's usual laconic and terse style. After an initial reading, I placed it in the tin box that holds so many of his papers at Cox & Co. in Charing Cross. Although Holmes has expressed to me a lingering doubt as to whether it should appear now, he reluctantly agreed with my judgement that its inclusion in the present collection was most appropriate, indeed necessary, if his Oriental adventures were ever to reach completion. The manuscript is undated, and I present it here without change.

My dear Watson,

I have decided to record for you, and perhaps someday for the public for whom you have chronicled a number of my cases, an account of events that took place shortly before I arrived here in Singapore. The heat here is intolerable, and I can write only in the early hours of the morning, but I must finish before I leave.

In the spring of 1893, I travelled south in Bengal to Chittagong, where I had booked passage to the Dutch Indies on a ship called the Matilda Briggs. *I had chosen it because of the rather circuitous route it was scheduled to take to its ultimate destination, namely Batavia, the capital of the Dutch colonies. From Chittagong, the ship was to enter the Bay of Bengal, calling at the Andaman Islands, then at various ports of call, first along the southern coast of Burma near Pagan, then proceeding on to Malaya and Singapore before reaching the island of Java. The trip was to last at least three weeks and perhaps longer, for such freighters move according to no fixed schedule and often stop in remote and unexpected places. This suited me well, for I was in need of a period of calm after my exploits in the Indian Subcontinent.*

The ship bore the American flag and, in addition to its cargo, carried a dozen passengers. I was happy to learn as soon as we embarked that, except for two people who figure in the events that follow, the remaining passengers were of no interest to me. Six of them consisted of an American missionary, a Mr. Blackton, and his family; another three were an aged Dutch couple and their crippled daughter returning to Batavia after a trip to Holland; the remaining two passengers I shall describe presently. Had I looked for intelligent stimulation, I should have been sorely disappointed, but I sought only the calm of the sea to soothe my nerves and limbs, by now exhausted by India.

For this voyage, I had again changed my identity. This was merely an added precaution, since it was not unlikely that some of my cleverer enemies, notably the criminal Anton Furer, now aware of my existence, might try to follow me. I travelled as William Redfern, a person with no visible means of support but one who professed an amateur interest in the archaeology of Asia in general and of the Dutch Indies in particular. In order not to cause undue comment, I dined every evening with the captain and the other guests but otherwise took my meals in my quarters, which were on the upper deck. The meals below were of tolerably short duration and, except for the occasional raucous behaviour of the American children, they were pleasant enough. The captain was a large Swede, whose overwhelming interest was first the sea, and second the food that was served.

It was toward the end of what was an uneventful voyage that I came to know two passengers, Baron Maupertuis, formerly of the Netherlands-Sumatra Company, and his wife, who, as I was to learn very quickly, was of English blood. It was not long into our first conversation that I realised that she was Ellen, née Hodgson, the youngest sister of the Oriental scholar Brian Hodgson, the tale of whose "ghost" I may one day relate to you. The Maupertuises were a witty diplomatic couple, and although I ordinarily tire of such company, I found their presence a relief from what had by then become the tedium of a hot and eventless voyage. I had ventured ashore on several occasions, however, particularly at Pagan, to satisfy my curiosity about archaeological monuments, and spent my late evenings in writing up my notes about them. You may have seen the work Ruins of Old Burma by William Redfern, a monograph published upon my return, which was entirely the result of this journey.

Baron Maupertuis was descended from an old Dutch family of Utrecht and had been in the service of his country for many years. After a term in Amsterdam, he had been assigned as Resident to the court of the Maharajah of Jogjakarta, and it was there that he and his wife were to reside.

On the last day of the voyage, they extracted a promise from me that I would visit and spend a few days with them in central Java. I agreed readily, for the voyage had taken far longer than I had expected. I was frankly bored now by the sea, aching for a fresh place for the eye and a new problem for the brain.

We parted in Batavia, they continuing on to Jogjakarta, and I staying on in this large city to see what I could of it in the short time that I had allotted to the task. It was the usual teeming Oriental metropolis, hot and filled with smoke like much of the East, but without that sense of mystery that I found in Calcutta. Islam had cleansed this once Hindu Buddhist island of much of its earlier beliefs and with them much of its artistic wealth. As throughout Asia, the Mahometan armies *and converts had defaced or destroyed much of what had lain in their path. After a week of desultory wandering, I decided to leave, the high point of my visit having been the apprehension of a rather silly pickpocket who, thinking to rob my purse, nearly received a broken wrist.*

I was rested from the voyage and now felt my old energy returning, despite the oppressive heat. So far, my stay had proved uninteresting. If nothing else, however, I wanted to visit the ancient monuments of Java before I moved on. It was then that I sent word to Baron Maupertuis that I should be arriving in a few days in Jogjakarta and that I hoped his invitation was still open. I received a reply the same day, saying that I would be most welcome to stay as their guest as long as I should like. I sent a wire with an immediate reply of acceptance.

I journeyed to Jogjakarta by train and was met at the railway station by the Baron's servants. Soon after I was ensconced in his palatial abode. The Residence is a large Dutch bungalow surrounded by wide gardens in the Amsterdam style. It was within walking distance of the kraton, or palace of the Maharajah, a large compound that dominated the city and stood at its very centre.

It was on one evening of my stay that I obtained my first glimpse of the society of Jogjakarta. The Maupertuises gave a lavish dinner party, to which the Maharajah himself paid a short visit. He was by now a very old man, very thin and frail, but his eyes were still bright, and his regal air commanded attention despite his advanced age and feeble manner. Much of the merchant community was in attendance, particularly those who made large fortunes in these tropical islands. Their round faces and stomachs told me all that I needed to know, and I soon found myself tiring of the glitter.

Maupertuis must have noted my discomfort, for at one point he grabbed me by the sleeve and pulled me across the room to a far corner, in which sat a rather professorial gentleman whom I had not noticed before.

"This is the gentleman I met on our last voyage, of whom I have already spoken," said Maupertuis, introducing me. "He is very interested in the archaeological remains on the islands. And this," he said, turning to me, "is Professor Van Ruisdael of Leiden."

Van Ruisdael greeted me with a slight nod. He did not rise, I think not out of any innate rudeness but rather because his bulk made it difficult for him to move out of his chair. He was an enormous man even seated, one who projected immense intellectual and physical energy. His face was round, his head bald with a fringe of long brown hair, and he had small, dark, but penetrating eyes. He motioned me into the chair next to him and we began to talk.

Van Ruisdael until then I had known only by name. He was one of the leading archaeologists of Europe and was by training a paleontologist, one who had made significant discoveries in the Pyrenees with regard to early mammals. He had been asked by the Dutch Government to lead the archaeological explorations of the East Indies, and had been in Java for over three years.

"I gather that you are an archaeologist," he began, with a slight tone of condescension. His English was almost perfect, but in the few words he uttered he communicated an overwhelming self-confidence.

"Not by training, only by continuing interest," I answered in Dutch, a language which I had spoken since childhood. My answer, in his native language, delighted him, and we both laughed.

"An Englishman who speaks perfect Dutch, a rare pleasure indeed!"

He seemed genuinely pleased, and our conversation continued that evening in both languages. We discussed the ancient ruins of India and the rest of Asia, comfortably isolating ourselves from the other guests.

Van Ruisdael had just finished the initial clearing of the famous Buddhist site known as Borobudur and had begun the preliminary investigation of a series of Hindu temples at Prembanan, a village not far from Jogjakarta. But at a certain moment, his voice took on a more serious tone and he said: "But the monuments have not much interest for me. I am interested in deeper things, what lies behind them, perhaps."

I asked him to describe these things, and without hesitation he answered: "These monuments, all of the historic period, all very recent from the point of view of mankind's long history, all lifeless stone even though some of them bear remarkably beautiful sculptures, are the result of long processes about which we know very little. They are of greater interest to the historian than they are to me, for I am interested in origins, in human origins and man's early society, in the earliest creatures man knew and domesticated, and his relationship to them. I am interested, in other words, in the origins of man's culture. As you know I began as a paleontologist concentrating on early mammals. It was only natural, therefore, that when I started to work on the Hindu temples of Java I became intrigued with their portrayal of animals and other fantastic creatures. Have you ever looked at Hindu sculpture not from the point of view of religious fantasy but from the point of view of reality, from its paleontological aspects?"

I said that I had not really ever considered the question, that I assumed the rich imagination of the Hindu had conceived these creations for didactic purposes, but that the world often turned out to be stranger than we first conceived it to be.

Van Ruisdael looked at me and said quite simply: "I too for the longest time shared your view. But my investigations have begun to lead me to see things differently. I believe now that these may be more than what we have believed them to be. These temples, with giant apes and monkeys, half-men, half-birds, elephant-headed god-men riding on birds, on rodents, on bulls, four-armed deities, what indeed does all this represent?"

"Surely," I said, "you do not believe that these are images of actual creatures of the past?"

He laughed and said, "In most cases not, though I do not believe that they are imaginary either. I believe, however, that they may be ancient forms later represented, even distorted, by religious life, the memory of ancient life-forms used in early prehistoric ritual and sacrifices, perhaps now lost to us. In some cases, however, I am not sure what to believe."

His face became quite serious, and he moved slowly in his chair, searching in one of his coat pockets, from which he took a small, circular silver box. He handed it to me and asked me to open it and examine its contents. In it I found a small whitish object, about a quarter of an inch long, that I immediately recognised as a tooth.

"An incisor," I said, "probably of Rodens communis or Rattus rattus alexandrinus, the common field rat."

"Yes, indeed," said he. "Now look at this." He then pulled a larger box from his coat and invited me to open it. Again, I found a whitish object, this time over four inches long, in form exactly like the first, only much larger. It was embedded in a black rock and had been partially fossilised.

"Extraordinary," I said, "in form almost exactly like the first, except that it is many times bigger. It is the tooth of a rodent, or a rodentlike creature, but one of enormous size. I have never seen anything quite like it. The collections of Europe contain nothing remotely comparable."

"You are obviously well versed in paleontology. You are correct. It is a rare find, from Sumatra in fact, where the species flourished millions of years ago but is now extinct. It is the tooth of a giant rat, an animal that may have been several feet long, an extremely dangerous and efficient creature, I might add. It is difficult to imagine what havoc could be wreaked by such an animal. One need only think of the speed of the common rat and add great size to it. There are few who could have recognised precisely what this is, and I compliment you. Perhaps you would like to visit my laboratory at some point and see some of my other specimens. I think you would find it most interesting."

"Indeed, I should like to very much," I replied. "Doch dieser Schwelle Zauber zu zerspalten, Bedarf ich eines Rattenzahns," said I, quoting old Goethe.

Van Ruisdael smiled. " 'To break through this magic door, I need a rat's tooth.' So said Mephistopheles. Let us see what magic doors we must break through, then."

Van Ruisdael explained that he would be visiting a pair of newly discovered sites outside the city and would be gone for several days. I would be welcome at any time after that. We continued to talk, and by the time we parted, most of the guests had left.

"I trust that you two had a pleasant and interesting talk," said our host.

"Yes, indeed," said Van Ruisdael. "Your friend here is well informed, an excellent archaeologist." He then bade us all good evening. My eyes followed his huge bulk as he made his way to the door.

When we were alone, Maupertuis turned to me and said: "A brilliant mind, that one. But he knows no limits and takes great chances with his life. On two occasions now, I have had to go into the remote interior of our islands here to rescue him. He is fearless and will do anything for his science. He has no family, no close friends. His life is devoted to his work and his work only."

"It is a devotion which I greatly admire," I said.

"He must have sensed that, for you are the first person in whom I have seen him take other than ordinary passing interest."

Maupertuis took out an old silver pocket watch and said, "It is late, and I still must prepare a document for the Maharajah's signature in the morning. Sleep well, my dear friend."

I watched the Baron as he slowly made his way up the circular staircase. I retired shortly thereafter, thinking that for the first time since I had left India something unusual was about to take place.

It was only toward the end of the week that I heard from Van Ruisdael. In a short note, which I received early one morning, he informed me that his trip had been unusually successful and that, if I were still of a mind, I could come over the following day at around four.

Finding Van Ruisdael's quarters took longer than I expected. He lived off the Marleboro, in a boardinghouse called the Peacock Throne on one of those winding alleys behind the bazaar. After passing through a long series of low archways, one eventually came to a dead end. There, to the right, was a small wooden signboard with a peacock carved on it.

I knocked on the gate and was immediately ushered in by a servant who took me to the professor's quarters. The courtyard just the other side of the gate was beautifully cultivated. Flowers bloomed everywhere, and the small hotel, which is what it was, was very tidy, unlike the rest of the city.

Van Ruisdael occupied a small white cottage at the back of the larger house toward the far end of the garden. It was a stucco building, with a green tin roof. There was a narrow porch, which ran the circumference of the house. High walls gave his residence almost complete privacy.

When I entered, he was seated at his desk in a very large room that served as both his parlour and his study. There were books and papers almost everywhere, and where there were not, there were bones, and specimens of every conceivable variety. In a quick glance at the shelves on the walls I noticed several large fossils, including the thighbone of an ancient ass, the skull of what looked to be an early ape, and several large specimens completely unfamiliar to me. One shelf contained enormous seashells, presumably of creatures long since vanished from the surrounding oceans. Van Ruisdael was apparently sorting through some of his latest finds, for there were boxes everywhere, some half-opened, in which I could see the fruits of his recent explorations. He rose to greet me and wasted no time in bringing me to a comfortable chair near his desk.

There was a troubled look on his face but excitement in his eyes, a contradiction set deep in his expression, as if he had found something of the greatest scientific interest, but at the same time mysterious and deeply troubling.

"It appears that your explorations were successful," I said to him, pointing to one of the open cartons.

"Beyond my wildest expectations, my friend. Just a few days' walk from here, I came upon a field of enormous richness in an unexplored area. Every conceivable kind of ancient form is to be found there. Look at this, a hitherto unknown form of Suinus selvaticus, an ancient wild boar, and this, a human-seeming skull, of unknown age and form. There is no end to it: an area of remains that covers several square kilometres that will need the most careful scrutiny."

Van Ruisdael became breathless as he talked, and beads of perspiration appeared on his forehead as he continued to move his great bulk animatedly through the room, with far more grace than I had at first thought possible. He continued to expatiate on his findings, throwing new ideas out as fast as he could utter them. There was much in his talk, much that I immediately had to reject as the first sketches of a brain hard at work, but I could not deny his genius: I was in the presence of a first-rate mind at work on material of the utmost scientific importance.

His face suddenly darkened. He turned toward his desk, picked up an object from it, and handed it to me. "Look at this," he said. "What do you make of it?"

As soon as I saw it, I realised why he was disturbed. It was a large tooth, exactly the same as the fossil specimen of the giant rat that he had shown me a few nights before.

"This is the same as the fossil," I said, "only it is modern. There is something wrong. If the fossil is what we think it is, then the creature has survived to the present from prehistoric times. But there is no other evidence for this. And no one has ever seen or described such a creature. Perhaps we have a coincidence of forms. This may be the tooth of a different animal, perhaps a member of another family."

"The fact that no one has ever seen or reported such a creature is no argument against its existence. I agree that it is strange that such a creature would have survived and its existence still be largely unsuspected, but it is not impossible."

"Let us eliminate whatever is impossible," I said, "and whatever remains, no matter how improbable, must be the solution. In this case, there is no absolute impossibility, but a near one. The idea of a giant-sized rat surviving in its prehistoric form would go against the entire evolutionary trend of the species. Yet, we cannot rule it out. Do you intend to return to the field where you found it? If you do, I should be most happy to accompany you. Whether this turns out to be as interesting as it seems or not, I would at least get to see the field as a whole and the place of this rather incredible series of finds."

"I would be most happy if you accompanied me, Redfern, for reaching the find spot entails a very difficult trip. It lies about fifty kilometres to the east of Solo in a deep depression in the central mountains. I do not know if any Dutchman has ever penetrated so far before, but I would prefer not to return alone this time. One never knows—a slip, a slight misstep, and one is down a precipice or into a chasm. A broken leg, or even an ankle, and one is doomed. And, besides," he said, "who knows what we will find?"

With the greatest alacrity, I accepted his invitation, and we made arrangements to depart early the following morning. A tonga was to pick us up at dawn to take us with our supplies to the next large town, Bulayo. There we would begin the walk toward the fields themselves.

The ride to Bulayo proceeded without incident. We passed through wide paddy fields and then entered the town. There we were met by two porters who were to carry our supplies. It was now about ten in the morning, and the sun already beat upon us relentlessly. Having given instructions to our guide, we began the trek, upward and eastward toward the foot of the central mountains. We were to pass over this first range to the valley that lay on the other side. It was here that the field Van Ruisdael had discovered lay.

The path we took went first through a large and dense forest. It was a well-

travelled track, clear of obstacles, and the undergrowth had made no inroads in it. Our progress was rapid for the first three hours, and we reached a clearing near the top of the range at around one in the afternoon. There we rested, shaded by some large trees, and waited for the porters to prepare our food.

"Another hour or so upward," said Van Ruisdael, "and we shall be at the top. From there you will be able to see our destination, the richest field in the world."

It was after we reached the top that I realised why Van Ruisdael had been so reluctant to return alone, for the descent lay by a steep and rocky path passing along the valley that stretched some five hundred feet below. One misstep and one easily fell straight down into a deep gorge cut by an ancient river. The valley itself, however, was a lush lowland, forested in part, in others filled with large rocks of what I took to be basalt.

Van Ruisdael pointed to a yellowish patch on the side of the hills opposite to us. "There it is," he said, "our destination. With luck we should be there by nightfall."

The descent was arduous, and I remember several times feeling that I should rather not tempt the gods so often in steep places. Except for blistered feet, however, we made it to the bottom without incident. There, after a rather harrowing cross over the gorge on a narrow footbridge, we began our trek through the valley, proceeding always in an easterly direction. We passed through a thick forest, slashing our way, until toward dusk, we reached the place that Van Ruisdael had pointed out from the ridge. Yellow earth, patches of elephant grass—it was exactly as he had described it to me. Night came almost instantly as the sun flashed gold behind the blue mountains in the west that we had just traversed, and we could see no more. We decided to set up our camp and retire early. The porters cooked our simple dinner, and we prepared for bed.

Van Ruisdael impressed me again with his physical energy and agility despite his great size. Silent for most of our journey, he now began to speak excitedly of his plans for the morrow.

"We have our work ahead of us," he said happily. "Tomorrow we shall begin our investigations. I have already measured the field and laid out our plans. In the morning we shall discuss them in detail. Our workers should be here by five. Local villagers, they are the people who helped me on my initial visit. Let us now get some rest."

In the early morning, just before five, the workers arrived, all residents of a local village save one, a fat, sweaty Javanese who appeared to have engaged the others.

We spent the next several hours with them, explaining the schedule of work, and the tasks that lay immediately ahead. The fat Javanese was named Uru, and it was he who acted as interpreter when needed. He spoke English, Javanese, and the nameless dialect shared by the others.

The next three days were days of deep engagement with the tasks at hand. Van Ruisdael had previously chosen the exact site where we were to work. It was promptly cleared, a trench laid out, and the excavation begun. We were soon absorbed in the relentless work of marking each specimen as it came forth, noting its size, nature, and location.

The workmen, five in all, arrived each morning at daybreak. Uru gave the necessary directions to them. Van Ruisdael and I supervised, and he alone almost effortlessly organised the packing of the specimens that we were to take back with us. We took a break from one to three during the heat of the day; otherwise we worked constantly until nightfall.

It was only after the first three days of excavation that Van Ruisdael and I began to discuss the pattern of the finds. It was evident to us that the site was a peculiar one indeed. Disturbed is the word often used, and the anomaly of many of the finds continued to perplex us. There were incomparable riches for science embedded in this field, of this there was no doubt, and much of it was destined to extend the frontiers of paleontological knowledge far beyond their present confines. But repeatedly we found the rather sinister problem that had presented itself in Van Ruisdael's study: we had found again not only teeth but various other remains of the large Sumatran rat in fossil form together with a variety of other specimens in various strata. But in a group of surface finds, remains of the exact same species of rat were met in unquestionably recent, and unchanged, form. Indeed, the number of recent specimens was far greater than the ancient.

"This large rat exists," said Van Ruisdael, one evening, "and continues to exist even now. This is the inescapable conclusion that we must face: the Sumatran rat has suddenly reappeared after a long absence from the fossil record. But how can this be?"

"I remain as perplexed as you," said I, "but we must continue to search for a rational explanation. It may be that its reappearance here is due to some recent event, and that the continuity of its record lies elsewhere and can be supplied from other sites. But the gap remains enormous. The oldest of these surface finds can be no older than a century at most. There is something else, however, that is equally, if not more disturbing, my dear Professor."

"And what is that?" he asked.

"It is this: that the Sumatran rat, whether of the prehistoric or more recent record, was apparently always killed in the same way. Have you noticed? The available skulls record a blow to the head that despatched the giant rodent almost instantly. We are apparently in a killing field, where the rat and other animal corpses were brought after death. If that is the case, then we are faced with an even more insoluble problem: how and why were they killed, for killing them was no mean feat. This was a fearsome creature, of the greatest agility and ferociousness. How was it killed? And, perhaps, most perplexing of all, by whom?"

My words seemed to disturb him, and he appeared doubtful, ready to take my thoughts as supporting his own theories but also unwilling to continue the discussion.

"Redfern, my dear Redfern, we are speculating without knowing, but your words tend to confirm my hypothesis. Is the rat wild, or domesticated? Perhaps it is both. If the oldest ones were killed in a uniform way, then perhaps they were killed by some early humans, in sacrificial ritual perhaps, after they were captured and raised for a time. Perhaps, as you say, we have stumbled upon a sacrificial field. It is in such ritual that we have the beginnings of religion—all later religions, the great temples, the great sculpture, and the great texts—all stem from these early original sacrifices. But enough, we must do our work, then analyse, and theorise, but only after we have all the evidence."

"Nevertheless, the rat is with us now," I said, "whatever its history. And it is not alone."

"You are right," said he quietly. He spoke no more but rose up silently, and went to his tent.

I sat for a few moments longer at the fire.

It was cool now, and I watched the dying embers for a few moments. What Van Ruisdael did not want to contemplate was the obvious: that nearby perhaps, in some hidden place, the giant rat and the humans around it lived still, bound in some mysterious and as yet unknown relation.

Entering my tent, I lay down but could not sleep. I continued to be disturbed by the perplexities of the finds. The jungle was noisy with the sounds of various creatures, and it was at about two in the morning that a complete silence, broken only by the occasional rustle of the wind in the trees, spread over it. Unable to fall asleep, I arose, thinking to read by my lantern for a while. But first, I thought, I must have a look round.

I could see Van Ruisdael blissfully asleep, lying not far from the campfire. There were clouds and a few stars, and a moon covered with mist, but there was enough *light to walk by. Our guides were sleeping softly and almost silently. The nearest path I could see went up a hill in the direction opposite to the dig. It was a path that I had not taken so far, and I decided to climb it.*

It was only when I reached the top that I realised how close we were to the sea, less perhaps than half a mile. I found myself looking through a cleft in the mountains to a small cove over which the moon had spread its silver light. I could hear the faint sound of the moving sea.

As I stood watching, I noticed a light blinking onshore. It flashed several times at regular intervals of a minute or two. Then I saw an answering signal, distant, on the ocean. I decided to go nearer.

As I approached the place of the first signal, the light at sea came closer, and I realised that a small boat had just landed. I heard the splash as several people left the boat and the low murmur of voices. Someone said in accented English, "Quiet, no lights now. Not until we reach the rocks. We are very close. Someone might hear."

The group moved close to me, to some rocks just to my left, where they lit a fire and talked. There were five men, four Europeans and one native. The native I recognised as Uru, our foreman. It was he who spoke first.

"Tomorrow night, no later. That is the time. There will be no moon. Come in the dark. Wait."

"Very well. How many will we be able to take?" said his interlocutor.

"Maybe two hundred, maybe more."

The light moved toward the European speaker, obviously the leader of the group, and I recognised to my amazement the Swedish captain of the Matilda Briggs, *the ship on which I had travelled to Batavia.*

"Good. We shall be here then. We shall come in plenty of time. Do not fail us, Uru. You have done well in the past. Here is your money."

As he spoke, he handed Uru a bag. Uru grabbed it greedily and clutched it to his chest.

The captain and his men rose, returned to the small boat, and began the trip back to their ship, now a dark shadow on the moonlit horizon. Uru slipped away into the night, and I went to my tent.

In the early morning, the men were there, including Uru. They told us that they would work as usual that day, but only until four. When pressed by Van Ruisdael, they answered that they had an important festival to attend that night. Van Ruisdael, disappointed at the delay, was forced to acquiesce.

"We shall spend the day speculating about this festival," he said in jest.

Uru, too, said that he was busy, and that he would not work that day or the next. He left, and I was relieved to see him go.

I said nothing to Van Ruisdael about the events of the night before, and I continued my silence, for I had not wished to disturb him or his work. He moved to his tent with his notes, and I remained at the site with the four workmen, with whom I had not tried in any way before to communicate, except in matters pertaining to the excavation. One of them, a young man by the name of Bulang, spoke some English, though he never spoke it in front of Uru. I motioned to him and asked that he accompany me for a moment. We walked away from the site and the others, and I questioned him about the festival.

He was reticent at first, concerned that I was merely trying to persuade him and the others to work on the festival day, for he repeated many times that it was a most important day for them. I reassured him, and told him that I was interested in his people and their history. That was all. He then began to talk, and although I understood only part of what he said, the main outline was clear. His tribe was a branch of the Batak of Sumatra, an ancient hill tribe that had tried to maintain its independence from the Dutch. They called themselves Norom-Batak, for they came from a place on Sumatra near Toba, called in their language Norom. His people were "sea gypsies," nomads who had had many homes and had lived in many places. This was one of the main *seron*, or domiciles. They had lived here for many generations, and had learned how to survive both the sea and the jungle. At first, their life on land was hard, for the wild animals were ferocious, particularly the giant rat, which attacked them. But their god, Kallo, entered the rat, and the rat became their friend. Kallo was worshipped then as the giant black rat, who protected them, and whom they protected.

One day, Kallo left and spoke to them from the sky, saying that they must return to Norom. And so, as they had done so many times in the past, the entire tribe left and returned to their ancestral home in Sumatra.

At first, their meeting with their kinsmen was peaceful. Kallo reappeared, and they were happy. But soon there was fighting, for Maharjo Dhirjo, the king of the Bataks, and Kallo were enemies. Kallo placed a curse on Maharjo, and as a result, Marjan, a white man, came. The white man was Kallo's friend, but Maharjo killed him in a dispute, and Kallo became angry. He said to his people that they should leave, taking his two youngest children, and return to Java. Because of Marjan's death, he told them that he would no longer be black but white. And so the tribe took to the sea, with the two children of Kallo, one female, one male, and came once again to this place. Here they raised Kallo's children, and succeeding generations. They worshipped Kallo daily, and tomorrow was his great festival.

I asked him where the festival was to take place. He pointed to a hill to the north. There he said was Kallo's great house and where they kept the descendants of Kallo's children. These were the last two, and they were old. Kallo had told them that there would be no more and that they would have to move again. So the tribe was assembling for the great festival, where Kallo would speak to them and tell them what they should do.

I asked him whether I could visit Kallo's house. He said that he would show it to me, but that I must not tell anyone. I could also come to the festival, he said, as long as I was hidden from view. Kallo would not want me to come to harm.

I sent word through one of the workmen to Van Ruisdael that I would be gone for a few hours. Absorbed in his cataloguing, he paid no attention, and in a few moments Bulang and I were lost from sight on the thick jungle trail up the slope of the northern mountain. Bulang moved quickly and silently, and I followed as rapidly as I could. It would have been impossible to find the place without him, for at a certain point the path diverged in several directions. Bulang took the one to the right, and we began a steep climb for several hundred feet. Then suddenly above our heads there appeared the first step of an ancient stone stairway. Bulang jumped onto it, pulled me up, and we made our way up the stairs to a clearing at the top.

What I observed thoroughly surprised me. This was an enormous stone temple complex, the likes of which had never been suspected in this part of the world. It was deserted when we entered. The main temple rose like some dark pyramid into the sky several hundred yards away. Directly in front of us were large sculptures of fantastic animals, large sea turtles, fish, and behind them jungle animals, elephants, tigers, snakes, and finally, at the foot of the temple, a column at the top of which stood a giant rat, its fangs bared, its claws ready to do battle. Its white colour stood in bold contrast to the blackened stone of everything else. Bulang told me that this was Kallo.

Bulang motioned me past the column, and I ascended the temple with him. The top was flat and contained nothing except what appeared to be an altar. He motioned to me to be silent, and we descended to a jungle area behind the temple. Once in it, I realised that it was merely a narrow ring of foliage hiding an enormous stone amphitheatre. In the centre was a large pit some fifty feet deep. Upon looking down into it, I saw what no one had ever seen before: a giant rat of Sumatra, alive but apparently moribund. It was attached by a heavy iron chain to the wall and appeared to be almost asleep. Bulang saw my look of horror, and said that there was nothing to fear. The animal appeared to be at least ten feet long, and while I realised there was no immediate danger, its size and look produced a re-

*vulsion that I have rarely felt in my life. A shiver of disgust passed through my en-
tire body.*

*Sensing something new, my presence perhaps, the rat began to move, and I saw
that it moved very slowly. Its eyes were cloudy and dull, and it was exceedingly fat.
It was old, old not only in years but in its form, for what I saw in front of me was
surely a relic of the evolutionary past, a path of ferocity that Nature in her mercy
had all but abandoned and confined to a remote corner of the globe.*

*The rat began to gnaw mindlessly at a large pile of vegetables and fruit left for
it. This was, said Bulang, Kallo's last offspring. There would be no more issue,
and he would be killed at the festival. When he died, his flesh would be shared,
and the bones placed in the sacred bone place. Without him, the tribe could no
longer remain, and they would have to journey again, perhaps back to Sumatra,
to find the new children of Kallo. He picked a flower off a nearby tree. This is
maja, he said. All of his people would eat these flowers after the sacrifice, and they
would walk to the sea, where they would sleep. In their dreams, Kallo would come
and tell them what to do, and when they awoke they would follow his instructions.*

*It was almost dark when I returned to our camp. Bulang had accompanied me.
As we approached, I realised that something was very wrong. The camp had been
virtually destroyed. Our two guides were lying dead near the cooking fire, both
stabbed to death. Everything had been taken, including the specimens, and Van
Ruisdael himself was nowhere to be found. The marauders had disappeared, leaving no trace. I, the lone survivor of our party, had no choice but to take refuge with
Bulang, who bade me follow him.*

*We retraced our steps to the temple. Bulang took me to a dark, wooded place
above the amphitheatre, where he said I would be safe. After dark, he said, no one
of the tribe was allowed to travel above the highest part of the amphitheatre. Kallo
did not like his people coming near his home, the sky, at night. But Kallo would
allow me to stay as a guest, he said. He then disappeared into the dark. I never
saw him again.*

*Permission of the god Kallo was small consolation for the situation I found my-
self in, dear Watson, for I was unarmed, and therefore helpless should I be found
out. But there I was, alone. I could only watch, hoping that what transpired
would proceed without incident. I would try in the morning to discover what had
happened to Van Ruisdael and who the villains were who had sacked our camp.
I could only hope that he had escaped or, if he had been taken captive, was still
alive somewhere.*

I looked down on the amphitheatre. It was dark, empty, and silent, except for the occasional movements of the great repulsive creature that lay in the pit. Several hours passed. Then, as if by signal, the amphitheatre began to fill with the Norom. They came in single file, passing first the column of Kallo. Then, climbing the temple, they descended toward the great theatre. They remained silent as they entered. A single light near the centre of the theatre was the only illumination. They stood in place until an aged priest entered, followed by several others carrying the image of the great white rat. They placed the image in front of the old priest, who touched the head of the image and began a slow dance. The crowd followed him in his movements, building in minutes to a frenzy that slowly subsided.

When the dance had finished, the priests produced long wooden spears and, jumping into the pit, watched as the aged priest, holding a stone club, rapidly despatched the great inert rat with a single blow to the head. The other priests drove their spears into the animal. What followed was a rapid dismemberment of the huge beast and the quick sharing of much of the flesh with the congregation. The maja flowers were then distributed, and the people began to leave as they came, in single file, led by the priests who carried the rat image at the head of the procession.

When the ceremony was complete, the great temple and its amphitheatre were deserted. I waited until the crowd had gone sufficiently far for me to follow unnoticed. I watched the procession by its own dim torchlight as it wound its way, first to the sacred bone place near our camp. Here the bones of the last giant rat of Sumatra were cast in the dark, and the crowd proceeded to the nearby cove.

I followed silently, and watched as they reached the beach. Each one kneeled and then lay down, as if in a deep sleep. The priests placed the stone rat in the shallow water, where it faced out to sea, awaiting Kallo's instructions. Then they too lay down and waited, in their dreams, for his word.

It was only then that I realised the terrible fate of the Norom, for whatever Kallo told them in their sleep, other forces were at work that would change them forever. After the last of them had fallen into a deep sleep, shadows appeared out of the dark. I saw Uru, and the great bulk of the Swedish captain of the Matilda Briggs, and many others that I had not seen before, perhaps the entire crew. They threw nets over the sleeping Norom, tying the hands of each of them. I knew only then to my horror that the ship in which I had travelled would now carry the most unholy of cargos, for two hundred human beings, asleep in the opiate of their belief, would awaken soon to find that their god had abandoned them.

If I have been frustrated in my work before, Watson, I can assure you that you have never seen me close to the sadness that I felt at that moment. I could do nothing. Indeed, if I interfered I could conceivably cause the death of many of those who, now bound, could not escape. I decided to leave, to return as fast as I could to Jogjakarta, and report the capture to Maupertuis.

I turned, and in the dark made my way back to our campsite, then started out on the trail up the side of the mountain. An hour into the march I decided to wait until dawn, for I could no longer see at all, and at the slightest wrong step I would have plummeted to the depths. I sat on the trail, awake with the horror that I had seen, until dawn, when the light sufficed for me to walk again. It was raining now, and the trail had turned to mud. I continued, however, until I reached the ridge, from where I could see the village of Bulayo. From there, my return to Jogjakarta was uneventful.

There is no reason to bore you with the rest, dear Watson. As soon as I related the events, Maupertuis, quite sceptical of some of my statements, sent a search party to look for Van Ruisdael, but he was never found.

As to the fate of the Matilda Briggs, I can tell you that shortly before its arrival in Pelambang, off the western coast of Sumatra, the ship was found drifting aimlessly near shore. A rebellion had occurred in which the crew and the captain were killed, the only survivor being a fat Javanese who died of his wounds shortly after he described the events to the authorities. It was he who started the rumour that Van Ruisdael had been sacrificed by the Norom to the great rat. I myself have no evidence of this.

So much then, my dear Doctor, of the incidents through which I have just lived. I write to record and to inform only you, for they form a tale that may yet unfold in strange ways, and for which I believe the world is not yet prepared.

Your sincere and devoted friend,
Sherlock Holmes

A SINGULAR AFFAIR

AT TRINCOMALEE

ARELY DOES LONDON BECOME SO HOT THAT ONE LONGS FOR THE cold, dreary winters that regularly afflict it. Thus it was, however, in the closing days of June 1897, a full three years after Holmes's return. It was the year of the sixtieth anniversary of Her Majesty's coronation and the very week of celebration throughout Britain. The festivities had brought hordes of celebrants from the countryside into the city, and the loud din of the revellers in the street below our open windows had stolen away the easy comfort to which he and I had grown accustomed.

"Impossible, Watson," said he, with uncharacteristic exasperation in his voice as he wiped his brow with his handkerchief. He had been lying on the couch attempting unsuccessfully to read the morning papers. "We should leave London to the rabble and retire to some tranquil place in the country—"

"A most welcome thought, Holmes, but a trip to the country would be unpleasant in itself. The trains are off schedule, and the cars are filled with the crowds that one wishes to avoid. And where is there to go? Where is there a tranquil corner on this sceptred isle? The celebrations are everywhere—"

"You are quite right, Watson. Let us not sit here moaning in discomfort, however. It is only eleven and already the heat is unbearable. There is a refuge close by—the Diogenes Club. My brother, Mycroft, will admit us, and we shall spend the day peacefully in its quiet rooms. If I am not mistaken, the Indian coolers recently installed there will reduce the temperature by at least twenty degrees. Come, Mycroft and a gin and lemon await us."

I applauded the suggestion, for I had spent many restful hours in Mycroft's club during Holmes's absence from London.

"Excellent," I said. "Let us be off."

As we left, Holmes turned and said, "You know, Watson, the heat and its attendant humid quality remind me of my days in Ceylon. Serendipitously enough, there is a tale, one which you have not yet heard, which relates to this week's festivities. Mycroft put the whole affair into motion, and it will be good for you to hear his part in it directly. If the heat has not sapped the last of his energies, he may be willing to relate how he came to be involved in the case."

"Splendid," said I. It was often in this incidental way that Holmes introduced his adventures abroad, and I suddenly forgot the heat in anticipation of what was to come.

The crowds were thick on Baker Street, and Holmes suggested that we leave our quarters by the back entrance. Once we were outside, his encyclopaedic knowledge of London's streets and alleys took us first through a series of narrow cobblestone mews of which I was previously unaware. We then found ourselves on Baring Street, from where we walked to Eaton Square. Here Holmes unexpectedly stopped in front of one of the more elegant houses, pulled a ring of keys from his pocket, and opened the door.

"The pied-à-terre of a most appreciative client," he announced, "one who has kindly granted me free access. It is one of a number of safe houses I have throughout the city. This one is among the best. If memory serves, the Duke of Wellington resided here for some days after his return from Egypt."

As we entered, I saw three men huddled around a small table in the sitting room to the left. They looked up in surprise as we passed, and Holmes nodded perfunctorily in response. Without pausing to converse, we walked through, quickly descending to the ground floor, where we exited into a small, well-tended garden. A gardener's ladder enabled us to scale the back wall, and jumping gently to the ground on the other side, we found ourselves again in one of London's many alleys. I followed a little breathless now, behind Holmes's rapid strides. He stopped in front of a large black door and rang the bell.

"This is the back entrance to the club," he said smiling, "one that I often find convenient, particularly if I have to disappear quickly."

A guard opened and, recognising Holmes immediately, took us directly to the large room in which the club's rules of strict silence were relaxed and one was permitted to converse softly. The room contained far more people than I had noted on previous visits, but it was still much cooler than our sweltering quarters on Baker Street. Mycroft Holmes was seated alone in his accustomed place at the end of a very large table. He greeted us with a broad smile, but without rising.

"Hello, my dear Sherlock, and dear Dr. Watson. Allow me to remain seated, for the heat is most unpleasant and unforgiving for someone of my bulk. I am about to indulge in something cool. Do join me. By the way, Sherlock, what do you make of the dark-skinned gentleman at the bar?"

Mycroft was perspiring greatly, and in weather such as this his corpulence must have been particularly trying. The great jowls hung from his face like soft pink pillows, and his enormous girth inevitably forced him to remain a fair distance from the table. But his grey eyes had their usual sparkle, and he grinned as he tested his younger brother.

"You mean the Ethiopian polo player?" Holmes asked.

"Yes, indeed, formerly a patriarch of the Coptic Church," replied Mycroft.

"Yes, and left because of his love of sport. Horses are in his blood . . . , " said Holmes.

"Probably of the royal family in Addis . . . ," said Mycroft.

"No, I think not, more likely a Galla tribesman. Note the thin nose, Mycroft. He has had a troubled morning . . . ,"

"An argument with his son . . . ,"

"True. The last match went badly, and he has not recovered from his defeat. He will leave shortly to make amends."

I looked over to the bar as they spoke, noting only a rather small, slender man standing there in conversation with several other people. That he was from East Africa I might have guessed from his fine features, but how Holmes and his brother arrived at the rest I could not fathom in the least.

"Too much too quickly for me to follow," I said.

"No matter, Watson. You merely lack practice, and the courage to make the necessary deductions. And besides, this is our usual fraternal form of amusement, one with which we are well acquainted. The inferences are of no lasting consequence, however. Hallo," said Holmes interrupting himself, "I see that the rules of the club have been further diluted. A woman in the Diogenes Club! Perhaps a first, my dear Mycroft."

A woman of regal bearing, dressed in the loveliest of Indian attire, had entered and begun speaking with our Ethiopian. She was covered with jewels, the most valuable of which were the diamonds and sapphires embedded in a gold tiara which she wore with the confidence of a queen. She appeared to be of the highest breeding and was, most probably, of royal descent.

"Just as we occasionally allow a break in the rules of silence, so in this case we have relaxed the strict misogynous rules that govern the Club. This occasional relaxation insures us against the dangers of fanaticism. The woman is a princess of Rajputana, descended in part, so it is claimed, from French and Portuguese adventurers of the fifteenth century. In England, she goes by the name of Marie de Benoît. Her family, alas, has recently come on hard times. She remains a favourite of the Queen, however, and I recommended that we give her and her retinue lodging here at the Club during these crowded weeks. Her Majesty has already expressed her sincere gratitude."

Holmes looked serious for a moment as Mycroft spoke. He took a quick glance round the room as if to make sure that no person or thing unfriendly to him was to be seen.

"Most interesting, Mycroft, but I promised dear Watson a story with which you had some connection—"

Mycroft beamed and sipped his gin. "You mean—"

"The adventure that we have referred to in the past as the singular affair at Trincomalee."

"And the Atkinson brothers," added Mycroft with a twinkle in his eyes.

"Perhaps for the good Doctor you might tell how it all came about, for I was in Java when I received your message."

"By all means, Sherlock, I should be most happy to. As you are well aware, dear Watson, I am on occasion consulted by Government on a variety of important matters, particularly on those subjects that the Cabinet finds too delicate or difficult of execution. It often requires the aid of intermediaries. In this case, I was seated in this very chair, some four years ago, when a distinguished member of the Cabinet arrived with a matter from the Prime Minister himself. If I recall, Sherlock, it was sometime in the fall of '93, in late September to be more precise."

"Indeed," said Holmes. "I had just lived through the bizarre events concerning the giant rat of Sumatra, of which I have already given Watson a written account."

"Yes," said Mycroft. "The matter presented to me concerned the Prime Minister and his relationship, uneasy at best shall we say, with Her Majesty. It is an open secret, good Doctor, that Mr. Gladstone has not enjoyed the full confidence and unalloyed affection of the Queen. To his credit, he has tried on a number of occasions to remedy this, but he has never succeeded in breaking through the rather cold reserve with which she has continued to treat him. It so happened, however, in that September some four years ago that discussions regarding the Queen's sixtieth jubilee arose in the Cabinet. Mr. Gladstone expressed his keen desire that the festivities go well, not only in Britain, but everywhere. It was his fervent wish that they be a worldwide tribute and a momentous success for her personally. Once again, he expressed his consternation at how clever Lord Beaconsfield had been in the past. What mattered most to him, however, should he be in office at the time of the celebrations, was that they should underscore the strong role that the Queen had indubitably played in the stability and the growth of the Empire. Let it be remembered, he said, that Her Majesty had acceded to the throne in 1837, at a time when it was not certain that the weakened monarchy would survive. Surely no one would have then predicted so long a period of progress and prosperity for England. No monarch in English history had done so much. Her Majesty deserved the very best that Government could conceive in her honour."

The Colonial Secretary spoke next, Mycroft continued, saying that the celebrations should indeed be worldwide. Not only in England but in all the great cities of the colonies, the festivities should be ample and unstinting. A large military tattoo should take place in London, with troops representing every country subject to Her Majesty.

"The Prime Minister and the Cabinet agreed at once," said Mycroft. "Mr. Gladstone, however, stated in addition that he wished to be able to bestow upon Her Majesty some extraordinary gift that would not only please her but also symbolise her great superiority to the other crowned heads of Europe. Had not the clever Disraeli presented the Suez Canal to her as if it were her very own?"

Speaking once again, the Colonial Secretary said that he had just received some news from abroad, yet unconfirmed, that was most pertinent to the Prime Minister's last remark. Secret word from our Resident in Colombo, Mr. Anthony Vansittart, had arrived that morning saying that in the recent pearl fisheries in Ceylon, considered to be the best in years, what appeared to be the largest and most perfect pearl ever found anywhere had been discovered. It was said to be a perfect sphere weighing over five hundred grains and possessing the most exquisite luminescence and colour. In size and beauty it far outranked the famous Cinghalese paragon acquired by Napoleon and now in the national collection in France. Why not acquire this jewel for the Queen and present it to her for her anniversary?

"Mr. Gladstone," said Mycroft, "was overjoyed at the Secretary's suggestion. Indeed, he went further and asked whether or not jewels of a similar quality might not be collected throughout our gem-producing colonies, all of which could be presented to the Queen set in a new imperial crown symbolising both the power of the Empire and the homage and affection that the native peoples showed her. The new crown would be given to her at a special ceremony and would be hers and hers alone. A new title might accompany it. Perhaps Regina Mundi et Imperatrix, Empress and Queen of the World."

In response, the Colonial Secretary agreed most heartily, and stated that South Africa, India, Ceylon, and Burma were the chief repositories of precious jewels. Given sufficient time, there was no reason why the requisite number could not be acquired. The first step, however, was the immediate acquisition by Government of this greatest of all Cinghalese paragons.

"It was at this point," said Mycroft, "having agreed to acquire the pearl, that the Cabinet sent the Colonial Secretary to discuss the matter with me. Our discussion was held at this very table, Sherlock. Here he presented to me the matter as I have just related it. He requested help in finding the person capable of completing the acquisition, of course in absolute secrecy."

"I assume," said Sherlock Holmes, "that the Colonial Secretary is the same gentleman who visited me in Florence with regard to the Tibetan affair."

"Indeed, my dear Sherlock. The first thing he asked was your whereabouts and whether or not you could be convinced to undertake this mission. I replied that we had been out of touch for several months, and that as far as I knew you were still in the Orient, perhaps on your way back, but that I would try to communicate the request to you as soon as possible. I of course reminded him that my confidence in you had only been strengthened by your exploits in Tibet and elsewhere, but that acquiring an expensive bauble for Mr. Gladstone was not exactly as enticing an affair as the Tibetan adventure.

"For his part, the Colonial Secretary agreed that the task itself would present few challenges for you, but that Government was prepared to make it worth your while with a handsome remuneration. For Sherlock Holmes, a series of simple if uninteresting tasks: to find the present owners of the pearl, to establish its authenticity, to negotiate its sale, and to deliver it to Mr. Vansittart for safe transport to England. You will recall, Sherlock, that in my message to you, I emphasised that though you might consider the mission to be without sufficient interest, the continued pleasure of the Queen and the deepening of her good feelings toward Mr. Gladstone would keep both home and Empire strong and firm as we moved, rather perilously I thought, into the last years of the present century."

Mycroft paused to sip his drink and wipe his brow. He was almost exhausted by his relation and sagged in his chair as if he had expended the last of his energies. Noting his brother's fatigue, Holmes broke in to continue the tale.

"I recall that I was quite annoyed when I first read your message," he began. "To speak in all candour, I had no interest whatever in the Prime Minister's difficulties with Her Majesty, and the procuring of a plaything to please her was not an especially inviting task. What, after all, is Mr. Gladstone to me or I to Mr. Gladstone? Surely, I thought, the entire task could be accomplished easily by Vansittart himself. But I was beginning to feel the pinch after my travels had depleted my pocket-book, and the remuneration was something I sorely needed. It is also true," he added quietly, without emotion, "that I have a special knowledge of precious stones, pearls among them, because they are so often the objects of criminal desire."

These last words visibly affected Mycroft. Despite his fatigue, he pulled himself up in his chair and said, "Come, come, Sherlock's modesty prevents him from setting forth all the reasons I had for choosing him for the task. His success in Tibet was only one. There are several others—"

"Enough, my dear Mycroft," said Holmes. "As you know, Watson, I have never considered modesty a virtue, for it only clouds the truth and misleads one into false positions concerning one's abilities. If I am reticent on the subjects to which Mycroft alludes, it is because there are still solemn promises of silence to be honoured. There are indeed earlier cases of mine which provided me with the rather unique experience necessary for dealing with the matter in Ceylon, and it would break no solemn oath to refer to them in a general way. One is of course the case of the black pearl of the notorious Count Batthyani."

"It was Sherlock," said Mycroft, interrupting once again, "who proved beyond the shadow of a doubt that this pearl had been stolen from the British Crown jewels a century and a half before."

"How it was finally found in a pawnshop in Budapest would make most interesting reading," said Holmes, turning to me with a smile, "as would the case of the pearl known as La Pellegrina, a gem once in the possession of the Zosima brothers of Moscow. Perhaps someday these stories will be told. In any case, we have the Trincomalee affair before us."

"But surely there is something else, Holmes," I said, "something even closer to this case, for I distinctly remember mentioning the Atkinson brothers of Trincomalee in my early chronicles, if I am not mistaken at the beginning of the affair concerning Irene Adler—"

Holmes became visibly annoyed by my mention of Miss Adler, to whom he still referred even after all these years as *the* woman. A dark look came over his face, but he recovered quickly and said, "Excellent, Watson, you have a most prodigious memory. There was, indeed, an earlier case in which I was consulted here in London involving some of the same principals, but I never visited Trincomalee before the present episode. Although the matter is of some relevance here, it too must re-main, for reasons of state, yet untold. Let it suffice to say that it too con-cerned a jewel, in that case a magnificent sapphire . . . and several murders."

Holmes broke off his narrative for a moment to sip his drink. A far-away look came across his face, one mixed with sadness.

"Think of it," he said, "the misery produced by these playthings. A pearl is merely the grave of some tiny parasite, sometimes a grain of sand, sometimes a worm, but in all cases a microscopic intruder into the private residence of a brainless mollusc buried fathoms below the surface of the sea, an intruder which annoys its host into secreting a substance that envelops it and buries it forever. Like all good gems, it is among the devil's pet baits. For every fifty grains of weight, there is often a monstrous crime. Who would think that such bonny things, with such humble origins, would be purveyors to the gallows and the prison? But there it is. And it was with the knowledge that this most beautiful of all pearls, if indeed it truly existed, would already be the focus of criminal intent that I accepted the task. Ah, this pearl, Watson! Despite my annoyance at the task, I knew that it would keep me in my element. Like fresh-killed prey, it would draw many of the worst to it, as hawks and buzzards gather in ever-narrowing circles above a wounded or dying animal. And I would be there watching, unseen, I hoped, as they gathered. The danger? The obvious. The closer I came to the prey, the greater the chance that I would be devoured as well. And yet, the scent of the criminal was so strong that I could not but stay close, with ever-increasing anticipation, I might add."

"I have always thought of you as a bit of a sleuth hound, Holmes," said I.

Mycroft laughed. "It is precisely that," he said, "which distinguishes me from my younger brother. It is what activates him, this ability to fol-low the scent, the total lack of which limits me to observations made from my chair."

Holmes did not reply to Mycroft but paused to sip his drink, and I took a moment to glance about the room. It had emptied for the most part. The beautiful Indian woman had left with the Ethiopian, and those who remained appeared to be regular denizens of the Club, ec-centric in appearance most of them, but all quiet in demeanour. The room had also cooled considerably. I noticed through a nearby window that the sky had begun to cloud over and that there was the welcome threat of rain. I turned toward Holmes again. The sadness that had come across his face had gone, and he continued the tale.

His reply to Mycroft's message, he said, was brief and affirmative. His final instructions came almost immediately. Mr. Gladstone's Cabinet had set aside one hundred thousand pounds for the purchase of the pearl, and the great Gniessen of Utrecht had already been commissioned to design the new crown. Holmes was to proceed directly to Ceylon, where he would meet with Anthony Vansittart, our Resident in Colombo, at the circuit house in Marichakudi, the small village near the pearl fisheries where the great pearl reportedly had been found. The Ceylonese authorities would provide every assistance, but he should know that in acquiring the pearl he would be largely on his own.

"I booked passage at once from Singapore to Ceylon on the *Susannah II,* a steamer out of Liverpool," said Holmes, "expecting to reach my destination within ten days. Two days out, however, our captain learned of several storms off of Ceylon. He therefore diverted the ship north, toward the Coromandel Coast. Here we came in sight of land south of Madras and set anchor. After a day of waiting, I left the ship, having decided that it would be quicker for me to complete the journey by land. I came ashore near Pondicherry, where I spent the night. It was here that I sent a message to my old friend Gorashar, now in Calcutta, asking him to join me in Ceylon. I conveyed no reason, but urged on him that I would need his aid in a matter of great importance. I wrote simply: 'If convenient, come at once; if inconvenient, come all the same.' In the morning I took the first train to Rameswaram."

It was on this portion of his trip that Holmes received confirmation of his early doubts about the secrecy of the recently discovered pearl. The train was crowded, filled with merchants and jewellers from all over India and from as far away as the Levant. They chattered constantly about the great harvest of pearls and the discovery of the greatest of all pearls at Mannar, the equal of which had never been seen before. Holmes listened to the talk in silence, anticipating now that the tasks set for him would be far more difficult than Government in London might have thought. The pearl had already received an unofficial name: the Moonstar of Mannar. Holmes avoided all comment, maintaining his disguise as a professor of archaeology from London, on his way from Singapore to Ceylon to study the celebrated ruins of Anuradhapura and Polonnaruwa. This scholarly disguise bored his companions instantly, and they soon lost interest in the apparently absentminded figure who sat with them.

"Among the many passengers, I recognised only one person," said Holmes. "She had appeared at the station in Pondicherry after I boarded, and I watched her arrival from my seat at the window in my compartment. Her name was Franziska van Rhede, a woman of unknown European origin. I first observed her in Banaras, but we had never met. She was a tall, slender woman, with long black hair, who often dressed in the clothes of a Punjab peasant woman. Most would have judged her beautiful, for her features were regular and her complexion light, but there was a look of cruelty in her eyes that marred her otherwise pleasing countenance. I had watched her unseen at the burning ghats, where she walked often by night, like some giantess, dressed in black, examining the fires, poking at them with a long stick, conversing with the cremation workers, over whom she towered, sometimes screaming at them in a high-pitched voice. Her most remarkable feature was her large hands, and her fingernails, which were exceedingly long and sharpened to dangerous points. I had seen her use them in a fit of rage on one of the cremation attendants, bloodying him badly. I made careful mental note of her presence on the train, then buried myself in my battered copy of Petrarch."

The train reached Rameswaram at dusk. It was the end of the rail line, and Holmes followed the crowd of passengers into the steamer that would take them across the Palk Strait to the Ceylonese mainland. As he alighted from the train, he observed that Franziska van Rhede, now somewhat ahead of him, instead of walking with the crowd, had stopped with her coolie as if in wait for someone. Holmes slowed his pace so that he could watch her as long as possible. A tall, handsome man, dressed completely in white, came up to her and embraced her in welcome. As Holmes passed, he recognised him: it was Colonel Sebastian Moran, the deadliest of his remaining enemies from the Moriarty gang. It had taken far longer for them to come upon each other than he had expected. Moran and the woman walked into the train station, and he then lost sight of them. Holmes smiled in the deepening twilight, for he knew then that his mission in Ceylon would be far more interesting than any assignment of Mr. Gladstone.

The crossing of the strait was a rough one, and many of the passengers became ill. The steamer was overcrowded with merchants and pearl workers, mostly Indians, but some from as far away as the Andamans. Luckily, the distance was short. After they disembarked, a waiting train took them south along the coast. Here Holmes looked out at the beautiful beaches and the sun setting into the sea. He knew almost nothing of the island on which he had just arrived. He had only a small map, which one of the passengers disembarking in Dhanushkodi had given him. On it, the island itself appeared like a pearl, gently hanging near the tip of the Subcontinent. From what he could see, it seemed to be a paradise. The rich Indian Ocean surrounded it, and its coast had many harbours, which served merchants and seamen from places as far away as Rome and China. Through the varied names of its geography, one saw the imprint of the invaders—the Portuguese, the Dutch, and finally the English. Intermixed with the local names were Adam's Peak, World's End, Foul Point, and other names that attested to the British presence.

Holmes arrived in Marichakudi the following morning and went, according to his instructions, to a small hotel on Chetty Street. The innkeeper handed him a note from Vansittart, which said that he would expect him at the circuit house at four that afternoon.

"My room was a misery," said Holmes, "hot and breathless, with only a small window blocked by a piece of torn brown paper that buzzed with flies occasionally, and placed there by some previous occupant in a vain effort to keep at bay the swarms of insects hovering outside. In the centre of the room there was a filthy bed, over which an old mosquito net had been hung. I climbed in to catch a moment's rest, but I quickly abandoned the notion as I felt the small but sharp bites of a variety of Asiatic pests. I left my room and went to have my first look at Pearl Town, as the central bazaar of the pearl fisheries is known. I soon saw that it was of no solid construction and displayed many of the shoddy aspects of a settlement that had gone up almost overnight. Little would remain of it after the fisheries were over, including my ramshackle hotel. The town was merely a row of cajang huts, thrown up temporarily to house the pearl fishers and the many merchants, with vile conditions for food and drink."

As he approached the main road, known as Tank Street, Holmes saw that he was only a few yards from the shore. There, hundreds of boats were engaged in complicated manoeuvres, some landing, others on their way out to the pearl beds, having disgorged their harvest onto the shore. The pearl fisheries he found grossly offensive, particularly to the olfactory sense, and to the eyes as well. The molluscs, collected from the sea by thousands of pearl divers, were delivered to the shore in large jute bags. They were then dumped from the sacks into large vats, or sometimes into small boats secured on the shore, where they were allowed to rot in the sun. The rotting process, he was told, softens the flesh in which the pearls are embedded. It is through the decaying slime that the searchers probe for the pearls, sifting the ugly oyster jelly for gems of the slightest weight, even of a half grain.

"Shakespeare was quite right, Watson," said Holmes. "A foul odour inevitably surrounds the pearl. The discovery of no other gem causes such a stench, and it is difficult to convey the odour produced by some twenty million sea animals rotting in the tropical sun and covered by large swarms of bluebottle flies and their maggots gnawing away at the sweet, rotting flesh. But this is the method chosen by the native pearl fishers and sanctioned by our agents, for the entire process is in Government's hands. Somewhere in that disgusting jelly, I thought, a human hand had entered and found to its great surprise the object of my journey. Now I had to find it once again."

From the rotting shore to the long line of pearl merchants was but a few feet. The shops were no more than lean-tos, sometimes no more than a large umbrella under which the jeweller sat to block the heat of the sun. It was there that the pearl fishers brought their share of the harvest, selling it to the dealers who drill the pearls, transforming them into the things of beauty that grace the heads and shoulders of the rich. No more varied group of faces could be found anywhere, for the merchants and their agents come from every civilised country. Holmes found himself accosted at every turn by hands extended, offering every conceivable size and shape of pearl.

Overcome by the stench and the heat, and tired of repulsing the touts and purveyors of these gems, he returned to his room, thinking to vary at least the discomforts which he saw were to be inevitably his over the next few days. Beyond the rudimentary aspects of the pearl fisheries, however, he had learned nothing of the whereabouts or even the existence of his quarry.

Once he was back in the hotel, locating the great pearl seemed far less important than coming to grips with his more immediate difficulties. His ankles were covered with already bloated leeches. His experience in the Himalaya had taught him that a lit cigarette, pressed strategically on their backs, often compels the worms to release their grip. Once this was done, and he was freed from this annoyance, he sat in the only chair in the room and began his battle with the flies. They came at him from every direction. Having had no experience with such devils, Holmes began to despair when there was a knock at the door. He opened to see his dear friend Gorashar.

"Lemon juice," he said as he sprayed Holmes's face and head with a squirt bottle. The flies disappeared instantly.

"I must say, Watson, that except for my happiness at greeting you on a number of occasions, I was never so pleased in my life at seeing another human being. After receiving my message, Gorashar had taken the first available train to Ceylon. Once arrived in Pearl Town, he had located 'the Englishman in the bazaar' in a matter of minutes. I had not seen him in almost a year, and after we exchanged pleasantries, I told him of my mission."

Gorashar's face darkened. "This pearl is no longer in Pearl Town. It is in Trincomalee, now in the hands of the Atkinson brothers, famous dealers in gemstones."

Gorashar already knew much, and Holmes asked him to pursue his enquiries as diligently and as discreetly as possible. Gorashar said that he would report to him that night all that he could discover. Holmes felt relieved, for Gorashar, unlike "the Englishman in the bazaar," could do many things and go many places without attracting inordinate attention.

Gorashar left, and Holmes took a rickshaw directly to the circuit house to his meeting with Vansittart. A peon informed him that Vansittart would see him in the inner garden.

Holmes found the garden of the circuit house to be a small English oasis, filled with flowers and trees, obviously well tended. In the shade in one corner sat two men dressed in white, the attire of the colonial servant. The older of the two nodded to Holmes as he entered.

"Welcome, Mr. Holmes, to Ceylon. I am Anthony Vansittart and this is my successor, somewhat recently arrived himself, Mr. Arthur Wellesley."

"My name should be used sparingly in public, if at all," said Holmes, "for even though some of my enemies may now have gathered that I am still alive, they do not necessarily know where I am. For all purposes here in Ceylon, I am William Redfern, archaeologist, here on assignment from the University of London."

"Forgive my indiscretion, Professor. . . ."

As he spoke, Holmes observed both men closely, and took a long look around the garden. Vansittart was the older, a large man, tall and stout, with a full head of white hair under his straw hat, florid of face, in many ways an unmistakable Englishman in the tropics. His speech was that of the seasoned government servant, knowledgeable and sympathetic, and his blue eyes appeared to be without guile. Wellesley, a far younger man, was far different. Holmes described him as in his early thirties, a kind of half-man, hair neither light nor dark, a face not unpleasant but of no strong character, and of medium build. He looked as though he had been ill, for he was overly pale, and his eyes were sunken and bloodshot. They showed a certain weakness, and when he spoke Holmes saw that his teeth had been ruined, most probably by the overuse of intoxicants and opium.

"You should know," continued Vansittart, "that I shall be leaving rather quickly, in one week, to be exact, for England. I have been here for three years, and I return home having completed this, my last assignment. In your work, you will be aided primarily by Arthur here. He has been briefed fully on the task given to you, and has my full confidence."

"Thank you. I often work alone and unaided, but I of course shall avail myself of your help as events unfold. What is the latest report on the pearl?"

"Our information is still rather sketchy and incomplete," said Wellesley. "And somewhat contradictory. The early reports, gathered by our agents in the bazaar, stated that the pearl had been found here at Pearl Town by a young Tamilean woman, Thyagamma by name. She had been assigned to sort through a large vat of molluscs by her father, an expert pearl diver by the name of Nelusko, in whose share of the harvest the pearl was located. She brought the pearl to her father as soon as she found it, and the two immediately left their quarters, a small hut on Tank Street not far from here, and absconded. They have not been seen, except for a report that said that they had been sighted travelling by foot on the road to Trincomalee."

"Trincomalee," said Holmes, "still then the home of the Atkinson brothers, the chief gem merchants of the Indian world."

"Precisely. I am astonished that you would know of them," said Wellesley.

"Some time ago I was consulted on the disappearance of a star sapphire, a case in which they played a large role," said Holmes.

"Since that time, there has been a change in the firm of which you may not be aware," said Vansittart. "The Atkinson brothers are gone, and the firm sold to an Arab jeweller, one Abdul Latif, who has shrewdly kept the old name of the firm. Latif is a stiff bargainer, and plays the game even harder than the Atkinsons. It is possible that the pearl is already in his possession. If it is, I would imagine that Nelusko and his daughter received next to nothing for it."

Vansittart stopped short as his eyes caught sight of a tall, thin figure of a man entering the garden and making his way slowly toward the shade of a large bamboo grove at the other end. He wore Arab dress, and as he took his seat, Holmes caught a glimpse of his face. His features and colour were neither Indian nor Cinghalese, and Holmes recognised him immediately.

"Arthur," said Vansittart, "please do the needful. See that he lacks nothing."

Wellesley got up, went over toward the bamboo grove, and sat down with the man. He took a deck of cards from his pocket, and the two men became immediately engrossed in the game.

"Arabi Pasha," said Holmes, "the Egyptian leader. I had forgotten that he had been exiled here."

Vansittart appeared somewhat surprised at his words. "Yes, indeed. You are most observant. He is now in his twelfth year of imprisonment in this paradise, shall we say. You know his story. He foolishly issued a proclamation to his countrymen that he was inspired by the Prophet to free the country of its foreign rulers. His forces were defeated at Tel el Kebir and he was taken prisoner. Condemned to death by our tribunal, his sentence was later commuted to life in exile. So far Allah and the Prophet have chosen not to free him. He has been one of my most onerous tasks, a heavy ball and chain, for in my three years here, he has been with me almost constantly. Wherever I have gone, he has come accompanied by two guards, who watch him while I sleep. Poor man, he wants nothing more than to return to his country, to spend his last days with his family somewhere in sight of the Nile. But Government refuses any commutation of his life sentence. For someone from the desert, the tropical climate of Ceylon is particularly difficult. And so he quietly plots his escape as he plays cards all day. Despite our best efforts, he seems to communicate regularly with elements friendly to his cause. How he sends his messages I haven't a clue. Twice he has almost made his escape, but he has not been successful in my time, thank God."

"He will make it this time easily, under Wellesley," said Holmes.

Vansittart's eyes narrowed. "Again, you are most observant, my dear Professor. Despite his illustrious lineage and my remark expressing confidence in him, Wellesley is really not up to the usual mark, I'm afraid. He arrived here just a month ago, sent in disgrace from Burma, where he became enmeshed in a scandal in Mandalay involving the Governor's daughter. Unfortunately, women are only one of his bad habits. The Foreign Office sent him here to keep him out of sight, with a severe reprimand that this was to be his last post should he fail to measure up. The Pasha's escape would of course end his career. But so far, Wellesley's behaviour has been impeccable, though I must tell you that, as I leave, I have some other more worrisome concerns that I do not think Wellesley will be able to deal with."

"What are they?" asked Holmes.

Vansittart leaned forward to make sure that he was not overheard.

"Ceylon, my dear Professor, as you must have seen even in the short time you have been here, has every appearance of an island paradise. I have come to love it and respect its people. But it would be the height of folly to pretend that our presence here is not deeply resented. Having defeated the kings of Kandy over a half century ago, we have managed the island for our own purposes, for tea, rubber, pearls, of course, and for men and women to do our labour. We delude ourselves about these dark-skinned natives. We love how they bow and scrape, with their heads bent low, their noses to the ground, call us master, and serve our every need. But given the chance, they would rise up and cut us to ribbons . . . as they once did in India.

"And there is now an evil presence on the island," continued Vansittart, "one who moves about constantly and is so clever that it is difficult to apprehend him or to fathom his intentions. He is in touch with every unhappy element here: King Rama IV and his family, who form the sad remains of the Kandyan dynasty, and the leaders of the growing discontented classes in Colombo and other cities, and the Pasha himself."

"To whom do you refer?" asked Holmes.

"One of our countrymen, a gentleman by the name of Sebastian Moran, late of the Indian army. You may have heard of him. He is an old India hand and shikari."

Holmes stopped a smile from breaking over his face. "Tell me more," said he.

"There is much still to learn," said Vansittart, "and precious little to tell, at least from my own experience. I met him soon after his arrival just a year ago. Before that, I gather he had been in the western Himalaya, his usual hunting grounds. But India became too hot for him. Wanted by the local police for attempted murder in Simla, he escaped and arrived here, where he has been protected by several friends in high places, who refuse to believe anything evil of him. Since he is faultless in manners and education, and his older brother was a loyal soldier who served heroically in Afghanistan, he is easily believed. He unfortunately has gained the full confidence of Sir Edward Gordon, the Governor. And Wellesley adores him. Moran was born here, in Colombo, the son of an early tea planter. He left after his father and mother were killed during the Kandyan rebellion. He joined the Indian army, following in his brother's footsteps, where he became one of its great marksmen. He is tall, powerfully built, and of great intelligence; it is only the cruel look in his steel grey eyes that gives any warning of his criminal disposition. Of considerable means, he returned here from London a year ago and purchased a large house in Colombo, which he furnished lavishly. He lived there alone except for a friend, a young Swiss by the name of Giacomo, who has since left on a tour of India. I met Moran at his house once. I was ushered into the library, where I waited for him.

He entered accompanied by two large wolfhounds, both of which he kept on tight chains. Otherwise they would have devoured me, I think. Our conversation began pleasantly enough. He had just been on an inspection tour of his property, he said, for there had been a burglary during the night. Alerted by his hounds, he had caught the thief, a boy of fifteen who had dared to scale the walls and enter the house. Moran caught him easily and brought him into the very room in which we were sitting. It was then that I noticed a frightening transformation in his face, for he proceeded to tell me in sickening detail how he had beaten the boy to a pulp before releasing him. It was the obvious and intense pleasure he took in a near murder that made me sense that something was deeply wrong with this man, and that he might become a danger to all of us. I took my leave as soon as I could, and I shall never forget the contrast between the civilised library and the cruelty of Moran's expression."

"No charges were pressed?" asked Holmes.

"A thief is a thief is the common attitude here. The boy was found on the road outside Moran's house and was taken to the local hospital. But he said nothing after his recovery and has since disappeared altogether."

Vansittart spoke quickly in a low voice. Holmes did not reveal his own knowledge of Moran and his crimes, however, for fear that he should interrupt Vansittart's account. But in his mind's eye, he returned instantly to the Reichenbach Falls in Switzerland, to the moment when Moran began throwing huge rocks down upon him.

"What else?" Vansittart continued. "He is an inveterate gambler, who plays constantly for high stakes. He rarely loses, but God help the winner, for Moran deals harshly with those who dare to best him. And he has a woman, some say a half sister, others a lover, known by the name of Franziska van Rhede, who aids and abets him in his crimes. Fortunately, she lives elsewhere, much of the time in Pondicherry, I believe, but visits on occasion. I have never met her, but the natives are terrified of her, saying that she takes on the form of a gigantic bird of prey at will and goes soaring in the sky in search of victims at sunset."

"Where is Moran now?" Holmes enquired.

"It is difficult to say," said Vansittart. "He rarely goes to Colombo these days, but spends most of his time camped at a place called World's End. It is one of the most beautiful and dramatic places on the island. It is in the southern highlands and is a kind of high plain, filled with the wild game that attracts him. At the end of the plain, however, is the sheerest precipice in the world: a straight drop of some five thousand feet. Moran hunts all day, feasts in the evening, and sleeps almost not at all. It is as if the inner cruelty dissipates somewhat in shikar. Otherwise, there would be more incidents like the one with the young burglar. Cruelty, gambling, shikar, high living. He needs constant replenishment of these nutrients, and he is not at all averse to criminal activity to meet his ends."

Wellesley returned to their table at that moment, and Vansittart seamlessly changed the subject. "Perhaps," he said, "the place for you to begin would be Pearl Town itself."

"The Pasha wishes to speak to this gentleman," said Wellesley.

"What about?" Holmes asked.

"Archaeology. He seems to have noticed some similarities between the pyramids in Egypt and the ancient ruins of Ceylon . . ."

"I shall be most happy to give him my views. By the way, Vansittart, please check the bottom of the Pasha's teacup before the bearer removes it. There is a message attached to it, I believe."

Holmes left Vansittart with a surprised look on his face and went over to where the Pasha was sitting.

"Welcome to Ceylon, my dear Professor," said the Pasha. "I hope your stay is fruitful . . . and not too long."

"I gather you would leave this paradise," said Holmes.

"Earthly paradises are difficult for a devout Muslim," he said with a smile, "and this one is more difficult than most. One of our great Arab travellers journeyed to India in the eleventh century. He begins his book by saying of the people in this part of the world that we have nothing to do with them and they have nothing to do with us. I am a man of the desert, who needs only enough water to keep alive and no more . . . but enough. Life has nothing for me now. My country is enslaved, and I, alas, shall never look upon the Nile again."

Holmes observed the man closely as he spoke. Although he lacked for nothing as a prisoner, it was the very servicing of his needs that was destroying him. The Pasha was very thin, almost emaciated, and was clearly not in good health. His eyes were dull, his skin an unhealthy sallow colour, and Holmes judged that he consumed large amounts of opium and alcohol. Scars on what he could see of the man's arms supported this conclusion. He was obviously a weak and sickened man.

"You are destroying yourself with opium," said Holmes.

The Pasha frowned. "You are right, but what of it? Before I came to Ceylon, I had never touched it, nor had I drunk a drop of liquor. Now they are my constant companions, my only relief from the tedium and pain of exile. I cannot live without them. Yet, because of them I have terrible dreams. I flee from the wrath of Brahma through all the forests of Asia. Vishnu hates me, and Shiva lies in wait for me."

"You know your De Quincey quite well," said Holmes.

"At last, a literate gentleman," said the Pasha. "Yes, I have much time to read and De Quincey is a favourite." He paused for a moment, and then said, "A French philosopher, perhaps the great Descartes himself, has asserted that one should travel in foreign lands but be mindful not to spend too much time away from one's homeland lest one find oneself a stranger upon one's return. It is now twelve years since I was separated from my people. My memory of them, of my own family, grows dimmer daily, and I am sure that few remember me. Surely, by now I should be permitted to return."

Holmes listened to this still proud man with great sympathy and said, "I cannot help you. I can only tell you what you already know: that your freedom can only be granted by Government after appeal of your sentence."

The Pasha's expression became more intense. "All appeals have failed to go beyond the Governor," he said. "I cannot rely on the mercy of those who placed me here. But you, my dear sir, can help me. Or to speak more correctly, we can help each other."

He looked Holmes directly in the eyes and said simply, "I have the pearl."

Holmes managed to conceal his surprise. The Pasha's words also told him that the Pasha knew of his mission and his true identity. All of this had been told to him of course by Wellesley.

"I have been authorised to spend money for the pearl, not to bargain the release of a prisoner for it," said Holmes.

"I am aware. We too have our sources of knowledge, and ways, devious at times, of learning things. Let me say that the pearl is a thing of incomparable beauty, and that my agents are prepared to deliver it to you in return for my release and safe passage to Egypt. If we cannot strike a bargain, we are prepared to deal with other governments, with which we are already in contact. My request is that you present my offer directly to those who have given you this mission and furnish me with their reply. You are of course free to tell Vansittart or Governor Gordon the whole of our conversation."

Here he smiled and said, "My request to you might lead to my confinement in prison somewhere . . . or to my execution. In either case, the pearl will be sold to the highest bidder and the funds used against you in Egypt."

Holmes said that he had no reason to doubt the Pasha's words. He returned to Vansittart and reported his conversation. Vansittart grew pale at the suggestion that the Pasha be released in return for the pearl, but he agreed that the offer must be communicated to London.

"That is when I received your message," interrupted Mycroft, who during Holmes's long account had listened with closed eyes but full attention.

"Indeed, my dear Mycroft," said Holmes, "it was precisely at this perplexing moment that I asked you to notify the Colonial Secretary. My message was brief: object of search located pending final confirmation; in the hands of agents of Arabi Pasha, who as owner demands his release in exchange. Ask authority to negotiate with Pasha, including granting his release, if necessary."

"An urgent Cabinet meeting was called," continued Mycroft, "which, I am told, lasted well into the night. All the arguments, for and against freeing the Pasha, were enunciated, including the possible outcry in Parliament should the real reasons be uncovered for his release. Mr. Gladstone listened to all arguments and then stated his views. In anticipation of the success of the Holmeses' mission, he said, the plans for a new crown and title for the Queen had been initiated, and it would be most unfortunate if the pearl were not secured at this juncture. The Pasha was now in possession of the pearl, and of that Holmes appeared to have little doubt. If the price was the Pasha's liberty, then so be it. He had been exiled for more than twelve years, and his return to Egypt after so long a time posed no serious threat to British rule in Egypt. An act of clemency by the Prime Minister, on grounds of age and declining health, quietly reported in the papers, would be enough to explain his release. When all was said and done, the Pasha might be more of a nuisance in exile in Ceylon than free in Egypt. There was no end to inimical parties, certain foreign powers need not be mentioned, ready to strike a bargain with the Pasha. Better free him than have him escape. Mr. Gladstone then added, to a resounding 'hear hear' from the Cabinet, that 'the saving of the one hundred thousand pounds that might have been expended for the pearl would have the firm support of the Chancellor of the Exchequer.'

"And so," continued Mycroft, "the Colonial Secretary came at once to me, with the message that Sherlock be notified that he had the necessary authority to free the Pasha if he indeed thought that the best resolution of the matter."

Leaving the circuit house, Holmes had returned to his Chetty Street hotel, where he awaited Gorashar and the response from Mycroft. The latter was first to arrive. One of Vansittart's orderlies brought the message from London. The Cabinet had agreed to the Pasha's release but with conditions: Once returned to Egypt, the Pasha would be under solemn oath not to engage in any public activity whatsoever. He was to remain a private citizen and to hold no public office. He would be allowed to leave Ceylon as soon as possible in the company of Mr. Sherlock Holmes and an adequate military guard. So that there would be no delay, arrangements had been made with the captain of the ship the *Susannah II,* now at anchor in Trincomalee harbour, to wait for the arrival of special guests of Government. Mr. Holmes was authorised to carry the pearl with him. In Alexandria, he was to deliver it to General Gordon, who would see to its safe transfer to London. Mr. Holmes was also to be afforded every facility for his trip to England should he desire to return directly from Egypt. In a separate note, Vansittart said that the Pasha had agreed to all conditions and was already preparing his departure. Holmes wrote out a short note in reply, asking Vansittart to arrange their travel to Trincomalee.

"It was just after I read the message, Watson, that I became aware of a great commotion in the street below. A large crowd had assembled, mostly Tamileans, and stood in almost total silence. After a few moments a small group of them moved from the back of the crowd to the front. They were carrying two corpses lying on bamboo stretchers. Once they reached the front of the crowd, the procession moved rapidly past and out of sight, leaving the street almost deserted. At that moment, Gorashar arrived and informed me that the dead were Thyagamma and Nelusko, the finders of the pearl. They had been brutally murdered in their rooms, and the sombre crowd was taking them to the shore for cremation.

"No one seems to know when the murders occurred," Gorashar said. "The bodies were found only a few hours ago. They had been stabbed and their faces horribly mutilated, as if the killer had been angered by something, perhaps by his inability to find the pearl. If the pearl was the motive, the two had been murdered needlessly, since they had already sold it to the Atkinson brothers and no longer had it in their possession. There are no suspects."

"Let us examine their rooms while the crowd is gone," said Holmes. "Perhaps we may learn something."

Gorashar took Holmes directly to the victims' hotel, one far more run down than his own. The lobby was dark and empty except for a sweeper working in one corner. Holmes placed a fistful of rupees in his hand, and the sweeper led them directly to the rooms, no more than two small, windowless cells on the second floor. There were beds but nothing else. Bloodstains were everywhere, but there was little sign of a struggle. Whatever had belonged to the victims had been taken. The prints of bare feet were everywhere, and whatever clues might have been were destroyed by the many who had entered after the bodies were discovered.

"We are too late. There is nothing to be learned here beyond the obvious," said Holmes. He turned toward the sweeper. Putting a few more rupees into his hand, Holmes asked him what he had seen. The sweeper said that in the dark of the previous morning, at about four, two people entered the hotel dressed in Arab costume. The sweeper saw their faces: they were European, a man and a woman. They went directly up the stairs to the second floor, remained there for a few minutes, then came down and left in a run. He thought nothing of their coming and going since nocturnal traffic in the hotel is common enough during the pearl season. It was only after the bodies were found that he associated the two with the murder. When pressed, the sweeper could say little more than that both of those who entered were very large. He added in a voice filled with terror that the face of the dead pearl fisher Nelusko had been covered with what looked like claw marks.

"Obviously, Watson, the bloodletting which I so feared but knew would associate itself with the Moonstar of Mannar had begun. Gorashar and I returned to my quarters. He repeated his judgement that the pearl had been sold before they were murdered and that it was now in Trincomalee. I told him of the Pasha's claim."

"The Pasha is telling the truth," he said, "for the present owner of Atkinson brothers is his agent and was here for two days bargaining for the pearl. He left with it while Thyagamma and Nelusko were very much alive. But who would have killed the two pearl fishers after the pearl was sold? Do you think the two seen by the sweeper are the murderers?"

"We do not know for sure," said Holmes. "Learn what you can in the bazaar. Then follow me to Trincomalee."

Gorashar left, and Holmes went directly to the circuit house. He spoke with the Pasha, who was ready to depart, and told him that they would leave as soon as Vansittart had finished arrangements.

There was no rail to Trincomalee from Pearl Town, and so Vansittart arranged horses and a small armed escort. For a part of the journey they also travelled by elephant. The trip took two days and was an unexpectedly gruelling one. Several times they were forced to take long detours to avoid the rebels under Rama IV, the rebellious king who lived in the jungles north of Kandy, and in whose hands no Englishman was safe. A few times they caught sight of these rebels, dressed in dark green, armed with rifles and daggers.

Despite the dangers, however, they arrived at their destination. Holmes and the Pasha went directly to the shop of the Atkinson brothers, called Les Portes d'Argent. They were led into a large room where they waited for Abdul Latif, the Pasha's agent.

"Notice the doors," said the Pasha, "jewellers must always have many ways of entrance and egress."

There were six silver doors in the room. The one directly in front of them opened, and Abdul Latif, a tall, thin man not unlike the Pasha in appearance, entered. He bowed to the Pasha and placed a small box in his hand. The Pasha opened it and gave it to Holmes.

"Here is the Moonstar of Mannar," he said. "It is truly fit for a queen.

You may test it in any way you like. Five hundred seventeen grains, a perfect sphere—"

It was indeed a beautiful thing, thought Holmes, one of the most exquisite examples of devil's bait he had yet encountered. He studied it under a glass for several moments, then returned it to its box.

"It is indeed what it has been claimed to be," he said.

"You may take it now," said the Pasha.

Holmes put the box in his pocket. The first part of the work was now finished, he thought. If all went to plan, the Pasha and he would board the *Susannah II* in a few hours and they would be on their way to Egypt, the Pasha with his freedom, and he with the pearl for Her Majesty.

Holmes paused for a moment, as if in deep thought. "And here, Watson, at this rather important moment, I determined to do other than what was planned. I decided that I would accompany the Pasha to the *Susannah,* but that once he was ensconced, I would return to Trincomalee to deal with Sebastian Moran. The pearl I would turn over to the ship's captain, for delivery to the authorities in Egypt. How could I not deal with Moran after all these years? I believed he was in Trincomalee, and I had to find him."

Holmes spoke these last words in deadly earnest, for Moran had been one of the chief reasons for his wanderings through Asia.

"But the unexpected happened, and I did not have to look for him," he said.

It was not far, Holmes continued, from the market of Trincomalee to the great harbour for which it was justly famous. As they approached the port, they could see the lights of the *Susannah II* as it prepared for departure. When they reached the dock, the Pasha turned to Holmes and said, "Thank you for your help, my dear Professor, but I am afraid that we must part here. It has all been arranged. Mr. Wellesley is to take your place onboard and will explain all to the authorities. Good luck tonight, my friend."

Holmes turned to see that the armed escort that had accompanied them had now trained its rifles on him. A fourth man, dressed in the dark green of the rebels, suddenly appeared from the darkness. Motioning to the Pasha to continue on his way to the dock, he said to Holmes: "Please follow. The King awaits your arrival."

Holmes watched as the Pasha lowered himself from the dock into a small boat that quickly took him toward the *Susannah.*

"In a few minutes, Watson, surrounded by the guard and their leader, I was led to a place known as Foul Point, a cliff that extends north of Trincomalee some three hundred feet above the sea. Here, my dear Doctor, was enacted, in this most beautiful of places, the final portion of the drama."

I noticed that Mycroft suddenly pulled himself up in his chair, for he had apparently not yet heard the end of the story from Holmes's lips.

"When we reached the top of the cliff, an unexpected sight greeted me. Seated in a row, as if at some great public event, sat an old man whom I took to be Rama IV, the leader of the Ceylonese rebellion, and on either side of him a large number of his soldiers. In front of him and his lieutenants, on their knees with their hands tied behind their backs, were Colonel Moran and Franziska van Rhede. As I approached, Moran glared at me with the greatest hatred. A soldier approached him, and with a knife cut the ropes that held his hands. Moran stood up. Franziska too was freed and afforded a seat in honour of her sex. The rebels maintained a distance from her, however, for they appeared more afraid of her than of Moran."

Then, said Holmes, the King, Rama IV, stood and made an impassioned oration in his own language. He finished with a few words in English: "You feringhi have brought our island to ruin. Your stench is everywhere. You have fouled our soil. I live only to rid the motherland of your pestilential presence."

The King paused for a moment, then said, "But let us make this night a memorable one for us. Mr. Holmes, honoured guest, let the royal festivities begin here this very night for your beloved Queen. The pearl, please."

Holmes handed over the box. A soldier took it from the King's hand and placed it on the ground between two black rocks.

"You two will fight for the pearl—and your lives," said the King. "Strip them! Bring the hoods!" he ordered.

As the guards stripped them to the waist, Moran spoke venomously to Holmes. "I have waited for this moment as if for an eternity," he said. "When Moriarty went over the Reichenbach Falls, time stopped for me. All that I am—and ever will be—I owe to that great soul. I learned everything from him. His mind was the sharpest that ever thought on English soil, his heart the strongest and the cruellest. And you, you fiend, destroyed that great genius."

"My sincere condolences, old fellow," said Holmes, "but you must understand that I am of course of a very different view. Do not forget that Moriarty came after me at the falls. Had he pursued a more intelligent path, he would be alive today, albeit sitting in a London jail. But we should give our attention to present matters, should we not?"

I stared at Holmes in disbelief. A look of amusement came over his face as his glance met mine.

"Moran and I," he said, "now stripped to the waist, were to fight it out to the delight of the rebel army. There I was again, Watson, on the brink of an abyss with a mortal enemy bent on my destruction, the very one who had thrown rocks down on my head and almost caused my death at the falls in Reichenbach."

He stopped his account to light a cigarette. "You have heard, no doubt, of the andabatarian gladiators of ancient Rome?" he asked, putting his match out in the ashtray.

"No," I replied.

"A most interesting custom," interjected Mycroft, lifting his heavy eyelids with difficulty, "which may have derived in the end from the ancient Indians. Hoods were placed over the gladiators' heads to blind them. Without sight, they fought more amusingly and of course more cruelly, to the great glee of the Roman audience."

"Never did I think that I would ever find myself in such a position," said Holmes. "As we began our duel, I suddenly thanked Heaven for my hours of practice walking and living in the dark. As soon as the hood was placed over my head, my ears, my skin, came alive. I knew that Moran, through far stronger than I, would find me a difficult opponent. My other senses, so patiently cultivated in my training, became so strong that they more than made up for the lack of vision. I could sense Moran's slightest move. I could hear his breathing, the smallest sound that he caused, the smell of his breath and of his sweat. Without eyes I had no back, no front. All my senses were equal and functioned in all directions. Moran could not do the same. Indeed, as our duel continued, I made myself almost imperceptible. He could not hear my breath, for I dropped it to an inaudible minimum. I could feel through my feet the vibrations of his heavy step, but he could not sense mine. I waited calmly as he moved. Purposely, I taunted him, so as to let him know where I was. Then, as he rushed toward me, I moved out of his way and gave him a sharp kick to the stomach. It brought him down, stunned and writhing in pain. I pulled the hood from his head. 'Come, my dear Colonel, this will give you a better chance.'

"Despite his pain, I could hear his fury rise, and so deftly did he move that he caught me by the foot. I escaped from his grasp, however, but felt a rush of pain as I extricated my leg. Moran rose and rushed toward me, but I dodged and tripped him, throwing him off balance. As he fell, I delivered a hard blow to the jaw. He moaned as he hit the ground, panting in pain at my feet, no longer able to move. I tore the hood from my own head. I sat him up, and he revived."

"You fiend," he cried.

"Come, come, my dear fellow, one wins some, and one loses others. You unfortunately have just lost rather a big one."

Rama and his men sat and did not move. Holmes rushed to the pearl. All watched helplessly as he took it and threw it as high and as far as he could against the darkening sky. For an instant it caught the light of the moon, then fell slowly downward, glowing like a star before it began its descent into the void.

Suddenly, Franziska stood up, a look of horror and greed on her face. "No," she shouted. Like some great Stymphalian bird, said Holmes, she leapt into the air, almost flying directly into him, her hands and fingers spread wide, her sharp talons fully extended.

Holmes moved quickly aside and watched as she neared the precipice. For a moment, the pearl seemed to hang in midair above her. It shivered for a brief moment, then continued its inevitable descent. Franziska stretched forward. The tips of her talons touched it, and for an instant it appeared as though it would obey and come to her. Instead, she lost her balance and, with a frightful shriek, fell after the small white sphere as it disappeared into the abyss. Holmes looked down. There was nothing but the roar of the sea as it crashed on the rocks below.

Moran rushed to the precipice. Seeing only the sea, he turned toward Holmes, a shocked look of despair on his face. His defiance gone, he suddenly broke into a run toward the jungle and disappeared in seconds. Rama quickly despatched some men after him.

"It was only at that moment that the severe pain in my leg came to my consciousness," said Holmes. "I could not walk. My leg felt broken, and I stumbled to my knees."

Then, in an angry voice, Rama IV barked an order: "Fling him into the sea." Four men came forward. They lifted Holmes by his arms and legs and began to swing him to and fro over the edge of the precipice. His injured leg made a sharp sound as he was swung in the air, and he swooned.

"I remembered nothing until I awoke in the dark. Thrown high into the air, I had come to rest on a soft ledge about fifteen feet from the top of the cliff. I lay there unable to move, listening only to the roar of the sea below. In the distance, I could see the lights of the *Susannah II* as it began its departure for Egypt, carrying the Pasha to his homeland. As it disappeared in the night, I heard friendly voices. Gentle hands lifted me and carried me upward. Gorashar's soft voice entered my ears, and I blacked out for the second time.

"I awoke the following day in the fort of Trincomalee, or so I was told, since I had no recollection of how or how long I had come to be there. My head throbbed, and my leg was immobilised with heavy bandages. Gorashar sat at the window in a light doze. At the first sign of life from me, he was at my side."

Holmes paused for a moment and sipped his drink slowly. I could say nothing, so horrifying was his account. Even Mycroft, who had remained impassive through most of the tale, seemed moved now by his brother's pain and his nearly fatal encounter.

"It was a fortnight before I was able to travel. What I thought was a broken leg was fortunately a badly torn muscle, and I was able to travel sooner than I had anticipated. I had sent a complete account of what had happened to Vansittart. Attempts to intercept the *Susannah* were futile, for the ship's captain too was part of the plot. Before I left, however, Vansittart informed me that the Pasha had escaped from the ship in the Gulf of Aden and had been met by a group of followers on the Arabian coast. He was now said to be deep in the Hadramaut, planning his way back to Egypt. Wellesley also had boarded the ship. But he too disappeared sometime during the voyage, and it was not sure at the time whether he had been lost at sea, or whether he had gone ashore when the Pasha escaped. It was only several years later that I was able to deal with Mr. Arthur Wellesley. And as to the Pasha, we know that his efforts came to naught."

By now it was late afternoon, just before five. As Holmes ended his tale, there was a great thunderclap, and the rains poured down heavily for a few moments. The heat had broken, and the late afternoon sun now fell on a cooler and cleaner London.

Mycroft looked at his watch. "The festivities for the Queen," he said, "have ended. Let us therefore stand, for Her Majesty is about to enter Westminster."

The few eccentrics who remained in the Club stood with us. Throughout the city, church bells rang. Then, as if by command, the stately strains of "God Save the Queen" rose in the city and floated through the window. It was as if the whole country sang in unison. Even in the staid chambers of the Diogenes Club there appeared not to be a dry eye.

Except for Holmes, who rose slowly, his face impassive, his jaw set. He said nothing, sang nothing.

"No new crown for the Queen, Watson," said Mycroft when the music ended, "no pearl of course, either. But Her Majesty is well attired for the occasion, in brocade, hand-embroidered in gold in India."

I thanked him for taking the time to relate his part in the Trincomalee affair. Holmes graciously helped his brother to his feet and walked him to his rooms.

As we left the Club, Holmes said that he wished to walk alone for a while and suggested that we meet just before eight at Covent Garden for a performance of Verdi's *Nabucco*.

I agreed and watched him as he rapidly disappeared into the dwindling crowd.

MURDER IN THE
THIEVES' BAZAAR

HERLOCK HOLMES'S EXPERIENCE OF A WIDE ASSORTMENT OF crime, often in some of the most remote corners of the globe, had led him to speculate from time to time on the relation between the native world and the world of the criminal. Like all true scientists, he believed firmly that the laws governing the science of detection—primarily those of observation and deduction—pertained universally, and equally therefore, in the winding alleys of the Hindu and Mohammedan worlds and the broad avenues of Paris and London. What differences there might appear to be lay at the surface and could be ascribed to accidental differences in local circumstance.

"Take, as an example," he said one evening at dinner, "a murder in Delhi. There are red stains everywhere, what appears to be blood. The stains continue several yards from the scene of the crime. In London, one can be almost completely sure that they are blood and blood alone. In Delhi, or elsewhere in India, however, they may be blood and betel, a leaf commonly filled with spices and the like and chewed in India, the juice of which when expectorated often resembles the splotches of blood that one associates with a bleeding animal, human or otherwise. Here we have a simple case of the necessity to understand the place in which one finds oneself."

I could not help but agree in this instance. "But what of the criminal himself, my dear Holmes? Surely the Indian or the Chinese criminal must perforce be different from our English criminal. Could one not talk of criminal types?"

"I do not believe so, Watson. Cruelty and the commission of serious transgressions may be innate in many human beings, but I do not believe myself that criminals can be described in such ways. There are no criminal types, nor are there tribes that are criminal. Gunthorpe's work on the criminal castes and tribes of India, for instance, is utter nonsense."

I was surprised to hear him speak in such fashion, for I thought that the work of Gunthorpe and Sleeman had greatly aided in the apprehension of criminals and criminal groups throughout the Subcontinent.

"Then what about the work of Lombroso," I retorted, "surely his reasoning that physical type and crime are intimately connected hardly needs justification. His theories have already established him as the leading criminologist of Europe."

Sherlock Holmes sniffed sardonically. "Lombroso is a miserable bungler. His works on delinquent males and females have made me positively ill. He reasons from the poor specimens who inhabit the jails of Italy, innocent devils, fathers many of them, who have committed no crime except the theft of a loaf of bread to feed a starving child, and mothers, forced to sell their bodies and their souls for the same purpose. No, Watson, were I to follow Lombroso's techniques I surely would pursue the innocent, and perhaps the innocent alone."

I was annoyed at Holmes's cavalier dismissal of writers whom I judged to have a high place in the forensic world, but I knew that mine was no match for his intimate knowledge of the criminological literature. Still, I decided to continue the debate and perhaps to provoke him into another tale.

"But surely the jails in our Empire are not filled with the innocent. My own experience in Afghanistan led me to the conclusion that were we to win control of those areas we would be faced with an enormous civilising mission, considering the moral turpitude of most of the local population. Even educated Hindus have remarked on the enormous number of social pests found among the lower castes who, in a variety of disguises, commit the overwhelming majority of crimes."

Holmes laughed warmly. "Brilliant, Watson," he exclaimed, "not even Gunthorpe himself could have put it any better. But I know you well enough to know that you do not believe such twaddle. If you want me to relate another Oriental adventure, you should say so directly."

I smiled broadly at his remark. "I should have known better than try to provoke you. But perhaps you could give me a longer example of the universality of your science and the nature of the special circumstances to which you have just alluded."

"If you mean by circumstances what is usually referred to as circumstantial evidence, Watson, then we have much to talk about. A crime in England, one in Italy, one in Turkey, one in Japan, will all differ in local circumstances and the way they happen. What makes them similar is the view that the detective takes of the circumstances. Universality lies in the eye of the observer. You no doubt remember the case to which you gave the name of the Boscombe Valley mystery."

"I remember, indeed. Surely no one ever appeared to be as guilty of murder as young McCarthy. Were it not for your intervention, Lestrade would have had him led to the gallows without the slightest qualm."

"Precisely. In many serious crimes—murder, in particular—there are often no witnesses, nor other direct evidence of any kind. Hence it is the reading of the indirect evidence that leads to a conclusion. Shift one's viewpoint just ever so much and starkly differing conclusions may be reached. The guilty become innocent and the innocent guilty."

Holmes stopped for a moment. "There is, Watson," he said with a sudden look of recall on his face, "a case that speaks to our discussion, one with which you are not familiar since it occurred during my time in the Orient. Perhaps you would like to hear it?"

We moved from the table to our favourite chairs, and he related the following tale of murder in the thieves' bazaar of Bombay.

"You will remember, Watson, that in one of my recent relations to you I described the awful events of Trincomalee."

"Yes, indeed, I do."

"It was shortly thereafter that I left Ceylon and began the long trip to Bombay, where I fully intended to begin my journey back to England. I decided to travel up the west coast of India this time, and so my first stop was the pleasant Indian city of Trivandrum. Here I met a most interesting individual, an Italian nobleman by the name of Count Lorenzo Spinelli. We found each other compatible, and Spinelli suggested that we travel together since we had similar destinations. Spinelli, I learned quickly, had a profound knowledge of Indian philosophy, and even though I did not share his passion, I found our conversation to be a most welcome distraction, particularly on the rather desolate portions of our trip that often held nothing of interest. He had no travelling companions except for three servants, Lachman, a young man who served as cook and chief guide, and two porters, who were obliged to carry Spinelli's large collection of books and papers. As to myself, I told the good count that my name was William Redfern, and that by profession I was a barrister at law, travelling to Bombay on business.

"The tale that follows, Watson, concerns Lachman, who was, I could see from the first, devoted to the Italian. When Spinelli finally left India, Lachman was quite distraught. In age only about twenty, he had become totally dependent on his master. The boy was of a very low caste, Jogee by name, and had been born in a small village in the poorest part of central India, in the area known as Bustar, a place considered by some to be among the most backward of the Subcontinent. The boy had run from the village and made his way to Nagpur. Spinelli found him wandering the streets starving and took him on as his personal servant. To Spinelli's great fortune, the boy turned out to be honest, intelligent, and diligent in his duties. I found him of great help in our travels myself."

Upon their arrival in Bombay, continued Holmes, Spinelli gave Lachman a substantial sum of cash, to be used according to the Count's wishes for Lachman to send for his wife and to construct a small house on the edge of what is called the Chor Bazaar, the great flea market of Bombay. Lachman had no other income, and Spinelli, still concerned about the boy's survival, left another sum, this about five hundred Indian rupees, with Holmes, who promised Spinelli that before his final departure from Bombay he would visit Lachman and deliver the gift.

It was many weeks after Spinelli's departure, however, before Holmes found a moment to begin the search for Lachman. He had become entangled in a minor affair that had baffled the Bombay police, and it was only after that had been resolved that he began to look for the boy. Spinelli had drawn for Holmes a small map, and with it he found his way to the Chor Bazaar, or Thieves' Bazaar, and therein Lachman's modest abode.

When he arrived, he found only Lachman's wife, whom he had met but once previously. As soon as she saw Holmes, however, she burst into tears and began to tell in broken Hindustanee what had happened to her poor Lachman.

On the previous evening, she said, Lachman and she had gone to visit some close friends. Their friends had fed them well, so that when they reached home they felt no need to cook and sat in their small garden chatting until bedtime. Lachman had been out of sorts because of a quarrel that afternoon with a man who had rented their extra room, and she tried to coax him out of his mood, but without success. She had pointed to a spider climbing up the leg of a nearby chair.

"What do you call these little beasties in your village?" she asked.

"I don't know," he said. Angrily picking up a nearby shoe, he aimed it at the insect.

"Don't kill him, don't," she shouted. But Lachman did not hear her entreaty and despatched the helpless spider.

"May he rest in peace," he said mockingly.

Furious with her husband, she was about to go inside when they thought they heard voices from their rented room.

"Shhh, listen," said Lachman. "There is someone in there with him." Lachman became even angrier, but she calmed him and they retired for the night.

Because they were again short of money, the couple had rented one of their rooms to a retired soldier returning from abroad, and it was he whom they had just heard talking in a low voice to someone unknown. And it was with this soldier, said his wife, that Lachman had had a near violent altercation on the street that afternoon, for the soldier had made unwanted advances toward her. There had been many witnesses to the argument. So heated had it become that Lachman had threatened to kill the soldier and had to be restrained by his neighbours.

It was later during that night, she continued, after they had retired, that they were awakened by a loud thud coming from the soldier's room. Lachman jumped up and nudged her awake. He took his knife from its sheath, and lighting a candle, he and his wife went into the corridor. They heard a strange gasping coming from the soldier's room. Frightened, they opened the door to find the soldier lying in a pool of blood, his neck badly cut. A cashbox, filled with rupees, lay flung open on the floor. It was probably the box hitting the floor that had awakened them. Interrupted by the noise, the murderer had fled quickly. The open window attested to his escape. Lachman tried to help the dying man, by holding his head up and offering him water, but to no avail. He expired almost immediately.

Lachman told his wife to inform the police, and that he would notify the headman. She watched her husband, she said, now bloodstained, staring at his dead enemy for a moment. As she left for the police station, she turned and looked as he walked toward the headman's house and disappeared into the night.

"That was the last time I was to see him outside of his prison cell," she said. "I only learned later from his own lips what happened to him." It was a dark night, he told her later, and he walked slowly at first, thinking over the events of the day. This scoundrel, who had tried to touch his wife, was now dead, and he could not help but feel a certain satisfaction. But the sight of the dying man had changed much of his anger to pity, and as he walked on in the night, he lost all bitterness toward him.

Suddenly, his mind seized on a thought, and he was thrown into panic: What if he, Lachman, were to be accused of the murder? Had he not threatened to kill the man in front of a large crowd of witnesses? Sweating in fear now, he began to run toward the headman's house, but when he reached there, instead of entering, he kept on going. In a fit of panic, he ran into the night, forgetting everything, his wife, his very life.

She sobbed now at the recollection of her husband's words, and Holmes comforted her, saying that he would try to help. His words helped her regain her composure. She said that the police found Lachman not far away, cowering and shivering at the home of a friend who had pleaded with him to give himself up. His attempt to escape had convinced the police that he indeed had committed the murder. His wife's words were discounted, for it was believed that she would do anything to protect him. And so he was arrested and charged with the crime. He now sat somewhere in a Bombay cell, awaiting the next step of Indian criminal justice. She had been allowed to visit him, but she had no idea of what was to happen next.

Lachman's wife was crying softly but uncontrollably by the end of her story, and Holmes could get nothing more from her. He went at once to the local police station to find Lachman. He was immediately ushered into the office of the chief inspector, an old but experienced policeman by the name of Pushkar Shamshere. The inspector made it clear that he regarded the whole affair as unfortunate but as an open-and-shut case. The circumstantial evidence was conclusive. There was, he said, an unimpeachable witness who, as he passed their house that night, heard Lachman's wife cry, "Don't kill him!" and an angry "May he rest in peace" from Lachman's mouth. He had bloodstains on his shirt, his knife was not in its case, and above all, he had a motive: Lachman had threatened to kill his boarder publicly that very day. The soldier's cashbox had not been taken. Robbery was therefore not the motive. No, said the inspector, let us not waste our time. Lachman is guilty.

"There is nothing to be done, my friend," said Inspector Shamshere. "A most tragic case of anger leading to murder."

"Perhaps," said Holmes. "But I know the boy well, having travelled with him from Trivandrum. I am not convinced."

Holmes asked that he be allowed to visit Lachman, and his request was immediately granted. Because of the grim nature of his crime, Lachman was alone in a small, vile cell deep inside Bombay's main prison. The poor boy was overjoyed when he saw Holmes, for his first thought was that he had obtained his release. Holmes had to tell him at once that he would try to help in his case, but that he did not know if he would be successful.

"How is my case, Sahib? I did not kill that man. Believe me. And believe my wife. Someone else came into the house. Through the window."

"Then why did you run?" asked Holmes.

"I suddenly became frightened, Sahib. I could not think. I ran and ran. Then I realised I had nowhere to go. So I went to my friend's house and he called the police. That is all."

Holmes then asked Lachman to recount everything he remembered, from the time he met the soldier until he ran from the scene of his murder. Detailed as it was, he was unable to add anything to the story that his wife had not already related. Holmes asked him to try to remember the voice that he thought he heard coming from the soldier's room, but he could not. And the soldier had died before he could say anything.

"I had seen enough of Lachman on our journey," Holmes went on, "to believe in his innocence. I now had to find a way of proving that he had not committed the murder. This would not be easy. The circumstantial evidence was very strong. How to tear this web of circumstance and arrive at the truth?"

He comforted Lachman, telling him that he would do his best to clear his name. He returned directly to Lachman's house to examine the scene of the crime. He had of course by this time no chance of examining the murdered man where he had been killed, and the room had been ransacked by the police. Still, he went about his business, carefully looking through the dust, examining the meagre furniture, the string bed, and the various other articles in the room. The window was still open, and someone could have left by it in a hurry. The murderer, hearing the approaching Lachman and his wife, could have rushed through it into the night. What looked like smudged hand- and footprints were visible on the frame and the sill. But how again to prove that they were those of someone other than Lachman?

It soon became apparent to Holmes that his methods of observation and deduction depended very heavily on another set of assumptions, assumptions that involved not only criminals and the police but the society itself.

"What one observes and deduces in London," he said, "is based on what Londoners ordinarily do and think. And my experience in the Orient had been so far almost exclusively with the crime of Europeans, among whom the same set of assumptions held. Here in Bombay, particularly among the lower classes, I had suddenly to think in different ways. My questions were of the same kind. Who was this soldier who was killed? From where had he come? Who killed him and for what motive? But, I must say, as I gazed around the dusty room, I was totally without answers. If the questions I asked were the same as those that I might ask at home, could the answers be so different?"

Holmes arose and began to pace about the room. "I realised at once that this was a case in which the most minute examination of detail, the sifting of every word of Lachman's and his wife's testimony, the scrutiny of every piece of evidence, would eventually produce another hypothesis, an explanation of the evidence that told another story. I renewed my efforts at the scene of the crime. If I looked carefully enough and went over the room skilfully enough, something would be found of value. Again I scoured the room. Finally, under the bed, I saw two small pieces of reddish clay, fairly fresh. My hopes were increased when I noticed that the same clay was stuck to the end of the bed, where someone's feet may have deposited them, either those of the murdered man or those of the person who had killed him. I reexamined the windowsill and noticed to my great elation tiny traces of the same clay. Hoping that they did not come from this part of the city, I placed them carefully in a small envelope. I examined the rest of the house and all the shoes that were there. There was no red clay anywhere, none on any of them. I also found one other clue, significant for Lachman's wife's version of the story, but in itself not enough to change anything: in one corner of the room was a single chupple on the sole of which the body of a dead spider lay crushed."

Holmes still knew very little, only that the red clay may have come from the shoes of the murderer. He left immediately for police headquarters and spoke to Inspector Shamshere once again. Holmes told him that he wished to examine the body of the victim, his clothes, and whatever else there was. Since he had already helped the police in another case, the Inspector had no objections. He himself had made his decision about the crime and had no interest in trying to find the evidence of Lachman's innocence.

Holmes first examined the body of the soldier. He was in luck, for in a few hours the soldier was to be taken to the cremation ground, where he and a number of other unknown Bombay dead were to be burned in a mass fire. Holmes examined first the wound and determined that a long, sharp knife had been used with force to cut the main arteries in the neck. The soldier was still fully clothed except for his feet, which showed no sign of the clay. His shoes had been removed, and Holmes was informed by the guard that they had been stolen. He found no other wounds. Underneath the clothes, however, was a well-muscled, powerful body. There were marks everywhere, indicating much handto-hand combat. Large scars on his shoulders and abdomen were from more serious wounds, which must have kept him idle during long periods of convalescence. His features were not pleasant ones, and there was a hardness in the expression on his face that attested a violent death had followed on a life of violence. His hair was a steely grey, and there was a series of small scars on his left cheek. Even in death, a cruelty played about the lips. He was neither Gurkha nor Sikh, but most probably a Mahratta, one of the most militant of Indian tribes.

Holmes then searched the man's pockets and found two articles of interest. The first was part of a steamship ticket. The ticket noted his name, one Vikram Singh, and the port of embarkation: Aden. Evidently the soldier had been in the Levant and had recently come to Bombay by sea. The other was a document, partly in French and partly in Arabic. Badly bloodstained, it appeared to be a contract with an unknown employer in the Near East for military services. Our soldier appeared to have ended his career as no more than a mercenary.

"I was about to depart when I noticed that something had fallen from the soldier's jacket, and this, Watson, was a bit of real luck: it was a small piece of a broken silver earring, rather distinctive in its form, for it had been set with a small piece of lapis lazuli. It appeared to me not to be of Indian origin."

Holmes then asked to see the cashbox, a wooden box that contained a large number of Indian rupees. There was no clue here beyond the box and the notes themselves. What was of immediate interest was that the notes were well worn, not the new notes a person recently arrived would receive from a bank or exchange. Some of the money was bloodstained. Holmes laboriously counted it. There were a few large notes, but much of it was in small ones. They totalled almost 10,000 rupees, a princely sum for a soldier, far greater than any salary he could have saved. Holmes's curiosity grew. How had the soldier been paid for his duties? In what currency? Hardly in Indian currency. No, this cashbox represented something other than the soldier's wages, a different source of income. But what? Had he himself stolen it? And, if so, from whom?

Holmes examined the box closely, looking for clues. It was of a common Bombay type, and had a variety of uses. One often saw them in small shops placed next to where merchants sit. This one had a small lock, but the key was gone.

"There it was, Watson. I had no more. A bit of clay, a broken earring, a wooden box of ten thousand rupees, a steamship ticket that indicated the soldier had come from Aden, and a small piece of paper written in French and Arabic that I could not decipher because of the bloodstains.

I should say to you now, in hindsight, that I had enough to solve the crime right then, or less sanguinely, I had enough to find the path to the criminal. And here, may I emphasise, the next step in all solutions: one must begin to weave a thread, something that connects, through the brain, the various pieces of the puzzle. For what one must create must resemble a picture, or series of pictures, of what had happened. One must become, Watson, an interpreter of events, and relive what happened, very much as a historian must who wishes to solve the riddles of the past."

Holmes decided then to put the case out of his conscious mind for a time and went to the Gymkhana, where he put himself through a rigorous round of calisthenics, after which he received an Indian massage by one of the master masseurs of Bombay. He then dressed and sat on the verandah, sipping a strong cup of Indian chai, rich with sugar, spices, and heavy buffalo milk.

"It was then that the story of the dead soldier and its end began to present itself in a new way," he went on. "So quickly did it all appear to me that it was as if the solution came at once out of the meagre evidence itself without any deliberation on my part. In relating it to you now, I shall retell it as if I became aware of the steps individually.

"First was our dead soldier himself. Here was a man of military skill and experience who, I guessed, had started out some twenty years before as a recruit in the British army. After duty abroad, he either left or was dismissed from Her Majesty's service. He then entered the world of the mercenary, fighting for the French, I imagined, in a variety of North African campaigns. His body now filled with the wounds sustained in years of combat, he decided to return home to retirement and engage in some more peaceful employment. Two days before, he had arrived in Bombay aboard some transport ship, the identity of which I could easily ascertain by a quick trip to the docks. Landing on Indian soil, he decided to seek lodging close by. A few enquiries led him by chance to the house of our Lachman. Lachman's wife rented him the room, and our soldier proceeded to make advances toward her, just as Lachman returned home. He heard his wife's shouts, and a loud quarrel then ensued. Lachman threatened to kill the soldier, but a crowd gathered and separated the two before they came to blows. The soldier insisted that he would stay for the night since he had already paid, and would leave in the morning. Lachman reluctantly agreed, and the soldier, leaving his belongings in the room, departed and did not return until dark, just before Lachman and his wife returned from visiting the home of some close friends.

"It was clear to me at that point that the soldier, during that afternoon, had gone somewhere and had most probably met his murderer. The question was, Where? And here, Watson, one does not have to meditate on the problem very long. Here is a tough, mercenary soldier, arrived in Bombay after a long series of campaigns and a sea journey of several weeks. Where would he go at the first opportunity?

"It does not take a strong imagination to suggest, as an answer to the question, that the soldier's first destination would be the nearest brothel or opium den, where he could find solace in the pleasures with which a city like Bombay is perhaps endowed like no other. He enters, begins with a round of intoxicants, and then retires with one of the women who ply their wares in such establishments. He has no cash on him but presents her with a set of cheap earrings from abroad. No client has ever done anything like this. Touched by his kindness, she tells him of her desire to leave her trade and pursue a normal life. She has saved some money, she says. He suggests that they leave together. She goes to pack her meagre belongings, and he departs before she returns, stealing her money box. She is able to follow him to Lachman's house, where she murders him in his sleep. In his final agony, he pulls one of the earrings from her ear. It disappears into a crease in his uniform. The cashbox falls to the floor. Lachman and his wife, awakened by the noise, rush to the room. She barely has time to escape, and must leave the box behind. The rest presents no challenge.

"I must admit, Watson, in retrospect, that this story had its difficulties. And yet, I had nothing else but to follow the rather bizarre tale that I had invented. I left the comfort of the Gymkhana and proceeded to the brothel district of the city. I began in the section that was not far from Lachman's house. I started with the main street. I stopped in several establishments and asked whether someone fitting Vikram Singh's description had been there. My questions were greeted with laughter. Everyone looked like that was the reply. No one recognised him from my words."

It was only when he reached the smaller gullies that Holmes saw what was to bring him to the solution of the crime: in front of one of the brothels were two men digging, for what purpose he did not know. As he approached, he realised that they had produced a large pile of red clay, undoubtedly the same as those small pieces that he had found in the soldier's room. He perhaps had found the place that he was looking for. He ascended the narrow staircase and came into a room of garish velvet. A woman sat at a small desk. He told her that he wanted to see her women. She obliged him by parading before him several of the poor inmates of her establishment. Dressed in flamboyant saris, the women cavorted in front of him, laughing, teasing, their faces the colour of flour paste, their eyes filled with pain and resentment. Holmes looked at each closely, hoping to see a wounded ear, but he saw nothing. He waved them all away.

"What is wrong? You have refused my best," said the woman at the desk.

To Holmes she was quite a horror in her own right, a fat, rather loathsome creature with orange hair, skin powdered to a thick whiteness, dressed in a red velvet gown, a large necklace of fake Bombay pearls around her neck.

"I want the one with the wounded ear," he said in answer to her query.

She frowned, hesitating for a moment. "She is not here today. It is her day of rest."

"I will pay well," he said.

"Very well. I will fetch her. Wait here."

Holmes waited for several minutes. The room was suffocatingly hot, and the smell of incense and cheap perfume made him want to retch. The madam returned, accompanied by a youngish woman, who was dressed not in her professional attire but in a simple sari. She wore no powder on her face. Her right ear bore a bandage, however, and the other a silver earring like the fragment he had found. Luck had brought him to the end of his search very quickly.

Holmes extended his hand and gave her the fragment of the earring that he had found. She looked at it with great surprise and then fear. She motioned for him to follow, and they went to her room. The madam chuckled as Holmes passed her.

"Let me speak frankly to you, my dear woman," Holmes said in Hin-

11

dustanee. "I have reason to believe that you murdered one Vikram Singh in cold blood last night. Why you committed such a deed is not of any consequence to me at this moment, for a young friend of mine has been unjustly accused of what you have done. I must clear his name. And so I must ask you to accompany me to police headquarters."

She stood there, silent, motionless for what seemed to him to be an eternity. Then she spoke softly: "You are right. I did kill Vikram Singh. But why I did it is important for you to know, and for the police to know. Before I go with you then, I wish that you listen."

Holmes sat on a chair in the corner of the room. She turned and said, "I have lived and worked in this room for eleven years. I was brought here when I was thirteen."

As she spoke, Holmes soon realised that the story he had imagined was hardly the truth, even though it had led him to the murderer.

"I was born in a village to the south of here," she said. "We were a poor family of farmers, and much of the time there was nothing to eat. My mother had five children and died after I was born. My father raised us as well as he could. One day he said that I was to become a devadasi, a temple dancer, and that this was to be a great honour. I was to become a wife of our god, Shiva. I was very proud, for I had no idea what the word *devadasi* meant, but marriage to the god was to me the greatest happiness. In a few days, I was dressed in fine clothes and taken to the temple, where the priests uttered prayers in Sanscrit and anointed me into the temple. I remained there for several days. Then my father fetched me and told me that I would go to the city. My uncle, his cousin-brother, would take me there. I would do the work of a de- vadasi. I would have much to eat, and I would earn much money. My life would be good.

"My father's cousin-brother came one day and took me with him. I cried as we left, but my father did not hear me. Nor my brothers. They all turned away. My uncle and I travelled to Bombay by rail. As soon as we arrived he brought me here and sold me to the woman you met below. I soon was taught my present trade and became a woman of the night. I have been here ever since. This is how I learned what it means to be a devadasi.

"During all of this time, I have never seen my family. My father came several times, but he came only to collect the larger part of my earnings.

My uncle was a soldier, and he left for battle, never, I thought, to return.

"Two days ago, a man came. I did not know him, but he asked for me. There are so many who have come and know me that I did not think it strange that he asked for me by name. He was drunk and wanted opium. At first he was kind: he gave me a pair of earrings, which I put on. He told me how beautiful I was. He caressed my face tenderly. Suddenly his mood changed, and he seized me and forced me into his embrace. I submitted, and when he had finished he threw some money in my face. He laughed. Then he told me: he was my father's cousin-brother, the very uncle who had brought me here. He had come for my wages. In disbelief, I told him that I had nothing. But he searched the room and found the money that I had hidden over the years, the money that was to make me free. He took it and left. I followed him, but when we reached his room, he threatened me with death and pushed me away. I returned here in despair, determined to obtain vengeance. As soon as night fell, I went back to his lodging. He had left the window open, and I could see that he was fast asleep. The liquor and opium had put him in a stupor. I climbed into the room. He must have heard something, for he mumbled in his sleep. Frightened that he would awaken, I rushed at him and slit his throat with all my strength. He awakened long enough to see my face before he died. Blood shot from his neck onto the bed. He tried to grab me, and I pushed him back. But his hand had reached my ear and pulled the earring from it. I almost cried out in pain. I tried to grasp my money box, but it fell to the floor. I heard people coming, and I ran to the window without it. Once outside, I no longer cared about the money. The death of this man brought me the greatest happiness I had known since I had been forced to leave my village. Now that you know my story, I have no fear in going with you."

Holmes arose once again from his seat and began to pace to and fro. "How wrong I was, Watson, in the basic details of the story. I had merely established a possible thread between pieces of evidence, its only virtue being that it led me to the true version."

As soon as she had finished her story, Holmes decided on a course of action. He asked that the woman remain there in her room until he returned. She agreed. He then went directly to police headquarters, and again to Pushkar Shamshere, the Chief Inspector, in whose hands Lachman's case had fallen. Holmes told him that it was most urgent that he listen to the version of the events that had just transpired. The inspector listened attentively to all that Holmes had to say.

"Mr. Redfern," said Shamshere, "it seems to me that you have cast sufficient doubt on the evidence adduced to convict young Lachman, and therefore I shall release him as soon as I corroborate your version of events. I am an old policeman, and I must see things for myself. As to the young woman whom you have described to me, I believe that in her case justice has already been done. There are," he said with a smile, "cases from which we police, no matter how old we are, should remove ourselves."

The inspector shook Holmes's hand, and asked that he deliver the money box to the young woman. This Holmes did. He learned before he left India that she had fled Bombay for good. Lachman and his wife were happily reunited, and Holmes heard from time to time that their lives had been happy and uneventful since the events recounted here.

My friend sat back in his chair and looked for a time in my direction but without seeing me.

"And so, my dear Doctor," he said, "there was a series of interpretations of the evidence: Inspector Shamshere's, Lachman's, and mine. And finally, there was the real version. Or, so we might think."

THE MYSTERY OF

JAISALMER

I HAVE ALREADY ALERTED THE READER OF THESE TALES ON SEVERAL occasions to the deep melancholia suffered by Sherlock Holmes during the first months after his return to England in 1894. That depression began to abate, however, as soon as the opportunities for him to exercise his profession increased. Beginning with the case of the Norwood Builder in 1895, almost to the very end of the century, Holmes was constantly occupied. The need for me to keep his mind active waned, therefore, and the opportunities to learn of his adventures in the Orient became severely restricted. Often I would catch the merest glimpse of a tale, sometimes only odd fragments, out of which I could piece together nothing complete.

The present episode remained a series of bizarre and fragmentary references for the longest time. They were conveyed to me between Holmes's adventures in 1895 and '96, and I have edited them into one continuous narrative. During this period, Holmes had travelled frequently to the Continent, his now considerable fame having brought him into the employ of kings and other heads of state, and even the Church of Rome. It was during a short gap in his schedule, after the notorious case of Lusoni's daughter, to be exact, that he gave me the portions of the account that enabled me finally to put the story in order.

Holmes's extensive travels in the Orient for a period of almost three years had led him to contemplate the final voyage homeward. His plan was to begin his last journey in India from Delhi, travel westward through Rajasthan and Sind, and then board a freighter in Kurrachee bound for the Mediterranean.

It was in Delhi that he met a Frenchman, one Louis Benoît de Boigne, who was travelling to Rajasthan with his companions, Shiva, his Indian servant boy, and a young Swiss painter, known only at first by the name of Schaumberg. Finding the company congenial, Holmes, again in the guise of Roger Lytton-Smith, suggested that they travel together for a time. Benoît acquiesced enthusiastically to the suggestion, for he had already made arrangements for a trip through the desert, and thought that the addition of a third member to their party would increase the interest of the journey. Having overextended himself a bit financially in his previous travels, he was happy to have someone share the costs of his latest adventure; a third traveller he thought would make little difference to their hosts along the way.

Benoît had prepared a varied route that included the chief cities of Rajputana—Jaipur, Udaipur, and Jodhpur—and some of the least-known ones, including Jaisalmer, a city far to the west into the desert. Few Europeans had visited it, and the descriptions of its fabled beauties had led Benoît to make it a destination of his long journey. Holmes too saw it as one of his stops before going south to Kurrachee. Little did he know that his visit there would bring him into a chain of events that would threaten to delay indefinitely his return to England.

"Our journey really began once we had outfitted ourselves, Watson," said Holmes as he commenced his narration. "In Nizamuddin, just outside the old city of Delhi, we hired porters and guides who knew the desert well and bought our supplies. We were to travel on horseback to Jodhpur. Once there we would continue on by camel for the rest of our journey, for according to our guides, the desert becomes a sea of shifting dunes once one leaves that city. Our last destination together was to be the city of Hyderabad in Sind, where my companions and I were to part company, they to journey northward to Lahore, and I south to Kurrachee, where I planned to board the first ship bound for Europe."

I interrupted my friend at this point.

"Surely, Holmes, there was more to it. I find it difficult to believe that you chose merely to tag along with these two."

Holmes grinned.

"Your power to see through my accounts has increased, I see. You are quite right, Watson. I could easily, and preferably perhaps, have made the journey myself. Except for an Italian count by the name of Spinelli, I had had little luck with travelling companions either on the high seas or in the mountains and found myself often bored into the dullest of conversations. But in this case I was intrigued immediately by the discrepancy between their account of themselves and what I could observe. Here were two European gentlemen travelling through India, one a painter, the other a writer, or as he put it, a diarist. Their story as they told it was quite unremarkable. They had met casually in Marseilles as they boarded the steamship that was to take them to Bombay. Finding each other compatible, they decided to journey together and to produce a book of travels, one of the kind that now commonly adorn the bookshelves of the English middle class."

On the face of it, said Holmes, there was no contradiction. Their behaviour was impeccable, and their relations with the native Indian extraordinarily proper. Both were well attired, spoke English tolerably well, and did precisely what they said they did. The young painter, Schaumberg, spent every morning setting up his easel at his newly chosen site, and returned only at midday. The other, Benoît, arose before dawn and wrote until they were ready to travel.

"So much for the untrained eye, Watson. But for him who not only sees but also observes, there was much more. And here, dear Doctor, I must say that I saw much that did not agree with the account my new acquaintances had given of themselves. Their story was meant to mislead, and though I had no evidence as yet, I felt a sinister motive lurking beyond their quite innocent demeanour."

Schaumberg, Holmes judged to be in his early twenties. He was of average height and very thin, almost gaunt, but wiry, with his hair cut quite short. He walked with a slight limp, the only physical infirmity Holmes observed. The limp he judged to be the result of a wound of some sort, and later this was confirmed when he saw a scar that was clearly from a recent bullet wound. His eyes were blue, but he avoided direct contact with them, as if there were something he was trying to hide.

Benoît was much older, in his early forties, not quite as slender, but taller, almost exactly Holmes's height. He had deep scars on his hands and one long one on his neck. His English was perfect except for a slight French accent that occurred from time to time, which he suppressed with great effort. He spoke softly and appeared extraordinarily calm, but his tranquillity seemed to Holmes to cover a deep tension that might erupt at any moment.

"Both men were muscular, their faces worn and hardened by long periods in the sun," said Holmes, "and their military carriage unmistakable. Their hands, strong and rough, spoke of the same life of heavy physical activity. There was nothing of the painter or writer in the body of either. And so, Watson, from the time that I first heard their story, I knew them to be something other than what they represented themselves to be."

For the first few days, Holmes continued, their trip was uneventful. They stopped at the end of the first day just outside Bharatpur, then continued on to Amber, where they spent the night in the great palace. In the morning they greeted the Maharajah of Jaipur in the Ram Bagh. Like the succeeding monarchs whom they visited, the Maharajah of Jaipur was exceedingly courteous, British in his education, and most forthcoming in his generosity. He invited them to stay as long as they wished, but they begged leave after a few days and continued on their journey south toward Udaipur, stopping in the kingdoms of Kotah and Bundi and visiting the fabled wooden city of Tonk.

"It was in Tonk that I had my first inkling that something was newly amiss with my travelling companions. I must say, Watson, that despite the natural beauty that surrounded us, I was already becoming a bit bored. We were by now six days out of Delhi, out of touch with the world, and had arrived tired and hungry after a full day's journey in the hot sun. Tonk appeared toward evening, and we pitched our tents just on its outskirts. While the servants were preparing our food, we walked into the town, which lay about a half mile from our camp."

By this time, Holmes and his companions had become accustomed to being importuned by a variety of touts, mainly small boys in the employ of merchants in the city, who surrounded one, hoping to lead one into the greedy, wretched hands of some thieving shopkeeper. But here in Tonk the expected touts failed to materialise and the three entered the city almost unnoticed. The town was silent, its streets and arcades empty of any persons, and only after they saw the entrance to the central mosque did they realise that they had entered at the time of evening prayer, and that the entire population was on its knees facing Mecca.

"Tonk, unlike the other kingdoms of Rajputana, Watson," said Holmes, "is Mohammedan, and is alone in this respect in the vast deserts in which a militant Hinduism holds sway. It is, unlike the other marble and stone cities of the Rajput, entirely constructed of wood, ornately carved and painted in greens, golds, and reds, and a variety of other hues."

As they stood staring at the palace, Schaumberg took leave of his companions. He said that he wished to wander alone through the town in order to sketch, and that he would meet them back at the camp. Benoît and Holmes sat for a few minutes under one of the arcades, delighting in this mirage of a kingdom. They then began to wend their way back to the main gate of the town. It was with some surprise, therefore, that Holmes saw Schaumberg stealthily entering a small house not far from the mosque. He said nothing to Benoît, for he thought that it would serve no purpose. They returned to the camp toward sunset, and retired immediately after a light supper.

Toward midnight, Holmes awoke to voices in the dark. Benoît and Schaumberg were seated by a small fire, trying to keep their voices to a low whisper.

"We have to get rid of him," said Schaumberg. "We should never have allowed him to come along. It was a big mistake, I tell you. Something about him makes me uneasy. Captain Fantôme is upset that we have a stranger in our midst, or so the agent told me in Tonk this evening. They are already investigating who he is. If he finds out what we're up to—"

"Don't be so jumpy, and be quiet or you'll waken him, you fool," said Benoît excitedly in a whisper. "I told you he will be with us through to Sind. He is harmless enough, a colourless chemist from London. His presence is good for us. He is an Englishman—that keeps the Maharajahs happy and unsuspecting. They see and hear him, and they see and hear nothing else, least of all us. And he gives them medicines for their ills. How many times do you think we can make this trip without discovery? No, I will be the one to decide when he goes, if he

goes before Hyderabad. And to hell with Fantôme! That bloody crew in
the desert will take orders from me! When we arrive in Jaisalmer, then
we shall decide, only then."

"A most interesting conversation, Holmes, if I say so myself," I interjected. "You must have been elated at the developing mystery—"

"Well put, my dear Watson. I am no lover of landscape for its own
sake, as you know. And the Maharajahs and their palaces are a bit trying
after a few days. Their pieties as well as their crimes are well known.
There is nothing to observe or deduce about them beyond the com-
monplaces that pertain to royalty. But, with this conversation in my ear,
I smiled in the darkness of my tent. My two companions then retired
for the night, and I heard their heavy, peaceful breathing as I too fell
asleep in the brisk desert cold."

When Holmes awoke at dawn, Schaumberg was already at his easel,
trying he said to capture on canvas the first rays of the morning sun
across the desert. Benoît was writing in his diary a short distance away.

"You have slept well, I trust," said Benoît, in greeting.

"Very well, indeed," Holmes replied. "You both are most industrious
this morning."

"Perhaps more than you will have noticed, my dear Roger. I have already been out, hunting up our breakfast. Look, three wild partridge
and a peacock!"

Benoît pointed to a large pile of feathers the cooks had plucked from
the unfortunate birds that were already roasting on spits over the fire,
and it was not long before the three companions set upon devouring
them, washing the meal down with large cups of Indian tea.

Invigorated by this most luxurious of breakfasts, they mounted fresh
horses and proceeded toward Udaipur. Here the royal palace faces a
beautiful lake and is surrounded by a ring of low hills. The city itself is
a cluster of white houses that lies nestled in a small valley, visible from
the top of the palace. The Maharajah insisted that they stay as his
guests.

After several days, they were loath to leave this happy vale. Holmes's
companions appeared, more and more, to be what they said they were:
two travellers on tour in the desert. Benoît explored every alley of the
city, bargained for trinkets, and wrote constantly in his diary. Schaumberg sketched and painted incessantly, never, it seemed to Holmes,

approaching the true beauty of the landscape, but every so often producing a few strokes that gave some intimation of the place.

Benoît reiterated to the delighted Maharajah that his diaries would form the text for a book about India and that he would include in it Schaumberg's sketches as illustrations. No more benign labours could be imagined, and Holmes resisted the temptation to equate exterior behaviour with the reality of his companions' true but hidden mission. Being somewhat of a literary bent himself, the Maharajah expressed keen interest, opened his vast library to them, and ordered his chief scholar, one Shyamal Das, to produce whatever Benoît needed to embellish his accounts.

"It was during one of our visits to the royal library, Watson, that I learned something, purely by accident, that gave me pause to reflect and brought me back to an ever more serious contemplation of my companions," said Holmes. "While idly perusing a large tome dedicated to the history of the Moghul Empire, I learned that there had been several soldiers of fortune who had served in the armies of the Moghul Emperors in their long battles with the Maharajahs of Rajasthan more than two hundred years before. These soldiers of fortune were mostly French and some Portuguese. The most famous of these was one Jean de Grimault, who had served the emperor Akbar. My interest, and my consternation, were prodded even more when I learned a few paragraphs down that two others of these early adventurers had borne the names of Captain Fantôme and Benoît de Boigne."

"How extraordinary, Holmes. What a strange coincidence! A name from that nocturnal conversation that you overheard and the name of one of your companions—"

"Coincidence, yes, Watson, but a coincidence in its most basic form: the names were coincident, identical, but I knew that this was no mere chance. Once again, a piece of unexpected luck from an unsuspected source, a dusty old book. Thank the gods for the memory of mankind, however imperfect. I said nothing to Benoît, of course, who at the moment of my discovery was fortunately deep in conversation with the royal librarian. I closed the book, filed the information in my brain, and decided to let it do its work in the attic of my mind: there were, then, two Captain Fantômes, two Benoît de Boignes."

For many days, neither Benoît nor Schaumberg showed any desire to leave Udaipur. It was on the evening of the tenth day that Benoît announced that they had been there long enough and they should move on. He said this with some urgency in his voice, but gave no reason. They informed the Maharajah, who grieved at their imminent departure, provided every convenience, including fresh horses for the onward journey.

Jodhpur, said Holmes, was their next destination. That desert city lies three days from Udaipur, in the middle of a desiccated landscape in which only thorny scrub plants survive. It was there that Holmes began to observe a rising tension in young Schaumberg, one that showed itself through his barely controlled anger in speech and his irritation at every mistake of the hapless porters. Several times he struck them. Benoît warned him quietly to control himself. Holmes said little, and kept slightly apart so that he could observe what transpired between them.

The Maharajah of Jodhpur was absent on shikar, and so they camped outside the city walls, where they bargained for the camels that were to carry them to Jaisalmer. They left the very next morning.

It was on this portion of their journey that they entered the true deserts of Rajputana. What had been up until then a dry, rocky landscape occasionally broken by the Aravalli Hills now became an undifferentiated mass of yellowish sand of the finest consistency, so that even a scant breeze blew enough of it into one's face to cause discomfort. It being winter, the air was cool, the sun intense, and the landscape barren of any living thing except an occasional caravan plodding east. The desert seemed endlessly smooth, effortlessly erasing every trace of their having been there.

By now it had become quite clear to Holmes that the progress toward their destination was timed very precisely by Benoît, for reasons that were still concealed. As if controlled by an invisible hand, they alternately raced ahead or waited for him to complete his diary entries, which became the chief pretext by which the time of travel was determined. Holmes made no complaint, content as he was to wait and see. Schaumberg was, however, alternately tranquil and agitated. He appeared impatient to arrive at their next destination and could not endure their slow pace without occasional outbursts to Benoît.

Two days from Jaisalmer, their guide informed them that the leader of a passing caravan had warned of sandstorms to the west so intense that they had best make a detour north, toward a town called Bap. From there, they could proceed without difficulty.

"Despite the danger, I believe that we should proceed as planned," said Benoît. "The storms may be over by tomorrow. And we have no guarantee that we will not run into them to the north of here."

"As you choose," said Holmes. "I have no preference."

Schaumberg, however, appeared frightened by the reports.

"I don't like sandstorms," he said excitedly. "I have seen one in North Africa, and I say let's take the detour. It won't add much, and we'll be much safer."

"No detour," said Benoît coldly. "We will proceed as planned."

Schaumberg said nothing.

"And so, Watson, we continued on our route. A few hours out, and the cool of the early morning had disappeared. The sun bore down on us mercilessly. Even more ominously, however, as we moved on, the gentle breeze which we had experienced thus far became more intense, and we felt the sting of the sand on our hands and faces. A storm was building, and we could see in the distance the tops of the dunes transformed into dancing swirls rising high in the air."

Toward dusk, they began to look anxiously for shelter, and their chief guide changed direction. In a short time, they saw something on the horizon. The guide had led them to a large, abandoned temple. The guides motioned them into it, and they took refuge just as the storm hit.

Holmes had never experienced anything equal to it. Sand swirled around them so intensely that it was as if all air had been sucked away. The temple was an open structure, and the only recourse they had was to turn their faces to the walls. But as the wind increased, sand blew everywhere, filling their eyes and nostrils, making it almost impossible to breathe without taking it into their lungs.

At the very height of the storm, Schaumberg began to scream in terror. "We can't stay here! We have to go on. C'mon! Are ye with me? We're going to die like rats here!"

He grabbed Holmes by the arm, but Holmes resisted. Schaumberg then leapt from the temple directly into the storm. Benoît sat silently, but Holmes rushed after him into the swirling sand. As he grabbed him and pulled him in, Schaumberg collapsed in tears. Holmes and Benoît pressed his face toward the wall. Benoît shouted at him to be still, but he kept sobbing to himself, and Holmes pretended not to hear as Benoît continued his remonstrances.

The storm subsided as fast as it arose, and Holmes looked out to see that it had passed, leaving nothing in sight but blinding white sand.

"The worst is over," said Benoît.

"Don't tell me to shut up," said Schaumberg, vehemently. "I have lived through too much in the Sahara. Don't you remember? This is the last time—"

Benoît slapped him hard across the face.

"Just remember who you are—and who I am," said Benoît viciously.

Schaumberg became calmer, and a morose look covered his face. The three men dragged themselves through the sand on the temple floor, into the desert. All that they had brought with them was gone. Animals, water, food, the guides—all appeared to have been buried. They had nothing.

"We're going to die," said Schaumberg. "I know it. This time, we're going to die."

"You bloody coward, shut up!" shouted Benoît.

Schaumberg sobbed uncontrollably, and Benoît shook him to bring him to his senses, but to no avail. Benoît left him and searched the horizon. As they looked out they saw campfires, not more than a few hundred yards away, toward which they immediately made their way. There, they found a group of Gujar herdsmen with their goats and camels. They had spent the day in Sam, they said, and had made a detour around the storm before returning to their route, their destination being the city of Jaisalmer. They offered the travellers food and shelter for the night and said that they would be welcome to accompany them to the desert city. And so, at dawn they awoke, and now provided with fresh camels to ride, they began the last leg of their journey.

For two days they rode through the dunes. A merciless sun beat down upon them from a monotonous blue sky. Toward evening on the second day, they saw their destination in the distance: a series of sand-coloured towers and walls rising suddenly out of the desert.

"I shall never forget that first glimpse, Watson," said Holmes. "We rode first among the many monstrous cenotaphs of the Rajputs, scattered as they were in the sand, and passed through the main gate at nightfall, lodging in our tents just inside the city walls. Our exhaustion made what little we saw of the population of the city that night seem even more unworldly than it otherwise would have seemed to be. The inhabitants were ghostlike, for all were dressed in long white caftans and white caps, with white masks over their faces. This was a city of the Jains. Fearful of injuring even an insect, they wear masks over their faces in order to avoid even the inadvertent inhalation of a fly or mosquito. Except for this oddity of behaviour, the population appeared quiet and tranquil, free of the many grotesque excesses that one finds in other parts of our Indian possessions. It was into this religious atmosphere of extreme gentleness that Benoît, Schaumberg, and I entered."

I interrupted Holmes at this point.

"I daresay, Holmes, that the contrast between the common citizenry of this strange city and its latest guests must have struck you as a very strong one."

"Indeed, it did, Watson, for Schaumberg and Benoît were tough men, bent on a mission of which I had uncovered little. Benoît was the leader, steady, cold, and calculating, with nerves of steel. Schaumberg was the follower, emotional, even more dangerous perhaps because of his unpredictability."

"Difficult at times, I should think. I must say that I greatly admire your courage and your forbearance."

"One tends to be courageous during the active crisis, Watson. As to my forbearance, there was nothing I could do but be patient. I knew too little, and I maintained an agreeable silence, shall we say, a bit British at times. I engaged in nothing but pleasantries, and even during the sandstorm I displayed only the usual British sangfroid. I was in all ways the English chemist Roger Lytton-Smith.

"Jaisalmer was as hot as any place in India," he continued, "so hot even in the night that I took to sleeping on the roof of a small Marwari hotel to which we had moved, where it was far cooler than inside. I awoke with the dawn and watched below as the city came alive with its morning rituals of bathing and lighting fires for the first foods of the day. It was on the fourth day after our arrival, toward evening, that a fortunate occurrence enabled me to progress toward a solution of the mystery of my companions."

Both of them suddenly appeared to be very agitated, said Holmes, and they ventured forth very little. They were obviously waiting, perhaps for some signal. The sun was intense, and Holmes had availed himself of a free moment away from them to purchase the cool white cotton clothes that the natives wore, including the mask. So attired, he walked up from the lower city to the high walls in order to view the desert, when glancing down, he saw, sitting together below him, Shiva and their two camel drivers, all of whom he had presumed to be dead or lost in the desert.

They did not see Holmes, and he watched as they talked. The camel drivers soon went off, and Holmes rushed down to follow Shiva to his abode. He walked so quickly that Holmes almost lost sight of him in the crowd, but he caught up with him just as he turned into the small, dingy doorway of a native hotel. Holmes followed him up the stairs and knocked on his door gently so as not to alarm him. He removed his mask, and when Shiva opened he turned pale as if he had seen a ghost. He tried to resist, but Holmes forced his way in.

"Do not be afraid, Shiva," he said calmly. Holmes told him that, despite the storm, they had arrived safely in Jaisalmer, and that he meant him no harm and only wanted him to tell what he knew of Schaumberg and Benoît.

"They will kill me if I talk to you," Shiva said.

"So you ran away in the storm. They think you are dead—and indeed, you thought that all three of us were dead, correct?"

"Yes, I thought you were dead, yes, and that I was finally free from them. I have been Benoît's slave for three years, and now I am afraid again."

"Have no fear, Shiva. I am not one of them. Tell me everything you can."

The man slowly gained his composure, and began to talk. "Three years ago," he began, "I met Benoît in Bombay. I had come there from a nearby village, and I needed work badly. There had been a terrible drought, and my children had nothing to eat. Benoît promised me good wages, enough for me to send money back to my wife to care for our family. And so I travelled with him through Rajasthan three times.

This is the fourth trip. He would come every year at the same time. We would take the same route, spend exactly seven days in Jaisalmer, then go on to Hyderabad in Sind, where he would leave me and continue on to Kurrachee, and I would return to Bombay.

"Toward the end of each stay in Jaisalmer, he would go to Mandor, where we loaded many horses with heavy bags of canvas. I did not learn what was in those bags until the third trip. This was last year, when one night there was a secret meeting with Captain Fantôme, the one who supplies the bags. Captain Fantôme came to Jaisalmer. He spoke not at all, wore a hood over his head, and merely nodded when addressed. Later some of the servants and workmen told me that Captain Fantôme was the head of the Landa, a strange people whose ancestors had migrated here many years ago and who owned much land. Through the centuries they grew in numbers and are now very rich. But they keep to themselves and do not mix with the Hindus and the Jains. Many men are employed by them, but no one ever returns from there."

"Where does Captain Fantôme stay?"

"In a large house in the centre of Mandor. That is his palace."

"Take me there," said Holmes.

"I will go with you only as far as the walls of Mandor, for it is said that it is easy to enter Mandor, but no one ever leaves without the permission of Captain Fantôme."

"Very well then, but let us hurry."

They walked from the hotel to the nearest gate. There they found a tongawallah, a rather robust old man, willing to take them the ten miles to Mandor. In the darkness, Holmes tried to get Shiva to talk a bit more, but he was silent in the presence of the driver.

When they arrived at what he thought was a safe distance, Shiva asked Holmes to step down, pointed toward the east, and then asked the tongawallah to return to Jaisalmer.

"I was now alone on the edge of Mandor, Watson. There was no one about. I walked in the direction that Shiva had pointed until I came to the city gates. There were no guards to be seen, and I walked through without interruption. Once into the city, I left the stillness behind. The streets were filled with people, and the city had the appearance of great opulence. It was as if I had left India altogether. There were street signs, and walled compounds with bougainvillaea overflowing the walls.

What I could see of the houses reminded one of French cottages from the Midi. The streets were cobblestoned and clean. It was as if I had entered a small town in Europe."

Holmes went into what appeared to be a café. The language he heard seemed to be a strange patois of French and Portuguese heavily laced with Indian words. As he sat down, however, all eyes in the crowded room turned toward him, and a great silence suddenly broke out. Holmes decided to throw caution to the wind and said in French in a voice loud enough for everyone to hear that he wished to meet "le Capitaine Fantôme." What had been until then a rather boisterous and happy crowd enjoying a late dinner stood up and began to leave. Holmes was soon left alone except for the proprietor.

"I repeated my request, and the proprietor came to me and said in the local language, 'Mandorme personne nahi jo s'appele Fantôme,' a perfectly comprehensible sentence if one knew French and Hindustanee— 'There is no one in Mandor by the name of Captain Fantôme.' He was lying, of course, and I decided to leave his establishment."

Now on the darkened street, Holmes lost all freedom to investigate, for he was suddenly surrounded by men with guns and sticks. They appeared to be a contingent of the local gendarmerie. They spoke to each other in the same patois, but this time Holmes understood nothing.

"I am here to meet Captain Fantôme. Please take me to him at once," he said loudly and firmly.

A nervous laugh moved through them, and they pulled the resisting Holmes with them to a small building. There seated at a desk was a gentleman with long white hair, a long, pointed moustache, and all the physical characteristics of a French inspector of police.

"Who are you, and why are you here?" he asked Holmes gruffly in English.

"Who I am is none of your concern," replied Holmes sternly, "but if you must know, read this."

Holmes handed him a letter from the Viceroy guaranteeing Roger Lytton-Smith safe passage through the Subcontinent and said, "I wish to see Captain Fantôme."

The letter appeared to have its desired effect, for a look of perplexity appeared on the old gentleman's face and he said: "Very well. Since you insist, you shall. There is no difficulty. The Capitaine is not far from here, and is always happy to meet strangers."

They left the bureau, and accompanied by a single guard, they walked through what had become by now a very quiet city. In the moonlight Holmes saw a large palace, very much of the Rajput form, but its gardens and decorations were distinctly European.

The police inspector handed Holmes over to a sentinel, giving him a quiet order in the local patois. Holmes followed the sentinel into the palace, where he was told to wait in a small antechamber.

"I waited several hours, and despite the precarious predicament in which I found myself, I must have dozed off. Just before dawn, however, someone brought me tea and breakfast, and I was informed that the Captain would soon receive me."

Holmes was led down a corridor, at the end of which he entered a large room. Seated in a chair at one end was a diminutive figure that he could barely see in the still dim light of the morning. As he approached, he saw that he was facing a rather short, stout, middle-aged woman, dressed in the attire of an Indian princess.

As she beckoned him to a seat near her, she said: "I am Captain Fantôme. I understand that you wished to see me."

"Most extraordinary, my dear Holmes!" I ejaculated with utmost surprise.

"Yes, Watson, I must confess that I was caught off guard and was not prepared for what I saw."

The Captain herself saw the look of surprise and said, "You seem, my friend, shall we say, a bit taken aback. What is it?"

"The name Captain Fantôme led me to expect someone far different."

"The name means nothing," she said. "It is the name of one of my ancestors, and is used to mislead the outside world. My real name is Elizabeth de Grimault, and I am the Queen of the Landa, and absolute ruler of Mandor. And you," she continued as she glanced at a file in front of her, "are not an innocent English traveller by the name of Lytton-Smith, but a spy of the British Government identified by my agents as Sherlock Holmes."

"I am indeed Sherlock Holmes, madam, but I am not an agent of Government. I am a private consulting detective. Why I am here is a rather long story, which I am sure you would not find particularly interesting—"

"To the contrary, Mr. Holmes, my men have learned much of your exploits," she said, pointing to the folder. "You are a most clever fellow, and your reputation precedes you."

"Thank you, madam, but I must say that you are far more clever. The existence of Mandor and the Landa is a most well-kept secret. Even the best of our Oriental scholars, who have mapped virtually the entire Subcontinent, have failed to report on you or your people."

"A well-kept secret, but not an absolute one," she said. "We are what we have to be in order to survive. We are known well by a very few and only vaguely by a larger number in India, particularly the Maharajahs. Our ancestors suffered greatly, and we had to learn how to live in a hostile environment. And so we chose to be by ourselves and to survive by our wits."

"Your name tells me that you are probably a direct descendant of Jean de Grimault," said Holmes.

She smiled and said, "Then you already know something, far more than most. Yes, I am directly descended from him, as is most of the population of Mandor. Jean le Grand, or Maha-Jean, as we call him, the founder of Mandor, was the brave soldier of Akbar the Great. Maha-Jean was given this place as a gift by the Emperor, and he settled here with his wives and family. But soon the local rajahs became fearful of their presence, for they were not Hindus but Christians. Maha-Jean was protected by the Emperor, but when the Emperor died, the king of Jaisalmer, leading an alliance of Rajput princes, attacked, and Maha-Jean was killed with many of his family. His oldest son, Piyer the First, fled with the remnants of the family to some caves in the desert, where they, hardened by the harsh life in the dunes, learned to survive on almost nothing. Then a most wonderful event occurred. It is celebrated as le din de la Neuvième Ratan, or the day of the Nine Jewels, the fifteenth of July 1686 in your calendar. It was there in those caves, where they had almost starved, that they discovered that their land would make them rich and powerful."

She extended toward Holmes her hand, on which she wore a ring with a large, lustrous red stone.

"This is the largest ruby in the world," she said, "a perfect jewel, found by Emile le Petit Rajah, the youngest son of Piyer the First. It has been worn by every ruler of Mandor since it was discovered. It was one of nine jewels found on the same day in a matter of minutes. Soon there were many more. It was not long before these survivors smuggled a variety of stones to the bazaar, where with the new monies they obtained, they began to build their kingdom and to protect it with a well-paid loyal army of mercenaries from Persia and the Levant, and even as far away as Africa. We became the chief suppliers of precious stones to all the potentates of the Orient. The Peacock Throne, stolen from India by Nadir Shah and upon which the rulers of Persia now sit, is encrusted with jewels from the ground upon which you walk. We are now rich and powerful. And unknown we move about the world pursuing our interests."

"And what are those interests?" asked Holmes

"Our own power and enrichment first. We the Landa are small in number, there being fewer than a thousand of us, but we travel from Mandor to Europe and America and the Far East with ease. We have our chalets in Europe and our network of agents who supply our every want. Beyond that, we are guided by Le Hukum Primo or First Command, expounded by Piyer the Third, who understood that the advent of British power into India could be disastrous for us and warned that we must fight it. And so we have supported the cause of rebellion throughout the world. We financed the French efforts during the American Revolution. We were major supporters of Napoleon, and we have tirelessly supported the French and German efforts in Africa. This we continue to do."

"Benoît and Schaumberg must be part of this game, then," said Holmes.

"Most observant of you. You are quite correct. Your travelling companions, Schaumberg and Benoît, are simply clients of ours, working against British interests in Africa. Schaumberg is really a Swiss raised in Africa, more Boer than the Boer himself, determined to rid Africa of the British. His family was wiped out a few years ago in the raids of Sir Leander Jameson, and so he bears the English the hatred required to make a good revolutionary."

"And Benoît?" Holmes asked.

"A legionnaire, working in Algeria to subdue the Sahara and to con-

solidate French gains in North Africa, a descendant of a close friend of
Maha-Jean, Benoît de Boigne the First, or as he is known here Benoît
le Premye Dost. He is different from Schaumberg. He bears the British
no hatred, and is merely a professional soldier doing a job."

"And their mission this time?"

"The export, shall we say, from India of diamonds and jewels. This
is their fourth trip to Mandor. This time they will take with them several million pounds' worth of raw diamonds destined for the markets
of Constantinople, where they will be sold and the monies used to fi-
nance armies of rebellion. These diamonds are our gift."

"In return for what?" Holmes asked somewhat sardonically.

The woman smiled. "Yes, you are right. We do expect a return, and
that is simple."

She rang a bell, a servant entered, and she said in the local patois,
"Ramon, porque est-ce que Schaumberg aur Benoît sont pahuncte?"

"Uiji, Mem Rani, ve sont pahuncte aj maten. Vos unko dekh ca-
hate?"

"Ji-oui. Unko isi fer ana."

In a moment, the servant ushered in Benoît and Schaumberg. They
showed no surprise in seeing Holmes. Rather, gleeful smiles appeared
on both their faces.

"So, dear Roger," said Schaumberg, "it is as I thought. You are a British spy."

"Hardly, my dear Giacomo; I am, shall we say, self-employed. I do
not work for the British Government, nor any other, I might add.
However, even as a private citizen, I do not look with favour upon your
activities in India. They will have to end."

His smile disappeared and a look of extraordinary hatred appeared
on his face. Turning toward Benoît, he said, "You see, you see, I warned
you in Tonk, but you would not listen."

Unperturbed by his associate, Benoît did not answer him but addressed the Captain: "When will our loads be ready for departure?"

"They are ready now. But word has come from our agent in Lahore
that disturbances have occurred in Hyderabad, and the British have de-
ployed several thousand troops along the major routes to Kurrachee.
Your departure will be delayed for at least five days."

Schaumberg became very agitated at these words. "But we must depart at the latest tomorrow. Otherwise our ship will leave Kurrachee without us. . . ."

"Calm yourself, M. Schaumberg. You are too excitable," said Captain Fantôme. "Your ship will not leave until you are on board. We have arranged that as well. And now, gentlemen, where are the documents assuring us of our remuneration?"

"I would prefer that our English friend leave at once," said Benoît quietly.

"Do not be concerned. Our friend will not leave Mandor. He is to be one of our permanent guests. What he learns here matters not at all."

"Very well, then," continued Benoît, "here are official secret documents signed by the ministries of France and the Boer Government granting the company Frères Les Comtes de Bruxelles exclusive mining rights in perpetuity in all of the French possessions in Algeria and the Boer states of Natal and the Transvaal. Frères Les Comtes we understand to be the exclusive agent and representative of the Landa of Mandor."

Benoît handed the documents to Captain Fantôme, who read them through.

"These are correct and well prepared," she said, and motioning to the servant for a pen, she signed them, returning copies to Benoît.

"And now, my friends Benoît and Schaumberg, please rest for the next few days, but be prepared to leave at a moment's notice. You will travel by foot in the dead of night before you are met by a group of our men who will lead you by a secret route to Kurrachee. As we have done since you arrived in India, we have planned every step of your way, alternately delaying and rushing you for your own security and for that of the treasures that will accompany you to Constantinople. You understand that our survival, and yours as well, depends on the total veil of secrecy that we have been able to maintain through many years."

Then turning to Holmes, she said, "And you, my friend, will be our permanent guest in Mandor. You will have the freedom to roam the city at will, but do not try to escape. Its border is well patrolled, and one can only leave with my permission. I shall, however, do everything I can for your comfort. Because your stay will be, shall we say, of indeterminate length, we will take extraordinary measures very quickly to ensure that, as you will see. In the meantime, if you have any requests, please let me know, and I shall honour them if they are within my capability."

"I have but one request," said Holmes.

"And what is that?"

"I should like to visit the mines."

"Easily done," she said. Turning to her servant she said, "Ramon, abhi he possible dekhvoir les mines?"

"Uiji, mon Capitaine."

"We shall go now. The entrance is only a short distance down from this room. Mes senhors Schaumberg and Benoît are also welcome. They have not seen the source of their wealth as yet."

Led by Captain Fantôme, they walked a short distance from the room of their meeting to a stair that led to a lower level of the palace. There, directed by Captain Fantôme, a guard opened a door and announced their entry.

"We entered what was, to my amazement, Watson, a small, beautifully appointed theatre, round in shape, with a large curtain that encircled us," said Holmes.

"This theatre," said the Captain, "was built over fifty years ago by one of our ancestors, so that the Familhe, as we call ourselves, could view in comfort the work in the mines, which hitherto had required that we actually enter them, a rather unpleasant task. Now from this vantage point, we can see all of it in comfort."

They were led to their seats in the first balcony, and as Captain Fantôme gave a signal to her servants, the curtain drew back on all sides. There below, in the light of large oil lamps, was a gigantic pit, filled with a groaning humanity, digging and sorting what it found. Men and boys from all parts of a far-flung empire, all almost naked, slaved through the earth in a sweltering hot darkness. The digging was completely disciplined, hundreds of pickaxes hitting the ground at the same time. Another group, on all fours on the ground, pulled the rubble toward them, loading it by hand into carts that were wheeled away by a third team. Over all stood tall, dark overseers, who carried whips and lathis, the deadly Indian hooked sticks.

"This theatre is the only viewing tower of its kind in the world," said Captain Fantôme. "Originally it was an English idea; we have adapted it to the mine. We sit exactly one hundred feet above the pit itself. This is our largest and most valuable mine, though hardly the only one. It is volcanic in origin, and its channels produce most of our raw diamonds."

Schaumberg and Benoît gazed in awe, for on their previous trips they had seen none of this. As Captain Fantôme spoke, Holmes could see that Schaumberg had become enamoured of the scene below. He plied Captain Fantôme with question after question, to which she gave immediate answers. The workers were recruited by agents stationed in all of Asia, she said. The more varied the workers, the better, for this made communication and rebellion difficult. Andaman Islanders thus worked next to Tamileans. The raw recruits were taken to a camp in a lonely area near Bikaner, where the strongest were chosen, the others released to die in the desert. This smaller group was then brought to a station south of Mandor, where they were trained in particular operations of the mine: digging, gathering, and sorting. They worked for exactly twelve hours each day, when they were relieved by another group. All their physical needs were met in order to maintain efficiency, and they were given a few hours per month of recreation and at least two hours in the sun on the surface. They had wives, but in common, and no attachment to single individuals was allowed. Male children immediately became part of the worker pool, and the females, except for the few necessary to the men, were sold in the bazaar in Bombay, where they worked as prostitutes. The best ages for work were between twelve and thirty-six. Those who reached the higher age of their service, if still healthy, became servants to the Landa. Otherwise, they were destroyed. No one of them, of course, ever left. In this system, she said, there was no waste.

"And who are the guards?"

"Ah! They are very special," she said. "They are the only remaining descendants of the Abyssinians brought in the thirteenth century by the Sultans. They are the infamous Hawbshi and have been in our employ for generations."

Captain Fantôme appeared suddenly to tire of the scene below. She stood up abruptly, motioned with her hand, and the curtain closed, hiding the dreadful scene that had just been before them. They followed her to the room from which they had come, and she dismissed them. Schaumberg and Benoît were led to their quarters, and Holmes followed a servant to a rather large room that was to be his home for the next few weeks.

"What an incredible experience, Holmes. Who would believe that such a place could exist under the very nose of Government?"

"And yet there it was, Watson. As you know, my nature and training forbid exaggeration, and you may take what I have told you to correspond to the literal truth. There, underneath the deserts of Rajasthan, laboured untold thousands of slaves brought from the four corners of the Empire for the benefit of a very few. And I was made to look upon their tragedy as if I sat in the luxurious comfort of Covent Garden viewing a performance of *Aïda*."

"Extraordinary, my dear Holmes, absolutely extraordinary."

"Yes, dear Watson, and I must add that at no time did Captain Fantôme show any sympathy to the people in the mines. It was as though they were not human beings but creatures of a lower order, separated from her by some invisible barrier greater than the one that separates us from the mere brutes of the natural world. Physically, Captain Fantôme was in all ways a French peasant woman, of no great beauty, plain in every feature. But her ordinary appearance hid a will of iron and a massive intelligence, both of which were in the service of an ever-increasing avarice and quest for power."

"You must continue, Holmes. I am most anxious to learn how this adventure concluded."

Holmes glanced about the room slowly, as if studying every detail of our quarters, and then said brightly: "What happened next was most surprising but led to the inevitable denouement. There is a new Turkish restaurant on Museum Street, Watson, and if we leave now, I can finish this tale for you over some rare delicacies from the Levant and a bottle of Syrian red wine. Come, let us hurry, for all of this talk has given me a bit of an appetite."

Before I could protest, Holmes had already bolted from his chair and donned his coat. We walked at his fast pace and reached the front of the British Museum in a matter of minutes. Then we turned to the right on Museum Street and entered the small Turkish eatery that Holmes had referred to. He had said nothing as we walked, and it was only after he had taken his first approving sip of the dry red wine that he continued.

"For the first few days of my stay in Mandor, I was in total isolation, except for the servants who brought me food and served my other needs. I saw nothing of Schaumberg and Benoît, and nothing of Captain Fantôme. I was allowed to take some exercise in the garden adjacent to my room, and I read several bad novels that had found their way into the Mandor Palace. Escaping I knew would be difficult, but escape I must. From the garden I could walk to the palace wall and peer out at the city. There were no guards or patrols in the direct vicinity, but I immediately became aware of sentinels who were placed in the buildings across from the palace. Nothing could escape their notice either by day or by night. And so I continued to observe, to let my eyes and brain put things in order. Schaumberg and Benoît, I learned from the servants, had yet to depart, and since stopping them was inevitably part of my goal, I was content to bide my time, for I knew that escape would not be easy."

Several weeks passed, continued Holmes. During that time, he ventured forth little. He spent it in deep contemplation of his eventual escape. He finally formed a plan, but it was risky, and he knew that it might not succeed.

Beyond the servant who attended to him regularly, he now saw only Benoît and Schaumberg. They had been delayed indefinitely by the troubles in Sind, and they felt almost as imprisoned as he.

One day, Holmes was summoned to Captain Fantôme's room.

"You will recall," she said with some amusement, "that I promised you extraordinary comfort during your stay here. I am sorry that you have been confined to a single room for so long, but our agents have been slower than I would have liked in preparing your permanent accommodations. You will move now to what I trust will be satisfactory quarters for you through the coming years."

"She smiled," said Holmes, "with the smile of one who greatly enjoys her handiwork. I bowed, not without an ironic look in my eye, and followed the servant to my new quarters. I was filled with a certain wonder as to what they would be—an Oriental queen's view of an English Heaven perhaps. The servant stopped before a door, handed me a key, and left. As soon as I saw the key, I knew what she had done. I opened the door, Watson, and walked into what appeared at first glance to be a perfect replica of our quarters, a copy of 221b Baker Street. I laughed as I entered and threw the key on the table, sat in my armchair, picked up my violin, and began to play—and to think. Overall, the quarters were well copied, and I could not but marvel how the Landa and their agents, in a matter of only a few weeks, had been able to perform such a feat. Obviously, someone had entered our quarters, and secretly enumerated and described its contents, possibly photographing them as well. Then a band of local craftsmen were made to copy as much as possible. Not only tables and chairs, Watson, but pipes and tobaccos, the Persian slippers, my cocaine bottle and syringe, and a slight scent of the disorder that we live in were there. I found myself smiling with pleasure at what I saw, for I momentarily had the feeling that I had already extricated myself from my predicament and that miraculously I was back in London."

Holmes confessed that he soon came to his senses, however, and began to observe the minute differences between our quarters and this replica. As he went through, noticing pictures on the wall which the taste of neither of us would permit, he realised that there were some large faults. Much of the contents of the library had been duplicated with the exception of the rarer items, but there had been no attempt to reproduce his files. All weapons, his pistols, his knife collection, and his poisonous experiments, were absent, no doubt as a necessary precaution, since he remained a prisoner. As he went through the clothes and other things, he realised how thoroughly the agents of the Landa had gone through our belongings. But there was little of mine, he emphasised, mostly his possessions very selectively chosen.

As he ruminated over this unexpected gift, there was a knock on the door. He opened and found Schaumberg and Benoît there to greet him: "Captain Fantôme has asked us to visit you and bid you farewell since we depart tonight."

"Come in, my dear friends. Welcome to my London abode."

They entered, and Holmes could see a look of amazement cross their faces.

"Not bad, especially for this godforsaken place," said Schaumberg.

Benoît was as usual more reticent, but Holmes watched him closely as his eyes went over the room, occasionally resting on some object. They sat and talked as friends do who are about to leave each other and may not see each other again.

"We have been through a lot together," said Schaumberg, " 'tis a pity that we are on opposite sides in this bloody fight. I shall miss you, my friend, and thanks again for pulling me in during that bloody sand-storm."

"My duty, dear chap. As to our being on opposite sides, well, we can do nothing about that, can we?"

Benoît looked at his watch. "It is almost dark, and the time for us to go approaches. We shall leave in a few hours," he said, "and travel in the dark until morning. By then, we should have passed through the Brit-ish patrols safely into Sind."

"They left, Watson, and departed for Sind that night. And Sherlock Holmes remained in his quarters."

Holmes stopped talking, as if the story were over. He looked down at his plate, took several bites, and then took a long drink with obvious delight from his glass.

He laughed and said, "Or so it appeared, Watson. For it was in those very moments that something happened that enabled me to escape from Mandor. After Schaumberg and Benoît left, I sat for a moment wondering whether to put my plan into action or to wait. My eye fell on the cocaine and some narcotics when suddenly there was a knock at the door. It was Benoît. He came in, and for the first time he appeared distraught."

"You must help me," he said.

"How?" I asked.

"I need your cocaine for the journey."

"You shall have it," said Holmes.

"I seized the opportunity, Watson, and before he could change his mind I had made a strong mixture, though not of cocaine, and plunged the syringe into his arm. He did not resist, but immediately went into a blissful stupor. I helped him to the sofa and quickly set to work. In preparing the replica of our quarters, the agents of Captain Fantôme had been unaware of the use of some of the items they reproduced. And so I found most of the paraphernalia of my disguises there ready for use. Wigs, powders, all my actor's magic was there. I worked quickly transforming Benoît into a fair version of myself while he slept, and then, switching our clothes, I transformed myself into a fair ver-sion of Benoît. As I studied my face in the mirror, I smiled, for I knew that I had made myself into a good likeness, good enough even for

Schaumberg in the dark. I delighted in anticipation as I glanced about 221b Baker Street, with Sherlock Holmes fast asleep in a trance. To Captain Fantôme I penned a short note, which I pinned to Benoît's shirt: 'My compliments and thanks to you for your hospitality. Herein lies a gift of appreciation, only a copy within a copy perhaps, but a rather good one, I trust. Sherlock Holmes.' "

Holmes ran out the door in time to meet Schaumberg as he left his room. They walked in silence to their caravan and without further ado began their long march. Holmes breathed a sigh of relief as soon as they passed through the gates, and a few miles into the desert, he left them and returned to Jaisalmer. There, he sent word to the British agent of the existence of Schaumberg's party. It was apprehended as it entered Sind that morning. At some time that morning, the replica of Sherlock Holmes must have awakened and was taken to Captain Fantôme by a rather perplexed servant, who judged that his somewhat changed appearance was due to sudden illness. Captain Fantôme read the note pinned to his chest, realised what had happened, and escaped before our soldiers could apprehend her.

In the next few weeks, Mandor was captured despite the heavy defence by its mercenaries, the mines were closed, and the workers released. Captain Fantôme fled to South Africa, where she oversees the new diamond mines there.

"And what happened to the Landa and the rest of the population of the city of Mandor?" I asked.

"Many of them moved to other parts of India, and some, Watson, have, I gather, come to England, where they move silently within the upper circles of society. Their town is but a ruin, sitting now unproductively above the large, silent caverns below. Considering my role in its destruction, I doubt if I have heard the last of the Landa. Captain Fantôme is not the kind of person who forgets such injury."

Holmes became silent, then said: "And of course, Watson, dear Giacomo Schaumberg was the young Swiss lad who gave you the false message at the Reichenbach Falls, changed by his experiences in the meantime, but recognisably the same."

"Good lord, Holmes, I should have realised this. When did you recognise him?"

"Immediately, Watson. That is why I decided to travel with them.

But Giacomo did not recognise me until it was too late. Perhaps he was there at the falls for too short a time. He is now at large, having escaped from prison in Quetta, and I have no doubt that he will show up one of these days. Who knows when?"

AFTERWORD

THE READER WHO HAS TRAVELLED THIS FAR WILL INEVITABLY BE TEMPTED TO
speculate on the effects of the Orient on Mr. Sherlock Holmes and the
course of his work subsequent to his return to London. It will come as
no great surprise to those familiar with the chronicles of these exploits
that my friend's peculiar character has often eluded me. But since I remain close to him even now after these so many years, my own observations on the matter may still prove to be of some interest.

It was, I remember, in that small cottage where we often stayed near
Poldhu Bay, at the further extremity of the Cornish peninsula, that I
first questioned him and put my thoughts on the subject in order. It
was in the fall of 1894, a cool but bright October day. Holmes had
begun to display his curious interest in the origin of the Cornish language and had expressed for the first time his notion that it was related
to the Chaldean. He had just received a consignment of books upon
philology but quickly abandoned them for the morning paper, which at
our distant location arrived several days late.

I watched him carefully as he went about his business. To the casual
observer, I thought, the Holmes who had returned to London after a
three-year absence was very much the same as before, a bit thinner perhaps, and somewhat older of course, but if anything more energetic and
resourceful than ever. His near-miraculous brain, with its almost magi-
cal ability to see beyond the appearance of things to their underlying
causes, his uncanny power to deduce final solutions from the most trivial of details, and the tireless energy with which he pursued the most
minute of clues, all of this was as before, if indeed not heightened by his

many adventures abroad. He still disappeared on his nocturnal prowls about the city, the sleuth hound following the scent, and by day would sit in silent adumbration of the problem at hand. It was then, as he sat motionless in his easy chair, his eyes staring vacantly into space, that his brilliant reasoning power would rise to the level of intuition, forcing those unacquainted with his methods to look askance at him as on a man whose knowledge was not that of other mortals.

To my frequent consternation, he had added remarkable skills in disguise and illusion through his training in the Orient. This was indeed a new aspect to his art. Yet, he remained philosophically a direct descendant of Galileo and Francis Bacon, contemptuous of anything not grounded in experiment and the practical. All of that high metaphysic that flows from Plato and ancient India through the murky Germanic schools of the last hundred years was anathema to his sombre and cynical spirit. For him, it was all sophistry and illusion, to be cast into the flames, were it not for his great tolerance of opposing ideas and his strong belief that all arguments needed to be preserved as well as heard. And yet, I sensed at times a deeper questioning of larger problems, the answers to which he had previously taken for granted.

In his outward personal life, the same abstemious habits prevailed, and he maintained his habitual clutter in the same inventive ways. The violin was still there, played as beautifully as ever. Inwardly, however, I sensed a difference. I have remarked in describing his singular character on its dual nature. The swings of mood still took him from extreme languor to devouring energy, and his great exactness and astuteness represented, as I have often thought, the reaction against the poetic and contemplative mood which occasionally predominated in him. But, as the reader well knows, Holmes had been subject to severe bouts of melancholia from the time of our first meeting. Before his long sojourn abroad, he had relied on various cures, which he administered himself. One was abstract reasoning, which led him to abstruse mathematical and logical problems that often, on a more practical level, became problems of cryptography. Another was his incessant probe of the world of chemistry in search of more precise tests useful in his criminal investigations. A third, more treacherous treatment was, of course, cocaine, in which he indulged frequently before his stay in the Orient, to my great displeasure.

After his return, however, I knew him to use cocaine but once, and to my knowledge, he never went near it again. Nor was he any longer content with the abstract puzzles which had entertained him and pulled him back in the past from the brink of depression. Although his despair at times was if anything stronger upon his return, he used nothing external to himself to relieve the black moods that descended upon him. He came out of them himself, never falling completely under their sway.

When I queried him about the difference that day as we sat looking out at the bay, he broke his usual reticence about himself and noted in explanation that the death of Moriarty was a far more significant event in his life than he had previously thought and it was only in the narration of some of the tales presented here that he realised how significant indeed it was. Until Moriarty's death, he said, he had seen crime very much as the creation of the individual gone wrong.

"You will remember, Watson, what I said so often in the past. There are some trees which grow up to a certain height, and then develop some unsightly eccentricity. You will see it often in humans as well. I had a theory that the individual represents in his development the whole procession of his ancestors, and that such a turn to good or evil stands for some strong influence which came into the line of pedigree. The person becomes, as it were, the epitome of the history of his own family. In the evil professor, I believed I had found the supreme example of this: the genius gone amok, preying always upon the innocent. With Moriarty gone, I believed that some part of evil itself was also eliminated. It was a simple matter of subtraction: remove Moriarty and we have a net gain of good for humanity. But, as I fought the good fight in the Orient and elsewhere, I realised that Moriarty's death meant nothing, that any number of criminal minds, some equally talented, his own brother for one, were available to take his place. Evil remained, therefore, as prevalent as ever: it was not a mere fact that could be changed, but something different. My theory of the evil genius explained nothing. I looked for a new explanation."

"And did you find it?" I asked.

"Let us put it this way, Watson. I speak in all candour. As you know, I have never been convinced by the deliberations of the metaphysicians. In my youthful career, I believed simply that I could eradicate evil, or large portions of it, for it had simple if commonplace origins in the hearts of men. When I felt thwarted in this, I suffered immediately from melancholia and boredom, the signs of an underemployed brain. It was then that I took cocaine until a new problem obviated the need for the drug."

He smiled broadly and continued. "But in Asia, Watson, I began to see things with a different eye, and it was in the early narration of these tales that I became most acutely aware of the profound effects of my Asiatic travels upon my thinking. Surely, so many of our countrymen who came to woe in these tales would have been far better off had they never left. Indeed, had Hodgson never left England, there would have been no Moriarty."

"Come, Holmes," said I, "surely you can't mean that we are to blame. Has Sherlock Holmes as well become another épateur of the bourgeoisie in the end?"

"I cast no blame, Watson. You know me far better than that. Nor do I insist on my theory. But as disagreeable as it may sound to you, the Orient begins in London, and it was in Banaras one day, while sitting on the banks of the Ganges, that I realised that my Oriental adventures had begun long before I ever left England. As I stared at the murky water and the thousands of naked worshippers bathing in it, one of the chief villains of our early adventures together, Jonathan Small, suddenly came to mind. Surely, you have not forgotten him."

"No, indeed," I said, "you mean the nasty little man from the Sign of Four."

"Nasty indeed, but it was in the very holy waters that I then contemplated that he lost his leg to the bite of a crocodile, or so he thought, a loss which so embittered him that he had little mercy left in him for his fellow man. Small's miserable story and his hateful image remained with me as I travelled."

He paused briefly to light his pipe, and then said, "On my way to Java, the ship stopped for a few days in the Andamans."

"Where Small was imprisoned for his part in the murder in the Red Fort in Agra. But you omitted your stop in the Andamans from the account you gave me," I said.

"Ah, Watson, there is much that is omitted in my narration, otherwise your simple tales would rival those of dear Thackeray in length.

Suffice it to say that I was allowed to disembark at Port Blair. I roamed the island at will, thinking often of Small and the other plotters in that godforsaken place. I climbed Mt. Harriet and probably rested close to Small's mud hut in Hopetown. I saw dozens of men like Tonga, the Andamaner who helped him to escape and do his evil deeds in London. Small called him the bloodthirsty little viper, did he not? The inhabitants I saw went about their business as calmly and methodically as any Londoner. I mingled with them feeling no fear. Our observers have cast them as godless, numberless, primitive without fire, and savagely cruel, ready to kill any foreigner. And yet during my stay, I felt no threat.

"As I left, I noticed that a whole group of them had been placed in a small shed near the shore in preparation for their transport as labourers to the Dutch Indies. I was told by our captain that there were one hundred ten men and women stuffed into the small shed, over one hundred Tongas to be taken from their island to unknown places. How many of them arrived at their destination alive?"

He stopped for a moment in thought.

"Later, on my way north from Ceylon," he continued, "I stopped in Agra, reliving the horrible events that Small related to us, of the Mutiny, of his fellow conspirators, and the murder of the merchant Achmet. My interest in certain cases never leaves me, and in Jaisalmer I saw many of the same small brown Andamaners at work in the mines of the Landa, the slaves of Captain Fantôme and her ilk. It was here that I began to distinguish between the scent of the criminal and the stench of empire."

He grinned as he tossed the morning paper in my direction. There on the front page was the report of the grisly murder of the Viceroy on his visit to the Andamans. The shocking crime had been committed by a man from the Punjab imprisoned in the islands. He had acted so quickly and with such force that the Viceroy and his party were taken completely unaware. The Viceroy himself mumbled something about a slight pain in his back and fell forward, dead in the water.

"What a ghastly affair, Holmes," I said.

"Yes, Watson, another gruesome crime, pointless in itself, but one that will have various repercussions. I have no doubt that Government will, as it usually does, act in such a way as to make matters worse. You see, Watson, it is no longer a battle from which I hope to emerge victorious. I fight simply because I must, and it is in the knowledge that there is no final victory to be had that I find solace. Shall we say, dear Doctor, that we are all entrapped in an iron cage, the exit from which is hidden from us? I sense an east wind and the coming of a dark polar night. But let us not despair, lest we do nothing at all."

He said no more. He removed his shoes and went out to the beach, where I saw him striding rapidly in the surf, his trousers rolled up to his knees, his shirt hanging loosely about his waist. For the moment, I thought, he seemed free of all care, only waiting for the world to engage him once more.

—John H. Watson, M.D.

A FURTHER NOTE

THE READER DESERVES A WORD ON HOW THESE PAPERS CAME TO BE IN MY possession, for it has long been assumed that all that Conan Doyle had written concerning Sherlock Holmes had been published long ago. Even Christopher Morley, one of the great Holmes enthusiasts of the last century, believed that many of the tales Watson had alluded to in his accounts as well as others unmentioned would never appear. Having whetted our appetite, Doyle departed this world and with him all chance of having them. His promises to communicate from the land of the dead were never kept, the tales never written, and Morley wrote sadly in his introduction to the complete Sherlock Holmes that "we shall never have them now."

My own tale with regard to these papers and how they came into my possession will explain, at least in part, how they were recovered and published only now. In late December 1962, I set sail for London. I left New York on December 27 on the USS *United States* and arrived in Southampton four and one half days later after a brief stop in Calais.

The crossing was a rough one. The North Atlantic was one large winter storm, and the sea battered the decks constantly, confining us to our cabins or to the main rooms inside. Long ropes had been placed everywhere along the corridors so that we could hold on to them and not be thrown down by the ship's sometimes violent motion. Eating in the dining room was an exercise in balance. Bringing a fork or spoon to one's lips was an almost impossible feat at the beginning, but by the third day we had learned to cope very well. In the few hours of respite that the storms occasionally gave us, the more adventurous among us ventured out onto the decks, but we were soon driven back by the icy cold wind, the ominous silver-gray sky, and the black, viscous sea. Despite the storms, the captain had refused to slow the speed of the ship. So confident was he in that incredible vessel that we arrived in Calais in almost record time. We landed there in the middle of the night and left just before daybreak for Southampton. I arrived in London by train that very evening.

In spite of the discomfort of the voyage, I had come to know several passengers, one of whom was a Londoner returning to visit his mother, who was ill. His name was Maxwell Smithson. I never saw him again, but I learned much about London from him, for there was little to do during the voyage except to talk and keep one's balance. I had been to London once before, but only for a brief visit, and so I was essentially a stranger to the city. I told Smithson that I was going to London to study at the School of Oriental and African Studies and that my initial problem would be to find suitable lodging. I was poor. My fellowship covered my travel expenses, and left just enough to survive. Smithson was sympathetic and suggested that I not try to live near Russell Square, where the school was located, but farther east, in Finsbury, where rents were lower. It would mean a longer walk to school, but I did not mind that in the least.

When I arrived, I went first to a boardinghouse in Cartwright Gardens. Smithson had suggested this as a first stop since it was close to the school and I could look for long-term lodging while staying there. The winter was one of London's worst—cold and wet, with deep snow soon covered with soot. The boardinghouse was a dingy rooming house inhabited mainly by African and Asian students. This was the interesting part of it. But it was filthy and noisy, and the fat, slatternly landlady, Mrs. Hudson (yes, Mrs. Hudson), gave us vile food and no peace. She ranted and raved about costs, about unpaid bills, dishonest students, lazy servants, and the high cost of running her establishment in London. It was no place to work or to write. The only pleasure I derived from my stay there was warming my frozen, wet feet at the large wood-stove that heated the large sitting room.

At the first opportunity, within a day or so of my arrival in fact, I began walking through Finsbury. My route was down Bedford Street to Grey's Inn Road and then up the hill on Wharton Street. On my second visit I went into a small grocery store at the foot of the hill. The shopkeeper was a middle-aged gray-haired woman by the name of Mary. It has stuck in my mind that she wore a blue dress, something akin to a uniform, that made her look like a nurse. She had a Cockney accent and immediately recognized mine as American. The shop was a poor one, but the only one in the neighborhood, and so Mary knew almost everyone. I told her that I was looking for lodging, and she said that I should talk to Miss Bertha Mills, an old spinster who lived in Lloyd Square at the top of Wharton Street. Miss Mills rented out rooms occasionally, and the only difficulty was that she was "one who liked to talk and did go on a bit but otherwise was a good soul."

I thanked Mary for the tip, climbed the hill on Wharton Street, turned to the right, and knocked on Miss Mills's door. When she opened, I introduced myself and told her I was looking for lodging. She invited me in. She had one room available, she said, her best room, which had just been vacated, and if I was staying for a long time (at least six months or a year) I could have it for two guineas a week. The room was pleasant, well furnished, and overlooked the square. I decided on the spot to take it. Miss Mills asked me down to her dining room, where we had tea and biscuits and finalized the arrangement.

It was the first of many teas, for tea in Miss Mills's household was a daily ritual. At four o'clock she was there, the silver teapot in front of her, placed almost in the middle of the old round table, together with a dish of plain unsalted crackers, butter, and marmalade. And, of course, cigarettes and an ashtray, for Miss Mills was a chain smoker. Both her lips and fingers were stained by the tobacco that had been her lifelong habit.

Miss Mills was already old, then in her late seventies I think, and except for the tobacco stains around her mouth, there was almost no color in her face at all. With white hair, pale complexion, and very thin, she usually wore a tattered black sweater over her shoulders. She was extremely animated and energetic, however, and spoke in a loud, deep voice that always surprised me when I heard it come out of her delicate frame. She used that voice endlessly, her talk a ceaseless flow that often made my eyes and brain glaze over in a late afternoon torpor.

After a few sessions, I began trying to avoid her, but she was relentless. If I arrived at teatime, which was my habit, she was there at the door with her invitation. If I was in my room, I heard her loud voice shouting, "Teatime!" How the other boarders managed to avoid her I learned only much later, for invariably at the beginning of my stay I was the only one at her table unless I brought a friend.

Finding avoidance almost impossible, I decided to enjoy my meetings with her, and instead of listening to her babble on about her neighbors—the latest goings-on in number such-and-such, a house owned by a Mrs. Travis, were her passion—I began to question her about her family and the house in which she lived. She told me that the house had been that of her parents, and that when they died they left it to her and her sister, also unmarried, who died young. Her whole life had been spent in that house with the friendship of her lodgers. Her only trip had been a long excursion twenty years before to visit a cousin in New Zealand, the cousin being her only living relative. She had led a quiet life of reading, gossip, tea, and cigarettes, and moreover was content with it. She had a bright look to her eyes that told me she was a happy person despite her occasional loneliness, and that her fortune had been to be content with what was close at hand. She had no need to look further. She was also an inveterate letter writer, and spent many hours in correspondence with her friends, who were scattered everywhere, living where she had never been and had no desire to go. The world she knew well but through the newspapers and the BBC. It was there to be talked about and had no other relevance. The only time it had impinged on her was during the Second World War, when one of Hitler's "bloody doodlebugs" had landed in front of number seven, shattering everybody's windows.

The teas became a habit, and then a ritual that I looked forward to, for I found that Miss Mills had recorded in her head every detail of the lives of her boarders and their activities in London. Some of them had lived in her house for a long time, others occasionally on their trips to the city. Some were famous. Sir Alexander Fleming had lived there in and out for several years. For her, however, the greatest joy was to talk of Sir Arthur Conan Doyle and his comings and goings, not the Conan Doyle of Sherlock Holmes but the later one, the one who was interested in psychical research. She remembered one evening that Doyle had demanded that she, Alexander Fleming, and he hold hands seated at that very table in the hope of calling up some spirit. "Nothing happened," she said gleefully, "and Doyle was a bit miffed."

Doyle was an occasional boarder, staying there when he lectured and wanted to hide from the swarms of Spiritualists who flocked to him in his last days. He could no longer stay at the large hotels in the city, which he could well afford. Instead, he hailed a cab, leaving his crowd of admirers behind, and came to Miss Mills's in Lloyd Square. I began to imagine him sitting at the same table, this powerful bull of a man with his great mustache, talking to a frail, young, perhaps then beautiful Bertha Mills, telling her of his beliefs in the afterlife.

One night, early in 1930, she said, and then paused, for there followed the usual internal argument—"it was February, of course, but was it a Wednesday or a Thursday, he usually came on a Thursday, but . . ."—that lasted through at least a half cup before she continued the thread. One night, then, early in 1930, on a Wednesday (this was more important to Miss Mills than the exact date), Conan Doyle appeared at her door in a considerable state of agitation. He had with him more than his usual small overnight bag. There were several suitcases and a tin trunk. He came in, saying that there had been a fire at Charing Cross in the building where many of his papers had been stored. Luckily, most of his belongings had been spared. He wondered if he could leave them with her in the cellar, where he knew they would be safe. He would eventually come and sort them out and take them off her hands. She welcomed him and told him to leave the bags in her hallway and she would find a place for them. There was no room in the cellar, she said, for Fleming had put most of his possessions there, including much of the equipment from his laboratory.

Doyle's agitated state of mind seemed to go beyond the fire and his papers. He had aged greatly since she had last seen him, and did not appear at all well. Before he left, over tea at that very table, she said, he made her promise that should anything happen to him before he retrieved his things, she would not disclose their existence to anyone, and that somehow later on, after his death, he would communicate with her. She agreed, but reluctantly, and said, "How in God's name you expect to communicate with me after you are dead is beyond me, but if that is your wish, then I shall abide by it." He smiled, she said, and gently admonished her, saying that if there was a difficulty, it was his and not hers.

After that evening, she never saw Doyle again. A few months later, she learned of his death. She kept her promise. Several years later she received a letter from Doyle, obviously written before his death but mailed (she did not know how or by whom) years later, instructing her to dispose of his belongings. The suitcases, he wrote, contain nothing but clothes and they should be given to charity or thrown away. The trunk, however, she should hold on to until she heard his voice telling her what to do with it. She laughed, for she was still waiting to hear from him, she said.

After that conversation, we rarely talked of Doyle again. Miss Mills and I, however, continued our almost daily meetings throughout my stay in London, and we became lifelong friends. For a number of years after my departure from England, we continued to correspond. Her hand, which had always been strong, suddenly appeared in one letter to weaken, and I heard nothing from her for a very long time. Then, one day just a few years ago, I received a letter and a notice. The letter was from a lawyer from London, notifying me of the death of Miss Mills at the age of ninety-six, and that in her will she had bequeathed to me a tin trunk in her possession and all its contents. She had also left a note of instruction, and it was her wish that I would abide by what she had written. The note was written in what must have been her last days, and it said, in part:

I am finally feeling my age (I will be ninety-five next month) and must dispose of some of the things that mean something to me. The house and the furniture I am leaving to charity, for I have no heirs and no one I know is poor enough to need my little fortune, however much it is. There is one thing that I am entrusting to you, however. And that is the old tin trunk that Conan Doyle left here. He never did communicate with me again, and I have yet to hear his voice telling me what to do with it. So I turn it over to you to do with it as you wish. Except do not destroy it or its contents, for Doyle may still show up. This morning I threw out several boxes of Alexander Fleming's old tubes and vials. Glad to get rid of it all finally.

It was hardly a letter of instructions, but there it was: a few words telling me that the box was in my care. When it arrived a few days later, I opened it and found that it was the tin trunk that had sat at Cox & Co., Charing Cross, with Watson's files on the unpublished cases of Sherlock Holmes. There were notes, drafts, and whole manuscripts, all written in a firm, clear hand. A first quick look revealed that, among others, the stories that Doyle had mentioned in the published tales but never saw into print were there. One can imagine my delight when I saw in front of me the manuscripts of the Paradol Chamber case, the case of the aluminum crutch, the giant rat of Sumatra, and the other fifty-odd tales that he referred to but never published.

The stories in this volume cover some of Sherlock Holmes's adventures during his years of absence between 1891 and 1894. Watson's preface described their circumstances. They are undated, but it is apparent that they were written over a long period of time, and that Doyle never edited them for consistency. In publishing them, I too have refrained from any attempt to edit them beyond the minimum necessary for editorial accuracy. They are presented here in the order in which Doyle arranged them in his file, which is not necessarily the order in which they were written. Doyle, it seems, wrote them at different times, and may have intended to publish them individually rather than in one volume.

In a short time, I hope that all that remains will be before the reader. I do not know if this is what Doyle would have wanted, but it is certainly what Christopher Morley would have desired, and it is more for his ghost than for that of Doyle that I have begun the publication of these tales.

—Ted Riccardi

ABOUT THE AUTHOR

TED RICCARDI is professor emeritus in the Department of Middle East and Asian Languages and Cultures at Columbia University, where he taught for thirty-two years. His special interests are the history of India and the cultures of the Himalayas. He lives in New York City with his wife, Ellen Coon, and their children. They spend as much time as they can in northern New Mexico. *The Casebook of Sherlock Holmes* is Ted Riccardi's first work of fiction.

ABOUT THE TYPE

This book was set in Bembo, a typeface based on an old-style Roman face that was used for Cardinal Bembo's tract *De Aetna* in 1495. Bembo was cut by Francisco Griffo in the early sixteenth century. The Lanston Monotype Company of Philadelphia brought the well-proportioned letterforms of Bembo to the United States in the 1930s.